T0286969

Beyond & Within

DISCONTINUE
IF DEATH ENSUES

Tales from the Tipping Point

Edited by Carol Gyzander
& Anna Taborska

Beyond & Within

DISCONTINUE IF DEATH ENSUES

IF DEATH ENSUES

Tales from the Tipping Point

by STOKER AWARD NOMINEES

Carol Gyzander, Kyla Lee Ward, Lee Murray,
Cindy O'Quinn & Anna Taborska

Edited by Carol Gyzander & Anna Taborska

FLAME TREE
PUBLISHING

Publisher & Creative Director: Nick Wells
Senior Project Editor: Gillian Whitaker

FLAME TREE PUBLISHING
6 Melbray Mews, Fulham,
London SW6 3NS, United Kingdom
www.flametreepublishing.com

First published 2024
Copyright in each story is held by the individual authors.
Volume copyright © 2024 Flame Tree Publishing Ltd.

'At Māratotō Pool' by Lee Murray previously published in *One of Us,
A Tribute to Frank Michaels Errington*, Bloodshot Books, 2020.
Reprinted with permission from the author.

'The Thing I Found Along a Dirt Patch Road' by Cindy O'Quinn
previously published in *Shotgun Honey Presents Volume 4 RECOIL*,
Shotgun Honey, an imprint of Down & Out Books, 2020. Reprinted with
permission from the author.

24 26 28 29 27 25
1 3 5 7 9 10 8 6 4 2

Hardback ISBN: 978-1-80417-937-6
ebook ISBN: 978-1-80417-938-3

The cover is created by Flame Tree Studio. Created specially for this
edition, the frontispiece and image detail is *On Her Shoulders*
© 2024 by Lynne Hansen, LynneHansenArt.com.
All other images © 2024 Flame Tree Publishing Ltd.

A copy of the CIP data for this book is available from the British Library.

Printed and bound in China

We dedicate this anthology to all our Sisters, wherever they may be, and to those who stand by them.

Don't let the bastards grind you down!

About the Title

(and That Tipping Point!)

SOME OF YOU might recognise the title of this anthology, *Discontinue if Death Ensues*. It's a line from the poem "For your information—from your pharmacist" by renowned writer and activist Marge Piercy from her 2020 volume *On the Way Out, Turn Off the Light*.

Those of us who aren't blessed with perfect health have probably, at one time or another, experienced the disbelief and quiet desperation of reading a patient information leaflet for a new medication and being confronted with a list of caveats and potentially fatal side effects. But of course, the poem is a metaphor for just about any aspect of life in the modern world – from rampant consumerism to life itself – as revealed in the final two lines: "Continue until medication is completely consumed, or you are."

It is also a metaphor for the exploitation and overconsumption of the Earth's natural resources, which have led to climate change and which manifest in the wildfires and floods we are increasingly seeing the world over. Scientists warn of a possible domino effect of climate tipping points (the destruction of ice sheets, forests, coral reefs, and so on), leading to a global tipping point – a speeding up of global warming and the resultant "hothouse" Earth, large swathes of it uninhabitable. This, unfortunately, is scientific fact.

But what if – and we are now entering the realm of the speculative – what if this is somehow linked to another tipping point? A point at which the female body can no longer passively withstand all the violence and atrocity that has been unleashed upon it since time immemorial?

Our responses to such a tipping point, presented in the stories that follow, open the door to new horrors but also, we hope, reveal the potential collective power of women and of those who stand by them.

Content Warning: Although there are no graphic descriptions of sexual violence, this is nevertheless a major theme throughout the anthology, and mention is made of rape and other forms of gender-based violence in many of the stories. It is not our intention to offend or to upset: rather, to inform, speculate, occasionally entertain, but always give food for thought.

Editorial Style: The stories in this anthology retain the respective authors' English of preference.

Contents

Editors' Preface
Anna Taborska and Carol Gyzander 10

Part I: Lee Murray, New Zealand
Withering 15
Goddess..18
Glow: An Oral History...26
At Māratotō Pool 65

Part II: Carol Gyzander, United States
Bobblehead 90
Wearing White Out of Season................................93
Because, Science..141
Storm Warning..149

Part III: Kyla Lee Ward, Australia
Circling Hecate 181
Maleficium 184

Part IV: Anna Taborska, United Kingdom

The Last Woman 259

Mummy Miya 262

An[n]us Horribilis 282

Fat 301

Thin 307

The Queen is Dead. Long Live the Queen 311

Part V: Cindy O'Quinn, United States

Pardon Me While I Hum 331

The Thing I Found Along a Dirt Patch Road 334

Rolling Boil 349

Everyone 400

BIOGRAPHIES 410

BEYOND & WITHIN 415

FLAME TREE FICTION 416

Editors' Preface

ON 24TH JUNE 2022, the Supreme Court of the United States overturned the Roe v. Wade ruling, thus stripping American women of the right to bodily integrity and fundamental aspects of reproductive healthcare. The US joined a vast body of countries – mostly in Africa and Asia, but also in Central and South America and in Europe – that deny women and girls the basic human right of access to safe and legal abortion. Countries such as Poland, where, on 14th March 2023, sentence was passed on a woman tried and convicted for giving her own abortion pills to a desperate woman with pregnancy complications, and where the suffering and deaths of women denied abortion are too gruesome to write about even in a horror anthology.

The court ruling in the United States was one of three things that culminated in the idea to create *Discontinue if Death Ensues*. This was the big thing, the thing that has already had a negative impact on the lives of hundreds of American women and will personally affect thousands more if it isn't rectified as soon as possible. The other two things that brought this anthology to life were little things, affecting only a very small group of people.

On 23rd February 2022, the Horror Writers Association announced the finalists for the 2021 Bram Stoker Award® for Superior Achievement in Short Fiction. For the first time in the Association's history, all five finalists were women. We already knew of each other thanks to social media and from having read one another's work. As we waited to see who would be chosen by the HWA membership as the ultimate winner, we started talking to each other online and came to the conclusion that, regardless of the outcome, the situation was a win-win for all of us.

The other little thing was an article written by Ken Brosky for his regular *Cemetery Dance Online* feature, "Dark Pathways", which was published on 8th April 2022. It was a fascinating and informative piece on the use of foreshadowing as a storytelling technique, which utilised the five 2021 Stoker-nominated short stories as examples. Ken titled his piece "A Frightening Sense of Foreboding", and that's how the Sisters of Foreboding came into being. A bit of fun in response to a kind article by another author, a group of five women thrown together by the support of fellow HWA members, and a turn in world events that has seen women stripped of the right to a peaceful, healthy, private existence.

The Sisters of Foreboding come from five different corners of the world: Australia, New Zealand, the United Kingdom, New York, and West Virginia. (You might be wondering about my description of New York and West Virginia as being different corners of the world, but I am told by friends in the know that these two fine places might as well be on different planets.) So, we made the decision to set our stories, where possible, in our respective geographical locations – in the places in which we live or were raised and which are familiar to us. But, in many ways, our stories could just as well take place in Asia, in mainland Europe, or indeed anywhere, and could have been written by authors from any part of the world.

In an ideal world, most of the stories you are about to read would not have been written. We would all have full control over our bodies and what other people can and cannot do to them. Nevertheless, here we are. And things being what they are, we are happy and excited to share with you our volume of Tales from the Tipping Point.

Thank you for being with us.

Anna Taborska, August 2023

IN THE SPRING OF 2022, the five finalists for the Bram Stoker Award® for Superior Achievement in Short Fiction realized something exciting—we were all women horror writers. The five of us—Carol Gyzander, Lee Murray, Cindy O'Quinn, Anna Taborska, and Kyla Lee Ward—began chatting among ourselves after the ballot announcement.

We wanted to support each other, particularly since we were from all around the world and would not all be able to attend the Horror Writers Association StokerCon banquet in Denver, Colorado, that year. Those who follow the Myers-Briggs personality types will understand that as an ENFJ, I love to bring people together as a team. During the banquet, I opened a Facebook group chat for the five of us.

"Hello to my fabulous Sisters of Foreboding! I wish we were here together at Stoker! I just wanted to say that it's been an honor to be nominated along with you all. I almost (ALMOST lol) don't care who wins, as all of the stories are terrific. Hugs to all!"

We cheered together as Lee received the award!

Our subsequent, ongoing conversations showed that we five all had a particular perspective on the power and abilities of women that we brought to our individual work. Combined, it was awesome.

That summer, I invited all to contribute to *A Woman Unbecoming*, the horror anthology from Crone Girls Press. Rachel A. Brune and I co-edited this work immediately upon the reversal of the Roe v. Wade decision in the United States that removed a woman's right to abortion. Lee, Cindy, and Anna had pieces to share in the short timeframe. The charity anthology's focus further clarified our mutual belief that women are powerful.

The team's ongoing discussion soon turned to how things stand for women in the world, and—as authors are wont to do—we slid right into the idea of putting together this anthology. Lee did some research and verified that we were, indeed, the first group of finalists in a Stoker category where all identified as women, but we knew we would not be the last.

The Sisters of Foreboding collective was born. We five brainstormed our topic together. Anna and I agreed to be co-editors of *Discontinue if Death Ensues*.

And, we were right—the finalists for the 2023 Bram Stoker Award® for Superior Achievement in an Anthology? All women again.

Carol Gyzander, August 2023

Part I
Lee Murray, New Zealand

Withering

Lee Murray

when they refused to bend
we hung them from the trees
left them to wither

unbecoming women
their mealy mouths too full of teeth
we let their corpses desiccate

let them bake and blacken
stark warning to the wanton
do this, and you will suffer

that was the messaging
to all those hungry, grasping whores
not so many now, of course

well, they had it coming

only, we hadn't counted on the trees
their heads bent together
like crones over their knitting

the trees who willow-wept
tears trickling downwards
rootbound to decay

we forgot the trees
forgot about the trees

it was the tipping point
the line in the sand
yes, yes, we'd heard it all before

but the giants withered
mothers of our first breath
who fed and nurtured us

in a stand with their sisters
their heartwood splintered
in solidarity

do this, and you will suffer
we got the message—just too late

so now, we grunt and grasp
hell's breezes searing in our throats
to our unbecoming end

Goddess

Lee Murray

IT WAS WILD. For weeks, the club had been heaving with people desperate to make the most of their last moments on a dying planet. Who knew exactly how long we had? Weeks? Days? It was The Party at the End of the World: 24/7 drinking, dancing, snorting. Fucking. Anything to help us forget the storm that was coming. Anything to feel alive.

Then word got out about the underground bunker in the NightRealm's basement, and how it was stocked up and strong enough to survive the end times. Everyone wanted in. Even me. Like sheep, they came to the club in droves, leaping over themselves for a chance to impress Hine-nui-te-pō[1], the NightRealm's proprietor, the only one with the key to that precious inner sanctum, the only one with the power to hold back Death. And it

---

1   Hine-nui-te-pō (Māori): Great woman of the night, goddess of Death and the underworld.

was fitting because my Hine is an absolute goddess. I loved her from the first moment I saw her all those years ago, the way she emerged from between the beer-sticky tables, cutting through the smoke, her broad hips swaying, and with a smile that could melt your insides.

Māui[2] appeared among the wave of opportunists, a player if ever I saw one. Had a rep too. The girls at the club reckoned the man could prise *tio*-oyster from a crag in a rock with that tongue of his. But when I saw their dark heads touching at the bar that night, Hine chuckling over something he'd said, I figured she'd have his measure. No way would she be taken in by a pair of tōtara-trunk thighs, thick lips, and mellow crème-de-menthe words. I left the pair of them to it.

But later, she brought him home, blundering through the front door in a bluster of whispers and giggles. Not going to lie, I was pissed. I didn't want his Lynx deodorant and peach vape stinking up our Te Atatu flat. This was *our* place. He had no business being here. I got out of bed, cracked the door a slit, and peeped out.

Pressed up close behind her, Māui's hands were roaming all over her, grasping and groping at her breasts and her mound, even as he ground his hips into hers through his Friday-night jeans. Hine didn't push him away. Instead, she threw her head back, exposing her throat, and laughed from deep in her belly.

2   Māui: Polynesian demi-god, a known trickster.

19

I choked down a bolus of longing. I had no right to be jealous. Hine wasn't mine. *She wasn't mine.* She could do what she wanted.

Māui growled and fumbled for her zipper – all finesse gone. Fingers plundering, plunging.

Hine twisted her torso and swatted him away. "Shhh," she said. "My flatmate. Pīwakawaka[3]. She's sleeping."

Fuck. Did she know I was watching? I pulled back, hunkering into the shadows, and stilled my breath.

"Aw, come on, baby," he whined. "Who knows if we'll get another chance?" He pulled a puppy dog face.

Hine laid her hands on his chest. Smiled. "No. Not tonight." Her voice was firm. "You said you'd hold me."

He grinned, then took a step forward, and she stepped back, in that age-old ballet, until her buttocks were pressed against the hardwood table. "And you said you wanted someone to help you sleep," he purred. "We both know what that means."

My hackles rose, and I put my hand to the door, ready to bust into the room. As if I could do anything. Māui was a big guy, and I was a small and flighty woman. I was no match for him, but I would do anything for Hine…

She lifted her knee, and that first flinch was enough. Māui's reflexes were as sharp as a blade of *toetoe* grass:

---

3 Pīwakawaka (Māori): fantail, tiny bird endemic to Aotearoa-New Zealand, a messenger from the gods.

he stepped back before he copped it in the crotch. "Okay, okay. Can't blame a man for trying, can you?"

And it seemed she didn't blame him, because she took him by the hand and drew him down to the couch until he was spooning her. Then she picked up the remote and flicked on the television. She did this a lot lately. I would come out of my room on the way to the bathroom, or just to check she was home, and would find her dozing on the couch, the television flickering a neon-blue dreamscape on the ceiling. These days, she wasn't getting much sleep.

"You think we'd be sleeping like the Almost-Dead, wouldn't you, Pī?" she joked the night Europe went dark.

It wasn't just the global fallout. It was the NightRealm and her newfound power over life and death. That kind of responsibility changed a person. Plus, I knew she'd seen things, ugliness she wouldn't reveal, not even to me. Instead, she'd numb her sorrow by binge-watching some re-run or another. In the morning, she couldn't even tell me what it was.

I longed to comfort her. If she craved human contact, *I* could spoon her. I was here, alive and warm and willing. But Hine didn't know, could never know, how I felt about her. So, I hovered in the gloom, feeling sorry for myself, as she fell asleep in Māui's arms, then snored softly, her top lip trembling.

I was about to creep back to bed when Māui rose from the couch. I hadn't realised he was still awake. He padded across to the kitchen, where his shadowy form coalesced in the silver moonlight. Getting himself a drink of water? Or something else? I cracked the door a little wider.

He was fumbling in the darkness. A cell phone glowed, illuminating his face in ghostly white. "Yeah, I'm here with her," he whispered. "Nah, not happening. Not tonight."

Straining to hear, I crept down the hall and ducked behind the credenza.

"Dad, you don't understand. There's something different about her. She's not like other women." He leaned against the kitchen bench while the phone hummed with insistence. "Okay, okay, yeah. I'll get it done." He snapped it off and turned back to Hine. Lifted his arm and rubbed the back of his head. All at once, the room zinged with menace, and the air turned cold. It was as if Whiro[4], the lord of darkness himself, had entered the room, snaking his evil tentacles through the slats in the air conditioning. The moon shuddered. I held my breath.

In that moment, Māui changed before me, his thick man-neck contorting into bulbous, brutal forms, which shifted, shrivelled, shrank. He dropped to his hands and knees, his skin darkening, and his spine extended at his tailbone.

He became a lizard, cloaked in reptilian red. Well, he would choose to take the form of a cursed harbinger of ill luck, wouldn't he? When the ugly son of Punga[5] had shrunk to the size of a football, he turned his yellow eyes on Hine.

---

4 Whiro or Whiro-te-tipua (Māori): god of darkness and evil.
5 Punga (Māori): god of sharks, reptiles, and ugly creatures.

His tongue darted in and out, and he scuttled towards the couch. I panicked, trembling behind the credenza like a coward, as Māui climbed the couch, latching on to the fabric with his curved lizard claws.

What was he doing? But I knew. *I knew*. He wanted to take her power from her. To claim her body and a place in the NightRealm sanctum. Already the foul creature was burrowing behind Hine's zipper, plunging head-first into her jeans until only his tail coiled and thrashed outside. It wriggled and writhed until her pants slipped past her hips.

Hine moaned softly in her sleep.

The lizard lifted his head and flicked his tongue, then plunged again.

No, no, no!

"Hine," I screamed. "Hine!" I threw on the lights.

She opened her eyes, blinked, then looked down at the lizard thrusting and thrashing between her legs. I had expected her to be surprised; Hine merely laughed. The apartment rocked with her laughter. She clamped her thighs firmly about the lizard-man's head, then twisted and coiled. I'd never seen her like this. She was like a crocodile wrapping her prey in the deadly roll of her hips.

Māui must have known he was outclassed because he shrieked and squirmed to escape her vice-grip. Hine relented then, opening her legs a little, perhaps to infuse the creature with a hint of hope. That's when I glimpsed the slick of blood and the black obsidian teeth of her vagina. Teeth! But she closed her legs over him and clamped down again. I imagined those black needles piercing Māui's lizard scales, the shards sliding into his eye socket and passing through his skull. All the while, Hine held on, gripping the armrest, her lips pressed together and her eyes glittering in the dim light.

Moments passed. Inside her body, the battle raged on.

I was in awe of her. It wasn't the first time a man had violated her – her father among them – but this new power of hers, and the calm confidence with which she wielded it, made my pulse thunder in my veins. I knew then that I both loved and feared her.

At last, Hine's shoulders slumped, and her fingers relaxed. "Hine?" I whispered.

"It's okay, hon." She parted her legs again, and the lizard's bloody carcass slithered off the couch and onto the rug. In death, it transformed into its true form. Just another man bedazzled by Hine's power, who thought he could take it for himself. Well, she had chewed him up and spewed him out until he was nothing more than a mound of pulped flesh.

Hine stood, wiped the smear of blood and brain matter from her inner thighs, then bent to roll the body in the rug. "You can't say anything about this, Pīwakawaka," she said. She gave me a hard look. I nodded, but inside my soul was singing.

We shared a secret. Hine *trusted* me.

I helped her as best I could after that, flitting ahead of her, opening doors, and checking that we wouldn't be seen, as

Hine lugged Māui's body downstairs on her shoulders. We loaded the trickster into the car, then ditched the body in the dumpster behind the NightRealm.

"What about the authorities?" I said as we climbed the stairs to the club, the dawn light sparkling on gum-spattered concrete.

Hine tossed her head. "What about them? In two days, a week, they'll all be dead."

At the top of the stairs, I pushed open the door and stepped aside so she could pass ahead of me. Like a breath, her hips brushed mine as she entered that darkened realm.

It was intoxicating. It didn't matter to me what she'd done. What she'd become. The world could end tomorrow; I was hers forever.

Glow: An Oral History

Lee Murray

Trigger Warning: Contains material
some readers may find offensive.

Lisa Selter, former CNN journalist:
[We meet her in the lobby of a Motel 6 – "We leave
the light on for you" – but conduct the interview
in Selter's room. There are only two chairs, so she
sits on the bed, her boots on the orange protector.
By now, her trademark blonde tresses have been
cropped short, and even inside she wears oversized
glasses, the sort you buy at charging stations. She
doesn't allow us to open the windows.]

Selter: I was reporting at the Paris Climate Summit the day
the Glow phenomenon was first observed. Reluctantly, as
it happens. I'd been asked to cover the California bushfires
– the fire front had travelled south to Lake Morena by that
stage, and the ash was thicker than a bowl of grits, choking

26

off crops as far away as Santa Fe – then the network changed their minds, decided they wanted an action hero-sort for that role, so they'd given Harrison Anderson a quick jarhead haircut, trussed him up in fire fatigues, and sent him out into the field, and I'd scored the summit instead. Speeches and posturing by politicos and corporate types droning on with the same tired old promises. It was drier than Australia. No wonder Thunberg refused to attend. We weren't even covering the main event, just a roundtable on environmental protections in one of the break-out venues. I'll admit I was annoyed about being relegated to the conference backrooms. Who could've known that the wind would turn in my favour and that I'd get the scoop of the decade? It's not every day a girl gets to capture the moment humanity hits Her tipping point.

I was lucky to have cameraman Cal S. Moore with me for the event. Cal's one of the best. Award-winning, respected. *Male.* And that last mattered more than you'd think, because later, there was so much mud flung, ugly trolling about my underlying agenda, so having Cal in my corner helped some when people, influencers and commentators whose sponsors had deep pockets, screamed for my head. There were claims that the original footage had been tampered with to frame certain players. People said I was a raging eco-feminist bitch (their words), that I had gone in there intending to stir up a shitstorm, and that the whole event was the culmination of an extreme leftist conspiracy. Well, it's no secret the social media furore the Glow caused worldwide. I disconnected my accounts; it didn't stop the death threats. In the aftermath, CNN benched me. They called it a sabbatical, but we all knew they wanted to deflect the heat they were getting from the powers-that-be, some of whom were affected…

We've seen the footage. What can you tell us about the day?

Selter: It's well known by now that the roundtable took place in one of two *grands appartements* of the Château de Maintenon, the quaint little castle where King Louis XIV housed (and humped) his favourite mistress – a fact that didn't go unnoticed later, given the gender dynamics of the day, and the fact that people were expected to turn a blind eye to the transgressions of their monarch. That said, there was no doubt it was a gorgeous venue, despite the lack of air conditioning, the way the ornamental gardens had been ravaged to make way for food production, and the fact that the aqueduct over the Eure River – which the guidebook said was situated at the far end of the domain – was completely obscured by pollution. The meeting room retained its grandeur though, with its 1700s *style chinois*, all polished black lacquer and gold trim, with heavy embroidered drapes in damask rose. Not that Adam Reitz – yeah, *that* Reitz, CEO of Giga – could've cared less about the historic surroundings, the way he flicked his cigar ash on the parquet floors. At a climate change summit. The irony, right? You can see it on the footage in the lead up, although distributors tend to edit out anything but the moment of that first Glow. Still, my job was to cover the news, to give the facts as they presented themselves, and to keep my personal view out of it.

[She snorts.] I mean, is that even possible? There's always a slant, always a spin, isn't there? The timing, the ad content, who's at the helm of the network, *everything* contributes when you're delivering the news. Nothing is ever entirely objective. But I want to say right here, the footage that Cal and I sent through was clean. Sure, it was doctored and edited by other sites afterwards, and by venues who should have known better, but the original reporting we sent through to the network – the lighting, the sound, my commentary – it was all exactly as we recorded it in real time. [Selter pauses to glance at the pendant lamp fixed over the bed. In the oversized glasses, we see the reflection of a moth, flitting around the bulb inside the globe.]

Besides, Cal and I were there. We saw it all…

The French conference organisers stationed us in the rear, in an area roped off for the press (velvet-tasselled rope no less) along with a couple of blog-news folk – who verified everything in our report, by the way. You'll want to talk with them as primary sources. I have some contact addresses, although, like me, they've been hounded by the original Glowlights, and for all I know they may have moved on after all this time. Anyway, ours was the only network to televise the summit out-takes. The meeting was wrapping up and it was clear to everyone that there would be no concrete outcomes. Nothing that would slow the creeping pollution that was nearing... had reached the point of no return. Watchdog committee. Ha! In hindsight, it's laughable. Did anyone truly expect the corporations holding the biggest slices of capitalist pie to call time on themselves? Oh, those pillars of the Earth knew how to sing from the song sheet; they made noises like they cared, as if they wanted to see change, when, in reality, they were the ones who'd had the most to gain from the US government decision to lift all environmental regulations. Don't take my word for it. The full transcript is available as part of the conference proceedings, and even without their grunts and sighs, the careful hesitation, and the nervous laughter of the audio recording, their obfuscation jumps off the page. They were laughing all the way to the bank, and they knew it. Anyway, the committee chair, a French grocery tycoon by the name of Pascal Alain, declared the meeting closed and asked the delegates to congregate at the front of the room for a publicity photograph. Just the delegates, mind, not the secretaries or the translators. So, they were all up there, a flock of self-satisfied roosters, buttoning their suits and straightening their cuffs, and, for some reason that no one ever ascertained, one of the conference minions opened a window, assailing us all with a gust of hot air.

And that's the instant we first saw the Glow.

Those six powerful men, all beacons of industry, suddenly beamed with fluorescent white light. Their skin was luminescent, translucent. Shining like proverbial Christmas trees, they were, but with solid white light. I blinked at the intensity. I remember Reitz checking out his reflection in the French windows, holding up his hands to his face. His expression was incredulous, but there was this indelible flicker of fear. He staggered back a step and dropped his cigar. (One of the conference minions stamped it out, leaving a nasty black scorch on the wood.) But in all my years of journalism, I'd never seen Reitz unguarded like that. You know the image he projected. Confident. Casual. The smooth manner with which he navigated the media, and the way he oozed that 'consummate man of the world' branding. But in that moment, as he tried to grasp the reality unfolding before his eyes, I realised just how curated his persona was. Here was one of the world's most influential free-market industrialists experiencing something he had no control over. He'd been reduced to the level of any other mortal. I guess that explains why he was among the first to refute the initial poison-in-the-water-carafe theory, going straight to the success-gene narrative. At least he could maintain some control over that. No, you won't see his reaction captured in the footage. Reitz was out of shot at this point – Cal had the camera trained on the committee Chair; you'll remember the close-up – but if you contact the blog-news folks, if you can get hold of them, I know they'll bear me out.

* * *

Jason Kelly, 65, global digital services billionaire:

[The following is a transcript from a studio interview with ABC morning television host Maryam Chan a full month after the Glow phenomenon was first observed. Kelly and Chan are seated before an indigo blue backdrop with the only lighting provided by the glow of Kelly's body. Although Chan wears a suit in crisp white, the three-time BAFTA nominee appears lacklustre, bordering on dull, when compared to her distinguished guest. Additional notes from the recorded interview were supplied by the network.]

Chan: So, I gather you agree with the 'genetic marker of success' theory?

Kelly: Look, Ms. Chan… [Kelly straightens his tie.]
Chan: Please. Call me Maryam.

Kelly: It's not that I'm vain, Maryam. [All charm, he flashes a glowing smile at his host.] But I know for certain that on the day in question, I simply didn't drink the Kool-Aid.
Chan: You're talking about the carafe of water provided for the conference delegates.

Kelly: Exactly. [He coughs theatrically.] Forgive me, Kool-Aid was an unfortunate choice of words. The thing is, Maryam, given the world's stretched food resources and the consequent high percentage of non-food additives in the foodstuffs offered by certain unscrupulous players, I'm careful to bring my own food and drink to events like these.

Chan [Leaning forward in her chair.]: Even to the Paris Climate Summit?

Kelly: I like to do my bit to support ethical business practice.

Chan: But surely you agree that not every man exhibiting the Glow monitors their eating in the same way you do.

Kelly: You're right, of course. Which is why, for me, the 'genetic marker of success' theory appears to be the most plausible explanation. But, even if we accept that likelihood, there are still so many questions to be answered. What biological factor or factors cause the Glow to manifest? Why are we seeing this phenotype now? And in such high numbers, since there are now around a hundred million men affected globally, according to recent estimates. Since the Glow appears to be sex-linked...

Chan [interrupts]: Meaning that the Glow only appears in men...

Kelly: Yes, good point, Maryam. The effect is sex-linked, not linked to sex [Kelly chuckles] and therefore it's important to consider the long-term effects on men's health, and ultimately, on the human population. We won't know for sure until the scientists have completed their early research, which won't be for several months yet, and since research begets research, I'm sure there will be other trials to follow.

Chan: I understand you've funded some of the initial trials yourself.

Kelly: Not just me. I believe all the men whose inner glow was revealed at the summit have invested heavily in the studies. We are the Patient Zeros of the Glow phenomenon, the pioneers, if you like, and as such we feel a responsibility to get to the bottom of it.

Chan: Yes, if only the same funds could be applied to breast cancer.

Kelly: Maryam, I couldn't agree with you more.

Chan: Are you aware that more has been spent researching Glow in the four weeks since its onset, than in four decades of breast cancer research?

Kelly [Clapping his hands to his chest.]: Really? It's appalling when we make those kinds of comparisons. As I said, I don't want you to think that I'm vain, but the very fact that the phenomenon appears to occur in men who have achieved a certain level of success has given us a big advantage in getting ahead of this thing, because sufferers have the resources to invest in answers.

Chan: Sufferers?

Kelly: This might be hard for people to believe, but it's tough to be singled out as a successful man. There are plenty of gold-diggers out there. Sycophants. Opportunists. Even terrorists. Wearing the Glow isn't always a good thing for a man.

Chan: No one has actually been injured, though.

34

Kelly: Have you seen how bright I am? It's intense. I'm barely getting any sleep! [He turns to give the audience a conspiratorial grin.]

Chan: One final question before we go to the break, are you aware that commentators are calling you the Glowlights?

Kelly: Glowlights? Really? Is that a fact? [Another chuckle.] Well, if the shoe fits…

* * *

Chris Schofield, Acting Director General of Prisons for the UK:

[We interview Schofield in his London office. No cameras are permitted.]

Schofield: Prison populations are often the subject of empirical research to determine the prevalence and possible causes of diseases, and the Glow phenomenon was no exception. Inmates' involvement in any trial is always voluntary and non-exploitative, you understand, but the benefits can be wide-ranging, offering, for example, opportunities to improve individual well-being and prison management best practices. They can also offer valuable insights to inform and underpin social development programmes. When Professor Silvester and the Cambridge University group approached the department for access to both male and female prison populations for their

Glow trials, we had already noted significant numbers of Glowlights in our male detention centres. Since so little was known about the disease, the first concern of my predecessor, Director Bentley, was the risk to the men in our care and the potential implications for their safety. Was the Glow a response to a viral infection, and, if so, how was that infection transmitted? How contagious was the virus and what were its other symptoms? Once our executive team had ascertained the Glow wasn't a virus and that it presented little risk, or no risk, to the greater population, we were happy to be involved. In fact, our ethics committee studied the proposal and concluded it would be inappropriate to exclude our prison populations from the sampling.

So, can you tell us what the Silvester trial entailed?

Schofield: I assume you've read Professor Silvester's findings? I have the paper here somewhere. [There's a rustle as Schofield picks up a stack of papers and momentarily leafs through the pages, clearly searching for the document. Eventually, he replaces the stack on the desk and steeples his hands.] Well, the results are available online and excerpts published in all the major newssheets, and you probably saw Silvester's op-ed in the *Washington Post*.

And from your perspective?

Schofield: Look, I'm no scientist, but as I understood it, Silvester's group believed the Glow was a simple case of survival of the fittest – with rapidly evolving extreme weather events causing equally rapid and unprecedented selection pressures. They assumed the Glow was a response to the prolonged drought and heat waves being experienced globally, beginning in the most industrially developed countries where the species has the best chance of surviving. They claimed it was man's equivalent to growing a peacock's tail.

Would you care to explain the metaphor?

Schofield: Sure. Simply put, it's a means of attracting mates. The peacock's tail, which the male uses for sexual display, entices the peahen, and, if she finds him pleasing, ultimately results in the replication of the male's genetic material. Professor Silvester's study examined the intensity of the Glow – the relative lux given off by an individual – against his attractiveness, that is, as perceived by women.

Except the analogy became a key criticism of the research since, unlike a peacock's display, a Glowlight male doesn't light up only at times of sexual display. And clearly opportunities to attract females are limited in prison facilities intended for men.

Schofield [Grinning.]: Silvester's team had an answer to that, too. The reason the Glow intensity never wanes, they said, is because human males are *always* up for sex.

* * *

Glowlight Paul Golden, New York Times bestselling author of Strike Two:

[Comment recorded during a panel session at Baltimore's Readers & Writers Festival six months into the Glow phenomenon.]

Golden: The high incidence of Glowlights in prisons? It doesn't surprise me at all. There's a fine line between heroes and villains. Often, protagonists and antagonists share the same or similar desires, and many of the same qualities – passion, drive, skill, power. They might have the same flaws and come from identical backgrounds – for example, in *Strike Two*, the hero and the villain are brothers – but it's the choices they make which ultimately determine a story's resolution. It comes down to the old Sorting Hat dilemma: are you going to be a Gryffindor or a Slytherin?

* * *

Glowlight José Ippolito, actor:
[Interviewed by Vanity Fair reporter Casey Maria Triana (in Spanish) about the sudden appearance of his Glow the day after his 2028 Academy Award win for Best Actor in a feature film for The Kingdom.]

Ippolito: It's definitely life-changing, winning one of these. Most actors would agree that it represents a measure of success. As far as sexual attractiveness goes, well, that's not for me to say, but I've never had any problem with the ladies, if you know what I mean?

* * *

Glowlight Taylor Morrison, Grammy Award-winning country music singer:
[In a post-Grammy social media comment.]

Morrison: Of course, it's about success. Darling, you should see the girls fucking falling over themselves to get in my pants.

* * *

Lisa Selter, former CNN journalist:
[A continuation of the Motel 6 interview.]

Selter: The Silvester research was significant because it was one of the largest trials conducted, but it was clear from the outset that the work had numerous flaws. While the research group assumed that the Glow was a sudden and irreversible evolutionary response to rapid climate change – as we're now aware, this assumption was correct, at least indirectly – Silvester's focus was on the population outcomes, rather than the underlying causes. And then later it was discovered he had his own agenda, which led him to deliberately falsify his results.

He falsified the results?

Selter: No, no, not falsified. Please don't print that. I shouldn't have phrased it that way. Omission is a better word. He *omitted* important details revealed in the trial, and that omission obstructed our understanding of the phenomenon, which meant it took us much longer to reach the conclusion we did. Imagine if we had learned the cause sooner, the lives that might have been affected, girls we might have saved… [Selter removes the oversized glasses and pinches the bridge of her nose, placing the glasses on top of the Bible laying on the bedside table before continuing her testimony.]

I met him once, you know? Silvester. It was not long after the New Zealand group published their results. Bewhiskered and upright, he had that old public-school charm. Like your typical grandpa, but with an added air of authority, like he wasn't used to being refuted, which only served to make the story he was telling all the more appealing. Of course, by then he was showing signs of the Glow himself, which people were attributing to the success of his work and the news that he was in the running for *Time Magazine's* Person of the Year, but Silvester must have known what triggered it, or at the very least, he would have suspected. [There is a pause as Selter accepts a glass of water from our producer.]

That said, Silvester's trial being among the first, it was important work, and it showed the complicity of women, the willingness of some groups to accept the success narrative being peddled by the Glowlights and their networks. It became a kind of self-perpetuating prophecy – a chicken and egg situation – because once women associated the Glow with 'successful' men, they naturally found them more attractive. The Glow emerged as a marker of success just like an Armani suit, a seat on the board, or an Ivy League degree. I think it is fair to say plenty of women think a man with a convertible is more attractive than one driving a beat-up Corolla.

But half the men in the trial were in prison. It's hard to argue that they were successful on any scale.

Selter: It just goes to show how social media and influencers have impacted human biological development, doesn't it? According to Silvester, there were no end of prisoners who were 'successfully' running empires from their cells. And we all know girls who love themselves a bad boy, right? In the end it came down to society's definition of success, and the Glowlights worked hard to ensure we all bought into their version of it.

What about the men who never showed any sign of the Glow?

Selter: Well, as the Glowlights said, what about them? The Glowlights ostracised anyone not demonstrating the Glow, flooding the media with the notion that Noglows were losers. It was just another facet of the Glow phenomenon, the way Noglows were marginalised, another tipping point in the balance of power.

Ms. Selter, could we back up for just a moment? You mentioned some trial results that Professor Silvester omitted to publish...

Selter: Well, for one, there was no evidence that the Glow waned over time. Men in both the general and prison populations who demonstrated the Glow, continued to show the same or higher intensity after manifesting. And secondly, practically no one showed an increase in intensity of the Glow while incarcerated, and it was this point in particular which Professor Silvester failed to report. Men came into prison with or without the Glow, but for those who demonstrated the Glow, the intensity typically did not change until after they were released.

Then the Kiwi team published their research, and it was game over for Silvester.

* * *

Taika Jamieson, Principal of Canterbury Private School for Boys:

[Conducted in the first year of the Glow phenomenon, in Jamieson's second-floor office. The principal is a Glowlight of medium lux. He agreed to the interview on the provision that we promote the school's accomplishments in any outcomes.]

Congratulations, Principal Jamieson. We understand that Canterbury has always had a strong reputation for excellence, but in the eight months since the onset of the Glow phenomenon, your students have achieved some of the highest academic and sporting outcomes in the school's history, making it the current school of choice for England's young men.

Jamieson: Thank you. Yes, our School Board of Governors, all esteemed Glowlights, were keen to get ahead of the curve. In fact, it was just weeks after the Paris Summit that they changed the school's mission statement to reflect the Glow reality. I have our new prospectus here – including the specific objectives – if you'd like to take a look. [He locates a copy in a drawer and passes it across the desk to our producer.]

Producer [Offscreen.]: These seem rather draconian. [She reads from the prospectus.] "While students may enrol without a Glowlux recording, any boy not achieving required lux regulations for their year level by the given date will be expelled."

Jamieson: Draconian perhaps, but as you say, the results speak for themselves, and just think of the stakes: the Glow has become a fundamental measure of success, a key measure of a young man's future prosperity.

Producer: Surely, it's just a new kind of Old Boy's Club?

Jamieson [He shakes his head.]: That's the kind of uninformed comment I'd expect a woman to make. What you have to understand is parents are desperate to get their sons into this school. It's about improving the confidence and standing of an entire generation of young men who have been harangued and marginalised by feminist lobby groups bleating on about glass ceilings and trans bathrooms. The truth is, parents want more for their sons, and they recognise our establishment can give their boys an edge, make them shine. And, believe me, they're prepared to put their money where their mouths are. Last month, for example, we had a family offer to fund a new library, *including all the books*. And this term just gone, a Glowlight parent – I'm not at liberty to give details, suffice to say he's a household name – paid for his son's French class (and the entire French faculty) to go on a month-long retreat in France. In fact, they stayed not far from the Château de Maintenon where the Glow first manifested. And do you know, every one of those boys returned with the Glow. One lad even outshone the teacher! Canterbury might have been the first, but I'm sure we won't be the only school to make the leap to these Glowing Standards.

Producer: The only boys' school, you mean. [Jamieson shrugs, and the producer reads from the prospectus again.] "Henceforth, all Canterbury's hires will be Glowlights." There must have been some objections to these changes? Legal challenges, maybe?

Jamieson: Well, the Noglows objected, obviously – sour grapes mainly – although any legal challenges were avoided when the Board offered them all a tidy severance package. As for the parents, there were some who didn't like the rapid adjustments to school policies, but in the end, people came around. They saw the writing on the wall, didn't they? The Glow is the future. Institutions will either embrace it or fall by the wayside.

* * *

Lisa Selter, former CNN journalist:
    [A continuation of the Motel 6 interview.]

Can you tell us about the Kiwi connection?

Selter: Cal and I travelled to New Zealand to get the scoop. I'd gotten wind of it through the women's resistance – just whispers, mind. At first, I thought it was just wishful thinking. It had been four years by then, and the Glowlights had the world firmly stitched up with their male success gene narrative. It was the story of the century. I was as surprised as anyone when the Dolly Foundation sent Cal and I tickets to go down and interview Aroha Carpenter.

We understand Carpenter asked for you personally.

Selter: Maybe. I can't say for sure. I'd already had one scoop of a lifetime. Maybe she saw it as a way for me to put the record straight. Both Cal and I had been 'let go' by that stage and the job offers weren't exactly coming in thick and fast, so we weren't about to look a gift horse in the mouth.

Anyway, the two of us toddled off to New Zealand or Aotearoa as the locals call it. It's truly the end of the Earth down there. Took us three days to get there for two days of shooting. But those two days: it made me wish I'd seen the country before, because even with the drought, even with half of Australia's dustbowl carried across the Tasman on the wind, the place was beautiful. Desolate and haunting, and there was this uncanny sense of the supernatural, like

45

anything could step out of the haze... Did you know New Zealand was the first country to give women the vote? It was fitting then, that an all-women Kiwi team should determine the cause of the Glow. [She pauses, staring at the moth again.]

The breakthrough came, not at the laboratory bench, but from a friend of Carpenter's. Her name hasn't been revealed and you won't get it from me – there are children involved – so let's just call her Sara. Thirty-eight and a part-time administrator at a retirement village, Sara was divorced and sharing custody of three children (then aged 11, 8, and 6) with her ex. One Friday afternoon, the ex came to Sara's house to pick up the children for his scheduled weekend, but he'd forgotten the kids had an after-school activity that day, so they weren't home yet. The guy got angry, figured he'd take it out on Sara, and he raped her. By the time the kids arrived home, he'd buttoned up, washed up, and was waiting for them on her couch. That's when Sara saw the first twinklings of the Glow in him, and in her bruised and battered state, she made the vital connection.

Of course, Cal and I interviewed Sara. The *sang-froid* of that woman was incredible. Imagine watching your children leave with a man who has just raped you in your own home? She said it was his casualness that was the worst thing. Even while he was pounding into her, he kept talking, maybe convincing himself he had the right, because he was saying things like they'd been in a relationship for years and they had three kids, so he could do what he liked and who was going to believe her. She'd let him fuck her before, so why not now?

46

Maybe she'd been lonely.

Maybe she was hoping they'd get back together.

Maybe she was just another whore.

Well, Sara hadn't let him. She's a tiny woman, barely 5 feet 2 inches, and I reckon she weighed less than 100 pounds straight out of the shower, but it didn't stop her thrashing around, twisting and bucking, trying to throw off her attacker. She scratched his neck – borne out by the DNA found under her fingernails – and she kicked and screamed. She did everything she could to stop him. And before you ask, yes, she told him, "No, I don't want this," so there was no ambiguity regarding consent. She begged him to stop, to please think of the impact on their children. And when none of those things worked, she promised to call the police.

Sara claimed the bastard had laughed at that. "If they ask me, which they won't, but if they do, I'll just tell them that the lady likes it rough." Can you believe it? That's what he said to her. Then he punched her in the stomach. (I saw photographs of the bruises. They were date stamped and included Sara's tattoo.)

Later, when he'd left with her children, Sara kept her promise and called the police, but she called Aroha, too. Demanded they both take a vaginal sample from her for their respective labs, and that brave act resulted in an injunction against Sara's ex, and the breakthrough that Carpenter needed. Sara became *their* Patient Zero, her sample allowing Carpenter's team to isolate the substance which stimulated the Glow in men – a protein named α-23Dinah. Since the police had taken their sample at the same time via an independent consultancy, it helped to corroborate the findings.

Ironically, α-23Dinah did turn out to be sex-linked, only not in the way the Glowlights claimed. Instead, it was a woman's physiological response to forced vaginal penetration, her autonomic defence mechanism, which was the underlying cause. The α-23Dinah protein secreted vaginally by Sara during the rape, once absorbed through her rapist's penis, stimulated the luminescent Glow proteins to manifest.

It was just one sample, and in no way statistically significant, so Carpenter's team immediately set about conducting the studies that would prove Sara's case was not unique. They worked all hours during those first months, their trials carried out in secrecy and funded from their own pockets. Carpenter had a couch set up in the lab, so she could be there to process the middle-of-the-night rape kits and the clandestine lux recordings sent in by victims via the women's resistance. Her colleagues will tell you she practically lived there. They were following a fragile trail of breadcrumbs to the truth, but those initial trials paid off, revealing that Sara's case wasn't merely a coincidence. There was a definite correlation between a woman's rape and the appearance of the Glow in her rapist. It was shocking, and also not. Despite the personal risk to themselves, Carpenter's team resolved to push on.

The thing is, nothing about Carpenter's work was easy. There are strict regulations governing any research relating to human health. You have to get the participants' informed consent, for example, and any published results have to be fully anonymised. Both these requirements were problematic with the Glow, because while men were happy enough to submit to testing when they believed the Glow was success linked, they would undoubtedly spit the dummy if there was a chance they might be shown (even anonymously) to be rapists. Plus, Carpenter's group knew they had to tread carefully to protect the safety of the women.

In the end, it was a stroke of genius that helped the team get the Glowlight data they needed: they purchased anonymised success-gene data from the Johns Hopkins extensive Glowlight database – from trials commissioned and paid for by some of the world's most influential Glowlights. The beauty of it was that the men in those trials had already consented to their data being used for research purposes. Their DNA, blood results, and their lux results – proudly updated every time the men saw a jump in intensity – it was all there on file, giving Carpenter's group the complementary data they needed. That, coupled with Silvester's prison data from convicted rapists, allowed Carpenter's group to show that the intensity of the Glow – that is, the Glowlux demonstrated by an individual Glowlight – is proportional to the number of rapes he has perpetrated. But Sara's case, her rape, was the lightbulb moment – if you'll excuse the pun. [She smiles despite her apparent fatigue.]

49

But why are we only seeing this now? After all, rape is nothing new.

Selter: Rather than asking why now, the question might be why this evolutionary change hasn't appeared sooner, because you're right, women have been the victims of rape for millennia, ever since Eve stepped out of the Garden.

According to the Kiwis, the antecedents were always there, encoded in our DNA, but it took a certain set of conditions for α-23Dinah and the Glow to manifest. Look around: those conditions have been coming to a head for decades. Forest fires, drought, hundred-year storms, Arctic melt, the subsequent loss of ecological diversity; these things have all contributed. Our global Doomsday Clock is well past midnight. The world has gone to shit. There's your tipping point right there.

* * *

[Redacted], Illinois mother:

[The speaker phoned the Women's Resistance Network (Wren) and gave the following testimony. Redacted names and dates have been verified.]

Redacted: Hello? Are you there?

Wren: Yes. This is the Women's Resistance Network. You're speaking with Terry.

Redacted: I… I don't want my name to be publicised.

Wren: I understand.
How can we help?

Redacted: It's about my son. His name is [redacted]. He's 17. A couple of days ago, he was accepted to Northwestern. He won a scholarship to study Finance, like his dad. The thing is, the night he got the news, he went out with his girlfriend to celebrate. We took ourselves off to bed, so I didn't see him come in, but yesterday when he came down to breakfast, he was Glowing. My partner was over the moon. He said it proved the success gene theory was correct, that our son was showing his true potential. [She sobs.]

Wren: Hello?

Redacted: I'm sorry, Terry, I don't think I can do this.

Wren: Would it help just
to get it off your chest?

Redacted: You won't do anything?

Wren: Not without your permission.

Redacted: I think he might have forced himself on his girlfriend. Oh my god. I can't believe I'm saying this. I'm his mother. But they've been going out for years, ever since they were both 14, and she's like my own daughter. Over breakfast, [redacted] said they'd broken up – he's going to Northwestern, and she's going to UW, so it just made sense to go their separate ways, and it was all amicable and everything – but the way he said it, I don't know, it just wasn't right. It was too... too convenient. Something happened that night. Something off. I know it. Because he hasn't called her, not even to stop by and drop off her things.

>*Wren: Could you speak to the girl?*
>*Encourage her to undergo a rape kit?*

Redacted: On what pretext? It was two days ago. Anyway, if I'm right then I'm the rapist's mother. I doubt she'll talk to me. I know I never could have... Look, I shouldn't have called. It's probably nothing. It's just I... I...

>*Wren: Did something*
>*like this happen to you?*

Redacted: [Muffled crying.]

>*Wren: I'm so sorry. You didn't*
>*deserve this. It isn't your fault.*

Redacted: [More crying.]

>*Wren: A rape kit can be carried out up to*
>*72 hours after the event. If there is any way—*

[The caller hangs up.]

* * *

Madison Ruth, disciple of the Temple of Light:

[Madison Ruth is the wife of Pastor Jimmy Ruth, who is currently serving a forty-year term for multiple incidents of rape and assault, including on minors. We are ushered into a small annex at the back of a modern church complex for the interview and are not permitted to tour the facility during our two-hour visit, although we catch

occasional glimpses of members of the Temple of Light community through the windows – mainly women and young girls, all dressed in long floral dresses and old-fashioned poke bonnets. Wearing an equivalent dress (somewhat faded from frequent washing), Ruth herself is a tall woman in her early sixties with greying hair plaited in two braids that reach to her waist, lending her a youthful air despite her austere demeanour. She allows us to film the interview, providing her face and voice are obscured in any eventual documentary footage, because, as she says in her testimony: "taken out of context things can get twisted around like a tornado, and the last thing the Temple needs is more of those denier crazies on our doorstep." Questions were pre-approved by the Temple of Light clergy (whom we did not have the occasion to meet, but they appointed member Mary Tenet to provide oversight on their behalf). An excerpt from the interview is transcribed below.]

Did it surprise you when your husband was recorded as having the highest lux of any Glowlight on Earth, at least in the developed countries where records are available?

Ruth: Not at all. Pastor Jim is a guiding light in our community, a father to all, and appointed by God, so it makes complete sense to me that he would glow like the Glory itself.

*The Temple of Light community protested the Blasey Act,
working in collaboration with politicians and lobby
groups and purportedly investing millions of dollars to
overturn the bill –*

Ruth: I saw it coming. I did. From the moment the Glow
appeared, I expected they would come for Pastor Jim,
that he would be hounded and persecuted. Made to
suffer for our sins. It's always been thus for truly holy
men. And Pastor Jim foresaw it too, because even before
the Glow manifested, he'd been preaching about the
end times, hadn't he, Mary? After all, what is this ongoing
drought but a period of tribulation, and the Blasey Act
was just another sign. We had no choice but to fight it.
We are soldiers of the Lord.

*So, I take it you don't agree with the findings of the Kiwi
research team?*

Ruth: No, I don't agree. What those women scientists
suggested is disgusting. Abhorrent. Using the Glow
to excuse their whoring. The damage those women
have wrought on the world. I know I should forgive
them, poor lost souls that they are, but they...
they... they just don't know Pastor Jim. He is a
Bringer of Light. He couldn't hurt *anyone*, let alone
the several hundred women the prosecutors said
he did. I am his wife. I was here the whole time; I
would've known.

*But didn't several Temple of Light members come
forward to testify against him?*

54

Tenet: Please don't answer that question, Madison. It isn't on the list. And for the record, they are *ex*-members. Disbelievers. We don't speak of them anymore.

Right... [From offscreen comes the rustling of papers, and a whispered conversation (indistinct) before our interviewer proceeds.] If you reject the science, how then do you account for the Glow?

Ruth [smiles]: It's the Rapture, isn't it? What else could it be?

Wait. The rapture. Are you implying then that Pastor Jim, the world's brightest Glowlight, is the Messiah?

Tenet: Another unapproved question.

Ruth [placing a hand on her companion's arm]: It's fine, Mary. I'll answer. [She clears her throat.] If you ask him, Pastor Jim will never admit to it – he's far too humble to call himself the Messiah – but yes, that is exactly what I believe.

But he's in prison.

Tenet: Unapproved.

Ruth: So was Jesus.

* * *

Lisa Selter, former CNN journalist:
[A continuation of the Motel 6 interview. Selter is nursing a disposable cup of vending machine coffee.]

Selter: After the research, after the peer review punch-ups, the Insta-family break-ups, and the Twitter explosion, then came the legal-political battle. It was all anyone talked about. A lot of people reasoned that if the Glow was able to shine a light on the rapists, then it was only right that those men be convicted for their crimes. The Glowlights were horrified. Even the shiny elites were shaking in their boots. They may have denied it in public – let's face it, most of them are *still* denying it – but deep down they knew what they'd done. There was a very real chance some of them would go to prison.

The Glowlight elite did what rich men always do when faced with a problem. They threw money at it, engaging a legal dream team to go in to bat for them. Their lawyers (including some women) contended that rape is a crime against an individual, and therefore, in order for a man to be convicted, a victim or victims would have to come forward. Glowlux data on its own shouldn't be sufficient to convict. That put the Glowlights back on familiar ground. After all, these men had spent their lives destroying any woman who might have had the courage to accuse them. The smear campaigns came thick and fast.

We think they did other things, too. Murders. Kidnappings. I don't know about you, but I find it hard to believe that several hundred serial killers suddenly sprang into action during that time. Look, you can't print that, obviously. I don't have anything concrete to support those last statements. They're all conjecture and speculation. But, off the record, if you haven't already, you should try and find Cal because I know he had some evidence, photos and film clips and the like, that you might find helpful. A certain Hollywood actress found in the barrel of a concrete mixer, for example… [Selter takes a sip of her coffee while that last statement sinks in.]

Remember rape isn't only a sexual act. It's about power. More than one woman told me that the Blasey Act made things worse, as Glowlight men simply turned to other forms of sexual violence, other ways of exerting power…

Then Senator Marlie Hodge swooped in. Amazing woman. I love her. Clever, articulate, and sharp as a tack. I was a journalist, so I had a pretty jaded view of politicians, but that woman was a breath of fresh air. I know, I know, the classic bob haircut and square-cut suits made her look like a throwback from the 80s, but maybe that was the reason the Glowlights took their eyes off the ball or maybe it was because they didn't expect it to be a daughter of the Grand Old Party who would throw them a curveball.

Hodge's idea was to consider rape as a crime against society. To look at it in the same way that a specific blood-alcohol limit would trigger a DUI, or possession of a narcotic over and above what might be considered for personal use meant you were a dealer. It was brilliant. While the Glowlight elites were distracted waging their menace campaign, Hodge tabled her Blasey bill. In that document, she suggested that a man with a Glowlux threshold equivalent to three or more rapes was a danger to society and should be incarcerated. That sent the Glowlight elites reeling, especially since the long-suffering Noglows and LGBTQ representatives, fed up with being sidelined and eager to give the Glowlights their just desserts, made it clear that they would be voting with the women. For a moment, it looked like Hodge had the votes she needed.

[Selter giggles.] I'm not a proper journalist anymore, but I have to say, watching the onscreen debates, seeing those Sparklers squirm, was some of the most compelling television I've ever seen.

But then the Glowlights rallied, countering with the Grand-daddy Clause put forward by ninety-year-old independent senator, Randolf Myers. That's the loophole which precluded historic Glowlights from being prosecuted. Only those Glowlights who showed increased Glowlux from the date the Act came into force would be subject to prosecution.

All across the resistance, women were up in arms, and rightly so. Even the MADD moms were disgusted. It was a bit like allowing an alcoholic to drive drunk, simply because he can hold his liquor better. But in a way, it made practical sense, because there were literally millions more Glowlights than there were prison cells. The clause remained, the votes were counted, the President signed it, and that was that.

[Selter exhales deeply.] I wish they'd put Adam Reitz in prison. The man has more Glow than a mall in December, and still he's walking around scot-free. That's not the worst of it. Every day he picks at the scab, looking for ways to reverse the Act, refute the research, and discredit the women. It's no secret that he's been lobbying for the imprisonable lux threshold to be raised, and my sources on the dark web tell me he has Myers working on a Minor Amendment to the Blasey Act, a clause that will exclude teens and youth from prosecution because they're too young to know any better. I mean, boys will be boys and all that. [She snorts.] Tell that to all the little girls who are abused. [She laughs bitterly, then mutters.] Boys will be boys. I'll bet bloody Myers can't even remember that far back.

[A pause.] Sometimes, when I think back on that day at the Climate Summit, I think Reitz really did drink the Kool-Aid.

Do you believe the Act has made things worse?

Selter: It's prevented some rapes, I'm sure, but perhaps it's also made the rapists sneakier. Meaner. Increasing the incidences of sodomy and violence… [Sighing, she plucks at a piece of fluff on her jeans.] There is one good thing, though.

Yes?

Selter: Oddly, the Glowlights have been so desperate to dim the lights that they've started taking steps to mitigate the climate crisis. Too little, too late probably, and it will be light years before they can reverse the pollution that provoked the appearance of α-23Dinah and the subsequent Glow proteins (if the phenomenon even is reversible), but studies suggest there's been a definite slowdown in carbon emissions. There you go: a beam of light in all this gloom.

* * *

Adam Reitz, billionaire CEO of Giga:

[This interview took place on the sidewalk outside Giga's New York HQ the week the Blasey Act came into force and the day the major phone companies pulled their lux apps in protest. Ardent (and arguably self-interested) objectors to the Act, Reitz and his inner circle of Glowlight elite (which includes two members of the royal family) are credited for the Blasey Act's Grand-daddy clause, the reason the billionaire isn't currently behind bars.]

Reporter: Sir, what's your reaction to the global removal of lux apps from sale?

Reitz [Straightening his tie.]: In my view, CEOs like my friend Jason Kelly have taken the right step. Today's outcome is an important milestone for men's rights. You don't ask a woman her weight; I don't see why a man's Glowlux is anyone's business. It's a gross invasion of privacy.

Reporter: With all due respect, sir, being overweight isn't a crime.

Reitz [Eyes flashing dangerously.]: Being a Glowlight shouldn't be a crime, either. [He raises his voice.] I'll tell you what's criminal, it's the indecent speed with which the legislation was passed. That Kiwi research was based on flawed assumptions. Not all Glowlights are rapists. I'm convinced that Professor Silvester's latest research will bear that out and his findings will lead to the Blasey

Act being repealed. When that happens, believe me, heads are going to roll.

Reporter: Any words for whistle-blower Lisa Selter now that the Act has passed?

Reitz [Frowning, he pushes past the paparazzi.]: No comment.

Reporter [Calling after him.]: Any idea of her whereabouts?

Reitz [Mutters.]: No, but when I find the harpy bitch…

* * *

Yasmin Bhagwat, 26, social commentator:
[Excerpt from a vlog published on Yasmin Bhagwat's TikTake-over, August 22, four months after the US Congress passes the Blasey Act.]

Bhagwat: Ladies, I implore you, this is no time to be complacent. Thanks to the sterling work of women like Senator Marlie Hodge, we have the Blasey Act, and while it's a great start, we all know the abuses against women and girls haven't ceased. Far from it. We owe it to our sisters, to our mothers and our daughters, to keep up the fight. More especially, we owe it to the women whose rapists will never be charged, whose rapists are still at large in the community, still living in their homes and sleeping in their beds… Remember, the Blasey Act allows a man to rape three times with impunity. Three times! One of those unfortunate women might be your sister or your daughter.

[She points at the audience.] It might be *you*. So, if you have a few dollars to spare, please consider donating to the Dolly Foundation and the work of trailblazing Kiwi scientist Aroha Carpenter as together they search for a way to connect the Glow proteins with the α-23Dinah proteins that stimulated them. Vital research, which, like a DNA fingerprint, will allow police to categorically identify a woman's rapist. To donate, text the number on your screen or call…

* * *

Lisa Selter, former CNN journalist:

[A continuation of the Motel 6 interview. At this point, Selter has been talking for close to seven hours. Her face is drawn and there are dark smudges beneath her eyes. Our team is exhausted too, but given the importance of Selter's testimony, no one suggests calling it a night.]

Selter: Obviously, there were women who knew what was happening even before the Kiwi team announced their results. Before all hell broke loose. Before Reitz and his Glowlight cronies started their private war. But the very means by which women knew, well, it meant they had little power. They were frightened. Angry. Tired. Confused. Many just wanted to put it behind them and move on. Still, there were people who were prepared to call it as they saw it.

Who asked questions. Brave women who stood up to the Glowlight moguls.

Women like you.

Selter [Snorting]: I was a journalist. It was my job to get to the truth. But even in those very early days, there were people who understood what we were up against. It seemed so simple. Like all we needed was the evidence, and things would get better. [There is a silence while Selter wipes her face with her hands.] When I think of those women... Women who willingly submitted to the rape kits – married women like Deborah Marie Marshall, Linda J. Jackson, and others – broken women who rose from the floor to measure the increase in their partners' Glowlux intensity even while they slept, sending the results through to the Women's Resistance. Those who couldn't risk having lux apps on their phones, who hid the bulky lux meters in their underwear drawers or in their children's closets. Women like poor Reese Dreamwalker, who was murdered by her Glowlight boyfriend when he woke unexpectedly. They were the brave ones. Not me. My job was to make sure their sacrifice meant something.

[As the first triangle of dawn shines under the blind, Selter gets up, arching her back and stretching her legs. She puts on the oversized glasses, then fumbles in the side pocket of her bag for a slip of paper (contact details for the blog-news team) which she hands to our producer.]

Selter: Thanks for listening. Good luck with your doco. Hey, would you guys mind turning out the lights when you leave? And if you find Cal, give him my regards, will you?

[Selter checks the corridor, verifying no one is there before she steps out. She wheels her carry-on down the corridor to the stairs. Once she descends, we can no longer see her, and nor do we hear from her again. When we send her the transcript of the interview for her approval, the email that we'd contacted her on bounces. Recent reports on social media suggest she is dead. One idiot on the dark web claims he's throttled the lying whore, bagged her up, and left her in a dumpster, but the FBI follows that up and it proves to be false. A year after this interview, a member of our team swears he saw Selter in the car park of another motel chain, this time in Michigan. It was 6 a.m. and he'd pulled an all-nighter reporting on a shooting incident. He said he recognised the glasses, but how could he be sure?]

At Māratotō Pool

Lee Murray

⌒

Maratoto: garden spring
Māratotō: river/gushing lifeblood

I'D CARRIED the bike for a kilometre through the sun-brittled hardwoods, forced to put it down each time I helped my mother manage the dusty inclines, or step over the dried-out ponga trunks. She was nearing seventy, after all. I would leave her to catch her breath while I went back for my trusty Trek.

"For God's sake, just dump the damn bike, Viv," she shouted after me.

I refused to give it up. It was all I had left; the only thing connecting me to home. Instead, I slipped my arm through the frame and hoisted the bike up, ignoring Mum's whinging and the pedal digging into the middle of my back. When I reached her, she made that *tsk*ing sound, like some vintage schoolmarm. "You're so bloody stubborn. Just like your father," she grumbled.

He hadn't been stubborn enough though, had he? Not enough to go the distance – taking his own life mere months after my brother Michael had got himself riddled with holes in a senseless shootout. So now there was just Mum and me, trudging through clouds of dust, towards an imaginary sanctuary somewhere up Māratotō way.

"Come on. Let's just keep moving," I said. "How much further to this lake, anyway?"

"Not a lake. Māratotō is a waterfall. Or at least it was, when I last visited."

"When was that exactly?"

"I don't know. A few years back, in thirty-four or thirty-five."

More than two decades. I didn't bother to roll my eyes. "Everywhere else is dry," I said.

"There'll be something there," she insisted. "Māratotō is Māori for 'gushing lifeblood,' so there has to be water. Stands to reason, doesn't it?"

There was no *reason* about it. I imagined an arid and dusty hole, its steep banks crumbling with desiccated moss. "Tell me again what they said at the water tap."

I'd missed the story, leaving her to hold our place in the line while I'd tried trading our last two Paracetamol caps for food.

Her tired eyes brightened as she told the story again. It had been nothing more than a whisper really, rumours rippling down the line at the township's last remaining water tap. The tale of a place with water where they welcomed everyone, not just able-bodied folk who could pay with their labour. Well, people talked, didn't they? What else was there to pass the time while they waited for their daily ten… then five… and now three litres of water, the quantity strictly enforced by two men with guns.

Of course, the sanctuary was a myth. It had to be. Because if a nirvana like that really existed, why would anyone leave it to come back into town and tell the story? It was just another rumour to add to all the others. A dream to dwell on while people wished away the hours. When I'd said as much to Mum, she'd just shrugged.

"Well, I'm going," she'd said, proving that the stubborn gene existed on the Braid side of the family, too. She waved her hand about what was left of our garden. "What's left for us here, anyway?"

I'd glanced at my precious crop of runner beans, shaded beneath their wilted too-white leaves, everything blanketed in dust, and pressed my lips together. The beans had been doomed, but I hung on another week – until someone broke down the fence and got away with half the crop.

After that, going to Māratotō was all Mum talked about. "If you don't like the place, you can always come back."

I helped her over a rut in the track and wondered if she'd have got this far on her own. An *easy* half-day bike ride from home. I stifled a snort. Life was full of paradoxes, wasn't it? Nevertheless, I hoped Māratotō still had its waterfall. A waterfall would be something.

We rounded a corner and my breath caught in my throat.

Tents of all colours. People. So there *was* a commune here. And I couldn't see any weapons either. But the people turned to look at us, and there was something slow and glacial about their movement. Their smiles were too wide, and their demeanour screamed of practised casualness.

The skin on the back of my neck prickled. "Mum," I said, hoping she would catch the warning in my tone.

"Shhh," she replied.

"Welcome to Māratotō, the garden spring," said a woman. She was my age and unremarkable – mid-thirties, brown hair pulled into a ponytail – but standing beside her was the most beautiful man I had ever seen. Not hard like the men in town. I could barely keep my eyes off him.

"So, is it true, then?" Mum's eyes glistened. "The falls are still here?"

"They're up the track a bit. In a grove of trees."

My knees trembled and I had to steady myself against a tree. There *was* a pool. They had water here!

The beautiful man smiled. "The falls might not be exactly as you remember them – they're hardly Niagara – but the pool is still there. Marelle and I will take you up there if you like."

They were going to let us see it! It had taken us three days to climb into the hills. We were weary, dusty, and as parched as stone, but we had to see the waterfall.

I left the bike behind, and we walked a kilometre to a grove of four solid fruit trees, their trunks as wide and straight as young kauri. Beneath the trees was a pink-

68

brown mud pool fed by a dribble of water which trickled down a narrow incline on one side.

Half a dozen people, mostly older women, lounged in the mud, their heads laid back on the flattened stones at the edge of the pool.

I felt myself colour as Mum took off her clothes, dropping them where she stood, and climbed right in. "Mum!"

Marelle touched my arm. "It's fine. There's a well further up the valley that we use for our drinking water, so we allow the older folk to indulge," she said. "It reminds them of the past."

My heart did cartwheels in my chest. There was a well! Not just this muddy wallow, although I could understand Mum's urge to get in. I'd only been small – maybe four or five years old – but I remembered swimming in fresh water. We'd gone to Lake Taupō, Mum, Dad, Michael, and me, before the crater lake had been pumped dry to slake the thirst of the country's six million gasping citizens. We'd walked an hour over the pebbly sand to the water's edge, where my brother and I had plunged into the icy water and come up shrieking and laughing. Our whole bodies, *immersed* in the water. I could still recall the sensation, so cool and calming on my skin, and with no crusty seawater sting. Just thinking about it raised goosebumps on my arms.

Mum lay back in the pool, mud rolling over her shoulders, and closed her eyes.

I'd never seen her so serene.

Marelle said, "Why not let her soak while Phillip and I find a place to set you up back in the village?"

They are going to let us stay. Why? The goosebumps lingered.

Mum's eyes barely fluttered. "Go on, Viv," she said. "I'm not going anywhere."

Marelle, Phillip, and I trudged back along the track to the cluster of tents, Marelle veering off to chat with someone when we neared the commune, while Phillip showed me to a dusty grey tent. A couple of camp beds had been stacked to one side, clean bedding folded on top.

"Surely this belongs to someone?"

Phillip shrugged. "They left."

Not knowing what else to say, I busied myself setting up the beds, relieved when Marelle returned carrying a basket of fruit resembling pomegranates. She offered me one.

I hesitated.

"I don't blame you," Phillip said. "Can't stand them myself."

Perhaps to reassure me, Marelle bit into one, its red juice staining her teeth and lips crimson. "Blood fruit," she explained. She showed me the inside: the flesh blood-coloured with sharp white pips.

I couldn't help narrowing my eyes. None of this felt right. It was all too good to be true. *The well.* This tent. The beds. And now this offer of food. Even with New Zealand's population dwindling to less than a million, there was still barely enough to go around. No one gave away food. Not without getting something in return.

"They say you let anyone in here," I said warily. "Is that true? You'll welcome anyone who turns up?"

I caught Marelle's shifting glance. "Not just anyone. We're careful."

"Why us then? You don't know anything about my mother and me."

Marelle pulled that slow smile, the one she'd given us when we arrived. "Well, that's just it, isn't it? You were willing to bring an elderly woman to a sanctuary this far into the mountains with no idea of what you might find here. That kind of thing says something."

"Yeah. It says she's a bossy old woman and I'm an idiot."

Phillip grinned. "Well, yes. There is that. But it also showed us that you're kind."

It didn't seem nearly enough.

In years gone by, a commune of sorts would pop up anywhere people located a water source – survivalist groups, religious nuts, even a few local authority regimes, all demanding you toe the line for a share of whatever resources they had on offer – but with so much demand, overcrowding and disillusionment meant many communities had imploded in violence. When munitions had still been available, people with guns had rampaged through the settlements. It hadn't been so much survival of the fittest as much as survival of the armed. Thousands had perished in that Great Cull. Nowadays, almost no one had bullets, but there were other ways to die, so people remained cautious.

Marelle's giggle cut across my thoughts. She handed me a blood fruit, then picked up the basket. "Well, if you *had* planned to kill us in our beds, you could hardly make a quick getaway with a seventy-something in tow, could you?" Smiling, she left in a swish of brown ponytail.

I had to admit she had a point.

When she was out of sight and we could no longer hear her chuckling, Phillip leaned over and nudged me with his shoulder. "If you must know, it was your bike."

"My bike?"

"Remember, that well we were telling you about? The one further up the valley? We drag the water buckets up by hand."

Understanding dawned: properly harnessed, the mechanical power of my bike would make it easier to bring the water to the surface. My unease dissipated. *Of course.* For all Marelle's talk of kindness, the bike had been our ticket into the commune. The quid pro quo.

I took a bite of the blood fruit and let the sweet juice drip down my chin.

Every day for the next few weeks, I walked the two kilometres up the valley to the well with Phillip, helping him to rig up my bike so it could be used to pump well water to the surface, and then taking my turn in the saddle to contribute to the commune's daily supply. During those walks, and over the course of our days together, I learned a lot about the commune.

"It's not so much a commune as a retirement village," Phillip joked as he adjusted the bike seat to accommodate his height. "There are close to sixty residents, most of them living in tents in the village, but one or two live dotted about on the surrounding ledges and plateaus. Half of our residents are in their sixties or above."

"I haven't seen any children."

His expression grew sombre. "No, you won't have."

Had they set up a school somewhere? Was that why? Surely, I would've heard the kids playing?

Phillip climbed on the bike and pushed down hard with his legs to get the wheels spinning. "There are no kids at Māratotō."

None at all? Children were rare enough, but in a community this size, I would've expected a few.

"Dunno why exactly," Phillip said before I'd even asked the question. "For some reason, new arrivals tend to be older. The drought taking a toll, I guess." He puffed heavily, getting into the cadence. "Or maybe it's our Māratotō population that's skewed. It was bound to happen; while we don't advertise it, people hightail it here pretty fast when they find out we don't require our seniors to work."

I arched a brow. "Nice life for some," I quipped.

My mother was certainly revelling in it; getting up earlier and earlier every day to make the one-kilometre trek to the falls where she would while away the hours, lounging dreamily in the mud pool like some kind of hallowed hippo. It was a wonder she hadn't dissolved, she spent so much time submerged. Marelle said there was something protective in the mud. A tourism industry had been founded on it. Way back in the 1900s, apparently. Then, last night, when I'd gone to collect Mum for dinner, she'd refused to get out and come back with me.

"Let her stay," Marelle had said kindly. "It can be a long walk for our older members. There are a couple of tents up here for those who prefer to stay close."

"But she hasn't eaten anything since breakfast."

Smiling, Marelle had laid a hand on my arm. "You're a good daughter. It can't have been easy looking out for your mother all these years. A lot of people took the easy way and abandoned their parents, you know? You deserve some time out. Cassie and I will make sure she eats."

So, I'd left my mother there and walked back to the village with Phillip. Then, after we'd eaten, the two of us had spent the evening beside the fire. We didn't talk much; just sat there enjoying the crackle and tangy scent of burning mānukā. From time to time, Phillip added another log, which stirred up the embers, sending frenzied sparks into the dry air. Bathed in flickering firelight, his skin had turned a dark bronze. Today, under the sun, it gleamed gold. He'd been pedalling a while now and the sweat was beading on his shoulders and back, fascinating me.

"Is that why elders get indulged here?" I asked, handing him a cup of water. "Because there are no kids to dote on?"

Phillip sat up in the saddle, his feet braced on the pedals, and took the drink. "Possibly. I never really considered it that way. I always thought it was because Marelle's great aunt Eremia founded the community and the old lady was part Chinese, part Māori." He handed me the cup and went back to his pedalling.

I had some Māori in me too, so I got his drift: in both Chinese and Māori cultures, elders were revered and respected. They were cherished family members to be nurtured into their old age, not just shunted into retirement homes. Since the drought had started, those values were wearing thin. It was refreshing to find they still existed here. Marelle's great-aunt must have been a force to reckon with.

"Did you get to meet her?" I asked.

"Eremia?" Still pedalling, Phillip wiped the sweat from his forehead with the back of his hand. "Eremia is still here. In a way. The spirit of her, at least. She's like a kind of overarching presence. But no, I didn't get to meet her in person. The old lady was long gone by the time I got here."

I didn't ask him to elaborate. Once upon a time I might have, but it had become impolite to ask about people's origins, and even more rude to inquire about their past. These days, everyone was entitled to a skeleton or two in the closet.

The bucket reached the top of the well and Phillip stopped pedalling. I tried to lift the bucket off the crossbar, but it slipped through my fingers, precious water slopping on the ground before I could recover.

I stared aghast as the silver droplets seeped into the earth.

"Here, let me help," Phillip said quickly, hopping off the saddle, his fingers brushing mine as he grabbed the bucket.

"Sorry I wasted some," I said.

"It was an accident. Don't worry about it."

I held the container steady, while he poured the water from the bucket, his reassurance not making me feel any better.

Phillip hooked the bucket back to the pulley. The rope creaked.

"Where does the water come from, anyway?"

"No way of knowing," he replied. "An underground stream. Maybe an aquifer."

"Aquifers are finite."

"All water is finite."

He must have seen my alarm because his face softened. "Let's hope it's not an aquifer."

We didn't speak again until we'd loaded the last filled cask onto a wheelbarrow-contraption, each of us lifting a handle to push our cargo along the trail back to the village.

Three months after our arrival, Mum emerged from the pool, brushed the drying mud from her skin, and hitched a ride on one of the wheelbarrow-contraptions for the kilometre journey back along the track to our tent. I hadn't been expecting her, so her arrival sent me into a frenzied panic. Mum sat on a camp stool and clucked her tongue while I separated the camp beds, changed the bedding, and shooed Phillip off to another tent to make space for her.

Mum rolled her eyes cheekily. "Don't mind me."

I was too happy to let it bother me. I suppose my relationship with Phillip had been inevitable given the time we'd been spending together. Perhaps it was because for the first time in my adult life I'd gained some independence – *I'd taken control of my own life* – now that Cassie and Marelle and the rest of the commune were helping to take care of Mum. And despite looking a little thinner than usual, Mum appeared to be thriving, although she moved about less, and when she did, her gestures were slow and graceful as if she were practising tai chi. I watched her with fascination as she teased drying mud from her hair. Perhaps this languidness was my mother's natural state, and it being so long since I'd seen it (if I'd seen it at all), I no longer recognised it.

"It's good that you're happy with your young man," Mum said, stopping her grooming for a moment to lift my hair off my shoulders. "I'm happy for you. For both of us. Coming here was the right thing to do: the people and the pool…"

I crouched beside her. "What's it like in the pool?"

She curled a mesh of hair around her fingertips. "Viv, it's blissful. Almost sinful." She breathed deeply and beamed at me, a rapturous schoolgirl describing her first crush. "I can hardly describe it."

"Try me."

She took my hands in hers and closed her eyes. "Being immersed in the pool makes me feel youthful again. My skin feels soft, even smoother than yours is, and my bones don't ache anymore. The pool, the mud, it lifts me up. *Uplifts* me somehow, cradling me to it. It's as if your father's still with me and holding me close." She sighed softly, then went on. "I'll spoon him, my cheek warm against his back, and breathe in the scent of him. It's so wonderful, the two of us lying there together in the cool where everything feels solid and safe. It was always meant to be like this." She opened her eyes, tears welling at the corners. "It's how our lives would have been, if the drought had never come."

My heart lurched with sorrow for her. What she was describing was pure fantasy. For a moment, I considered preventing her from going back to the pool and forcing her to face reality. But I stopped myself. If she'd said these things while we'd been back in town, I might've done exactly that, but now that we were here, it seemed too cruel. After years of hardship, my mother was finally content. What harm did it do to allow her to daydream? After all, I had Phillip now.

"You're sure you're not bored spending all day up there?" I asked her.

"Bored? Of course not. There's so much to talk about! We're always chatting."

I smiled. The times I'd been to the pool to see her, she'd almost always been napping, her body in the mud and her head resting on a stone, eyes closed and her chest gently rising and falling. More often than not, she hadn't even registered my presence. Although, lately I hadn't been there as often as I would've liked. Perhaps I'd just picked the wrong moments.

I lifted my hand to her cheek. "Well, if you're happy, then that's all that matters."

Tilting her head to one side, she covered my hand with her own. "Viv, I really am. It's why I made the trip here to the village. I wanted to let you know that I plan to stay out at the pool permanently. I love it there."

My skin prickled. "You want to leave me?" My voice sounded petulant, needy.

"Viv." My mother pinched me gently under the chin. "You're thirty-six years old. A grown woman. You don't need me under your feet playing gooseberry."

Since she'd already made her decision, all that remained was to make the most of her visit. I prepared her a cabbage tree heart wrapped in an omelette and told her about the commune's poultry farm and its skinny yet overconfident rooster. I made her a tea of steeped mānukā bark and told her how some of us were rediscovering the Māori process for making glue from tarata bark, which we hoped might come in useful for mending the aging tents. When I asked if she'd like to finish her meal with a wedge of blood fruit, she shook her head.

"Too sickly," she said, and I smiled because Phillip and I didn't eat them either. I didn't care for the way they made me feel; some compound in the fruit made my head spin and my teeth go numb.

After dinner, Mum said little, content to sit by the fire and let me natter on about this and that. Indulging me, I guess, since she was moving away.

The next morning, after she'd left and I was changing the bedding, I found the note. It had been written on a sliver of stick and hidden in the hem of one of the blankets. I might not have discovered it at all, but the stitching on the hem had unravelled and the stick had worked its way out. Someone had written shakily in purple biro: *Beware Māratotō!*

"What's this?" I asked Phillip.

His head whipped up and he snatched the stick from me. "Is that your mother's writing?" he demanded. Last night's tent mate had been a snorer, so he was crotchety from lack of sleep.

I shook my head.

Phillip threw it in the fire pit. "Buggered if I know. That stick could've been there for ages. You nearly ready?"

Draping the bedding over a line to air in the sun, I hurried to collect the water casks for our daily trek to the well.

In autumn, I awoke one morning to learn one of the elderly women who shared the pool had died overnight, so I delayed my daily trip to the well in favour of a detour to the pool to check on Mum. As always, I found her with her head resting on a flat stone, eyes closed and her shoulders submerged, although this morning a thin line of pink-brown clay smeared her cheek.

"Mum?"

"Hmm?"

"They say one of the women passed on last night. I thought I would check you were okay."

"Okay," she repeated, her voice distant, as if she were waking from a dream.

I slid my hand into the lukewarm mud and squeezed her shoulder. "I wanted to make sure you weren't upset about losing your friend."

"It's fine. She's fine." Beneath my hand, her shoulder twitched. Perhaps she'd intended to raise her arm but found the effort of lifting it out of the mud too much and changed her mind. In any case, she didn't open her eyes.

"I suppose she's gone to a better place," I said. It was a platitude, but what else could I say? I hadn't known the dead woman.

"Something else springs forth," Mum murmured. "Decay and renewal. It's the cycle of things. She's still here with us." She opened her eyes and stared hard at me. "Just in a different way."

I jumped backwards, startled. Could she tell? Did I look so different? I left her, heading across country to meet Phillip at the well. My detour hadn't taken long, but already he'd filled and loaded a barrow of water casks.

"Everything okay?" he asked when he saw me.

"Yes."

"You don't sound so sure."

"I'm pregnant," I told him.

When Phillip announced he was leaving the commune, my heart skipped a beat and my knees buckled.

"Not for good. Just for a few days," he said, gathering me to him. "Marelle has asked me to go down the mountain to get some supplies. Someone goes every six months or so to trade."

"Why you?" I whined. "Can't someone else go?"

He nuzzled my neck, hands on the small of my back. "They could, but Marelle's asked me because she knows I'll be careful about what I say. If news spreads about the commune, we'll be deluged with people looking to join us."

"Let them come," I said flippantly. It was how we'd come to be there, after all.

Phillip stepped back. "You're too trusting. Not everyone appreciates the way we live here."

That's when I remembered the stick hidden in the bedding. The people living in the grey tent before us had decided to up and leave. What hadn't they appreciated exactly?

Still, I didn't want Phillip going into town. Things had been bad enough when Mum and I were still living there, and no doubt they'd have deteriorated since. "What's in town that we can't make here?" I said. "We've got everything we need."

"Well, medicine for one."

"What's wrong with the old Māori remedies?"

"There are other things." He read off a list written in the margins of a page pulled from a textbook. "Firelighters, a new chain for the bike, a pair of tweezers…"

"Phillip—"

"I have to go, Viv," he insisted. "Whatever you do, don't lift any water casks, and don't go getting in the pool – we don't know what the mud might do to the baby."

The days were endless without him. I couldn't get any peace. Since ours was the first baby born to the commune in close to a decade, everyone fussed about me. They meant well, but it was stifling.

"Sit down, Viv," they said.

"No reaching."

"Here, let me leave this water here for you."

I sat cross-legged outside my tent and made twelve flax baskets, ground a mountain of pikopiko fronds, and mended a craggy hole in the fly sheet. When I couldn't bear it any longer, I walked up the track to the pool to sit with Mum, only to face a scolding from Marelle the moment I got there. But even she could see I was going stir-crazy, so she let me hold the basket while she harvested blood fruit from one of the trees.

A week crawled by.

Phillip had been gone ten days when the fire broke out. I was napping and might have slept on, but the shouts and screams woke me. I emerged from my tent to find the village shrouded in smoke, the plastic smell of burning tents polluting the air. And everything was ready to light up like touchpaper. Already, half the tents were engulfed in flames.

A man staggered from the wreckage of his tent, burning fabric seared into his shoulders, and plunged into the bush, a trail of fiery carnage spreading in his wake. Charging through the commune after him was Cassie, her hair ablaze.

"Cassie!" The smoke choked me. I pointed to a cask of water, but either she couldn't see it, or she was too crazed with pain and fear because she ran right by. Only a few tents remained now, the fire melting them like candyfloss. I'd waited too long. It was closing in. I needed somewhere safe from the fire. Somewhere Phillip would find me.

There's only one place, and it's a kilometre away.

I couldn't just run. The fire would get me first.

Dashing back into my tent, I snatched up a blanket and carried it out to the water cask, where I leaned on the container, tipping it over and drenching the wool. Then, pulling the damp fabric about my head and shoulders, I ducked under the smoke and crouch-galloped clumsily up the track.

My lungs were heaving, and the blanket was dry by the time I reached the pool. I didn't hesitate; dropping the blanket, I stepped in beside Mum and the others, mud squelching through my toes. My shoulders had only just slipped beneath the surface when the fire arrived, hissing and cackling and burning the bush in patches of blurred orange.

I dowsed my hair in the muddy ooze, leaving only my nostrils and eyes on the surface. Still, the hot smoke stung my throat and eyes.

Suddenly, at the edge of the pool, the largest of the blood fruit trees groaned, the sound loud despite the mud caked in my ears. Was it really crying or was it just the sound of the wood drying and splitting in the heat? Cringing, I cradled my belly in my hands and did my best to close my mind to the tree's desolate shrieking. With no escape, the tree dragged its limbs back, away from the heat and the creeping, licking tendrils.

84

Then Marelle was there, running up the scorching track, her bare feet slapping on the dirt and a bucket thumping at her hip.

I dragged my already heavy body up against the sucking mud and lifted my shoulders from the pool. "Marelle," I shouted. "Get in the pool. Quickly!"

But either she didn't hear me, or she chose to ignore me because, taking her plastic bucket, she scooped up a load of mud from the pool and slathered it over the trunk of the tortured tree.

What was she doing?

"Marelle!" I could only sputter.

"I'm here, I'm here," she crooned.

But the fire was here too, and her ministrations were not enough to prevent it from razing everything in its path. The crafty flames bounded from a nearby treetop, jumping across a gap to devour the blood fruit's papery leaves and bite into the white flesh of its trunk.

"No!" Marelle screamed.

She took off her cardigan and slapped at the trunk with the fabric, desperate to beat out the fire. All she did was fan it, the flames leaping and ducking out of reach. It caught her by her hair and in seconds she was burning. I expected her to run, like the man and Cassie had done. Instead, she sank to her knees against the blood fruit tree, her body overrun by fire, and howled.

If her screaming was agony, her silence was worse.

I lifted my eyes, unable to watch any longer. Above Marelle's immolating corpse, blood fruit blistered on their stems, eventually shrivelling to black pits which rained into the pool. I thought I heard my mother moan, but with mud in my ears, I couldn't be sure. I sank further into the warming mud. *Please!* I begged the pool. *Help me! Save my baby.*

My skin tingled and a feeling of calm swept over me. It was as if I was stretched out in a hammock, rocking gently, with the cool air lifting my hair and tickling at my neck.

Phillip wrapped his arms about me. "We're going to be a family," he said.

No, that couldn't be right. Phillip had left Māratotō. He'd gone to town to scrounge for supplies. We'd squabbled and he'd gone...

Perhaps I was dying. People have delusions when they're dying, right?

"It's Eremia who has perished," someone whispered in my ear.

"The pool will sustain us yet," another said. "Others will come. We'll survive."

"Yes, yes, Māratotō will go on."

Someone giggled. I was missing the joke. I tried to turn, but I couldn't move.

The trees reached into the pool, their roots smothering me, suckling from me. Soft mud enveloped my limbs, flooding me with warmth. Somehow, the pool could leach away the pain.

Did I want this?

"Why must you insist on being so stubborn, Viv?" my mother said. "Give in. It'll be easier."

No.

A feeble protest because I didn't really mean it. Phillip's bronzed limbs stroked my stomach and my thighs. In the end, I lay my head back on a stone and let myself drift.

Someone dragged me out. Cradled in mud, I fought against them. My limbs burned. *No.* I couldn't leave the safety of the pool. I didn't want to breathe in the baked air. I didn't want to die. Let me alone. *We're safe here. We're fine...*

Water splashed over me. Water? My eyes flew open.

It was Phillip.

"Viv. Baby, we have to get this mud off of you."

"But it's nice in the pool," I croaked. "Soothing. Get in with me, Phillip. Try it."

Phillip just pursed his lips and threw more water on me. The cold was shocking. I shivered even as warm blood sluiced down my thighs and mixed with the water at my feet. The slurry seeped into the ground. Seeing it, something in me stirred. Letting fluid drain away like that? It was wasteful.

Phillip's slap stung my cheek. "Viv! Come on. Snap out of it!"

Barely able to lift my head, I gazed around us at the devastation.

The trail to the village was nude, the trees scorched to the ground leaving only an occasional black stump, wisps of white smoke rising from them to curl into a grey sky.

I turned, though it took all my strength to do it, my movement slow and sluggish. Why were my limbs so heavy? I felt like a Golem, with ponderous limbs fashioned from rock and mud. At last, I was facing the pool. I shuddered. To one side, near the largest blood fruit tree, Marelle's body was little more than a pile of dusty charred bones beside the tree's burned-out husk. Three sister blood fruit trees still remained, although their leaves were singed, and the fruit was shrivelled.

"You were lucky," Phillip said. "The wind shifted."

"The baby?"

He shook his head.

I'd lost her. Deep down, I'd already known it. I wasn't going to be a mother after all.

Mother!

I dragged myself to the edge of the pool, plunging my arms back into the mud, searching for her. "Mum!"

"No!" Phillip yanked me back and doused me again with water, washing away the mud.

I struggled against him. "Mum!"

He grabbed me by the chin and forced me to look into his eyes. "The pool has her, Viv. The blood fruit trees have taken her in. She's one of them now. They both are."

I stopped fighting, trembling as the water dripped off me. "You knew?"

He dropped his eyes. Nodded. "These communities," he said. "There's always a contract. I'm so sorry, Viv…" He sank to his knees and buried his face in my stomach. "How was

I to know? I'd already promised; made my trade before I met you."

I ran my hands through his hair and held him to me. I didn't blame him. I'd known it too, had done it myself. All those years, just surviving. I'd been so tired that I'd let down my guard in favour of an easier life here at the commune. "We should leave," I said, but I didn't move.

Phillip got to his feet and grasped me by the arms. "Or we could stay? Rebuild. There are more people on the way. It's why I went to town."

"The myth at the water tap? That was you?"

He nodded again.

It all made sense now: the trees, the dizzying spell of their blood fruit, Marelle and the generations of her family who had settled nearby to nourish the pool... and Phillip, Mum, even me – we'd all been complicit.

Above me, the leaves of the blood fruit trees whispered in my ear. The people weren't gone entirely; their lives had simply been extended. They'd evolved into something different. *Something new.*

And my mother had been happy, hadn't she? She was *still* happy.

Phillip's auburn eyes burned into mine. "Viv?"

"What was it like in town?"

"Worse," he said. "The desalination plants have broken down."

I lifted my chin to the blood fruit trees, feeling strangely lighter. "Okay, then. We'll stay."

Part II
Carol Gyzander, United States

Bobblehead

Carol Gyzander

You do your job well that day
Only to be corrected by a man
Who is not even your boss
    You smile and nod

You love art class after work
But the studio guy critiques your piece
Before it is even done
    You smile and nod

You pull away from Uncle at the family party
When he passes by too closely

And laughs as he pats your backside
    You smile and nod

You try to refuse Uncle's offer
To escort you home after the gathering
But he insists it's for your own safety
    You smile and nod

You gather your torn clothes after he's done
As Uncle says to consider yourself lucky
That he even paid you any attention
    You smile and nod

You become restless in your own body
A different energy courses through you
No longer your own—no longer alone?
    You smile and nod

You talk to the doctor about your fears
Show him the home test kit since
The extra line must be a mistake, right?
    You smile and nod

You should have used protection, he says
Of course, this happens all the time
Now it's your responsibility to bear
    You smile and nod

You ask about alternatives, please,
Because surely you can't be expected to—
No, he says, that's against the law
   You pause and nod

You feel your body change as something else
Takes control and changes how you walk home
Passersby move out of your way for the first time
   You shrug and nod

You gaze in the bathroom mirror with wonder
Pull back your lips and turn your head
The light glints off what it reveals
   You grin and nod

You stare at Uncle when he laughs
And asks, aren't you getting a bit fat?
You run your tongue along those multiple rows of teeth
   You bite off his head and smile.

Wearing White Out of Season

Carol Gyzander

ADA LOVELACE held out a hand to steady herself as she materialized in the London workshop. The room swirled around her momentarily and then solidified to reveal several long worktables covered with small gears and minute pieces of metal. Hundreds of bins perched along the far wall, one on top of the other to the ceiling, each meticulously labeled with numbers.

An intricate machine loomed in the center of the room, eight feet wide and seven feet tall and clearly under construction. *Finally, I get to see it again! The initial Difference Engine, the inspiration for his Analytical Engine we have worked on together.*

A man in his late fifties bent over some papers at the other side of the room. He wore dark trousers, a matching waistcoat, and a shirt with an upstanding collar.

"Charles?"

Charles Babbage turned and blinked owlishly at her as she suddenly appeared in his workshop.

She felt self-conscious. Ada considered herself plain but in good health at thirty-five. She wore her brown hair pulled back in a bun with a lace head covering. Layers of crinoline petticoats supported the skirt of her gray bell-shaped dress, giving the impression of a tiny waist.

"Excuse me? Who are you, and how did you get in here?" He looked wildly around the room, from the closed door to the complicated piece of machinery taking up most of the workshop.

"Charles? It's Ada. Ada Lovelace. You know me; we've met before and corresponded about your work and my mathematics. I'm terribly sorry to surprise you."

Babbage peered at her through bushy eyebrows. "Ada?" He blinked. "You're supposed to be in Surrey. And how did you get in?"

"Well, it's a rather long story. But I wanted to tell you about my plans." She hurried on when she saw his frown. "And, of course, I hoped to see the Difference Engine before I go. It's been such an inspiration to me... in so many ways. The first machine to calculate polynomial equations correctly."

"Yes, of course." His eyes lit up. "Let me show you again." He talked her through the different parts of the enormous calculating machine in front of them, explaining all the workings and the little pieces that numbered in the thousands, which all had to be precisely the same. It had taken years to create the manufacturing capability to replicate identical parts.

As he finished, she nodded. *It is indeed a shame that the British government stopped funding its manufacture.*

"Why are you here, Ada? Does it have to do with our work?"

"Well, yes. In a way." She took a deep breath. "I've been working on my mathematics and how your Analytical Engine can be programmed to compute Bernoulli numbers. But everyone else assumes that my only interests are embroidery and household things. It's terrible being a woman with a brain. And frankly, my mother only arranged for my mathematics schooling to help keep my mind busy so that I would not go mad like my father, Lord Byron."

Babbage raised his eyebrows. "Go on."

She clenched her fist, hidden in her skirt. "I resolved to discover how other ladies have handled themselves throughout history. I can't be the first one with a brain and a vision. Other women before me have had notable success and careers where men have listened to every word they said."

"What are you getting at? What have you done?" He guided her to a seat at the worktable and took the chair next to her.

Will he believe me? She clenched her fists. *Well, either tell him now or go home and give up this idea.* "I'm going to go back in time. I've designed a device that transports me through time and space. That's how I got here."

"That's impossible!" Babbage cried. "I have often thought of trying to do something like that, but the

95

mathematics involved was daunting. And the size of the machine required! Compared to the Difference Engine here, it would be a behemoth."

Ada pulled a small cube from the purse on her wrist. About the size of a deck of playing cards made square, she balanced it on her palm. The light from the window gleamed on the smooth surface of the cube; miniature dials covered the top, which bore a clockface in the center. "Here it is. My Time Traveler. I tinkered with watch parts to make it portable." *There. I've shown it to him. There's no going back now.*

"My dear, that little thing?" Babbage chuckled. "Look how large my Difference Engine is, all of it required just to calculate numbers. There's no way this tiny box could take you through time and space."

"Charles, I often tell my husband that size is not important. It's what you do with the device that is significant."

As Babbage dissolved into a blustering coughing fit, she held up one finger and continued. "I just wanted to inform you of my plans in case I don't return. I am about to go back and visit a woman with immense power. Someone who commanded the world around her and was worshipped as a goddess."

Babbage finally caught his breath enough to reply. He raised his eyebrows. "And who, pray tell, could that possibly be?"

Ada experienced less dizziness this time as she materialized on a low, wide party barge. Lush greenery lined the river, and several stone pyramids pierced the horizon. Sweat trickled down her spine, and she immediately realized her clothing was too warm for the location. Flute music floated from the front of the barge. *I made it to the Nile! I think I'm getting the hang of this. Now, did anyone see me?*

She scanned the empty deck, breathing a sigh of relief that no one saw her arrive. Tall statues marked the corners of the square tent in the middle of the barge. Then, footsteps coming closer glued her in place. *No! Please don't see me, don't see me.* She pressed herself against the tent wall, standing rigid like the statue next to her.

A young person wearing sandals and a linen tunic padded down the deck, carrying a tray with empty cups. They deposited the tray near the stern, their gaze sweeping right over where Ada froze. A moment later, the servant disappeared back around the tent.

Ada sagged against the wall. *How did they not see me? Just because I didn't want them to? How ironic that while I'm searching for how women can have power, I become invisible.* After a moment, she collected herself, then studied the tent bearing the royal mark she recognized from her studies. One deep breath and she slipped inside, then melted into an alcove beside the door.

She peeked out at a lavish dressing room filled with racks of long linen tunics. Shelves filled one entire wall, containing various headdresses and display stands that bore beautiful necklaces of snakes encrusted with gems.

In the middle of the tent, looking at herself in a large mirror, Cleopatra ran her hands up and down her torso over the slender sheath dress. When she saw Ada in the reflection over her shoulder, she turned, glowering. "*Ti esti?*" she said coldly as she walked toward the alcove.

The device in Ada's hand echoed the words in English. "Who is it?"

It works! "I'm Ada Lovelace. I come from your future. I wanted to speak with you." *There, I hope it translates correctly.*

"From my future? Is that what women will be wearing?" Cleopatra drew her out of the alcove, poking and pulling at Ada's pinched-in figure. "I think this thing you have about your waist must make the stomach smaller. Although, I'm getting a bit soft in the middle after so many children. I'm afraid that Antony is starting to lose interest."

Is she serious? That's what intrigues her about a visitor from the future?

"Cleopatra, I came back to talk to you about your powerful position as a woman who rules over Egypt."

The Egyptian snorted. "A woman who rules, yes, but always at the permission of powerful men. I have had to carefully plan and negotiate every step of my public career to ingratiate myself with some man or other who is in power. I even married my own brother for a time. It chafes me to have to do this instead of simply using my leadership gifts."

"Oh, my," Ada replied. "I didn't really think of it that way. I have seen pictures of your statue where you are depicted as the goddess Isis, and I thought—"

"As what?" Cleopatra frowned. "I don't understand your words. Can you mark it down?"

Ada blinked, then turned a dial on the top of the Time Traveler. A small strip of paper printed out a string of hieroglyphics.

Cleopatra glanced at it and chuckled. "Oh, you've made a common mistake. It's Ibex before Egret, except after Camel. So, great, you've seen my statue. But I've had to play the men around me like a lute all my life. I had to wrap myself in a carpet to get in for a dalliance with Julius Caesar. Of course, we became lovers and allies for years, but still."

"Ah yes, you met him back in 48 BC." At Cleopatra's raised eyebrow, she frowned. "I mean, before Christ." *Oh, darnation. She has no idea what I'm talking about because Christ hasn't been born yet.*

Ada sank onto a bench and thought furiously, her brow furrowed. *It seems that men have always controlled women, even one I thought was a strong female leader. What about going forward?*

She looked up at the Egyptian. "It is much the same in my time. Perhaps you can help me understand someone I peeked in upon in the future. Well, the future times that come after mine. Would you like to come with me and see?"

"You mean, leave here and go somewhere else?" Cleopatra's eyes, emphasized by the dark eyeliner, widened. "I wouldn't mind having a night off from entertaining Antony."

"Not just some*where*. Some*when*. Come to the future with me, and let us see if women have gained a stronger voice." She held out her hand to the Egyptian ruler, who paused just a moment before grasping it in her own.

She gave Cleopatra the Time Traveler cube to hold with the other hand while Ada worked the controls. The tent swirled into a dizzying stream of people, places, and events speeding past them. The clock on top of the cube spun so fast they couldn't even see the hands move.

Ada leaned in to be heard over the whooshing sound that surrounded them. "I'm taking us into my future to search for a brilliant woman. Be sure to keep ahold of the Time Traveler, and you will learn some of what transpires after we leave your era. But it will go by fast, so you won't catch everything."

They traveled the time stream over two millennia past Cleopatra's age. Periodically Ada slowed the stream and peered into the surrounding array. Several times she cried out in delight.

Cleo peered out as well. "How do those lights work without fire? Amazing!"

"I was right!" Ada said at one point. "They finally created computing machines like Babbage's Analytical Engine and computing programs as I designed!" She dipped her little finger into the time stream, scanning the content at fantastic speed. "Oh, *she* looks interesting…" After a moment, she reversed one of the dials and headed back down the time stream just a touch.

The pair materialized in a woman's dressing room. Like on Cleopatra's party barge, racks of clothing lined one wall, primarily low-cut dresses made of satin. The Egyptian staggered when the room became substantial around them. Ada helped her to the couch and made her sit down with her head between her knees for a moment.

"Sweet Isis," gasped Cleopatra, finally sitting up. "What have I just seen? So many wars and so many men trying to conquer the world. But good people as well. Where are we? Or should I ask, *when* are we?"

"I believe we're in the 1950s, about 2,000 years after we left your barge." Ada looked around the room. "One of the things I read in the aether along my way to you was of a woman who came from nothing yet commanded much attention with her acting and public persona. I'd like to see how she accomplished this. Clearly, she must be brilliant."

"How does she do this trick?" asked Cleo.

"Something called a 'movie,' which seems like a play or lantern slide show. I don't know how it works, but this looks like a theatre, so we must be backstage. Is there a curtain that opens? I wonder where the audience sits." Ada moved around the room, examining the books that covered the coffee table. One by Albert Einstein fell open to a section on the theory of relativity. She immediately got so absorbed in reading that the opening door made her jump.

A stunning, voluptuous woman with platinum blonde hair entered and stopped short at the sight of them. She recovered her composure in a beat and slid across to sit in the chair in front of the lighted mirror. "Well, my, my. That is indeed the most amazing pair of costumes I've seen together. Are you from wardrobe or"—she broke off and stared at Cleopatra's face and eyeliner—"from makeup?"

"Miss Monroe? Marilyn? We're actually…" *Can I really say this? Oh well, she's supposed to be smart.* "This is Cleopatra, and I'm Ada Lovelace." Ada held her breath, waiting for a reaction.

Marilyn stared at her for a long moment. "You don't say. But hey, who am I to argue with someone wanting to reinvent themselves? You go ahead and be anyone you want to be, sugar, that's what I say. You just have to, you know… *convince* them. Put your heart into it. This kind of method acting and going around in costume should really work for you." She turned her attention to touching up her hair in the mirror.

"Well, thank you. I think." Ada blinked a few times. "I've… read about you on the way here. They say you are very smart, but people don't seem to realize this. Could you show us what it is you do here? We don't know much about the 'movie' business."

The actress looked at Ada in the mirror. "Don't know much about movies, and yet you're so much into the costuming? Well, I suppose I can show you. I'm about to watch the dailies from my current movie, *Some Like It Hot*. Since starting my own production company, I've gotten much more say in how I play a scene. Come along."

She led them out of the dressing room, outdoors, and across a road between huge buildings. Cleopatra grabbed each woman by the arm as they neared the other side of the street, stopping them in their tracks. A strange rattling sound came from the shadowed base of the opposite building.

"Wait!" The Egyptian bent forward, scanning around them, then moved slowly toward a thick brown and yellow shape coiled on the ground. The spear-shaped head lifted slightly, the tongue moving in and out, and the rattling sound increased as the tail raised into the air.

"A rattlesnake!" Marilyn whispered tensely. "It must have gotten away from one of the Western sets. Be careful. They can strike really fast!"

Cleopatra held up both hands, palms toward the snake. The vibration slowed, then quieted as the rattlesnake lowered its tail. Then it uncoiled, undulating rapidly away and disappearing around a corner of the building.

How did she do that? Ada gathered her wits and led the other two into the building. She faced the Egyptian woman. "I know you've studied toxins and various poisonous tinctures, but I didn't know you were a snake charmer!"

Cleopatra blinked, then looked at her two hands. "I... I've never done that before. At least, not before I came on this trip with you."

"Well, I don't care how you did it as long as the snake left." Marilyn embraced her, then pulled them down the hall. They entered a darkened room filled with several rows of seats. Ada sat between them, unsure of how Cleopatra would react.

"Roll it please, Harry!" the actress called to someone over her shoulder. "And notify security that there's a rattlesnake outside."

A screen in front of them lit up with a scene from the movie. The handwritten names Jack Lemmon and Tony Curtis appeared for a moment, then two men dressed as women played instruments in a band along with Marilyn, who wore a low-cut dress. Ada's heart raced. *Oh my... oh, my! What is going on?*

"What is this devilry?" the Egyptian queen hissed in Ada's ear.

Of course, she's amazed. While I've never seen people behave like this, she's never even seen a photograph. "Hush. Just watch. Have you ever made shadow puppets on the wall with your hands? Well, I think this is a story done with shadows, just more realistic than we've seen before." Ada's voice trailed off as she became mesmerized by the images.

When the day's scenes finished, the film flapped around the reel, momentarily making the screen blink. The lights came on in the viewing room.

"Well? What do you think?" Marilyn asked.

"I am... confused," Ada blurted without thinking. "So those are all popular stars of the stage? Then why are the men dressed like women? And why do you act like such a silly thing?"

Marilyn gave a sly smile. "Well, you see, it's sort of a play on our roles. People, especially men, like to see me act vulnerable and, I don't know, *available*. And if they want to see that, well then I'll sure as hell give it to them."

Ada frowned. "Can you tell us more about your production company? We came here because I saw in the aether, er... I read that you, a woman, were instrumental in breaking up the stranglehold that the powerful entertainment consortiums held over filming and actors. How did you do that?"

"Oh, sugar, I was already very popular. Back then, I just told them that I was 'tired of the same old sex roles' and declared the studio had broken their contract because they weren't paying the bonus that they had promised me. Said I wouldn't act in any more of their movies, moved to New York, and started my own production company. Pretty soon, they were begging me to come back. And on *much* better terms."

Yes! That's what I've been hoping to see! Ada's heart soared. *Women controlling their own actions and destiny!*

But after a moment, her mind returned to the scenes they'd just watched on the wall. *She still has to play such an indecent kind of character.* "So now, you're still doing what the men want you to do, just getting paid more to do it, and you have more control. Correct?"

"True." Marilyn sighed. "Hey, where did you two say you were from again?"

Ada took a deep breath and decided to risk telling the truth. "The past. We are time travelers from your past. We are looking into our future to see how women can evolve and get control of their lives. How they can get men to listen to them for the content of their minds and not just what they can do with their bodies. Right, Cleopatra?"

At the other's nod, Marilyn looked back and forth between the pair. "Golly. I love reading Albert Einstein's work so much that it made me want to sleep with him, so I understand this could be *possible*. But you're serious. Tell me your name again, honey."

"I'm Ada King, the Countess of Lovelace. People often call me Ada Lovelace."

"You're the mathematician! I've read about you." Marilyn leaned forward and smiled brightly, any pretense of languor gone. "I have many different books and love to read anything that strikes my interest. Now I understand the things you say you've done."

Oh my! Someone in my future actually knows of me and remembers things I have accomplished? Perhaps all is not lost. But still.

"Marilyn, I thank you for your kind words." Ada laced her fingers together in front of herself. "You've read Einstein's book, but nobody would expect a woman in my

106

day to be able to do original work and get it published. The best I could do was a detailed translation of a foreign mathematician's work."

She picked up the Einstein book and stroked the cover. "When Charles Babbage persuaded me to write my own notes to append to the end, I created an amazing document that *should* have convinced the British government to invest the money and take up construction of our Difference Engine or Analytical Engine, but they did neither."

She held the book out to the actress. "Nothing happened."

"Oh my, sugar. I'm so sorry. Say, this book clearly holds your interest. Why don't you take it with you?" Marilyn pushed it back into her hands, and Ada paused momentarily before sliding the heavy tome into her soft purse with a nod.

"Thank you. But it seems like women have not yet achieved the role of equals in your time, as you must still pander to men's desires." She gripped the blonde's arm. "Would you care to join us on our voyage and see how women fare in *your* future? All of our futures?"

At her resounding grin, Ada instructed Marilyn to hold the Time Traveler cube in one hand and take Cleopatra's hand with the other. Ada held Cleo's free hand. Thus linked, she triggered the cube for a future date she'd already noted when they surfed up the timestream from ancient Egypt.

Blaring music shook her to the core. *My stars! What on earth could that be? Have I done something wrong?*

Ada shook her head, clinging to the other two women while they all tried to regain their equilibrium. As she blinked, the scene steadied—a beautiful garden behind a large restaurant.

"This looks more like home, at least." Cleopatra gestured at the palm trees that grew around the yard. "Where are we?"

People gathered around the lawn in small clumps, seated on chairs spaced wide apart and standing in small groups throughout the yard. A long bar ran along one side of the garden. A large, brightly lit screen dominated one end of the space, showing a podium on an empty stage flanked by two flags with white stars on a blue background and red and white stripes. In addition, banners of red, white, and blue festooned the screen.

"Judging by the flags and banners, I'd say we're in the United States of America. But those flags have lots more stars," Ada said.

Marilyn nodded. "Looks like California, near where we were at my studio."

"What?" The Egyptian held a hand to her ear, and Ada repeated the words closer to the translator so Cleopatra could understand.

Everyone held a beverage glass. *It's a party! I wonder what the occasion could be, for it surely seems to be some sort of celebration. Strange that everyone wears a mask covering their nose and mouth.*

"I see the screen. Is this another shadow puppet show?" Cleopatra whi

Ada shrugged.

Marilyn answered, "It looks like a live television broadcast. Someone's about to make a speech. But I'm amazed at the quality of the image!"

The back of Ada's neck tingled with the odd feeling that someone was watching her. She scanned the gathering. Most people stood together, chatting in small groups. Then she turned to the crowd's edge, where a young man with black pants, a white shirt, and a black bowtie waited off to the side. A shock of red hair fell over one eye, contrasting sharply with his light skin. He stared directly at the three, and when Ada looked in his direction, he slowly put out his tongue and licked his lips. Then a group of people walked between them, and Ada lost track of him in the crowd.

"Pardon me, but what is the date?" Ada asked a masked waitress moving among the groups. The woman's T-shirt bore "Biden and Harris 2020" on the front.

"November seventh, hon. But here, y'all need to wear a mask, even though it is a private party." The waitress peeled off three facial masks from a stack on her tray and handed them to the trio. "And here's your champagne! I'm glad I had time to bring you some before she comes on."

She? I wonder who the special guest will be. So many people are here to see her, whoever she is. This must be a significant event.

"November? How strange that so many women are wearing white," Marilyn said as she slipped the mask on. "It's way past the season for white, isn't it?"

"It's a symbol!" A middle-aged woman standing nearby called out to them without coming too close, gesturing at her own white suit. "Shirley Chisholm was the first African American woman elected to Congress in 1968. She wore white, as did Geraldine Ferraro when she accepted the role as Walter Mondale's running mate for his presidential campaign in 1984. And Hilary Clinton's signature white pantsuit is well known from when she accepted the Democratic presidential nomination in 2016. We even set up a wardrobe in the tent over there where women could borrow one for the party!"

She looked up and down at their attire. "I must say, though, it's a stroke of genius on this momentous occasion for you all to wear historical clothing showing women through the ages. Cleopatra and Marilyn Monroe, right? But who are you, dear?" The woman looked at Ada.

"I'm Ada Lovelace, ma'am." Ada gave a curtsey out of habit.

"Wonderful! The woman who designed the first computer program! Brilliant." The woman's eyes crinkled when she smiled, and her mask moved slightly to reveal a brown birthmark on the corner of her jaw.

Oh, my goodness! She knows my name and what I've done! But what is this momentous occasion?

The red-haired busboy came through the crowd, collecting glasses and plates. When he took Ada's glass, he moved his hand so that his fingers brushed against hers. She froze.

Marilyn handed him her glass, then flicked her fingers toward him as if he were a pesky insect or fly. The busboy tilted his head with a slight bow, then carried the tray back toward the restaurant.

"He actually touched me!" Ada declared after the young man left. She wiped her hand on her skirt.

"I imagine he's just intrigued by our costumes, sugar. At least, that's what everybody thinks we're wearing." Marilyn patted her shoulder. "Creepers like him are a dime a dozen. Don't pay them any attention."

The music blared louder. All eyes turned to the screen as a striking woman in a white suit and blouse strode confidently across the stage to the podium. The announcer said, "Ladies and Gentlemen, Vice-President Elect Kamala Harris!" The group in the garden cheered wildly, almost drowning out the cheers and applause from the screen.

During her acceptance speech, Harris spoke about several different aspects of equality. She also said, "But while I may be the first woman in this office, I will not be the last, because every little girl watching tonight sees that this is a country of possibilities."[6]

At the end of the speech, the crowd cheered again. Ada's heart soared. She looked at the woman on the screen and the women around her wearing the same clothing. *Now*

---

6   Kamala Harris's speech quoted from washingtonpost.com/politics/2020/11/07/kamala-harris-victory-speech-transcript/

I know what we have to do as we advance. We must stand together.

She pulled Marilyn and Cleopatra to her and spoke quietly but fiercely. "My friends, I understand now. Here's what we must do as we continue on our journey. No more pandering to the men by wearing alluring clothing or deferring to their supposed superiority. No more smuggling ourselves into their bedchambers to make a liaison so we can survive. We depend upon *ourselves*. And one more thing."

Ada gripped their hands with a smile. "We all need to wear white pantsuits."

Marilyn broke out in a grin. "I get it, sugar. Now, why don't you figure out how to get us some new clothes while I run and use the necessary."

"The necessary what?" Cleopatra blinked, looking back and forth from the cube to the actress.

"The restroom. Oh, you explain it to her." Marilyn threw her hands in the air and headed toward the restaurant.

Ada pulled Cleopatra along, and they caught up with the actress. "I really think we should stick together. But yes, bathroom first."

Together they entered the building and asked the red-haired busboy, the only one whose attention they could get, for directions. He escorted them toward a staircase and stood at the top, indicating the location with an extended hand but partially blocking the way. He watched them with a leer as they squeezed past him to head down the stairs.

Marilyn finished in the restroom first and headed into the dimly lit hallway, leaving the door partly ajar. As Ada washed her hands, the actress suddenly stopped and looked up from lighting a cigarette. *What startled her like that?*

Someone's shadow fell across the actress's face. "Sugar, you need to give me some space here so I can get this lit."

Ada cringed at the sound of a man's guttural voice from the hall. "I don't know how you made yourself look so much like Marilyn Monroe, but the effect is... quite *moving*, if you know what I mean. I watch that scene where her skirt blows up from the sidewalk grate when I... well, anyway, why don't you just come with me, and you can act it out?"

"I have no idea what you're talking about, and you can stop right there." Marilyn's voice came out ice cold, followed by a man's grunting and then a scream.

Oh no! Ada rushed to the door, followed by Cleopatra, who emerged from the bathroom stall. When they got to the hallway, Marilyn stood over the busboy, who rolled on the ground holding his eyes.

"What happened?" Ada caught Marilyn as she staggered back.

The actress's eyes showed wide in the dim light. "I... I'm not sure. He came at me, making obscene comments, and went to grab me and drag me down the hall. Then I just raised my hands to block him, and he fell. I didn't even touch him."

"All right. Let me see." Ada bent down and pulled the busboy's hands aside.

Red streaks lined his eye sockets, which now held glowing white orbs. As they watched, a black mark bubbled on his forehead, resolving into a single word.

ABUSER.

The women gasped and stared at Marilyn. Ada grabbed her in a fierce hug. "Oh, you poor thing. I don't know how—"

She broke off at the sound of footsteps coming down the stairs.

"I believe now would be an excellent time to depart. One quick stop by the clothing tent, and then we move on. Ladies?" She held up the Time Traveler cube.

Now dressed in white pantsuits, they reappeared under some flowering trees surrounding a majestic water pool. Fallen pink blossoms covered the ground all around them and the path leading around the water toward a white, domed building lined with columns. A tall, thin monument peeked through the cherry blossoms to Ada's left.

A massive, blocky white building loomed through the trees on the right, showing bare earth around the base like a construction site. "Oh, my lord!" Marilyn gasped. "They... they tore down the Lincoln Monument and put *that* ugly thing there!"

People walked along the path in small groups, and Ada blinked at the difference from the women at the inauguration. Pairs of women in long, white dresses walked together, small tote bags over one arm. All wore either a white bowed sash at their waist or a white scarf tied in a bow at their neck. Some carried a small book that resembled a Bible as far as she could tell. All kept their eyes down, speaking quietly to each other, if at all, as they moved sedately along.

This is not what I expected from women wearing white.

Cleopatra blinked, her black eyeliner gleaming in the afternoon sun. A pair of women approaching from the opposite direction moved to one side to get around them. One young woman glanced up briefly, her gaze falling upon Cleopatra's face. The young woman's mouth dropped open, her eyes widened, and Ada heard a small gasp as the woman clutched her companion's arm and pushed her to the far side of the path away from the three.

The pair averted their eyes and hurried past them, whispering to each other.

"What was that all about?" Marilyn asked. "She didn't even look at you closely. It's like she'd never seen anyone wearing makeup before!"

Cleopatra shrugged. "I have no idea. But look up there." She pointed to a spot on the path up ahead where the steady movement of white-clad women slowed. The traffic pattern eddied like the water in a stream flowing around a large rock or obstacle in its path.

"What's going on?" Ada stepped onto a rock beside the path and peered over the people. She blinked in surprise. "There's somebody up there who's not wearing white! I see two women in red dresses, and they're the only ones with their faces covered by a mask. I wonder why."

"What's the problem, sugar? So, somebody's wearing red. I happen to look pretty good in red." Marilyn vamped a bit, posing with her shoulders leaning forward and her lips pouting, then leaned back and laughed as she stared at Ada. "What do you see? What's everybody in a tizzy about up there? Come on, give!"

Ada blinked. "Give what? Oh, you mean the information. Sorry. I see several women in red coming toward us, and people are going even farther around them than those two did when they passed us. Some even stop and point. Shall we go see what's going on?" Cleopatra held out a hand, and Ada grasped it, then lightly hopped down from the rock.

"Something seems very strange here," Cleopatra said. "I just don't get why all these people wearing white are so upset to see us just because our clothes are different. I thought you said wearing white would be the way of the future."

Cleo clicked her tongue. "It doesn't seem to have gotten anybody anywhere. On the contrary, everybody looks very"— while she continued speaking, the translator paused, apparently searching for the correct word— "uptight." Cleopatra shrugged.

Ada tapped the translator. "Uptight. Well. It seems like this thing updates its vocabulary with every jump forward in time. I didn't realize I had programmed it to do that."

They headed toward the commotion. As they neared, a young girl in a white dress bent over, grabbed a rock

116

from the path's edge, and hurled it at the pair in red. It struck one on the shoulder, and she cried out in evident pain, then stifled the noise. Neither red-dressed woman retaliated. Instead, they grabbed each other's hands and tried to get past the growing throng.

"We've got to help those two!" Marilyn whispered fiercely. "This crowd is turning on them, and they're in danger."

She started toward the group, but an older woman in a long white dress stepped onto the path from under the trees and blocked her way, speaking quietly but intently.

"I don't recommend that. If you interfere, things will get even uglier, and the gender police will appear." Her gaze traveled up and down the trio of time travelers. "You need to learn how things are here and in a hurry. Come with me." She laid a hand on Marilyn's forearm, drawing her back under the trees. Ada and Cleo looked at each other, rolled their eyes, and followed.

She guided them to the park's restroom building nearby, took them inside, and turned to confront them. Her face showed even more wrinkles as she frowned. "Okay, I don't know what's going on. You look just like the women I saw at Harris's inauguration. It's been twenty years, but you haven't aged a bit. Yeah, you're wearing white pantsuits, but women don't wear pants now." She put her fists on her hips as if defying them to come up with a reasonable explanation.

"Everything you said is correct. And…" Ada peered at the woman. *She has that birthmark on her jaw!* "I do remember you! You're the one who explained to us about the political implications of wearing white! That's why we dressed like this... on our journey."

Marilyn crossed her arms and tapped her foot. "So why *aren't* you wearing pants? Why is everybody dressed like some kind of nun from the sixteenth century? What the hell is going on here?"

"All in due time." The woman held her hands up to them. "First, we have to worry about your safety. And mine, if I'm seen with you. You need to blend in. You need to be discreet. You need to be demure."

She pulled Cleopatra toward the washroom sink. "Here, you first," she said, yanking some paper towels out of the dispenser and turning on the water. "You need to wash all that makeup off your face. Proper women don't wear that anymore. Only the tramps and those hussies who invite the bad attentions."

Cleopatra blinked at her, mouth agape. But when Ada nodded and gestured to the sink, she said, "Oh, all right. It's important that you know this black eyeliner has its purpose. It's not just for appearance. It also helps reduce the incidence of eye infection through its chemical properties and—"

"Tell me when you're done. This is serious." The older woman shoved the towels into Cleopatra's hand, walked briskly to the utility closet, and pulled out three long white cloaks with hoods. "Here, you two put these on. We keep them here in case one of the proper ladies has been

118

soiled in some way. Can't give the impression that anyone is *dirty*, you know. And we're certainly not allowed to wear pants."

Marilyn opened her mouth as if she were about to launch into a tirade when Ada took the cloaks from the woman.

"See, this isn't so bad." She draped one around Marilyn's shoulders. "I've seen a lot of strange things in my travels, so what's one more? Let's just play along, shall we?"

Marilyn squinted at her, then sighed. "She does seem to think it's important."

Cleopatra stood up from the sink and dried her face.

Ada smiled. "Oh my! You look much less... intimidating now."

"I'm beginning to think that that's the reason behind all these ridiculous rules," Marilyn said. "Control women's behavior, control what they wear, control how they present themselves, and you take away their power. This is utter nonsense. Oh, and what is your name, anyway, sugar?"

"I'm Suzanne. You're absolutely right, Miss Monroe." She shook her head, smiling wistfully. "Yes, I do recognize you. Even though none of your movies are shown anymore, I remember."

"How did it all get like this?" Ada asked. "What happened?"

"Well, if I recall, we had a conversation back at the inauguration about Roe v. Wade, and y'all didn't know what that was. It's an important rule that was put into law by the Supreme Court almost fifty years before that inauguration, and it recognized a woman's right to have an abortion if she needed one. Two years after we last met, a bunch of extreme conservatives led by Leader Palmer started taking over the government, overturning Roe v. Wade. Then it became law that it was illegal to have an abortion or even give one."

Cleopatra stopped in the middle of draping the cloak around her shoulders. "What do you mean, illegal? All the women in my time know how to do that. It's nobody else's business what a woman does with her body."

"And that opinion is why I traveled back in time to find you, Cleo." Ada smiled tightly. "People in my days knew as well, but in some of my prior time travels, I saw things changing. Now we seem to have come to the culmination of all those changes."

"All right, if nobody's going to ask, I will." Marilyn still stood with her arms crossed. "In my day, before this Roe v. Wade decision, women knew people who could get abortions done, and it was done discreetly. But what's going on now? Is that related to those women not wearing white? The ones being stoned out there in full view of everyone?"

"Yes. The political and social pressures changed so quickly that anyone caught trying to get an abortion was singled out and targeted." Suzanne looked down, and her face sagged. "Then, it got worse; abortion-seekers, and then anyone getting pregnant or just having sex out of wedlock, were made to wear red clothing and mask their faces. They dressed us all in white to differentiate the 'good girls' from them. Took away our jobs. Took away our right to vote. Made us useless little ornaments wearing a white bow while simultaneously claiming they are all morally superior." Her voice grew more bitter as she spoke.

"I took this job as chaperone to the proper ladies here in the capitol area to get out and be in touch with more people. To start a resistance movement. Many women remember twenty years ago and want to take back our power." She clenched her teeth and banged her fist on the wall. "I'm thinking… maybe you can help. I don't know how you move through time, but you clearly have some power we need."

Suzanne led the three out of the park toward her home. As they walked, they came upon a scene in the street. Many men, and a small number of white-dressed women, filled the square—their attention on a woman in white tied to a pair of posts on a small stage.

Two men in black, wearing leather masks over their eyes, beat the young woman with long, thin sticks that whistled as they slashed through the air and wrapped around her back. The woman stifled a cry with each blow. Some men in the crowd leaned forward, their eyes bright and their heads moving up and down to follow each lashing.

"What the hell…?" Marilyn started forward, but her traveling companions held her back again.

Suzanne gripped her forearm tightly and whispered fiercely. "Remember what I said. Be demure. Be quiet. And don't interfere." She looked Marilyn in the eyes. "It will not end well if you do and will worsen things for her."

They skirted the crowd and followed Suzanne down the street. They kept quiet, but Ada and Marilyn looked over their shoulder at the woman being punished as they passed.

"So, what's that all about?" Ada's fists clenched as they exited the square. She wanted to rush up, grab the canes, and beat the men over the head and shoulders, but she recognized the wisdom of what Suzanne said. *What could we do to stop that, with so many men in the crowd going along with it or... actually enjoying it?*

A pair of preteen girls broke away from the back of the throng, following a short distance behind them. Suzanne turned sharply at the sound of their footsteps, then relaxed and smiled as the two approached. She drew them all into a small park behind some tall bushes and put her arms around the two girls, who burst out crying. "There, there. I know. It's hard to see."

The girls controlled their tears and wiped their faces as Suzanne loosened her embrace.

The older woman looked at the younger ones. "Remember, you can't let anyone see you upset. We have to act as if this is okay until such time as we can do something about it." Her glance flickered over the time travelers and back to the young women. "We have to stick together and be strong. I have a feeling that better times are coming soon." She patted each of them on the cheek.

"Now, off with you two, and I'll see you at reading class tomorrow, right?"

The girls nodded and slipped out of the park. Ada started to follow them, but Suzanne drew her back.

"Let's wait for them to get to where they're going. It's not good for us to be seen together in public too often."

"Reading class?" Ada asked. "I remember when my mother had to arrange special mathematics classes for me because girls didn't get any schooling. Do you mean to tell me that it hasn't changed in all this time?"

"I learned reading and writing and mathematics in school," Marilyn said. "But it looks like things have gone backward, right?"

Suzanne blew her breath out with a puff of her cheeks. "Absolutely. Over the last twenty years, they've canceled women's education. That woman in the square was being beaten because they caught her with a book that was not the Bible or a prayer book. One not allowed for women anymore." She looked out between the shrubs and gestured for them to follow her. "Coast is clear."

The four walked the rest of the way to Suzanne's place in silence.

Suzanne brought them back to her small apartment, where she was allowed to live alone as she was past menopause. At first, she told them stories of what she knew of their lives, but after hearing one publicity stunt she'd done, Marilyn asked her not to reveal any more—she didn't want to know how or when their lives ended.

Then over dinner, Suzanne filled them in on all the relevant issues in the current world. It wasn't just that the government forced "loose" women or the ones they caught seeking abortions to wear red. As the men in power acted increasingly pious and religious, they somehow took it upon themselves that they could have their way with any woman. They adopted the motto of their leader, Mr. Palmer: "Just grab them and do what you want." And yet, he often said that any man who abuses a pure woman is not worthy of being a leader or a member of their society.

Ada watched her fellow travelers as they listened to these tales. Each one's face grew stony in reaction—angrier and angrier, just as she felt.

How dare they?

"But what is our purpose here? Do we just want vengeance?" Ada tapped her finger on the coffee table.

"I want to make things more equal." Suzanne wiped a tear from her eye. "When I was younger, we were getting somewhere, at least. Then these men took power… and they took *our* power! I want to build a better society where everyone has rights."

"All right, then," Ada replied. "We have to come up with a plan…"

They were watching the news on the wall screen. The massive, pristine building of white granite they'd seen by the water, fronted by an imposing staircase, filled the background behind the reporter. A cleverly positioned spotlight on the roof pointed into the sky, making it seem like a beam of light shone down onto the building from above.

"He says there's a gathering here in the capital. Some sort of roundtable. What's that all about?" Marilyn turned to Suzanne. "Are these the people in charge of this stupid society now?"

Suzanne's grim smile answered. "You better believe it. They're all coming here tomorrow—it's the dedication ceremony for the new Leadership Hall, led by Palmer. Governors, Senators, even some of the Supreme Court judges... all men."

"So," Ada said, "they'll all be in one place. The question is... what are we going to do about it?"

Marilyn raised her hand. "I could start a relationship with the Leader."

"I can sneak in for a dalliance with one of the leaders. Roll me up in a rug and have someone smuggle me in," Cleopatra said. "What? It worked once."

Ada shook her head. "I hate to use the same approach—where we need to actually give ourselves to a man to get what we want."

"Women are limited in the jobs we're allowed to do, but we have some who work as support chaperones for any women the men bring to a meeting." Suzanne held up both hands and rolled her eyes. "Of course, the men think they can't be left alone, so many bring them along.

Several of our movement also work with the exterminator service; apparently, the glorious new building bypassed construction standards and has a continuing rodent problem. That means we already have several allies in the Leadership Hall. But I don't know how to do anything against the ones in power."

Marilyn said, "So you're telling me that many of those men there are abusers and rapists, right?" She traced her fingers over her forehead with a grim smile that did not extend to her eyes. "I think I have a way of beating them at their game by pointing them out without actually having to sleep with them."

"Oh my," Suzanne said. "You mean like that busboy who got the Foreboding at the Biden-Harris Inauguration!"

Cleopatra held her hand out to interrupt. "Foreboding? I don't understand that word, even with the translator." She gestured at the cube on the coffee table.

"A Foreboding is like an omen or a portent, dear." Suzanne looked from one woman to the other. "They found him on the floor, blinded and unable to speak, with a word marked on his forehead by some weird brand—so, the police investigated and discovered he was a serial killer who kidnapped and abused women. By the time the trial ended, everyone said he'd received a Foreboding, which entered the common vocabulary."

Suzanne leaned back, rubbing her forehead with both hands. "So goddam infuriating because this group of leaders uses him as an example of everything they claim they are not. Nobody ever knew how he got that mark."

"Well, perhaps he shouldn't have gone around assaulting women in white." Marilyn snickered. "Especially when they are developing powers they didn't know they had."

Suzanne lifted her head, her eyes wide. "Oh! It was *you*!"

Ada smiled fiercely. *At least he paid for his actions.* "Apparently, we change as we move through time."

"My allies and I want to do something on this occasion, but it's hard to plan when we have little power. Each of you has been significant in your own times"— she held up a finger as Ada tried to object—"and you appeared here, now, dressed in white for a reason. You represent women's quiet, unknown power. Together, we can do something that is *not* quiet. We will no longer be unknown."

She clasped hands with the two nearest her. The four women linked hands like the three travelers connected when traveling through time.

"Right, then. But how do we get in there?" Cleopatra asked, dropping her hands. "We don't know the building, and I don't know how to behave in this society. Plus, I need the translator."

"Yes. It would be best if you kept it with you because even though I may speak an outdated version of the language, I can understand what's being said," Ada replied. "And Marilyn, here, will just have to try not to sound too sexy. If she can."

They snort-giggled, which turned into bigger chuckles, and they were all laughing uproariously within moments.

Suzanne waved her hands to hush them. "Don't let my neighbors hear this! It's not *proper*."

"All right," Ada said as the group quieted. "Suzanne, here's what we're going to do. You tell me if you think this will work. First, we need to send Cleo outside the city on an errand, and Marilyn needs to visit the museum…" They leaned their heads together over the coffee table.

Ada stood in the corner of the entry lobby wearing a white cloak; one hand supported the purse containing Einstein's book that dangled from the other forearm. A steady parade of important-looking men entered the huge meeting chamber in the new Leadership Hall—built on the site where the Lincoln Memorial once stood. All she had to do was stay out of the way of anyone who might bump into her because she knew she could keep herself from being seen. *This is a ridiculous metaphor for how I've been treated my whole life.*

As some of the men came in with a white-clad woman, Suzanne and the other chaperones escorted the proper ladies down the corridor to another room to be served tea and cookies while the men talked about important things.

Ada moved across the lobby when the flow of incomers slowed. Then, when the last men entered the reception chamber, she slipped through the imposing double doors just as the guards swung them closed.

Made it!

She moved to the back corner. Once everyone found their seats, the attention turned to the front of the room, where two American flags on stands flanked the podium. Giant screens hung on the wall on either side of where the speaker would stand, displaying a view of the podium. *This looks a lot like that speech we saw from Harris at the inauguration.*

She looked for what Suzanne described as robotic television cameras, and one stood on each side, apparently recording the podium. This confirmed Suzanne's supposition that the address would be broadcast live to viewers nationwide and abroad.

The murmuring of the crowd died down. Ada saw the men sit forward at the edge of their chairs, leaning toward the podium as if willing their leader to appear. When the guards opened the double doors to the side of the stage, everyone leapt to their feet, applauding. The five-second delay before anyone appeared in the hallway served to whet their anticipation even more. The crowd roared as a man in a conservative dark gray suit emerged from the hallway, holding both hands up and waving at the group, followed by a pair of guards. One of the robotic cameras rolled nearer and broadcast a close-up of him.

There he is. Palmer. The leader of this supposed free world, not that you can call it that when half the population is controlled. She narrowed her eyes and observed the man in person. He projected an aura of supreme confidence mixed with profound humility, which seemed a puzzling combination—yet she could see how it could be attractive to those who needed something to believe in.

It took several minutes for the leader to make his way to the podium; he stopped to shake hands with those in the audience over the low wall along the aisle as he passed. Eventually, he climbed the four steps to the stage, where he posed alone, hands braced on the sides of the podium while the guards watched from the floor level. The cameras zoomed in on his face.

Smiling and looking around the crowd, he raised his hands to quiet the group. When the cheering and clapping finally stopped, he began. "My friends, my supporters, my colleagues. I thank you for traveling from all the corners of our glorious nation to join me on this august occasion, the dedication ceremony for our new Leadership Hall."

His magnetism seemed so strong that it even drew the guards at the back to move toward him, away from the doors. Another round of frantic applause made him pause and smile. He held his hand up and continued.

"Some have asked why we needed a new building. Why not just use the same tradition-bound edifices that our forefathers used? But this is the beginning of a new world order. A new world peace built upon moral superiority. Given this new perspective on our nation and society, it's only right to reflect this in our Leadership Hall."

He went on and on about how much better their new society was, what an improvement it was over the radical and dangerous times in the past, and that it was appropriate to remove term limits from his position. The audience hung on every word. Ada tapped her foot. *What's taking Cleopatra so long?*

A flicker of movement in the corner of the room behind the leader made her heart jump. *And there! There's some more.* The air vent at the base of the wall slid open several inches, and multiple copper-colored snakes came through. The audience, intent on the leader's words, did not seem to notice. Finally, after several minutes, a familiar voice carried from outside the chamber. The guards now stood by the back row of the audience, not next to the door, so it was easy for Ada to move toward the center doorway while projecting her desire to stay invisible. *Don't see me! I'm not here.*

She opened the door a crack. Her fellow time travelers waited; the floor around them boiled with motion. She flung the doors open wide, and Cleopatra stepped into the reception hall, hands aloft, accompanied by dozens and dozens of copperhead snakes that flowed over her feet and wriggled down the center aisle. She pointed to each side, and a group immediately split off to the left and down the far aisle, and the same to the right.

Finally, the guards and some of the people in the back noticed. When the uniformed men saw the surprising intruders, they went to pull their guns, but a pair of copperhead snakes struck in a flash and dropped the men to the ground, where they writhed momentarily before going still. Other snakes brought down the guards by the podium.

"They're faster than you." Cleopatra's voice rang out through the room from the translator. "I wouldn't take the chance." By that point, the snakes surrounded and threatened the entire crowd. Some men whimpered, and others pulled their feet onto the chair as snakes slithered down each row. Everyone froze in their places.

Ada nodded to Marilyn, who walked slowly and provocatively down the center of the aisle—ignored by the snakes. Her hips shimmied under the white cloak that she wore, holding one side over her chest. All eyes followed her seductive journey toward the podium, the snakes all but forgotten.

Palmer started down the stairs, but Marilyn got there first. She put two fingers on his chest and backed him up the steps to the podium with a coy tilt of her head. She smiled tentatively when she got to the front of the crowd.

"Some of you may remember me from movies in the past," she said into the microphone in a breathy voice. "Some of you probably dreamed about me when you were boys. Some of you..." She looked around the room, making eye contact with many leaders. "Some of you wished you could... *you* know."

A man in the front row gasped as she lowered the white cloak a bit, revealing the skin of her neck and shoulders. "But I am here with a special message for our Leader Palmer, to celebrate this wonderful new facility. I have a song. Do you want me to… sing it?" She held up one hand, palm up, asking the men in the crowd for their approval.

Many started to applaud and cheer.

It's like they can't help it! Ada studied the men, now sitting forward in their seats despite the snakes all around them, as she moved invisibly down the side aisle to the double doors through which Palmer had entered. *They want to… Well.*

"All right." Marilyn slipped the cloak off her shoulders, letting it fall to the ground and exposing the shimmering, bejeweled, skintight dress they had 'liberated' from the museum at Suzanne's suggestion. At the sight of her bare shoulders and barely clad body, the men in the room gave a collective gasp.

She started singing, "Happy… dedication day… to you…" She paused for effect, and several groans came from the audience.

Palmer's face grew red. He looked like he was having a fit or a heart attack. The leader stood slightly behind Marilyn, entranced, and swayed back and forth as if having trouble keeping his balance.

Most of the men leaned forward in their seats, mesmerized by the image of Marilyn as she sang and spoke in her breathy voice, enticing them in. Ada glanced at the television cameras, pleased to see the little light still blinking on the top. Their broadcast continued. A grim satisfaction grabbed her heart. *Let's see what this country thinks about its leaders in a few minutes.*

Marilyn finished her song with a breathy line. "Happy dedication day, Mr. Paaaalmerrrr. Happy dedication day... to... *you*." She drew out the words until Ada could almost see them hanging in the air.

Then Marilyn held both arms out to her sides, palms facing toward the sea of men. She threw back her head and closed her eyes. Ada heard the same grunting in the crowd she remembered from the busboy in the hall, which seemed like only days ago.

Then the screaming started.

A fifty-year-old man in the front row grabbed his face, holding his eyes. Blood streamed between his fingers. Ada squinted across the crowd, seeing man after man grab his face and scream. It passed in a ripple from the front to the back of the room.

She looked back at the one in the front row who had screamed first. A dark shape bubbled on his forehead, spelling something in raised letters that seemed to roil and change before her eyes. A-B-U... Black letters bubbled on half the men in the audience, leaving a word branded across their foreheads.

Some men did not change. She assumed those men were decent people who did not abuse or take advantage of women or children. The unafflicted recoiled in horror at the changes in their colleagues. "You have a Foreboding! You... and you!" A clean man in the front pointed to the ones around him who clutched their eyes in agony.

134

Then a man who carried the Foreboding stood up, clutching his eyes and paying no attention to the snakes. The ones near him struck like lightning, over and over, injecting their venom and then waiting for the toxin to take effect. Many other marked men froze in their seats as his screams filled the room but eventually died off.

Wait a minute. Where is he? Where is Palmer?

The leader had been positioned *behind* Marilyn when she held her hands up and thus escaped the effects of her abilities. Ada scanned the crowd and discovered him heading toward the hallway from which he had entered, motioning the remaining security guards to open the doors. She took three strides and vaulted over the low wall along the aisle, past where the snakes lay in wait on the ground. *Something to be said for wearing pants instead of a long skirt.*

Again, she willed herself invisible and reached the security guards just as they opened the door. She hefted her soft purse, weighed down with Einstein's tome, and swung at the first guard's head. He dropped to his knees. She repeated on the second man with a backhand swing. Both fell within the range of one of the copperheads, which struck twice rapidly. The first guard fell and blocked the door, exactly as she hoped he might. She ran back to Palmer as he staggered toward the doors—and stuck out a foot to trip him.

As he went down, Marilyn turned back from the podium, holding one hand toward where Ada stood over Palmer. "You're in the way!" Marilyn called.

I'm not worried. "Go ahead." She watched the leader at her feet as Marilyn raised the other hand. The television cameras moved into position and zoomed in. The screen overhead showed a split image of Marilyn on the podium and Palmer cringing on the ground.

"You can't affect me," he cried. "I don't know what witchery this is, but I'm a good man and pure. Those others, they don't deserve to be leaders."

He screamed. His eyes melted.

Letters bubbled up on his forehead as his face filled the screen.

RAPIST

Stunned silence blanketed the room. A few high-pitched shrieks came from elsewhere in the building, rapidly drowned out by the sound of women running down the hall, cheering and laughing.

This time, the facial brands—the Forebodings—are the portent of hope.

The footsteps and the cheering grew closer. Ada looked up from the suffering form of Palmer at her feet as Suzanne led a group of women into the meeting room.

The women stopped just inside the doorway. Their mirth died away as they surveyed the scene left from the interaction moments before. Several guards lay dead at their stations. About half of the men bore the Foreboding stigmata on their foreheads, some rocking in their seats with their arms wrapped around themselves, and some sitting in an apparent stupor. Their blind white eyes stared at nothing. None of them spoke.

"Right, then." Suzanne glanced at the women behind her. "Cleopatra, could you please get the snakes out of here? We have to help these people."

Cleopatra sent the snakes out of the room with a quick flick of each wrist. Some slithered back through the ventilation grates, and some undulated past the women, who stepped to one side and allowed them free passage out of the building.

A man stood up in the front row. He wore an American flag pin on the lapel of his jacket. He moved forward to meet Suzanne halfway up the center aisle. "Do any of you have medical training?"

A middle-aged woman stepped forward, gray streaks in her hair. "I was an internist in the Before Times. We need to do triage and check each afflicted man. Identify the worst wounded and get them to the hospital."

Another man from the front row stood up, frowning at her. "I don't think you should be the one—"

The man wearing the flag pin held up his hand. "Quiet, George. I am in charge now that Leader Palmer is incapacitated. I say we're going to work together. We need their help, and they need ours. This has gone too far."

As the women and uninjured men spread through the crowd, moving the Foreboded to different sections depending upon the degree of their affliction, Marilyn and Cleopatra joined Ada in the back of the room.

"Do you think they can actually work together now?" Ada asked. "Some of these young women have never known a world that even resembles equality."

Suzanne came up behind her. "That's absolutely true. But we're going to do our damn best." Tears showed in her eyes. "Thank you for what you've done. You've freed us, and we won't let it go to waste."

"It seems our work here is done, and you can take it from here." Ada hugged Suzanne, the two women holding each other tightly before pulling away.

Suzanne stroked Ada's hair. "Now, you three go back and see what you can do in your own times. Right?"

Cleopatra held out the Time Traveler cube to Ada.

The three materialized behind a screen in a stone temple.

Ada immediately pulled at the collar of her beloved white blouse, grinning. "Cleo, even this white pantsuit is too hot for your climate. I hope it doesn't cause you any trouble to appear in this clothing."

"I don't anticipate any problem," Cleopatra said. "Even though men have influenced my actions, some things will change around here. I wonder if anything I do now will affect you in the future."

"Good luck, sugar. It's been a pleasure." Marilyn leaned forward and embraced the Egyptian. Then Ada threw her arms around them both and hugged them close.

After a long moment, they pulled away, sniffing and wiping their eyes.

"Well, I would love to stay here and help you, but I'm feeling the urge to return to my own time and see what I can do there now. So, let's get going." Ada took Marilyn's hand, and the actress held the cube with the other.

"Sugar, we might as well. As they say, there is no time like the present!"

Ada manipulated the controls, and the room grew fuzzy as the pair spun into the future. The last she saw was Cleopatra's puzzled face as she tried to make sense of Marilyn's words, then burst out laughing and waved.

Ada and Marilyn re-entered the twentieth century at the side of a movie set where several cameras focused on a large wooden desk in an oval room. A woman in a business suit sat behind the desk, signing some papers as the cameras rolled.

"Cut!" cried a woman in black pants and a vest, sitting in a director's chair. Several men and women bustled around on the set, stopping to ask the woman questions.

Marilyn and Ada stepped outside and stopped short. Across the road, a giant sign rising over the enormous complex read "Monroe Studios."

Marilyn blinked. "Oh, my. I seem to have moved up a bit in the world."

Ada smiled at her. "Well, I don't know if this is Cleopatra's doing, based on how she was going to start changing her world…"

Marilyn grinned back. "I'm sure that's part of it, sugar. But I have a feeling that you're about to go make some major changes too."

A young woman bustled up to them, carrying a small, flat screen before her. "Miss Monroe, you have a meeting with the other studios in ten minutes. The reminder just came up on my Lovelace." She tapped the screen in her hands.

Looks like I've made an impact.

Ada's heart soared. *I already had a brain and a vision. Now I have a purpose. I will go back and make men listen to every word I say.*

Because, Science

Carol Gyzander

STILL RIDING the high of her recent college graduation, Emma clinked her glass against Rachel's bottle of IPA, ignoring the sour beer and sweat odors as they toasted their future. She didn't want to give up on the evening, although the rest of their graduating friends—three other young women, also technology and science majors—had already left the rural Pennsyltucky bar. *I knew we could all do it!*

She took a sip of her now-watery diet soda. "So, what will you be doing at the lab?"

Rachel grimaced. "Well, as the lowly summer intern, the best I can say is that it's great to have a job in the field, and I'm sure it will help me when I get to medical school in the fall. What about you—first day at the engineering firm tomorrow, right? Good thing you volunteered to be designated driver." She tapped her bottle against Emma's glass with a chuckle and took another swig.

"Hey, come on, Julie did too. We understand about drinking and driving—because, science!" She leaned back on her barstool, stretched her arms over her head, then sat forward. "Golly, could you have imagined back in high school that all five of us would be science majors and graduate top of our classes?"

"Right?" Rachel asked, taking another sip. "So, what's the story with that hate mail you got?"

"Beats the hell out of me." Emma threw her hands up in exasperation. "Some idiot sent me a snail mail saying I should find a more appropriate job if I knew what was good for me. Good for me? I worked hard for four years, graduated summa cum laude, and landed an ace job… and now some asshole is telling me what to do. What is this, the 'fifties? *Snail mail!*"

Rachel choked on her beer as she laughed and leaned forward to grab a napkin—then grabbed Emma's arm and pointed at the television screen over the bar. "Look! Holy crap, isn't that Julie's car?"

Emma swiveled to check out the late-night news. The headline read: "Another group of women report seeing The Man." The hazy image showed Julie's crumpled ten-year-old Toyota wrapped around a huge pine tree. The vehicle perched off the edge of a dark two-lane road running through a forest. Rain poured down the car's back window, obscuring the interior, but the camera moved around to show the smashed windshield.

Oh my God—Julie! Where are they? Are they… are they dead?

"Hush, everyone! Hush! Can you turn it up?" Rachel flagged the guy behind the bar. "That's our friend's car!"

The bartender surveyed the small crowd nursing their drafts, then shrugged and increased the volume.

The reporter's voice came on. "… and the three young women involved in this accident are from Smithville, just home from graduation at the Science College. These three are luckier than some of the earlier accident victims. Two girls are in intensive care, but we spoke to the third in the hospital."

Amanda's face filled the screen, a bandage covering her forehead and one eye. Her other eye showed red and puffy, mascara smeared underneath. Blood splatters on her shirt collar, now dried and dark, contrasted with her gray skin. A voice offscreen asked, "What happened? You say you saw The Man?"

She nodded, lips pressed together tightly. "We didn't believe any of those stories we heard at college. Thought it was just a hoax. But then, on our way home, Julie suddenly yelled and stomped on the brakes. I wasn't watching the front. I'd been talking to Amy…" She stifled a sob and drew a deep breath.

"… I was talking to Amy in the back seat. I turned when Julie screamed. A man in a trench coat stood in the middle of the road. Right in front of our car! We could have killed him. Julie did the right thing. She swerved. The car went into a skid. There was nothing we could do. I thought I was going to die. The road was so slick. We slid off the road. And then…"

Her hand came to her mouth. "The car hit a tree, and everything went dark. Julie was slumped over the wheel

143

when I came to, but the airbag hadn't gone off. Amy was unconscious in the back, and her head was bleeding. And there was nobody else there. The Man was gone."

She stared directly into the camera. "Where did The Man go? *Why didn't he come help us?*"

"Third incident this week involving 'The Man' and female graduates from scientific institutions," blared the newscaster. "Officials speculate that it's a backlash to this year's class that featured record numbers of women graduating with science degrees, and women now make up 70% of all new science hires."

The weather report came on next. The bartender sneered with a tilt of his head, lowered the sound, and served another patron down the bar.

"I saw those girls here with you." An older man seated near them leaned over, glowering. "They were just asking for trouble. Women shouldn't be trying to work in science, and they certainly shouldn't be out on their own in bars. The Man was just trying to teach them what's right."

He crossed his arms and sat back with a satisfied nod.

Emma stared at him coldly. "You have no idea what you're talking about, buddy." She turned her back on him and faced Rachel, who stared at the silent screen with her mouth hanging open. Emma patted her friend's shoulder.

"Are they going to be okay?" Rachel blinked and wiped her eyes with the back of her hand. "And what the hell is going on? What's wrong with women doing science?"

144

Emma's fist tightened. "I'm not surprised that he came for some of us. After all the other things people say he's done. But Julie and Amy are in intensive care. The police have to *do* something!"

Rachel grabbed Emma's arm, her fingers digging deep. "Look! There he is again!"

On the television, the weather report blinked and rolled a few times. The set made a sparking sizzle, like electricity running through wire. Then a man in a trench coat and dark sunglasses filled the screen. The image buzzed and zapped, flickering like the flames licking up over logs in the restaurant's fireplace.

The bar's patrons went silent. The bartender tried changing the channel, but the same image appeared on each one. The buzzing sound grew louder until he finally turned it off.

The set darkened for three heartbeats. The image appeared once more.

People's phones started buzzing. The jukebox played three songs at once.

Emma and Rachel looked at each other.

"What's happening?" Rachel wailed. "How is he doing this? He must have hacked the TV station."

"I can't stand this anymore," Emma said. "He's got a lot of nerve. There must be a group of them or something."

Rachel's sobbing suddenly stopped. She looked up and stared at Emma, her face set in hard lines. "Why doesn't he ever bother men?"

Emma hugged her friend, then pulled back. "I'd say we're threatening them, and hurting women is how he makes himself feel important. But no way in hell are we going to give in to fear. Let's go."

They paid their bill and ran toward Emma's Volkswagen across the rainswept parking lot. Rachel wobbled a bit, and Emma helped her into the car.

Rachel slumped in the passenger seat, and Emma reached over to fasten her seatbelt. "Can't forget that!"

"Where are we going?" Rachel roused a moment. "Can we go see them in the hospital?"

"No, I'm sure visiting hours are over. Let's go home." Backing out of the parking lot, Emma put quiet jazz on the radio and tried to relax as she pulled onto the dark, rainy road. "Hey, you can go see them at the hospital tomorrow while I'm at my first day of work. Find out all the details, okay? You'll feel better when you see them again."

Strident words broke into the soothing jazz. "We interrupt this broadcast. Police are asking women to take care on the roads and, where possible, travel with a father or brother while 'The Man' is still at large."

"Oh, for Christ's sake," Emma said. "Seriously, that's their answer?" Static filled the car. She turned off the radio. The crackling continued. *Huh. Humidity from all this rain must be messing with the connection.*

Rachel leaned back against the headrest, closing her eyes. Emma negotiated the road as it wound through

146

the tall pine trees. Her ears throbbed with the static's increasing intensity.

What the hell? This can't be real. I turned the damn thing off. Must be my nerves... this dark road in the rain. Starting the new job tomorrow. That news report about the accident.

A diamond-shaped yellow sign warned of an approaching S-curve. Emma started into the first turn. The steering grew strangely sluggish.

No! The power steering is dead!

Manhandling the wheel, Emma dragged it around, barely making the curve.

Breathing out, she shot a glance at Rachel and chuckled. *Sound asleep.* Emma looked back to the road just as it started to straighten out between the curves. A dark shape suddenly appeared before them. She shrieked and automatically jammed her foot on the brakes.

A man blocked the road. Wearing sunglasses and a trench coat, he held his arms out to each side and raised his hands.

Her spine tingled. The Volkswagen skidded out to the side.

Not putting up with this. Emma clenched her teeth. *I studied physics.* She kept her foot off the gas, using all her strength to turn the steering wheel into the skid and keep the car on the road. The wheels caught the pavement, and she straightened out, careful not to overcorrect as she approached the second turn—heading right toward The Man looming ahead.

"Leave us all alone!"

She waited for the thud. Instead, the front of the car passed right through The Man. He exploded in a shower of sparks. The headlights blinked out with a zapping buzz. The engine sputtered. Static crackled, pulsating like a heartbeat as the car careened into the curve.

Emma hauled on the steering wheel, barely keeping them on the asphalt in the darkness as the road banked through the second curve. As they hurtled along the road, the headlights lit up again, and the engine flicked on with a gentle hum. The pavement ahead glistened. She looked in the rearview mirror and saw only the dark road and trees.

Emma hooted and pumped her fist in the air.

"You can't keep me from my new job, asshole!"

Storm Warning

Carol Gyzander

MIRANDA lay on her pallet in the cave, her belly tight with cramps. *What is going on?* She rolled onto her side and then onto her knees, sitting back and rocking. The motion had relieved the cramps when they'd started the previous day but now offered only slight relief. She pulled herself up, pushing her dark curls from her face.

She made her way through the network of caves to the open stone room where she and her father took their meals, lit a fire in the cooking area, and put on some water for tea. She gazed into the fire, waiting for the water to heat. Her head drooped as the warmth enveloped her, and the red glow of the burning wood grew brighter. Suddenly she tensed, realizing she had been staring into... *Is that an eye?*

She shook herself—*I'm imagining it*—and then poured the tea into their one remaining porcelain cup. Sipping the warmth helped ease the cramps. When her father strode in from his office, she asked him about the discomfort, but he brushed aside her questions with a wave of his hand.

"Come along, girl. My plan is in play after all these years of preparation, and I must ensure supplies are in place before I finally call the storm. The body is unimportant, as the mind is the only thing worth pursuing." Prospero drew her outside. They headed down the rocky path and around the base of the cliff that held their palace, a series of interconnected caves in the mountainside.

Miranda walked alongside her father, pleased that all his hard work and study would come to fruition for him. As they approached a wide, open spot on the path, she let him take the lead as he always did when coming to speak with his servant.

"Caliban!" Prospero roared. "Come out of your cave so we can consult upon the tasks at hand. Great things are afoot, and I need everything to be settled ahead of time."

The youth's tousled, curly dark hair and broad shoulders emerged from the small hole in the cliff. Miranda held her breath as Caliban straightened to his full height, equal to that of her father and greater than her own. Barefoot and shirtless as usual, he wore her father's torn pair of hand-me-down pants and a knife in his waist sheath.

The brute grinned at her, and she took a half step back behind her father before realizing she was moving.

Prospero raised his chin, giving him the effect of speaking down to the youth. "Caliban, some guests will arrive shortly on our island during the upcoming storm. I ordered that extra wood and food be gathered and stacked in the palace. Have you accomplished this task?"

Guests? On our island? He's always talked about it, but it hasn't happened yet.

Caliban scuffed the sandy ground with one foot, glowering as he looked aside for a moment. Then, raising his eyes to stare directly into her father's face, he grunted. "I have done all you said. Had you looked, you would have seen stacks upon stacks of wood. I always do as you say, knowing your power and how you would punish me."

An image of the two men on the island's shore, one young and one older, suddenly flashed into Miranda's mind—her father leaning forward at the forest's edge with his arms crossed, brow furrowed, and smile tight while an insect cloud pursued Caliban across the shorefront. The winged pests buzzed and stung his exposed skin. They swarmed around his face as he screamed and cried, wildly batting them away with both hands—until he leaped into the water. The vision disappeared as abruptly as it came.

Her breath caught, and she pressed against her abdomen with both hands as a wave of cramps ran through her. *Can this be true? I've never seen this before.* From her safe vantage point behind her father, she examined the skin of Caliban's chest, seeing myriad small welts she'd never noticed before and long, thin lines of red extending over his shoulders from his back.

He stepped to the side and peered back at Miranda. When his gaze met hers, her heart lurched, and she gasped.

What is it that connects me to him? He has no couth, is not part of the court my father speaks so much about and lives in squalor among the island's creatures.

Caliban reached out a hand toward her. "I found some more rabbits if you want to see them."

A few years ago, Caliban had crossed her path with a sack containing something that moved. When she'd inquired, he'd opened it to show her a litter of baby bunnies. He had plucked one from the sack and deposited it in her arms, along with instructions on how to care for it—but the rabbit had escaped from her palace bedchamber and run past the door of her father's study chamber, further and deeper into the cave that was their palace. Into the deep caverns where her father did not allow her to go, no matter how much she begged.

"No, my dear," her father had said. "That area is not for you. We live on this side with my books and my studies."

She shivered in rage at the memory of not being allowed to rescue the poor little rabbit, then snapped her attention back to the present, unclenching her hands.

"None of that, you wretch." Her father held out an arm to block Caliban's approach. "You have done your tasks. That is enough."

Caliban scowled and disappeared through the hole in the stone wall. Miranda was surprised that her heart ached when he left as if some part of her were gone. *How can Father be so careful with me yet so cruel to Caliban?*

She suddenly felt bolder than ever before and turned to her father. "How did we get here, Father? Why is Caliban so different from us? I don't understand."

He looked at her long and hard, then inclined his head as he seemed to come to a decision. "I haven't told you the story of how I—we—arrived on the island, but now you seem to be old enough to understand. I was the rightful ruler, the Duke of Milan, but I lost my title to my brother and had to flee in a boat containing just my books and some simple necessities. It landed here. I found Caliban as a savage orphan child, wandering the island, and brought the wretch under my power to help save the boy. He has been helpful, but he is not like us."

<*I was not always here.*>

Miranda gasped and looked around for the speaker.

Wait, what? Did I think that?

"Why do you ask about Caliban, Miranda?" Prospero's voice cut through her confusion.

She blinked to clear her mind so she could answer her father.

"I don't like to look upon him, Father," Miranda said with a frown. "I know I taught him to speak, but I feel confused in his presence. There is something that draws me to him. I do not understand."

Her father tilted his head to the side as he took a few steps away. "You did indeed help him learn how to communicate, but I fear that is the most accomplishment he will get. Not like you, who will someday have a place in court if you follow my teaching."

He held up one finger when she opened her mouth to ask another question. "I am sure of it. Finish your sums before I return."

How can he always be so sure of things?

"Now I am off to find Ariel the sprite, get them set on their duties, and then call the storm." Prospero left her by the cave, taking the trail to the cliff where he did his weather magic.

She watched him go, clearly focused on the tasks ahead of him and no longer noticing his daughter. *He says we are not the same, and yet he controls me as much as he does Caliban.*

Miranda used the chamber pot in her stone bedchamber and was shocked to discover blood. She steadied herself against the wall and raised one trembling hand to her forehead. *What is happening to me?* Then she blotted herself with dried moss and stuffed some fabric scraps between her legs.

<I was not always as I am now, either.>

Who said that? With a whimper, she dashed mindlessly into the long cave that served as a hallway between the bedchambers and her father's study, running to him for help as always. He had not returned to his office. She grabbed a lantern and dashed out, continuing farther down the forbidden passage, hoping to find him to help quell her panic.

154

As she went deeper into the cave, the walls narrowed, and the path descended. Putting one hand on the stone, she was surprised to find it warm—the walls in her room were always cold. She trailed her fingers along the rock, feeling a slight charge enter her fingertips.

Taken aback at first by the tingle, Miranda soon found that she liked it.

I want more. Is that wrong?

At a fork in the tunnel, she followed the left-hand path. It seemed to head back toward the surface, and the charge dissipated after only a few steps. She turned and took the other branch. The sense of energy grew more vivid, the wall grew warmer, and a faint, earthy scent filled her nostrils.

Within minutes, she entered a small, round cave. Red crystals glowed in the walls, lighting the space with a gentle, even warmth. In front of her, the bodies of many small animals lay at the base of a high stone ridge and scattered around the room. A ledge formed a seat on the right-hand side.

Panting and very close to tears, she sank onto the ledge, feeling the blood seep from between her legs against the rock. Soothed by the warm stone, she leaned back, resting against the wall. It almost seemed to pulsate.

A footstep grating on the stone startled her. Caliban entered the round cave. He stopped and stared at her, fingers opening and closing as his arms hung loosely at his sides.

"You're here." He smiled at her. "We've waited a long time."

We?

She wiped her face with her hand, trying to clear the fog of confusion enveloping her since she discovered the blood. "What is going on? Why was I drawn here? Why do I feel such a pull toward you?"

He shrugged. "I guess it is time."

"Father always tells me not to be alone with you anymore. Ever since…"

He threw both hands in the air with an exasperated cry, then reached out to her. "I never would've hurt you! I just wanted to spend time with you. To be together with you."

"It's odd to hear you talk so freely." Miranda sighed. "But if not for me, you wouldn't have any words at all."

Caliban nodded, his lips tight. "You did indeed give me words. Words that I can use to curse the man who binds me here, who holds my mother in thrall, who teaches you in his manner but omits the important things."

"But what does this all mean? Why do I feel so funny?" Miranda leaned forward, searching his face, then jumped as she caught motion in her peripheral vision. She looked across the chamber and saw her reflection on a smooth sheet of quartz in the wall: tousled hair, a streak of blood on her cheek, and her eyes wide.

Caliban grunted. "What your father told you about how he came here is not right."

"What?" She looked back at him. "How do you know that?"

"Your words. Learning words from you helped me connect to my mother, Sycorax. We are with her now, and she tells me things." Caliban held out his arms. "We are deep in her circular center."

Miranda frowned. "Your mother? But how did she get here?"

Even as she spoke, her heart thrummed as she drew energy from the stone under her. She pressed against the granite at her back, and the feeling grew. She kicked at some of the tiny animal carcasses as she stretched her legs forward to get better contact with the stone.

<He will tell you in his own time.>

What? Miranda's head snapped up. "Did you say that?"

Caliban smiled. "No, I didn't, but I am happy you also heard her." He grasped one of her hands, going down on one knee before her. "Do not fear. Since I learned the words, she speaks in my mind, and it seems she now speaks in yours. Show her, Mother."

The quartz panel displayed an image of her father as a younger man, yet still bent over his papers the way Miranda often saw him.

<I once was part of Prospero—the part with earth magic. The part that had a heart and compassion for others. He buried it long ago, immersing himself in his scholarly studies and ignoring his responsibilities of rulership while he was the duke and should have been dealing with the people.>

Tears brimmed in Miranda's eyes, and she stroked the stone bench next to her. The image changed to show a small boat landing on the island's sandy shore, one single male occupant on board among a stack of crates and barrels.

<When Prospero arrived here, he was alone. All he had was his books and enough food and supplies to get him started. But he could not accept his loss of power. He raged against me, this part of himself connected with the people and the earth. All he wanted was to study the weather and his books, especially that book of magic.>

Miranda pressed her lips together. She knew the book and wasn't allowed to touch it.

The voice grew louder and more vehement. <Somehow, he used my book to turn my earth powers against me and split us in two. I was consigned to live in this round cave, divorced from my intellectual self—which he retained for his own.>

Miranda pressed her free hand to her throbbing temple as the words edged into her brain. "Where did I come from, then? And what of Caliban?"

<It was the one blessing of splitting my soul from his intellect. Once separated, once divided, somehow I was with child: twins. The two of you were born. Caliban, gifted with my connection to the earth, and you, my daughter Miranda, with your father's intellectual ability.>

She looked at Caliban, trying to picture him as her twin, her partner, and felt a jolt of completion as his gaze met hers. It traveled through her heart, down her torso, and out to the ends of her limbs—leaving her fingertips and toes

158

tingling. Her hair rose on her scalp, swirling as if in a breeze, even though the air was still.

Suddenly, she doubled over and cried out as her abdomen spasmed with fierce cramps. The warm flow gushed stronger, spreading across the stone ledge beneath her. The red crystals embedded in the walls glowed with soft light that grew in intensity until the room blazed red. She straightened up, the cramps gone. *What's happening? I feel so... so powerful!*

She pointed at the remains of the tiny creatures laid out at their feet and sent them sliding across the floor with a twitch of her fingers. Then, throwing her chest out, she stretched out her arms and raised both hands, lifting herself and Caliban off the floor. The cave vibrated, and a crack appeared in one curved wall.

All her life, she had followed her father's dictates and gone along with his complete control over her. Now connected with her mother—with the earth—the forces at her command freed her spirit. She sucked air into her lungs, ready to release a shriek of repressed rage and power.

Her eyes glowed bright red in the wall's quartz sheet like the embedded crystals in the rest of the cave. She turned her head and watched the reflection move, the eyes widening even further. This startling image broke through whatever possessed her just as the stone ceiling overhead groaned and dust fell from a crumbling section in the corner.

She had to rein it in—the whole island would be destroyed if she went off like a star! In the quartz reflection, the light in her eyes flared momentarily, then ebbed to a gentle twinkle in one eye. She gently sank back to sit on the ledge.

This changed everything. "We can make our lives on our own terms now. Go where we want."

The same red glow ebbed in Caliban's eyes as his feet touched the ground. He paused for a moment as if listening. When no words came from their mother, he smiled and shrugged.

"Some part of Sycorax will be with us wherever we go." Caliban's lips twisted. "Your father conjures up a storm that will bring men here from his own land. I heard him agree to release Ariel from his control once the sprite tricks one of those men into marrying you so that Prospero would regain his position."

She wrinkled her brow the way she did when concentrating on something in a book. Her father always spoke of their return to civilized society, but this last part was news to her. Being used as a tool to regain his position rankled her. *Doesn't he care about what I want?*

"He has indeed taught me to want more than this island," she said slowly. "I have followed all his rules— studied all his books and learned how his society works. But... I've never had a chance to decide what I want. I cannot be a pawn in his game."

Caliban nodded. "I would also like to see more than just this piece of rock in the water. And what of Prospero?"

Her heart and brain warred within her. "Although he did keep me as only half of myself, separate from you and our… mother, I don't want to abandon my father. If we can bring him in with us and reunite him with what we have now become, perhaps all will be right with the world. But if we cannot…"

She straightened and rose, gripping both of his hands in her own. "If we cannot, I shall grieve for my father. But together, we will take what is ours and claim it as our own. I can rule in my *own* name." Miranda took a deep breath.

"Because together, we are the future."

Miranda snuck back to her bedchamber after watching Caliban head toward his cave. She sat on her pallet, feet drawn up and arms wrapped around her knees. Everything seemed different—yet it all fit together. Her father, a stern taskmaster, always insisted she do her schoolwork.

The rumbling of her belly roused her from her ruminations. Unsure how much time had passed, she leaped from her bed and dashed toward the kitchen to start cooking dinner. Prospero insisted that food be ready at specific times, even though he often got involved with some project and forgot to come out and eat.

She reached for the flint to start the fire, then paused and searched deep for that power she'd felt in the circular cave. *Can I do this? I don't want to burn everything.* Extending one hand into the fireplace, she touched the wood and concentrated… and it caught fire!

Smiling, she chopped some meat and set it to cook. Next, she filled the other pot with water and hung it over the fire to heat in preparation for boiling some greens.

The cooking was well underway before Prospero's footsteps sounded in the stone hall, so she wouldn't get in trouble for being slow. But what would he think of her discovery—this new version of herself? Tension gripped her heart again. She jumped to her feet as Prospero entered the cooking area. *Will he look at me and know? Does the red light still show in my eyes without Caliban around?*

Her father entered, his focus on the book in his hands. A side glance at the fire, then a nod. "When will the food be ready?" Finally, he turned to face her.

"In about fifteen minutes, Father." She curtsied as he had taught her to do—she never knew why. Many of her required actions made no sense, but he always said that was how people did it in court.

She'd never thought she would see this court. But Caliban said her father was plotting to bring a ship here—in a storm—to marry her off and regain his position. *How dare he not tell me?*

Her father made no reaction. "All right. Call me when it's ready. Don't burn anything." He turned on his heel and headed toward his office.

Miranda sank onto the rock ledge they used as a bench. *No reaction whatsoever! Couldn't he tell that I have found the other half of myself? I always thought him so powerful.* She stared at the wall, unseeing—until the crackling of the cooking food jolted her back to her surroundings. She stirred the meal before it burned, narrowly avoiding her father's wrath.

As they dined together, Prospero focused on his book and paid little attention to Miranda. She still felt power surging through her after finding Sycorax—her mother?—in the cave and joining with her. The strength emboldened her. "What are you reading, Father?"

He looked up at her, eyes wide. "You have your own work to do, my dear. Leave me to mine. Have you finished your mathematics assignment?" Now interrupted, he frowned. "You'll have to show me your progress after you clear the table."

"The mathematics is easy. I understand the concepts and can easily do the practice equations you set for me." She lifted her chin as she spoke, perhaps for the first time with her father.

He nodded and rubbed his chin. "I see. So, perhaps you are ready to move on to the next phase of your schooling. This book"—he gestured at the tiny print on the page before him— "contains the combined writings of experts in their field, who write about the physical world and how it can be controlled."

She smiled inside, careful not to let her amusement show on her face. She suspected that she now knew so much more about the physical world through Sycorax and Caliban than could ever be in one of his books.

"What is this to be used for, Father?" She fluttered her eyelashes just a bit, as this usually made him warm to her and share his thoughts.

"My daughter, you've worked hard and learned well. You have a good head on your shoulders for business, not that anyone in court will allow it of a woman, but I expect you will do well when you marry into the royalty."

"But how can I marry into royalty when there is no one here but us?" She kept her face impassive.

"That's why I'm looking at this book. Others will be joining us tonight. It is time for you to check your wardrobe and lay out your finest clothing so that you can make a good impression."

Her eyes widened. *So it is true!* Not that she had disbelieved Caliban; she simply had not known how soon it would all come about.

He laid a strip of cloth in his book and closed it up, then rose from the table and held one finger in the air. "Also, we must prepare for a storm such as we have not seen on the island since just before your... birth. I'm sure of it. Strange things are afoot, my dear."

She cleared the dishes and scrubbed the cooking pot as fast as possible so she could sneak out and meet Caliban as they had planned. She tried to resolve these different versions of her world and her father—how his actions didn't match his intentions. Strange things, indeed—he would see just how strange.

As the winds abated, she waited for Caliban in one of the exterior caves as they had planned, alternately pacing and tapping her foot. With her bleeding contained by dried moss and no more cramping, it was no longer a distraction.

The storm raged all night, the winds buffeting the surrounding trees so that they shook their arms as if in warning. Of what? Miranda wasn't sure—only that a ship was coming. With people. Men from her father's country. What would it be like to see others, as she only knew her father, Caliban, and Ariel? *But a sprite doesn't count as people.*

Her increased confidence once Caliban entered the cave amazed her. Was this just what she had read about—that a female needed the male to protect her? She tapped her chin as he shook the rain off his cloak. No, it wasn't that. Now she understood how incomplete she'd been without the other half of her psyche, which her father had split from her.

Caliban turned toward her, and the huge grin revealed that his response was much like hers. They touched their fingertips together.

"So, the storm is abating. Do you think Prospero's plan has worked?" Caliban searched her eyes.

She lifted her hands. "I suppose we should go and find out. I saw lights down by the shore."

They decided to cut through the woods toward the beach. As they walked, she chuckled at how well they worked together to make their way in the dark. First, one would go ahead and hold a hand to help the other over a difficult spot; then, the other would hold back branches that blocked the trail. All worked well to strengthen their connection.

We must be near. Did you hear that? I thought I heard voices ahead. She pointed ahead and off toward the side.

He bared his teeth. [I suspect they are in that clearing where the deer sit in the sunshine on a nice day. Shall we go and meet them?]

I shall watch from the bushes in case they are not to be trusted. She frowned at the dull ache in her belly.

When Caliban reached the clearing, the winds abated, and the sky cleared as the first light filtered through the trees. He sat on a large rock and cast his cloak over his head. Miranda made herself comfortable behind a large tree with low-hanging branches that gave her a protected view.

Presently, a pair of men in bedraggled velvet clothing crashed through the trees from the opposite side of the clearing.

One cried, "Daylight! Enough of this eternal forest. Stephano, here is a clearing! Perhaps we can rest here."

The other surveyed the grassy area. He pointed toward the hump on a rock that was Caliban. "Look! Almost like a tent for us to sleep under." He took three long strides and threw back the cloak. Caliban looked up, blinking at the sudden light.

"Oh," cried Stephano. "What have we here?" He eyed Caliban's bare feet and muscular calves and his tousled, long hair. "Some sort of monster? Who knows what creatures are on this island."

Caliban started to speak, but the first man moved before him, sniffing. "He smells rather gamy. He can't be a man, for he doesn't seem intelligent. More like an animal. I do believe this is a man-calf. How now, man-calf?"

Stephano grabbed a stick and prodded Caliban in the haunch, yelling, "Go on, get moving! Show me and Trinculo what you can do. Lift this rock, man-calf!" He tapped a massive stone with the stick.

Why don't you go along with them and see what they want? We may learn much from these two without them being any the wiser.

Caliban gave an imperceptible nod without even flicking a glance in her direction. He bent and lifted the giant stone and tossed it aside, then stood before the two, speaking in simple words. "Don't hurt me! I am but a plain soul. How can I help you?"

"Well," said Stephano. "We landed on this shore after a storm, and our master, Antonio, has told us of the one who lives here—Prospero, correct?"

"Yes, I have been his slave since almost before I can remember. He treats me poorly, beats me, and tricks me into doing what he wants."

Trinculo cried out at this and capered about the clearing. "We thought as much! We have heard that Prospero is the rightful Duke of our land, but we would take his place. Will you help us, man-calf?"

I can't say that this is a very good way to convince people to offer help. Who likes to be called a monster?

"Our master is the brother of yours!" cried Trinculo. "He is the Duke only because your master Prospero disappeared. He would not like to give up his power. But—"

"But we would take his place," interrupted Stephano. "Take both of their places. With our master gone and yours out of the picture, one of us would be next to rule our homeland. So, man-calf, what do you say to that?"

"I'm not sure what to say," replied Caliban. "I certainly have no fondness for Prospero, for he has mistreated me my entire life. When I didn't do tasks on time, he beat me. When I did, but not to his satisfaction, he sent plagues of biting insects to torment my eyes and skin. So I care nothing for the man."

"Then you can work with us," declared Trinculo. "Help us to get rid of our master and yours. And we shall find a place for you in our court."

"So be it." Caliban nodded, and the two clapped him on the shoulders.

"That's our man-calf, for sure!"

I cannot understand why they would treat you like an animal and yet expect you to help them.

[It seems odd to me as well. This is how people behave?]

It doesn't seem right to me. I don't trust them. Do you?

The two men were still celebrating.

[If they would turn against their master, they would just as quickly turn against someone they don't know.]

I have a solution for this.

She stepped into the clearing. The newcomers turned at the sound of her footsteps.

"Well, now! And who is this? You didn't tell us you had a lovely lady, man-calf." Trinculo eyed Miranda, a lascivious smile crossing his lips. His eyes gleamed a shiny black.

"I am not yours to enjoy. I am my own person. As is Caliban here. Why do you treat him like an animal?"

She stood with her hands on her hips, a tingling in her chest. A hint of red glowed in Caliban's eyes. He nodded at her.

"Oh, ho! A feisty maiden. This will be fun." Stephano took a few steps toward her.

Miranda held up one hand, and he froze midstride. His eyes now shone as black as his partner's.

"You must be fond of animals," she said. "What did you call him? A man-calf? I have read about cattle and cows. The calf is their baby. If you call him a baby and would be his superior, then you must be a full-grown animal. Unfortunately, we have no cows here on the island, so I can't replicate that, but there is an animal that I know very well."

She crossed her arms and extended them toward the pair. Their form shimmered and grew vague. Both men's faces bulged and shifted as they hunched and dropped upon shortened front legs. Their clothing fell away, and their faces changed. Each grew a long snout, ending in a pair of quivering nostrils.

Trinculo opened his mouth as if to speak, but only a squeal came out. He froze as his companion made the same noise in response. Both ran frantically around the clearing on all fours, leaping and bucking as they tried to stand up on their two hind legs but couldn't balance. One toppled over and landed at Caliban's feet.

Caliban grabbed him by the neck. "Ho, what do you think?" He pulled the knife from his belt.

She pointed two fingers at the other boar, freezing it in place with her will, except for the frantic quivering of its nose and labored breathing. "I think we should take a wonderful feast to my father's brother, wherever he is, so as to be welcome in his company. Do you agree?"

Caliban bared his teeth fiercely, then slit the animal's throat. It let out a frantic squeal, then fell to its side. Blood spurted and burbled from its neck, pooling onto the grass where it soaked into the ground in moments.

Knife still dripping in his hand, Caliban advanced toward the boar that Miranda held in thrall. The monstrous beast snorted and whimpered as he approached.

One swipe of Caliban's arm and the second man-pig lay next to his friend, bleeding out from a gaping wound in his throat. The light faded from his black eyes. His tongue rolled out, and his head and body went slack.

Caliban gutted the pair, then bent to wipe the knife on the torso of the nearest corpse.

"I think we are different now, Caliban. Remember how we used to save the little rabbits? But now we are looking to save ourselves."

"These two will make a fine feast. I can carry them both," said Caliban.

Miranda put her hand on his arm. "No. I will lift them, and you guide them. Let's head toward the shore. We might find more men from the ship." She gestured with two fingers, and the boar corpses rose, their hindquarters in the air so the blood could drain.

"Strange to see these two after knowing only you and your father my whole life." Caliban touched the two floating carcasses gently to guide them along the trail. "Of course, look how it turned out."

"I know what you mean. All my life, my father has been promising me a better future was coming. Who would want to spend more time with the likes of these two?"

"We know so little of people."

Yet Miranda'd had a feeling about Stephano and Trinculo when she first laid eyes on them in the clearing. Something had been... off about them. Was it her unfamiliarity with other people, or had something about them set off her warning senses? Their eyes weren't gleaming black when she first saw them. Perhaps that would be something to pay attention to as they met more outsiders.

"I'm ravenous," Miranda said after a bit. "That took a lot out of me. I wish we had brought some food with us to eat right now."

Caliban grinned and shook his head. "Think a moment. Connect with the land, and you will find what you need."

She focused inside herself, tapping into the warmth in her abdomen, then gestured toward the surrounding undergrowth. Branches laden with fruit leaned in front of them, and she gathered blueberries and blackberries, gobbling them as they walked.

Eventually, they reached a small clearing near the rocky shore, where Miranda had seen lights the night before. They stopped behind a large rock and peered through the undergrowth. A giant ship listed to one side in the small harbor. On the shore, several dozen men huddled around a tiny campfire against the cliff that extended into the water— probably too afraid of their location to gather more wood and make a bigger fire.

I'll have no problem with that! She drew Caliban back to safety, then swept her hands at the tangle of wood at the edge of the clearing, using her power to drag several logs into a pile. She fashioned a framework above them, then reached in and pointed at the wood with one hand. The power surged within her, and wisps of smoke rose from the pile's center. Tiny flames sprang up and traveled along the length of the wood so that they had a roaring fire within moments. She clapped her hands with glee, and her heart soared at her new abilities.

Caliban stretched the boar carcasses over the fire, and they sat down to tend the cooking.

As the meat roasted and the delicious aroma filled the air, muttering echoed from the shore area, followed by footsteps. A tall, imposing man appeared, leading a group of men. They stopped abruptly when they saw Miranda and Caliban.

"What is this?" the leader cried. "It smells divine."

Miranda beckoned to the speaker. "I am Miranda, and this is Caliban. We have a large quantity of food we cannot consume ourselves. You are welcome on our island. As long as you are honest and true, we shall count you as friends."

Caliban rose and helped the men drag some logs around the cooking pit.

Once all were seated, Miranda addressed the leader again. "Who are you, and what brings you to our island? We have been here on our own for so long."

The man squared back his shoulders. "I am Antonio, the ruler of Milan. A sudden storm came over us as we traveled the open sea—such a tempest we had never seen before. It drove us to this island and trapped our ship in the cove. Many of us were flung overboard. Sharks set upon us and ripped the men's flesh. I saw my navigator floating ahead of me and gripped his arm, but his head tipped under the water, and he had no legs. Those lucky enough to avoid those sharp teeth made it to the shore, some on this side of the cliff."

Antonio drew in a breath. "Our group was divided, and the current pulled some of the bodies to the cliff's other side. Many are unaccounted for, including my son. We cannot reach them, and we cannot return to our ship. So, your offer of food is appreciated. We are famished." He looked from Miranda to Caliban.

"I am so sorry for your loss," she said.

"My brother, Prospero, was lost at sea while traveling near this island." He leaned toward Miranda with raised brows and a black gleam in his eyes. "Do you know him?"

She tried to assess his manner and intentions. He certainly spoke differently than her gruff and direct father. Was his polite manner a reflection of his character or just an example of court manners? *If that's the case, he's putting on an act to achieve his goals.*

Caliban turned the spit over the fire. The meat sizzled and popped, dripping grease and juice into the flames, each drop crackling. Antonio breathed deeply through his nose and licked his lips.

"Tell me of this Prospero," she said.

"He is my brother, the ruler of Milan before he was lost at sea. I was urged to take his place. A dozen years since I last saw him, and my heart still grieves." Antonio raised his hand to his chest. "Would he were here so that we may be reunited. And how do you come to be on the island?"

Gleams of black formed again in his eyes.

He wants to know where my father is but doesn't want him as ruler. This one is not to be trusted, for his words don't match his intentions. She blew air out of her nostrils. *Two can play this game.*

"You speak of my father, Prospero, who is here on the island and doing well. We have been waiting to be rescued all this time. I will much enjoy returning to Milan as heir to the kingdom."

Half of the men gasped. They rose and bowed in her direction, but Antonio remained seated. She inclined her head gracefully to the men as her father had taught her but then looked Antonio in the eye, her eyebrows raised.

"My father must be on his way now that the storm has abated. If you wish, we can go and bring him directly here. Of course, although the food is nearly cooked, it would not be appropriate to eat before he arrives as he is the ruler of this island."

"We will follow your wishes." Antonio placed a hand on his heart, but his eyes flashed as he gazed at the roasting boars.

Miranda and Caliban left the men tending the spits while they fetched Prospero. They found him not far away, coming down the path toward the shore. Miranda explained that she had already met the castaways, including his brother, and where they were to be found by the cookfire—but didn't mention how they obtained the boars.

He looked at her as if seeing her for the first time. "I'm surprised you're so comfortable and bold with these men. I thought you would be nervous and afraid, having never seen other people. Perhaps there is more to you than I thought."

You have no idea, my father. You have no idea.

"Father, I made them swear not to eat the food. I am curious to know if they are true to their word." Her heart clenched. At least with her father, she knew where she stood—as a tool to regain his position.

Prospero pushed her aside. "Great changes are indeed afoot. But, for now, let's get to the clearing so I can meet with my brother."

Prospero took the lead, but just before they reached the clearing, he stepped aside and let Miranda and Caliban precede him.

Miranda pulled up in surprise as she entered the clearing. One roast boar lay on a pile of leafy branches, most of its flesh torn off and consumed. A cloth covered its head. The other still hung on the spit. Antonio looked up while chewing a massive mouthful. He froze momentarily at the sight of Prospero; then his features took on a happy expression—although he was forced to swallow before speaking. Gulping down the mouthful of flesh, he rose and wiped his fingers on the inside of his cloak.

"My dear brother! I don't know if we have come to save you or you have come to save us."

Prospero stared at him coldly. "Antonio, I see that you have taken advantage of my daughter's hospitality in her absence. Were you not to wait until I arrived?"

Antonio's breath caught with a gasp.

Miranda examined the others. Those who had earlier applauded and bowed were gathered in a clump, their hands and faces clean, while grease and meat juice smeared Antonio's contingent.

She stepped in front of her father. "Hold on, Father. Allow me. I am the one dishonored by their behavior. However, those who follow your brother will soon learn *they* have been betrayed."

Antonio glanced at his men as they hastily licked their fingers and wiped their faces. "Whatever do you mean? You took so long to return that I thought you weren't coming. My men were starving."

"You swore you would not eat until we returned. Did it not even occur to you that there could be a reason for that?" She crossed her arms. Caliban stood behind her, one hand on her shoulder. Energy coursed through her at the touch.

"There's another pig there. Untouched. What's the problem?" Antonio smirked.

"The question is, what kind of meat *is* it?" She gestured toward the fire and the hacked-up carcass lying on the branches. A trail of sparks left her fingers, flying toward the corpses. The roasted flesh of the boar on the spit bulged and stretched. The elongated snout, now crispy under the fire, reshaped into the face of Stephano.

A man near the roast shrieked and backed away as the ribs and remaining leg of the other boar reshaped into human form. Another man pulled the cloth off the head, exposing Trinculo's face. The seared eyes crackled and broke away. Crisp lips curled back and exposed the teeth.

The second man screamed. One sailor, gnawing on what had been the boar's hind leg, now held a man's foot and lower leg in his hand, part of the calf torn away by his own teeth. He vomited on the ground, triggering a wave of regurgitation that left most of the diners wheezing on their knees. Others screamed, thrusting the food from their hands.

Prospero chuckled at their reactions, covering his grin with one hand.

"What have you done?" Antonio demanded, his face pale and his hands trembling. "You made us eat our comrade!"

"No. You did that yourself. I turned them into wild things because *they* treated Caliban like an animal. They were not to be trusted. And clearly, neither are you, for you could not wait until we returned. So now you shall feel what they did." Her belly warmed with the power inside her.

The diners gaped at each other. Suddenly, one fell off his seat and began writhing in the dirt. Another dropped onto all fours and rooted in the ground with his nose as his legs shortened and his torso broadened. One by one, those who had consumed the tainted flesh transformed into boars. They squealed their fear and dismay. The nonstop chorus deafened the remaining humans.

Although Antonio had partaken, he had yet to change. "What have you done to my men?" His voice quavered.

"Again. I didn't do a thing. You did it all yourselves. And now that *you* have seen what your treachery caused, it's *your* turn." Suppressing a smile, she flipped her wrist in his direction with a flourish of her fingers.

He opened his mouth, clearly looking to make a retort, but all that came out was a high-pitched squawk. He stopped, stunned, then tried again. The shrill noise pierced the air as he buckled over, holding his midsection with both hands until the transformation forced his arms to extend into legs and catch his weight. He stamped his four little hooves on the ground and squealed furiously.

Miranda shrugged. "It matters not what you say now. We cannot understand the language of animals." *Caliban does. But these men are of no matter.* She grabbed a leafy branch and chased the boars into the forest. When she returned to Caliban and her father, Caliban nodded, a red gleam in his eye.

Her father watched the entire proceeding gravely—and eyed his daughter as well.

Miranda turned to the remaining knot of men clustered by the fire. "If we can get us all onto your ship, can you take us back to your land?"

Several of them nodded, and one stepped forward. "We can. Everyone knows Antonio was not the rightful Duke. While I am not happy to see this happen, I understand that he broke his vow." He bowed for a moment, then straightened.

"Antonio's son, Ferdinand, is still missing. We presume he's been lost at sea, or the sharks got him. He was a good man, unlike his father."

Prospero chuckled. "He will be here soon. I've sent him wandering around the island until he could find my Miranda here, for soon they will be in love." He raised one finger. "I am sure of it."

Miranda's heart froze at his chuckle. *He really has done something with his own magic or had Ariel do it.* Cold spread within her. A black gleam shone in her father's eyes.

They gave the son a love spell so that he would fall in love with me, marry me, and then Father would have his rightful place back through my marriage.

179

"No, Father. What you've done is wrong. You can't use me to get what you want. I am not your bargaining tool. You must have done this because you are missing part of yourself—the part that separated when you came onto this island. You cannot leave until you learn to be a full person again."

Her father gaped, then strode at her, growling. "How dare you, girl?"

She held up both hands, and Caliban gripped her shoulder again, feeding energy into her and warming her core. She raised an invisible barrier against her father.

Prospero bounced back when he struck it, blinking in disbelief. He grabbed a flaming branch from the fire and swung it at her head with a roar. "How can you stop me? I am—"

The branch stopped in midair and rebounded toward him so that he had to duck and shield his face from the flames with one arm.

"It doesn't matter who you say you are, Father," she said sadly. "You must go to the island's center—the red circle in the cave. Make yourself whole. We'll locate Ferdinand, go to Milan with the sailors, and I'll find my way."

Her father trembled. She pulled her shoulders back and stood taller than ever before, with Caliban now at her side.

"But I can't stay here by myself!" he cried. "I've already released Ariel. There will be no one here."

"Another boat will come along at some point, Father." She grinned fiercely, raising one finger.

"I'm sure of it."

180

Part III
Kyla Lee Ward, Australia

Circling Hecate

Kyla Lee Ward

For three times round the pillar I must pass,
Three times address the Goddess to each face
She wears. A supplicant in urgent need.
Sweet Maiden, by the bright torch in your hand,
And crown upon your head, I beg you see,
My motives are as pure as is the One.

As witch, I comprehend that Three are One.
No Christian through such sharp ordeals shall pass
As tutored me. I know your second face.
Strong Mother, in these fresh travails I need
Compassion's cord, that binds love hand in hand.
Let open Wisdom's eye and let me see.

Such horrors as but few would choose to see!
A doom that comes upon us, every one.
But those who through the underworld would pass,
Must honour sunken eye and shadowed face.
Great Queen! It is your power that I need,
The daggers that you bear in either hand!

These dogs that I have fed with my own hand
Now snap and growl. Shall I the Goddess see?
Or does the mob approach to make me one
More victim? For the second time I pass
And offer to the Maiden's marble face
A kiss, a sister's kiss of love, not need.

My mother was abandoned in her need,
So I let fall my tears upon your hand.
Good Lady, now our drear confusion see!
I offer up myself, I shall be one
Of those who will Medusa's judgement pass
Upon such men who think to never face

The consequences of their greed, to face
A land despoiled, and yet we live in need.
Hell's Mistress! Now that hell is here, my hand
I cut for you, my true devotion see!
The ancient carvings blur, becoming one.
Let all I will this midnight come to pass!

On my third pass, a cold wind whips my face
And now I need to brace me with my hand.
My fate to see, take one more step, just one.

Maleficium

Kyla Lee Ward

Monday, 8 August 20XX

SHOCKING DEATH OF KINGSTON
PROPERTY HEIR

Twenty-four-year-old Raynor Kingston, son
of property magnate Ragnar Kingston, was
rushed to hospital last night with a suspected
case of pufferfish poisoning. It is understood
the young man was comatose on his arrival at
Sydney Central Hospital and was placed on
life support shortly after. Despite the efforts of
the medical team, he was pronounced brain-
dead early this morning.

Dr Dinah Kogoya, the State Coroner, made a
public statement: "I cannot overemphasise the
danger of eating improperly prepared pufferfish,
or any fish that has not been identified and

184

cleared of contamination. Only certified, farmed seafood is safe. Although correctly prepared pufferfish or fugu is a great delicacy in some cultures, we cannot condone this dangerous practice. Tetrodotoxin, the poison found in pufferfish, is one of the most dangerous naturally occurring substances and there is no antidote."

A graduate of the Maddox University Business School, Raynor Kingston had recently commenced working in the land reclamation arm of his father's company. While still a student, he won acclaim for his work supporting R---- and other charities operating in the Drowns. A notable athlete, he played rugby for his school and won trophies for golf and sailing. Friends, teachers and colleagues describe him as "a wonderful young man", "the pride of a nation and the touchstone of our future", and simply, "the best".

Prior to his collapse, Raynor and a group of friends attended the Sheldou Club in New Harbour. A spokesperson denied that fugu ever formed a part of their menu; however, the club has been closed by court order while the matter is investigated.

* * *

Thursday, 11 August 20XX

"It's about my son."

Dr Xanthe Cosmo froze at the sound of the voice behind her. Her dongle slipped through suddenly clumsy fingers. The chink as it hit the concrete echoed through the vaults of the car park beneath the State Coroner's Office. The car park that was supposedly restricted to the staff and official visitors, but an official visitor wouldn't be prowling around her charging Perky at 21.00. It was all she could do to turn, sweat bursting from her brow and pulse banging, thinking *have they noticed?*

She was pretty enough for unwelcome attention – attention that could turn hostile very, very fast. She shared her sister's large and liquid eyes, her wavy black hair, although her face was squarer. She was wearing her slicker, and her regulation blouse and green culottes were hardly revealing. But if they noticed the thickness of her neck or the shape of her legs…

But the flavour of danger shifted as the pale visage loomed over her, Bubble pale, someone who seldom stepped outside a controlled environment. She recognised Ragnar Kingston – anybody would, from the billboards if nothing else – but she did not understand. It was unthinkable she should be standing barely a metre away from one of the wealthiest, most powerful men on the Eastern seaboard, a cold, wet gust from the street playing around her knees. Another man stood behind him, iTaukei diaspora in a long, black slicker, openly wearing a gun. His face bore just a trace of a smirk.

Xanthe lowered her hands to her sides. "Can I help you, Sir?"

She'd heard Ragnar Kingston described as "a duck's arse on stilts" – which wasn't helping her now. His face was long with a pointed chin and peaked forehead, set off by his trademark curl of white hair. His mouth was pursed and pink, and those pale grey eyes were not concerned with the shape of her legs, or the thickness of her neck, but with what she could do for him. In a flare of panic, she realised what this was. But *how* could he know? She hadn't even tried to obtain Raynor's autopsy report, let alone to examine his body. Kogoya had already shut her down.

"You're Dr Cosmo of the Sydney Morgue." Not a question.

"Y-yes, Sir."

"You've got a theory about what's been going on. The poisonings. I'd like to hear more."

Here in the garage, with a cold breeze and flickering solar lamps? This was insane, this was a doubled-down drug trip laced with alcohol and just a dash of neurotoxin…

Then she noticed the Tholstrup Magnum parked across the bays. It wasn't a regular model – its size was such that she simply hadn't registered it as a car, rather as a void. Its sleek black carapace was lightly pearled with rain. The blind gleam of the windows set alarms shrieking in her head, but there was nothing to do, no way to linger, and even had she found the words to refuse, she wouldn't have dared.

With as much dignity as she could muster, she retrieved her keys, shrugged out of her slicker and let the Smirk take it before ushering her in.

* * *

Thursday, 28 April 20XX

NEVER DIE ON YOUR SUPPLY – ALLEGED DEALER DEAD AFTER PARTY

A man and woman were discovered dead by paramedics called to a house in New Harbour early this morning.

The man has been identified as the house owner, Kaspar Vaughn. Vaughn, a sometime movie producer and chief executive of the Sunshine import company, had been arrested previously for possession of refined himbacine, popularly known as HiBac, although charges were later dropped.

Attending police found evidence of HiBac usage at the party and a number of arrests have been made. Witnesses say that Vaughn collapsed shortly after 2.00 a.m. He had been drinking heavily and allegedly observed using the drug.

The dead woman has been identified as Sibble Burns, a 19-year-old who lived locally. The same combination of drugs and alcohol is believed to have caused her death.

* * *

"You first raised the issue at the Vaughn inquest." Another non-question. Ragnar's voice was soft, that of a man used to being heard no matter his surroundings. He looked and sounded peculiarly unemotional for a man grieving his child. But then, people mourned in different ways.

"I was called as an expert witness," Xanthe said, although to her mind, it was more the Sibble Burns inquest. Burns had only been nineteen. She had been beautiful – golden skin and long, black hair, eyes that would have gleamed with life. She had died at a party held in the house of notorious fixer Kaspar Vaughn, at which Vaughn himself had also died. The assumption of the police, based on witness reports, had been a drug overdose, but Xanthe didn't make assumptions. Her examination disclosed the bruises on Burns's neck, arms and thighs, the broken fingernails snaring skin that turned out to be Vaughn's – the immutable imprint of rape and strangulation. That was what she told the Court, buttoned up in her best suit and sweating – no matter what precautions she took, she still sweated like a rugby forward when under scrutiny. And that, even if Burns had already been dying, she was still murdered.

She was sweating now, despite the air conditioning. They were cruising the Boulevarde, which at this hour was a revolving smear of coloured lights, a ride at some dark funfair. Rain driving in from the sea smashed against the left-hand windows – were they taking her home? *That* would be something to distract the neighbours from Melina. But by those lights, they were still skirting New Harbour. They had a good way to go before they were anywhere near Bayside.

Ragnar reached out to the air con controls and the passage of air across Xanthe's arms increased. "You're a PhD with a certificate in forensic pathology," he said. "And there aren't many people with your particular speciality. Why animal toxins?"

Her laugh came out shaky. "I know – when all the problems in the world seem connected with industrial pollution, it wasn't the smartest move, maybe."

"But it's where you shine. And in your doctoral thesis, you proposed a connection between the survival of amphibians and their own toxicity."

"Oh, well proving *that* would require a whole lot more study with substantial fieldwork and suitable controls—"

"You make an insulting amount at the State Coroner's Office. Why aren't you working in the private sector?"

"You mentioned the Vaughn inquest," she answered. "Sibble Burns was murdered. When my work reveals something like that, I feel that I'm achieving something."

"And Vaughn?"

She paused. "The official verdict was a *mix* of drugs."

"If I wanted the official verdict, I'd talk to Kogoya."

"There was tetrodotoxin in his system, along with the HiBac." When Ragnar did not respond, she continued. "Burns too, although it was less. The way Vaughn was described by the witnesses could have been that – the slurred speech and staggering, together with a kind of euphoria, before the paralysis sets in…" She trailed off, appalled she was describing the way in which this man's son had died.

Ragnar merely said, "Meaning, they were also poisoned. By pufferfish."

"I don't know." Ragnar looked at her but somehow the words just kept coming out. "Tetrodotoxin is highly, highly toxic, it only takes a small amount to kill. But there wasn't any seafood in their stomachs. What I mean is, pufferfish aren't the only source. There is the blue-ringed octopus, moon snails, the rough-skinned newt…"

"So how were they poisoned?"

She swallowed dryly. "In traditional cases of fugu poisoning, it is eaten, yes. The toxin is found primarily in the entrails and if the chef is not extremely careful removing them, it can leak into the flesh. But the blue-ringed octopus, as well as carrying the toxin throughout its body, can actually exude it from its skin. People can absorb it simply by handling the creature, even if they aren't bitten."

"Absorbed through their skin?"

"Y-yes, but there are plenty of other possibilities... and that's why I looked at Henry Haver."

"The rugby player? He's supposed to have died due to an allergy."

"Yes, he was allergic, but there was no seafood in his stomach either. And when I checked for it, tetrodotoxin."

"So, what's going on?"

"I don't know. But it seems possible, from what else I found... that there was human involvement."

"What do you mean?"

"I'm not sure," she said.

"Of course you are. Just because your boss has the scientific curiosity of a cinderblock doesn't mean the samples were contaminated. Or that you were attempting some ridiculous kind of deception."

Which was exactly what Kogoya had suggested, before instructing her to hand over the samples and keep quiet. She pressed her legs back against the seat, as her centre of balance shifted. The car was turning off the Boulevarde and, like a stage effect, the rain ceased beating against the left side of the windows and commenced hammering on the back. It was something to remember – no matter how bad things were in here, it was worse outside.

"What does this all come down to, Dr Cosmo?"

She took a deep breath. "Tetrodotoxin doesn't come as a pure substance, not in nature. There's a cluster of associated chemicals – histamine, taurine, dopamine. In these three samples, Sir, I also found acetylcholine, tryptamine, and adrenalin."

"Which means?"

"Sir, I don't think these samples came from any of the known sources. I think there's some kind of new organism. A parasite."

"Why?"

"Because they look human. Like substances found in a human body, especially the adrenalin."

"You mean we're looking at a murderer. A human murderer."

"Ah… not necessarily." Xanthe felt like her own diaphragm might be stiffening. "I mean, no human being could get it mixed up with their saliva, or blood – this isn't the kind of thing you can develop a tolerance for. It's just not possible, they'd die."

"So, what is possible?"

"That a parasite has developed the toxin, one of these new mutations that are happening, all over the world. A human parasite, at least at some stage of its life cycle. You see, some parasites develop a kind of, of *disguise* to fool their host's immune system."

Air conditioning. The battery's hum. Both sounds enough to conceal any quickening of breath from Ragnar or his bodyguard.

"Wouldn't it kill the host?"

"Not necessarily. Look, I found no trace of any organism in Haver, Burns or Vaughn. But it's the only thing that makes sense."

A sudden burst of rain against the right-hand windows indicated another turn. They were slowing now, another incremental shift of balance. Whatever their destination, reaching it had taken precisely the duration of their conversation.

For the first time, Ragnar shifted his posture, one long hand dipping over his knee. "I want to engage you, Dr Cosmo, to confirm your theory. No more, no less. You will have access to all the equipment you require and there'll be no impact upon your regular employment. You may expect Kogoya to be amenable."

Did he know what she was, who she had been? He had to. If he were considering hiring her. *My neck my legs maybe because I'm sweating...*

But then, lights showed through the tinting and rain spatter, disrupting her inner monologue. The band of blocky squares in that precise tinge of sodium green and the arc of white upon the signage was familiar. The glisten and flap of sodden dracaenas in the concrete planter. It was the State Coroner's Office.

They had driven round in a circle.

As the garage mouth gaped wide, Smirk leant towards her, slicker rustling. In his hand was a glowing screen.

"Work agreement and an NDA," he said. "Any

disclosure of confidential information will meet with the severest penalties."

She signed both with her finger, as the rain cut out and her Perky loomed once more into view.

* * *

Sunday, 24 July 20XX

RUGBY WORLD IN SHOCK AFTER SUDDEN DEATH OF "HURRICANE" HAVER

Henry Haver, prop for the Sydney Stonefish, has died at the age of 30. The cause of death is believed to be a severe allergic reaction.

"I just can't believe he's gone," said Stonefish Captain Budi Santoso. "Henry was the heart of the team, a fantastic player and a good mate."

Haver is known to have been allergic to shellfish but a mystery surrounds his final hours. His body was discovered early this morning in a car parked on the Boulevarde just outside of New Harbour. Doctors surmise that he began experiencing symptoms and pulled over, but was tragically unable to call for help.

Haver was born in the Drowns. His talent was spotted early by educational groups and his training sponsored by R----. Problems with alcohol and violence plagued his early career both on and off the field, but he overcame his disadvantages to become an inspiration. Haver was a legend of the game to his many fans. Tributes are pouring in from members of the local and overseas competitions and the Eastern Australia Rugby Association has proposed a prize to be awarded in his memory. He is survived by his wife Jessie, and children, Gemma and Garrick.

* * *

Xanthe stepped through the front door of her apartment, into air conditioning and the scent of the next-gen disinfectant she had stolen from work. Bayside wasn't the Drowns – no one would ever run that far, no matter what they were escaping! But when the wind blew the right way, she could smell them.

"Tonight," she announced to the dark, "was a doubled-down drug trip laced with alcohol and the neurotoxin was in Raynor too."

"*That* Raynor?" The dark replied unexpectedly and Xanthe panged, because there was no way Melina should still be awake. If her sister was speaking to her now, it meant the pain was bad.

196

"Are you out of arum?" Xanthe pulled the dongle back out of her pocket. "The Perky's still got charge, I can go out again..."

"Not the pain," Melina answered drowsily, "the rain. It's mainly the rain, again."

The topical painkiller made her slightly high. Xanthe stepped forward carefully till her knee knocked the edge of the sofa bed and sat down, her eyes now sufficiently sensitised to see her sister's curly head, and that her arms were wrapped round her knees. Their apartment had no windows, but the darkness was full of tiny lights, the white of the air conditioner, green and amber from the kitchenette, buttons, controls and alarms, all reflected in the door of the shower cubicle. She pressed her fingertips to Melina's forehead then ran a hand down her neck, checking temperature, pulse, whether there was sweat beading her skin...

"Was it that Raynor?"

"Can't say." Satisfied, Xanthe withdrew her hand. The operation had been a success, but subsequent infection was a significant mortality factor with ACOS.

"Oh poo. You see all the interesting things then won't tell me."

"If the arum didn't work, I'm getting you an ice pack. Can you straighten?" She helped her sister ease gradually out of foetal position. With Melina at home, instead of the hospital, she could see things were done right. "Now, what about the hormones? Did you change the patch?"

"Didn't want to."

"Melina, you *have* to. When they removed the cysts, your ovaries stopped producing things that you most definitely need. Believe me, without those patches, you'll feel a lot worse."

"Guess you'd know."

"Guess I would. Now, don't curl up again – I'll only be secs."

She took care of the oestrogen patches first. Then she grabbed the pack from the freezer and wrapped it in a clean face washer, before slipping it lightly against Melina's lower abdomen. Melina whined drowsily, and said, "You could at least bring me some of that neurotoxin."

"You don't want that. Really."

She remembered Melina's face, discoloured and sweating in the months, *months* before they were able to get a diagnosis (for no one wanted to be responsible for telling a woman that the only way to improve her quality of life was to remove the parts that to many, made her one), the wait for surgery and right down to the last minutes there were protests all round, threats from the family, suggestions from complete strangers that purified water and mangoes would put everything right. Underlying it all, the assumption that no kind of pain could be bad enough to merit the sacrifice of some nebulous maternal fulfilment. Acute Cystic Ovary Syndrome was recognised, had been established by WHO and the AMA as a direct consequence of the new bacteria strains that could be found in contaminated water, against which even the next-gen antibiotics were useless. Growing up in the Woronora Bubble hadn't preserved Mel. But nobody wanted to hear that. Not when they could shake fingers at Xanthe, glare darkly and whisper such horrible things…

That was why they lived here – why they both lived where the Drowns could be smelled if not seen by night. She patted Melina's rump with the patch in place, humming to comfort them both. In a few weeks, Melina would be truly well for perhaps the first time since puberty. Then all kinds of things would be possible.

When Xanthe was confident her sister was dozing, she took herself to the shower cubicle and wedged herself inside with her work screen. She got as far as calling up an article on traces of human-like cell clusters that had allegedly been discovered in a plant in New Zealand, before the enormity of it all hit her. She started shaking.

I just discovered that the pride of a nation was doing HiBac.

His father had known, obviously. And Kogoya – you didn't suppress that kind of scandal without the State Coroner getting involved. Kogoya had stood before the press straight-faced, talking about the correct preparation of fugu.

But the drug hadn't killed him either. Her examination of Raynor's body had confirmed what she suspected. No matter how it was delivered, he would have felt little at first and yes, a user might even have found it pleasant.

His first awareness that something was wrong would have come anywhere between ten minutes to three hours after exposure, as his body belatedly attempted to rid itself of an invader that had come softly, but was now blocking its sodium channels, retarding the communication between nerve and muscle. Starting in the extremities, the paralysis had overtaken him rapidly, followed by death. But there had almost certainly been a window where he had been aware, completely aware of his condition but unable to so much as scream.

What's going to happen now, what will Kingston do now he knows? And what if there are people weaponizing this? These deaths could have been going on for years! What will they do when they realise someone has detected them?

What's going to happen to me? To Melina?

There wasn't even room for her to rock back and forth, not without rattling the cubicle walls. She just had to sit and let the panic pass.

Eventually, she was able to breathe again and think. She was a small fish. She certainly didn't have the kind of reputation that would induce the police or media to listen, and thanks to Kogoya, her discovery wasn't even on record. Ragnor's approach had been discreet and she had done what he asked, no more, no less. In all likelihood, once he talked the matter over with his own scientific experts and her theory was thoroughly quashed, she'd never hear about it again. So long as she held her tongue, and Lady knows, she had enough practice at that.

She closed the article she had opened. Such a thrill it had been, as the prospect unfolded before her eyes. The idea that she had discovered something new.

The prospect of a new kind of human parasite evolving was, well, it was appalling. But it was an entirely possible consequence of flooding and overcrowding – as plausible as the ACOS bacterium. Or the cholera variant that had killed so many in the '50s. She could have been the first to identify it.

But she would keep her head down, and never think about it again. Everything would be fine.

* * *

Friday, 12 August 20XX

"Dr Cosmo?"

Xanthe nearly dropped her thermos of congee and pickle, as her alarm bells shrieked proximity. To a woman. Women could be no less dangerous to her than men, but in different ways.

The intruder stood in the partial shelter of the stairwell, enveloped in a long slicker of the greeny-grey shade adopted by people who wanted to avoid standing out, especially to police drones. But her hood was down, revealing cropped, greying hair and greenish eyes. Skin pale enough for a Bubble-dweller, though she didn't have the look of one. A filter mask dangled around her neck and she was too grimy, ragged around the edges.

"Who are you?" Xanthe demanded.

"Fliss Gleeson." That voice gave her raggedness the lie. Warm and rich, without a trace of diaspora burr or the local twang, that voice could have been Mamma's. Xanthe's stomach tightened and she turned away, as the woman continued. "I'm with the Ardent Investigation Agency."

By day, you could see the Drowns. The third-floor landing had no seals, actually gave onto the open air through blackened, salt-furred slats. Way out over the morass of rotting rooves, carious walls, mudbanks, rubbish and rafts, the thick, grey ocean furrowed and foamed.

"I don't think this is appropriate," Xanthe said, looking straight at the sea. "Any queries concerning the results of autopsies or other official records should be directed to the State Coroner's office."

"Yes, yes – if I were inquiring about something like that, I'd be way out of line. But this is more of a family matter." *Family*. Had this woman been *sent* by Mamma? "You know, fathers and sons."

Fuck. "I'm afraid I don't understand."

"I think you do. I think everyone attends on the prince."

"If that were so…" If she retreated to the apartment, then this *investigator* might force her way inside. Melina was still sleeping, not to mention what bacteria she might introduce. "If that were so, then obviously there would be nothing that wasn't in the official report. Please go away – my sister's ill." Perhaps that would be enough to dislodge her.

"Sibble Burns came from the Drowns, you know. She'd taken a job at Vaughn's house, hoping it would be a way out."

Sibble Burns? What did she *have to do with this?* "As it happens, yes, I did know that. Are you suggesting it should have made some difference?"

"Absolutely not. You were the one who proved Sibble Burns was murdered. That she wasn't an overdose."

"Any of my colleagues would have done the same."

"Would they?"

The stench of the Drowns slipped into her lungs like fingers. She said, "Look, Ms Gleeson, whatever you want, I can't help you."

"I want to know if privileged young men are taking advantage of desperate young women. You know about desperation, don't you?"

Desperation? The sense of being suffocated, that if you did not somehow escape from the life you knew, it would kill you, or all that mattered of you. But her desperation had been a fall, not a climb, an acceptance of fewer comforts rather than a struggle to survive. If that had been the story of Sibble Burns, she would never claim to know what it was like. "I do what I can within the law and the purview of my office."

"Only that's been compromised now."

Sweat bursting from her hairline and under her arms, Xanthe barged straight past her interrogator and down the stairs, expecting Gleeson to seize her sleeve or hood.

But she didn't, just followed her down the stairs, saying, "I need to know what Kingston thinks is happening – what happened to his son. Before more people are hurt."

"Like me?" It just slipped out.

"You think I'm part of some kind of security check. I'm not. And it's unfair of me to approach you like this."

Xanthe made no reply, save for the dull thud of her sabots on the plascrete steps. By day, she could also see the swirls of faded red and orange, and dull white nuggets scattered through the grey. There were cameras here, but they focused on the front door and the intermittently operational elevator. She kept going, down to the garage. The lamps were exhausted as usual – for this interval, she was walking in the dark.

"Lives are at stake, Dr Cosmo, and what's happening is being covered up. By his instructions."

"Any evidence of a crime should be reported to the police," said Xanthe. Then she felt a tug at her slicker pocket.

"I've just given you my card – an actual card, so no digital trail. The number on this should reach me directly."

"Please, go away!" Xanthe stumbled into the greater darkness of the garage – the cameras here would be useless – and with relief, saw that her Perky was showing a green light. She clicked the dongle and sprinted.

Gleeson didn't follow. It was the shadows in the stairwell that said, "You told the Court that Vaughn strangled Sibble, but not that he raped her. Why not?"

Xanthe paused with her hand on the car door. It honestly took her a moment to remember, and when she did, it was like a cold hand closing round her stomach. "She was dead," was what she said. "Why put her family through anything more?"

"You put your own family through a lot, didn't you? I believe your uncle described you as pure poison—"

She slammed herself inside. The Perky had nothing like the air conditioning of Kingston's car, nor its insulation. But she cranked up the radio until she could hear absolutely nothing from outside and drove out without looking back.

* * *

By the time Xanthe reached the Coroner's Office, she had almost calmed down. If Gleeson was a test, she had passed. If not, then the "investigator" was just one of the maniacs who used conspiracies to lever themselves just that bit further out of the muck than everyone else, though Lady knows how she knew about Kingston…

Stainless steel and gleaming white, her lab was a safe place. It was almost better than home, although right now they both smelled the same. Her lab was cleaned nightly, and the cleaners knew not to shift anything out of place. Everything here was exactly as she had left it the night before (before all this started!). Which meant, it was where she wanted it, from the precise order of her tools on the tray to her electron microscope and the autoclave, light on to indicate the sterilisation cycle had finished. Always, the fresh filter mask and coverall folded beside her box of latex gloves. You could not be too careful when it came to preventing the spread of infection or toxic agents, and a good part of care was order. On the bench top sat her reagents, clean petri dishes, boxes of fresh slides, and another box stamped with the insignia of Maddox University...

It was then she realised that, although nothing had been moved, some things had been added.

All of her confiscated samples had been returned, along with the exotic poisons she had ordered before being shut down. Her tetrodotoxin carriers, yes, but also platypus and slow loris, the only venomous mammals. A sample of the highly effective neurotoxin contained in the venom of the taipan. A quick check indicated the unexpurgated case files were all back in her workstation, including both Kogoya's and her own examination of Raynor. This made her check the fridge. Haver and Vaughn were back in residence.

"Looks like he's decided to keep you."

Dinah Kogoya stood in the doorway, gazing at Xanthe with heavy-lidded eyes.

That the State Coroner looked like a beluga whale was a standard joke that even the newspapers made from time to time. A bulging forehead and nose the filter mask could not disguise, were accentuated by a slight stoop or slump. The slump had been there for as long as Xanthe could remember, but today, for the first time, it struck her that Kogoya braced under a heavy burden.

Kogoya sighed. "I'm sorry, Xanthe. I tried to keep you out of it."

"And what is 'it', exactly?"

"The cover-ups. Raynor's little drug habit – it all comes down from above."

But it wasn't Raynor she wanted to ask about, it was Sibble. Her gaze slid away from Kogoya, around her augmented lab. "I'm supposed to find the parasite?"

Kogoya flapped a gloved hand – even though she had no direct contact with the various biologics, she always wore a mask and gloves to visit the labs. So strict was she about this, Xanthe had seldom seen her without them, at least in the flesh. "I told him the odds," she said, "but he's not acting rationally at the moment. Understandably."

"It's there," Xanthe said as steadily as she could.

"I hope so. I really do."

All right. All right – she knew that the poison existed. All she had to do was find its source. No simple thing by any means, but Kingston was right, *this* was where she shone. And going by the figure on the work agreement, if all went well, she and Melina might be moving sooner than expected, back to one of the nice, clean neighbourhoods where there was security to turn back the Fliss Gleesons of this world. Only this time, it would be on their own terms.

Why not rape?

Because she couldn't prove it. The samples from Burns's vagina were contaminated during the DNA testing. Even with the best procedures, in the best of labs, it could happen.

Only Kogoya was *right there*, leaning against the door frame and staring at her, and she couldn't help thinking, what if the contamination wasn't an accident? What if instructions had come down from above about Vaughn, or if Vaughn hadn't acted alone?

"Thank you for the poisons," Xanthe said.

Kogoya flapped a hand. "You'll get whatever you ask for, within reason. No one can know about this work – you don't go outside, not for expertise, not for samples, definitely not to conduct any field work."

"I understand."

"Do you?" But then she flapped her other hand. "Where are you going to start?"

"Fish catch records. Make sure I know what's turning up in the nets."

"Not bad. But that won't reveal dinoflagellates."

Kogoya was a lawyer rather than a doctor. But she was an experienced coroner, who had seen some of the worst this world could offer laid out on tables. Her opinion was worth consideration, and the microscopic organisms were known to carry toxins, just never tetrodotoxin. "There haven't been any recent shellfish poisonings, have there?"

"Wrong season," Kogoya replied blandly. "But I have bacteria samples from last summer's outbreak in the Hawkesbury farms. You could extract their toxins and compare to the university samples."

But Xanthe had turned to her workstation. "The Drowns are closer than the Hawkesbury estuary."

"I don't have samples from there."

"Look, if something new *has* evolved, can you honestly think of anywhere more likely?"

"No," said Kogoya, "I can't."

The next five hours were spent crunching statistics – from the catch records, yes. But also everything she could pull together from the Drowns for the past three years. The basics were readily available – that the average life expectancy was twenty years lower than on dry land, that cholera, resistant tuberculosis and the catch-all of secondary infections were the lead causes of death, followed closely by drowning. So far as parasites went, hookworm, tape worm, and sea lice led the parade.

But that was the tip of a very large, very dirty piling. Such records were notoriously incomplete, with chronically low reportage and statistics gained from charity clinics such as R---- skewed for the diseases they actually treated, which was in turn influenced by their funding. And what Xanthe was looking for would show only between the lines. Kogoya popped in and out, sometimes bringing new files or suggestions, such as examining the Department of Navigation's smack alerts and satellite photos of algal blooms.

By four p.m. or so, Xanthe's eyes were aching and she was seriously considering coffee, though that was expensive. She had abandoned the AMA annual reports and the Registry of Births, Deaths and Marriages, and was thinking about two other possibilities. The first was making a request to R---- for the records of the clinics they had in the Drowns: she was unsure if that would contravene Kogoya's guidelines or not, given that the charity was virtually part of Kingston's business. The other was the files the Coroner's Office itself kept concerning all its guests. She decided to pursue the latter.

It was an easy task to filter out those who came from the Drowns, and even a short glance at these revealed another side to the story. She leaned back from the screen, shifting her weight from leg to leg and gazing at the ceiling. It was to be expected, she supposed, that HiBac and violence would go together. But could ACOS really be that widespread, that this random sampling of the unlucky should show such a bias? Sibble herself had shown the signs, or so Xanthe seemed to recall. She called up her file and saw that she, too, had merely noted it in a sidebar.

She had downloaded the Department of Navigation's latest map of the Drowns and been tagging the approximate addresses of relevant guests, mainly clustered in the shanty town of Botany. Now she added Sibble's address as it had been given, also in Botany but toward the southern end. Where the barely liveable ground gave way to the nightmare of the ancient airport and oil refinery.

Then she saw it. Unlike Vaughn, who had been abandoned, Sibble's body had been collected. The signatory was Fliss Gleeson.

What did this mean? Despite referring to their pain, she had no idea what family Sibble had alive. She was, however, quite certain they would not have the means to hire a private investigator. So, that meant another kind of connection and what could that be? If Gleeson hadn't been working for Ragnar, there was another interested party in all this.

But that wasn't her mystery to solve.

* * *

Over the next week, Xanthe checked last summer's dinoflagellates and the university's samples, comparing them to her own. Molecular analysis confirmed her first results, that the poison carried human genetic markers.

On the sixth day, she asked very delicately if Kogoya could perhaps obtain material from R---- on her behalf. This turned out to be the work of ten minutes and resulted in not just their statistics but in copies of their monthly internal newsletter going back twenty years. She started with the year previous, browsing pages of self-congratulatory waffle and photos of team-building days for anything that might indicate the object of her search.

On the evening of the thirteenth day, Melina asked her what was wrong.

Xanthe had come home early and was preparing a proper meal of fresh vegetables and a sliver of beef (as expensive as coffee, but worth it). She had cleared the kitchen bench so as to lay everything out in the proper order. Melina had improved over the past week: the pain had subsided and she was able to sit up to read and watch streams. The titles suggested she was pursuing her interrupted degree.

"Mind you don't tire yourself out," Xanthe scolded, agitating the bok choy.

"Right back at you." Melina shifted on the sofa bed. "I know you're busy, and that what you're doing, it's beyond the ordinary – I'm not going to ask! But tonight, it's different. Before, you were stressed, yes. But now, you're really worried."

"I'm worried about you. Even though you're picking up, we still have to be careful about infections."

"Something happened today. If you can't tell me the details, at least tell me what kind of trouble it was."

Melina was going to make a good counsellor. Xanthe took the stir fry off the heat and checked on the noodles. Then, contemplating the boiling water, she spoke in a low voice. "I've discovered something. It's not what I'm looking for – at least, not in itself. But it's not good."

"How not good?"

"I think that some people, maybe a lot of people, have been described as drug addicts when they aren't. The examiner maybe got the cause of death wrong as well."

She had been back adding more guests to her spreadsheet, when she realised that of those guests from the Drowns noted as drug overdoses, *not a single one* had actually been tested for HiBac, let alone for other toxins. In some cases, HiBac had been discovered *on* the body, or its characteristic tells of patch dermatitis and bloodshot sclera

– as though that couldn't be caused by a hundred other things – had been noted. On one level, she understood – drug screening cost money and time.

What's happening is being covered up.

"That's like the girl back in April, isn't it?"

Xanthe nodded.

"Have you reported it?"

She paused, then said, "Let's eat."

The stir fry was good, rich flavours that made Melina exclaim. But Xanthe had to force herself to swallow. She hadn't reported the omission to Kogoya or anyone else, all because of Fliss Gleeson's words curdling in the back of her mind. There had been something about that woman, with her rich voice and sea-grey eyes, a danger of no common kind. What Xanthe had done, after wading through five months of R---- internal newsletters, was discover a spirited rebuttal of the claim made by one Dr Ariel Pandey last August, that people suffering from jellyfish and other stings had been turned away from the R---- clinic in Botany on the grounds they appeared intoxicated.

The R---- line was that they offered treatment to all in need, but they reserved the right to refuse entry to those obviously under the influence of alcohol, HiBac or other drugs. This was for the protection of their clinicians. There was little in the way of comment and no follow-up – Dr Pandey was a small fish too. Who practised at the Collins Shelter in South Botany.

"What are you going to do?"

For a moment Xanthe stared blankly at her sister, then shrugged, almost upsetting her plate. "I don't know. There may not be anything *to* do."

"Oh, I doubt that."

"Why?" And then a hand laid lightly upon her back.

"Because," said Melina, "it's you. You always do something. The right thing, usually."

A laugh that was half sob escaped. "Don't reckon Mamma would agree."

"She'll come round in time. And if she doesn't, screw her, it's my body. Just like yours is yours."

* * *

Friday, 2 September 20XX

Ragnar Kingston had built New Harbour up from nothing, all but literally.

First, all residents in that part of the Drowns nearest the city had been relocated. The R---- charity had been set up, originally, to assist them. Then the area was detoxified according to best practice, with thousands of tonnes of earth dredged from the tidal zone, thousands of tonnes of old brick and concrete ground into rubble, the whole panned, sieved and baked, before being placed over the remaining littoral, turning it into the curving bulwark of the city's newest district, cradling the excavated bay. The extracted plastics had formed the basis of construction in less prestigious areas, such as Bayside. But here, all was bamboo slats, blue and white canvas and carefully moulded white stone. It was passably sunny, though grey clouds piled in the south like a giant's frown.

It had been twenty-one days.

Xanthe had left the Coroner's Office slightly before lunch, claiming that Melina had called her and was feeling unwell. She drove home and parked her Perky in the garage. A week ago, she had commenced stealthily loosening the connections between the lamps and the solar panels, just to make sure she had a place to change into her brand-new green-grey slicker and filter mask. She climbed to the first floor and caught the elevator down, exiting the foyer anonymously and catching a tram back into New Harbour – she hated the crowding in trams, but if she really was going to carry out her plan, this was the least of it. Now she wandered the circular plaza at the base of the bulwark, where it budded off from the original waterline. Tower blocks and Bubbles loomed in the north, and the Boulevarde, here little more than a pleasant avenue, skirted one side before streaking away down the coast. The plaza was broad and open, and the general public were by and large permitted to enter, to browse the ring of food stalls and boutiques. A plaque at the centre commemorated Kingston's achievement. Xanthe bought fried plantain from a stall, and walked back and forth in front of the New Harbour pharmacy.

Having her hood up was acceptable here, but covering her face was not. The plaza buzzed with impeccably suited figures and cameras perched like obese seagulls on every shopfront – far more than she had to deal with anywhere else except at work. The sole dead spot, so far as she could tell, was a building with shuttered windows and no passage through the heavy, wooden door. She did not see why closing a business should mean removing the cameras, but there were none on any corner. Then she saw gleaming brass letters: THE SHELDOU CLUB. Perhaps, for such an exclusive venue, cameras were not required.

She pretended to people-watch, keeping her face turned as much as possible to the centre and the plaque. A trio of masquers obligingly caught her eye, the blue and white of their costumes marking them as officially approved entertainment. They slid through the crowd performing all the usual sorts of routine – cringing in fear from small children, miming infatuation with passing men, walking backwards before a woman heading towards the Land Titles office, mimicking each swing of her briefcase and tilt of her head.

This is a doubled-down drug trip laced with alcohol and a hefty chaser of stupid.

Problem was, she had nowhere else to turn. The restrictions set on her actions were firm but, failing another gangster being so gracious as to die, her only lead was Dr Pandey, who had no current work or home address, who did nothing, it seemed, except oversee a shelter so obscure that to find it you needed to tag its weekly delivery of medical and hygiene supplies. Tracking *that* down had taken the better part of a fortnight.

She had not neglected to look up Ardent Investigations, based in the Hornsby Bubble and largely concerned with background checks on potential spouses and surveillance of existing ones. But although there was a Ms Gleeson on their list of associates, no picture or address was available. What was *she* doing, mucking about in the Drowns? Hardly chasing an erring husband – although pursuing one to the house of Kaspar Vaughn wasn't quite such a stretch. Perhaps the other interested party was a wealthy wife.

I want to know if privileged young men are taking advantage of desperate young women.

All the victims she had discovered were male.

Xanthe dug in her slicker pockets for some way to clean the plantain off her fingers, and saw, surely, the person she was waiting for exit the pharmacy with a faded grey backpack.

Xanthe hurried, ducking through the crowd as the backpack bobbed and vanished between two stalls, one selling brightly coloured slickers and sunglasses, the other bibingka. A young, blonde woman in a cleaning coverall, she'd been told. The businesses in New Harbour hired cleaners and warehouse staff from Botany, so long as R---- cleared them healthwise. Pushing between the stalls, she regained sight of the woman, heading for the point where the nearest building met the south wall. Before her, the wall crested like a wave against the tumulus, which scowled even darker.

"Nemmy?" Strange name, but it was what she'd been told. "Please, just hold on a minute."

Nemmy glanced back but did not stop. The corner received her and she vanished.

Xanthe ran to catch up. The corner revealed itself as a narrow alley, containing a single, grilled door in the left wall – *The Sheldou Club Staff & Trade Entrance*. She hesitated, then remembered the lack of cameras. "Nemmy!"

This time, the girl saw the pack of arum in Xanthe's hand. She stopped, blue eyes squinting suspiciously from a broad, heavily freckled face. Xanthe displayed the rest of her offering – three packs from Melina's script, antifungal cream and another stolen bottle of next-gen disinfectant.

"This a donation?" Nemmy said, voice twanging. She was thickset, and the coverall was paired with rubber waders.

"More of a – a sample. I need to contact Dr Pandey, urgently. It's about something she wrote."

"Doctor P doesn't leave the shelter." Packets and bottle were taken briskly and stowed. "I can give you her email."

"No. No digital trail. I need you to take me to her."

Nemmy stopped, brow furrowed. "Not happening," she said.

"My name is Dr Xanthe Cosmo," she said, and saw Nemmy stiffen slightly, eyes sharpening. She knew her name – was that good or bad? "I work at the State Coroner's Office and I can only assure you this is very important. Lives are at stake. I swear, if you lead me there" – Nemmy was turning around

– "I'll not tell anyone. If my boss knew I was here, I'd be in as much trouble as anyone. Maybe worse."

Nemmy kept walking. Xanthe could see now, the alley ended in steps going down. Down to the south, the other side, the Drowns.

"Hurry up, then." The girl started down.

Xanthe drew a shaky breath. She followed Nemmy, pulling the filter mask over her mouth and nose. I'll touch nothing, she promised herself, except with gloves, and keep the mask on at all times. When I get back to the lab, I'll put my clothes in the hazardous waste and go through the full decontamination procedure. It'll be fine.

* * *

The rain began just as they reached southern Botany. No one had attempted to mug them, and she had almost stopped choking on the sour, metallic tang that worked through her filter.

If she were to be brutally honest, not that she'd ever *say*, the shanty town was almost a let-down. A lot of work had been done here, by whom she did not know, to keep the streets raised and the drains clear, the walls and rooves solid and square. She spied troughs of green, enclosed by plastic, and the snaking pipes of water catchment and filtration systems. Xanthe and her guide moved quickly through the outskirts, never angling towards the centre where other, more substantial buildings rose. If she glanced to her right, most of the time she could see the embankment at the top of which the Boulevarde ran out of sight and nor could she hear anything except the occasional distant rumbling. Between them lay a no-man's land of rocks and brimming sumps. It seemed to have been left as a kind of moat to discourage anyone from venturing the climb. Previously, she would have assumed that those at the top had done it; now, she was not so sure.

The people she glimpsed (walking with her hood down, avoiding eye contact), were no different to those she might see around her own building. There were even children, and though the thought of them growing up in the Drowns filled her with the proper horror, these ones at least were laughing and sprinting about the alleys. Still, she thought, they must be carrying outrageous levels of toxins and metals, with a commensurately increased risk of cancer, ACOS and other degenerative diseases…

A peripheral blur dragged her head around. For one ridiculous moment, she had thought she glimpsed one of the blue and white masks from the plaza.

Ahead, something equally ludicrous loomed through the murk. It was sufficiently intact to hold a shape, but that shape was a daisy. It resembled a collection of massive oil drums, each large enough to serve as a room, collected around a central pipe – the whole was topped with something resembling a giant pie dish and leaned drunkenly, one edge dipping into – had they reached the water already? Was this the *other* side of Botany? But for the most part, the structure hovered above, every drum a patchwork of plastic and canvas, coated and crusted. She saw now that it was supported by uncountable bars, girders, pipes, and other detritus, even palm trunks had been pressed into service.

"Here we are," said Nemmy. Xanthe looked carefully at the edifice – the remains of something from the airport? – before realising that she and her guide had been silently surrounded.

"Hey, it's okay," said Nemmy, to the slickered figures now filling the alleys. "She's got the good stuff."

Women stared at her, stony eyes over filter masks, or simple bands of ragged cloth. Some had no facial protection at all – she saw eczema encrusting limbs like barnacles might a rock, acid burns and deep pockmarks. But she also saw stitches, dressings, casts. A place for those who could not get to the R---- clinic? Who would not be accepted? She understood none of this, only felt her alienation in every fibre. She had no place here.

"I'm sorry," she said, "I'm from the Coroner's Office. Not officially, I'm just… looking for something."

"Something?" A voice behind her rasped like iron filings. "Or someone?"

"A parasite, I think." Xanthe didn't dare turn round. "Maybe dinoflagellates or snail larvae. I think it's killing people down here, only the authorities don't recognise it."

"And you do?"

"I'm Dr Xanthe Cosmo. I specialise in animal toxins, including invertebrates."

"Oh, that's right." A faint squelching, as the person behind them approached. "You did the frog thesis. Walk on, there's a ladder just behind those beams."

She followed Nemmy and the squelching followed her. The ladder was well-maintained and neatly concealed, leading up into a space that seemed small and blue. She climbed, her gloves slippery on the bars.

Now she stood in a rough decontamination zone – plastic curtains, slatted metal floor, rows of waders sitting in a trough of disinfectant that stung her eyes. Nemmy was unpacking the backpack, laying packets and vials out on a table beside Xanthe's donations. In the gleam of struggling solar lamps, the space beyond was large, the ceiling vanishing into shadowy nests of ancient cabling.

"Sorry about the damp reception." The shape of streaming water that was presumably Dr Pandey emerged – had she been *swimming*? "There's been trouble of late and we're all a little on edge. Now, what do you know?"

The filter was peeled away and Xanthe gazed down at shrewd, dark eyes and brown skin that seemed stretched to the point of translucence across the bone. Dr P was old, for all her agility – the kind of old that took no shit. She was enveloped in a slicker of a mottled grey that Xanthe realised she had mistaken for water as the light played across it.

"There's a massive gap in our records for the past five years," she said. "I haven't gone back any further. But on some recent bodies I've found traces of tetrodotoxin from a source I can't identify." No need to bring the human DNA into it just yet.

"So obviously it came from the Drowns."

"I believe that you're right, that a percentage, possibly a significant percentage of deaths ascribed to drug violence are actually stings—"

"Oh, that complaint to R----. A mistake on my part."

"How so?"

"Drawing the attention of any of those shits."

Xanthe felt her whole mission slipping away. "I don't want to cause you any trouble. If I can just find confirmation, maybe a specimen—"

"And what will *that* bring down upon us?"

"I don't know what's going on here. But if there's going to be any kind of remediation—"

"You brought us arum, Dr Cosmo. You know something about ACOS?"

"I do, yes."

"That's what we treat here, more than anything. R---- won't do that – too controversial, too unpleasant. And they won't even provide effective pain relief, they're so fearful of facilitating addiction amongst the *unfortunate*. If you're looking to take on the monolith, Dr Xanthe, there you are."

"Did you treat Sibble Burns?" That landed. She saw Nemmy flinch and Pandey glance minutely towards the curtains. "The man who murdered Sibble died that way, and he wasn't in the Drowns."

"We get stings and bites here from every kind of creature." Pandey stepped away from her. She lowered one boot, then the other into the trough. "I've seen children die after finding a blue-ring under some rock – its colour is a warning, but they think it's pretty." The old woman tipped her head again, to meet Xanthe's eyes. "Nothing new. I'm sorry." Then she waved to Nemmy. "Have a can, the both of you, and sit for ten. Then you go back."

"Please, Dr Pandey, I can help—"

She jumped as a piece of the roofing moved. There was someone up there, silhouetted against the suddenly revealed sky. "Got four cops coming in from the northwest." The voice was rough and female. "Looks like an inspection – there's a clinician with them and two of those black slickers. Reckon they're armed."

Black slickers. Xanthe's stomach clenched. She flinched at a loud chink followed by a rolling clatter – Nemmy had dropped a can of sweet tea. "Fuck! We weren't followed." She turned her head up to the silhouette. "I took her round the edge, no way were we followed!"

"You just had to be seen," opined the lookout.

"Then it was *her*! She tipped them off before she came after me!"

"No," Xanthe exclaimed, the clench tightening, "I didn't—"

"You know why I brought her here!" Nemmy was shouting. "You know what Gleeson said!"

Gleeson? Gleeson had told them – what? Xanthe turned to Pandey. "No one knows I'm here. I told the office I was going home to look after my sister."

"Your sister?"

"She's just had surgery. ACOS."

The old woman looked at her, as the up-down shouting match grew ever more heated. "Gleeson said," she spoke slowly, "that you're working for Kingston."

"Not outside of the lab, I'm not." *And Gleeson doesn't work for a suspicious wife but for these women. For whatever reason, a one-time Bubblehead is creeping around the Drowns in mask and slicker. Watching for Kingston's agents.*

But Nemmy was shrieking at the ceiling. "Oh, don't worry, I'll fight! I'll kill every fucking one before I let them take her!"

"We're not going to fight, we're going to be sensible." Pandey raised her voice along with her hands. "Now, where's Gleeson got to?" Nemmy shrugged and the silhouette shook its head.

"Nemmy, dear." The doctor turned. "Go get Silla. You can go out the back, along with Dr Cosmo."

"No!" Nemmy turned on her, face ablaze. "We can't take *that* with us!"

"Yes, you can. Take her out and show her the way back to Botany."

"We can't take the risk," said Nemmy, each word weighted. "You *know* why I brought her here."

"And here is precisely where she cannot be found." Dr Pandey was peeling off her slicker. Beneath it, she wore a robust coverall. "I believe her, Nemmy. I think she is here for exactly the reason she says. But you will do as you want, of course. I'll handle the cops."

And that, it seemed, was that. Xanthe picked up the tea and replaced it on the table – she didn't know why, only that she had to do something as Nemmy vanished behind the curtains.

"This inspection," she said, "who is conducting it?"

"It's an excuse. Here, put this on." Stepping out of the trough, Pandey thrust the grey mass at her. Then she went to the table, scooping up the arum and disinfectant back into the backpack along with certain other bottles and packets – things the inspection must not find?

An excuse for what? "What does Kingston want—"

Nemmy re-emerged. "Hurry the fuck up," she snarled, seizing the backpack. Xanthe stumbled forward, the foul-smelling grey slicker in her hands. She felt Pandey's gaze upon her as she passed through the curtains.

Beyond the curtains (though she hadn't been decontaminated, hadn't even pretended to) she saw a central space set up as a basic surgery. Lamps, couch, a steriliser and ECG. Around it (in each of the barrels, she realised), were beds, battered, heterogenous and the sheets patched, but clean and charted like any hospital. Women occupied them, haggard and drawn – she glimpsed the same marks she had outside, but these fresher, and often the feet were exposed. The growths and lesions on their soles and ankles were terrible, made her want to stop and advise, prescribe, even cut. She peeled her own slicker down to the waist and tied it off, pulling the grey one over the top.

In the opposite barrel were storage racks and a small kitchen. A slight figure waited, also swathed in grey. The light slid and ran down the folds – Xanthe realised that Silla, this *child*, was swaying, as though too tired or dizzy to keep her feet. She darted forward, as Nemmy clanked something in the shadows behind the fridge.

She caught the girl before she keeled over, feeling thin bones and feeble heat. "I got you," she said. "It's all right."

"Don't you fucking touch her!" Silla was all but torn from her arms. "Come, but understand I will kill you if you even *think* about giving us away!"

Raw, wet cold slapped her across the face as she leant towards the hole Nemmy's efforts had revealed. They were on the tilting side of the edifice, barely inches above the grey water. Even through the filter, she could smell it.

"Go," said Nemmy. Xanthe grabbed the rusted edge, tried to see how she could ease herself down into, actually *into* that toxic sump…

Then she saw her own eyes looking back at her, and then the path.

It was grey and glassy, looping across the water like some massive eel. Only by looking directly at it could she see – a hand's width to the side or a body length in front and the tenuous solidity was lost in the rain. She placed her foot gingerly upon the surface and then the next, as Nemmy growled behind her, and shuffled forward.

"*Move it!*" It wasn't easy – the surface was made up of disparate panes and sometimes plastic – it was slippery as a kidney and made sudden, sharp turns. But one thing she did grasp – in their grey slickers, in the rain, they were more or less invisible.

Ahead of her, a wall loomed out of the murk. The path headed for a doorway, a grey rectangle in a broken, black line drawn like a buttress against an invisible cathedral. She stepped from the path onto slick, algae-encrusted brick, but her relief at regaining solid ground was erased by what she saw through that doorway.

Dark veils of rain dragged across a nightmare. Crumbling towers that were once stairwells, expanses of roof now twisted and gaping. Jagged metal, the blade itself bleeding slowly into the muck but still tracing the outline of some gigantic building. It was the view from her landing, but here, *underneath*, it comprised a hopeless maze. What were those steel cabins, their doors rusted shut, still stacked three or four high, and who knew how many down? What gigantic structure, memorialised by shards clawing out of the water, had crashed down, clearing a path for more water to enter, seething and striking towards the defiant land?

She turned around. "I'll make my own way," she said "I'll go *that* way." She pointed west along the wall to where the embankment barely loomed.

228

"You'll step in a hole and drown," said Nemmy, propelling Silla through the door before her. "Worse, you'll make noise. Come on, this is the way."

She wanted to ignore Nemmy, turn her back on the mystery and the doctor and those wretched, wretched women, and splash towards home. She did not. She followed Nemmy and Silla, and silently they worked their way towards the ocean.

The black algae coated every surface. Xanthe had read that the mutant varieties outstripped all efforts to catalogue them. And not just of plants. In the polluted zones of other countries, there were reports of vast changes amongst invertebrate populations – many unsubstantiated, but all the same, if she only had time and tools, the solution could be right under her feet.

A sharp cry – Xanthe snapped out of her reverie. Ahead of her, one or other of the women had slipped and Silla hung in Nemmy's arms. Without hesitating, she stomped forward. "Let me support her on the other side. Come one, she's in pain."

"What do *you* know about pain?"

"I'm a doctor, and she shouldn't even be out of bed, should she? Let alone being dragged through this muck. Is this about the treatment you provide, that R---- won't?" The stony silence she took for affirmation. "What if she's bleeding? At least take a look."

Nemmy's glare could have holed the bulwark. Then she pointed to one of the cabins, one side peeled partly away, still smeared with the remnants of blue paint. "We'll stop there. Only for a moment."

Xanthe ducked underneath the jagged edge to see Nemmy unfastening Silla's slicker. "Wait," she said, and hastily shucked her borrowed skin. She laid it on the sucking black ground that grasped at her sabots with each step. Nemmy said nothing but allowed the girl to sit.

Silla could only have been fourteen, fifteen at most. Skinny she was, her skin a pale gold with wisps of black hair escaping her hood. She would have been beautiful, save for the bruises and swelling across the right side of her face and the terror in those huge, brown eyes. It went to the marrow, the fear of someone whose own body had become unfamiliar in its capacity for pain. She stared at Xanthe, who felt a terror all her own – not just because of the violence this child had suffered, but because bruised or not, she was a younger Sibble Burns.

"I'm Xanthe," she said softly. "I'm just going to stand over here while your friend looks after you, okay?"

She turned her back. Gazed out, straight over the wall which was steadily losing both height and integrity. The rain was so heavy that she couldn't see Botany, which she supposed was good. As the sounds behind her settled, she turned her head until she could just make out the dressings on Silla's arms and torso, as Nemmy lifted a threadbare T-shirt, pale patches resolving into a pattern that told her she was wrong. This was not ACOS but something else she knew only too well.

230

She had seen those marks on Sibble and a hundred women who had not survived their rape. She turned back to the rain, feeling sicker than any toxin could possibly make her. After what seemed an age, Nemmy squelched up and pushed past.

"What happened to her?" Nemmy ignored her, scanning the terrain. "Is she Sibble's sister?"

"Don't even *say*—"

"I don't know if you registered where I work. I had... care of Sibble. I saw what he did. Just tell me, was it his people?"

"People?" Nemmy snorted.

"Monsters. Why did they come after her, because of her sister?"

Nemmy rounded on her. "Because she's *pretty*. Used to be, if you were strong without any obvious growths, you let R---- check you out and got a job outside. I did and Sibble was trying. But all the pretty ones end up at the house or the club."

Xanthe froze. *Vaughn's house. The Sheldou Club.*

"So, girls stopped going to R----. That's when the inspections started. Now, sometimes, they'll just take girls off the street."

And no one knew where Haver had been that night, oh my god...

"This is what Gleeson meant," she whispered. "It's not just the drug use Kogoya's been covering up, it's this."

"Those *fuckers* didn't even know what they'd caught.

Not at first. Not until he stuck it in her. And now, if anything happens... oh fuck." This last was directed at the rain.

At the shadow in the rain, a black slicker using the remnant wall for cover as it closed, not from the west but from the *east*. From the ocean, where no one would be unless they had been placed there, deliberately, to cut off escape. Maybe there was even a boat, a whole launch of black slickers stalking through the ruins. She thought of Smirk, Kingston's bodyguard, who had threatened her with consequences.

Nemmy's arm was like iron, pushing her back inside the cabin.

In the dimness, Nemmy flashed a hand sign to the girl, who immediately rolled herself up in her slicker. Xanthe pulled her own up over her head. A moment's consideration, then she plucked up the edge of the grey slicker with both hands and attempted to flip it over. It came loose with a sucking pop, the underside fouled and dripping black. With what seemed a thunderous noise, she dragged it into the corner, but Nemmy didn't interfere, only watched her hunker down, pulling the mess over them both.

Now she was trapped. Trapped and absorbing particles of heavy metals, insecticides, detergents, petrochemicals. Despite her slicker, despite her filter, through her lungs and through her skin. She didn't extend a hand, merely sat slicker to slicker with Silla, and after a while, she felt the little ball press against her.

Prior to his collapse, Raynor and a group of friends attended the Sheldou Club...

Kingston *had* to know what his son had been involved in. Perhaps Smirk had found the same trail she had, or had followed her, tracked her, and now they'd come to root out the murderer. Perhaps he thought it was Dr Pandey, that she was breeding blue-ringed octopi in her clinic. And what did *she* think?

I think I'm going to die.

She hunched there, and the only sound was the rasp of rain against the metal roof.

And the rain.

And the rain.

What was happening out there?

"Silla," she whispered. No answer, save a slight shivering. Obviously, Ncmmy would attempt to draw the hunters away, but what if she had been killed or captured? Or, what if she'd succeeded? Were they supposed to just sit here until she came back?

The group who had gone to the clinic presumably wouldn't stay there forever. They'd want to rendezvous with their fellows, see what they'd caught. "Silla, would Nemmy want us to keep moving? Do you know where to go?"

"Down south, to the cluster house."

"Is that in Botany? Or further out…" She didn't want to consider that. "I'm just going to slide out of here and go to the opening. Just to sec," she addressed the frightened whimper. "I'll keep my head down and be really quiet." And perhaps that last was to calm herself.

Doing both turned out to be impossible. She ended up holding the skirts of her slicker up above her knees, stepping like some ridiculous, courting crane. But she stayed in the shadow and when she got to the opening, she pressed against the rusted metal, scanning the drear beyond. Wall, rain and algae.

After staring for a moment, she realised she could hear another sound. A different kind of rasping.

Xanthe worked with the dead, but she had served her internship at Sydney Central Hospital. She recognised the sound of impaired breathing, of someone struggling to drag air into their lungs, and it galvanised her. Sticking her head out, she looked right – left, then squelched along the wall towards the nearest gap.

It wasn't Nemmy.

He lay half on slime, half in water, limbs unnaturally lax and still, chest barely quivering as he fought for breath. A man with the bronzey skin and black curls of the iTaukei diaspora, lips blue, his face drained and grey. He showed no awareness as she hunkered beside him, hand reaching automatically for the pulse in his neck. She was gloved, but still it seemed erratic. This was a whole-body event, a toxic reaction as violent as anything she had ever encountered. A throat being cut cell by cell.

"You can't help him, Dr Cosmo. You know that." The rich, warm voice sounded directly behind her. "And knowing what I daresay you've discovered about who they are and what they do, why would you try?"

Xanthe remained squatting. "I'm a doctor," she answered.

"You don't save lives," Gleeson answered. "At best, you vindicate them."

"I collect evidence. I daresay this man has done horrific things and I would be so, so glad to catch him out. But I can't just sit here and pass sentence."

"You'd let Kingston do it."

"No! I took on his assignment, yes, to find out what killed his son."

"So what's your theory?"

"A parasite. Maybe the larval stage of a moon snail variant. They'd be the size of pin heads."

This man was dying. It was too late for any other intervention – if she didn't start CPR, he'd be dead within minutes.

Xanthe Cosmo removed her mask.

"A true doctor. Go on, then."

She saw his mouth, then, as the orifice of an octopus or snail, puckered and grooved. "It's on his lips, his tongue. That's why it's taken him so quickly, though it must have been a massive dose. If I touch him, the toxin will pass to me."

"A hero's death, some might say."

Smirk was no longer visibly breathing. His pupils were dilating. Options whirled through her head – an intubation, what could she use? Her hands were shaking, this man was dying and she was just sitting here!

"Saving people is hard. You have to make hard decisions." Gleeson's hand rested on her shoulder. Through the slicker, it felt cold.

"Who the fuck are you, Gleeson? What are you doing here?" Her gaze returned inexorably to the corpse, or near-corpse. Smirk might still be aware, able to hear and see but not to give one single sign. She stared into his eyes. *Did she do this to you?*

It was so, so clear to her now – these women, existing beyond any hope of legal redress, had armed themselves against their predators. Not with guns or knives, but with whatever came to hand. What killed their children. Perhaps they had even tried to report the parasite and been rebuffed.

Those cold fingers on her shoulder felt like claws now. Her every nerve was twitching, anticipating the jab of a hypodermic. But she did not pull away. "Silla's back in the cabin, the blue one. She's safe."

"Did you lead those men here?"

"I was careful." She recognised Nemmy's whine in her own voice. "I thought I'd covered my tracks. I can't imagine why they'd follow me – I haven't produced anything in a month."

"I must say I'm surprised to see you here, after our little chat. You were so certain as to your own helplessness, I'd decided you were safe. How'd you find us?"

"R---- gets real snarky when someone calls them out." Turning, knee-shuffling so she could see her potential murderer. "You told me there was a cover-up and there it was, right in front of my face."

"You didn't ask for this, I know."

"Thank you." Seeing surprise in Gleeson's grey eyes, she repeated her words. "If I'm going to be forced to lie, then at least now I can choose to whom and why."

"You'd lie to the most powerful individual in Eastern Australia about what you found here?"

"I've found nothing except a brutalised child."

"About what you surmise then. Because you aren't a fool, Dr Cosmo. I suspect you're already very close to the truth."

"Do I approve of what's been done? No." He lay there, becoming a corpse, within arm's reach. "Have I a better solution? No, of course not. But you should know that Kingston's not behaving rationally right now." She'd take Kogoya's word on that. "If he finds me here, with his bodyguard, I'm dead."

"That's probably true."

"Go, take Silla somewhere safe." She rose to her knees and felt Gleeson's hand depart. "I'll find my own way. Or end up in a hole."

"Almost certainly. But we are quite close to your apartment, as the crow flies. Was that your alibi?"

"Yes." Hardly daring to believe, she watched as Gleeson stepped backwards and then, the courtesy as incongruous as her voice, extended her hand to help her rise.

237

Those eyes, utterly calm. That clean, pink palm, at odds with the fringe of dirty fingernails – why wasn't she gloved? Her palm glistened, it looked like with spit. Lips pursed slightly, she leaned forward. Xanthe felt Gleeson's breath on her face and realised the hand was coming for her mouth.

Xanthe pushed her fist beneath Gleeson's slicker, grabbed the far side and yanked hard as she rolled, putting her whole weight behind it. It was a dick move, especially on a slippery surface, but done right, the little jelly blubber would fall on his back and you could drive your heel into his stomach.

You're a jelly blubber, Alex. A fucking fag loser.

She was on her feet now, but she didn't try for the stomp. Gleeson was on the ground, floundering beside her victim. Xanthe felt dizzy, but that was her own adrenalin like as not, not the poison. "Find Silla," she said, almost choking on it. "Keep her safe." And then she ran. West along the wall, retracing her own steps but this time on the unsheltered side. It was the only thing she could think of to dissuade Gleeson from following, or Nemmy from jumping at her like a spider. She risked being seen by Smirk's fellows, even shot, but she was a green-grey fish sliding through the rain, way too small to be bothered with.

* * *

"Don't come near me. Stay right there!"

238

Melina, who had been settled comfortably, reading, when her sister burst in the door, stared at her in shock. Xanthe cringed from the look and also from the knowledge she was dripping toxins on their own floor. The slicker and sabots had been kicked into the garbage downstairs, but she was still saturated, contaminated…

"Xanthe, what happened?" Melina rising, reaching for her.

"*Don't touch me!* I fell in a hole and then had to climb – look, I have to clean myself, can you get up? The disinfectant is under the sink."

Obeying this time, Melina tossed her the bottle and shrank back as Xanthe poured it over herself, everywhere except her face. The next-gen scent billowed and fumes stung her eyes. The skin of her torso was prickling. "Okay. Now toss me a bag. I'm going to strip, then shower. What you need to do…" Her left knee, the one she'd cracked on a rebar during her ascent to the Boulevarde, gave way and she swayed. "… you need to pack."

Melina understood. "No," she said, "I'm not going."

"You have to. I'm sorry, this wasn't the plan."

"I'm not going back there! Mamma will be unbearable and everyone else will be worse!"

"Better that than you pick up an infection! Look, just go to the Bubble, okay? See if Tarne or Verda will let you stay, only… make nice to Ma if you need to, if anyone comes after you… I'm in a bad spot, Mel."

"So let me help you."

"It's Kingston, Mel! Ragnar Kingston. I'm caught between him and some… other people. Please, you can help me by going."

Melina didn't say anything else. She took down a bag from the upper shelf (Xanthe winced to see her stretching) and started plucking items from her side of the clothes rack. Xanthe pulled off her sodden blouse, eyes on the shower capsule.

When that first burst of clean, warm water slapped her face, she started crying.

Gleeson was going to kill me. I know she was. And as for how… it's not important. None of those things I imagined, as I ran… it's like I told Kingston, impossible! Down there, everything is poison. I was crazy, I should never have gone!

Over the water, she heard the buzz of their front door.

"Don't answer it!" She punched out of the shower before she had completely turned off the water. She dripped across the carpet, pulling on her dressing gown, and wrapped a towel around her hair. Mel was in the kitchenette with her bag, dividing her glances between door and sister. Xanthe lifted the cover of the bed and waved at her, frantically, to get in. Mel did, pulling the bag with her.

Drawing a shaky breath, Xanthe glanced through the peephole. A black slicker – her knee nearly gave way again. *If they saw me in the Drowns, if they followed me, then this is it.* Then she opened the door.

"Excuse me?"

She gazed into the face of a man she had not seen before. This one was pale-skinned but kind of squicky-looking, as though nothing could keep him clean. "Dr Cosmo?"

"Yes?"

"Pardon me for interrupting." His gaze remained steady, taking in every detail of her dishevelment. "There's been a development – an important development. I'm here to collect you and take you back to work."

"Sir," she said, "my sister is ill. She's been vomiting all afternoon."

The scent of disinfectant rolled out onto the landing, overpowering whatever the Drowns might do. Squick wrinkled his nose ever so slightly in distaste. "I'm to tell you that a specimen has been acquired."

A *specimen*?

"What do you mean – you've found the parasite?"

"That's up to you to determine. Anyway, it's there, waiting for you."

The memories surged, of how her already-overburdened nose had twitched at something, not quite a scent on Gleeson's breath. The dizziness that had accompanied her as she ran, the slight tingling of her cheek where Gleeson's hand had brushed as if, as if…

Squick was saying something about Kingston being a good boss, but only if you proved yourself. "Chance like this, you don't want to let go by."

… as if the organism was not a parasite, but a *symbiote*. She said, "Ten minutes."

"I don't think you've heard me. See, he'll be there himself, he wants to watch—"

"Not me in my dressing gown he doesn't! Give me ten minutes to get dressed and to call our mother. She'll just have to come down and look after Melina herself."

Squick turned away, speaking into his palm. Without waiting for permission, she marched back inside and closed the door.

Melina sat up. "What the *fuck*, Xanthe?"

"Shush, stay down." Digging her fingers into the towel, she stalked to the clothes rack thinking, ring Kogoya and get her to confirm something, anything. Ring Mamma, beg her to take us both…

She had to go with him, didn't she? Smile and bow and keep up the pretence, if it wasn't already too late. Whatever they'd brought her, she would be timid and academic, the sort of researcher that *never* went into the field, and then do whatever they wanted. It was the only way.

But what if it's Silla? What if they've brought me Silla?

"I'll call Mamma," Melina said softly. "I promise. But you've got to escape out the garbage hatch right now."

"Tell her I'm sorry." Xanthe stared unseeingly at her neat array of blouses and her workaday slicker, a faint memory pricking at her. "I never meant that she should feel embarrassed, or like she did something wrong." Melina swore, but Xanthe was already digging into the slicker's pocket. Because as insane as it seemed to her, even now, when everything else was also insane, in all this mess there was only one person who might possibly be able to help. Who, despite everything, deserved to be told.

* * *

This was a room that should not exist. That did not, in any legal way.

Xanthe stood still, listening to her own heart drumming louder and louder in her ears. The room was one of the most lushly appointed she had ever been in, with rich carpet and creamy leather-covered panels on the walls. Air conditioning whispered against her neck; she had shed her shoes to enter, replacing them with pristine slippers. Here, well beneath the surface of New Harbour, the air was cool and dry, and smelt of sandalwood and jasmine.

When the Tholstrup Magnum missed the turn-off to the State Coroner's Office, Xanthe's hopes had shrivelled. She had been kidnapped after all, and the warning she had left in Gleeson's message bank meant nothing. But she had stayed sitting, straight-backed and feet clamped together on the mat, as though that would be enough to save her. As New Harbour came into view, she began wondering which of Kingston's offices he used for interrogations and executions.

It wasn't an office, at least not in any usual sense. It was the Sheldou Club.

There was no sign that the club was open as they crossed the plaza – the windows were still shuttered, the external lamps still dark. It had struck her that to anyone watching, she would look like an expert called in to verify the discovery of bacteria, or that the deep cleaning had sufficed and for just one moment, she had dared hope she was wrong.

A uniformed attendant manned the door they entered, and from somewhere back behind the bar, light and motion spilled. But they did not go that way. They went down.

Then this room. This room had a bed. The fact they had a bed here, with metal rings attached to the posts…

Ragnar Kingston was seated to the side on a luxurious couch. Spotless white cushions were piled around him, in an antique cedar frame, and a plate of appetizers rested on the arm. They had just been delivered by an obsequious chef. Ragnar sat straight, face as expressionless as if this was just another meeting with someone who might be of use. In this case, the someone was Nemmy.

The blonde woman was tied by wrist and ankle – thankfully, they had left her coverall on. Xanthe could see she was alive, though badly beaten, and a dirty and unravelling bandage marked some injury to her leg. Better get her on antibiotics, Xanthe thought absently. Then she realised that if she was here to be punished, then this was the perfect punishment – to be the one to enact Ragnar's will on this twenty-something cleaner, who was cleaning her way out of the Drowns but still ran deliveries to the Collins Shelter. Who had been willing to kill for Silla, if not die. No one was willing to die.

To enact Ragnar's will? Oh no, no, she was here to do what, in some corner of her brain, *she* still wanted. To uncover the truth, to discover something new.

Nemmy's not going to survive this. No one who witnesses this will – unless the world is so far gone that this is nothing. But the moment I refuse to obey him...

She stood there, in this room that should not exist, which should never have had a single woman in it ever, and the black slickers stood around, all four of them.

"What do you make of this?" Ragnar asked.

Xanthe kept her voice flat. "Do you wish me to examine her? To see if she's a host?"

"That would seem appropriate."

Silence crept between them. *Just say no, get it over with.* "I'll need my equipment," was what came out and part of her shrivelled to hear it, to note how she turned and followed Squick without even glancing up, until she was standing at the room's private bar.

"Is this everything you need?"

The bar had been covered with a white plastic sheet, clipped at the corners, and fragrantly next-gen. There was a tray of instruments, an autoclave plugged in and cooking, a box of gloves, coveralls, filter masks, electron microscope and boxes of slides, petri dishes, and those boxes of slides were stamped with the insignia of Maddox University...

It was her equipment. Her own. Not knowing precisely what she'd need, the black slickers that descended on her lab had brought everything. Including her samples.

The drumming in her ears grew faster. "Thank you. I think it is."

Am I really considering doing this, with them all standing around the walls? No, not thinking, hands moving of their own accord, going through her regular prepping of tools and slides, arranging everything how she liked it.

"What kind of examination will you be performing?" Kingston's voice startled her so badly, she nearly dropped a swab.

Keep him talking. Because when he's talking, you know damn well that he isn't looking at you.

Her gloved fingers slipped slides from boxes, some already stained.

"I will take samples from the ears, nose and mouth, also from vagina and anus. These I will place on slides and examine for visual evidence of the parasite."

"Do you enjoy poking around inside vaginas?"

"I... beg your pardon?"

"Examining them. Investigating those organs that you don't possess and never will. No matter how much oestrogen you take."

"I... I'm a doctor, Sir." She could feel their eyes, their grins. Looking at her neck, her legs, the breadth of her shoulders. Sweat burst out on her forehead and under her arms.

"I guess you've found a productive way to indulge, though you usually restrict yourself to corpses. Anyway, I couldn't have a woman doing this."

It only takes a moment for an accident to happen. For your very protection to become contaminated. And then, of course, there is the danger you will contaminate others...

A sound came from Nemmy. Xanthe thought, I should sedate her. If she sees me, if she says *anything...*

"Gentlemen," she said, pitching her voice much deeper than usual, "we are dealing here with an unknown biological organism."

"Oh fuck yeah," said one of the slickers. *Snide, let's call him.*

"For preference, I would be doing this in a sterile area behind glass. Do you have any more of these sheets?"

Squick and Snide removed themselves from the walls, aiming towards the stack of white rolls in the corner. She held up her hand for them to stop. "First, please use this sanitiser. That's right – now put these on." Gloves and masks followed. "You'll need to place the sheets around and as much as possible beneath the subject."

They obeyed. She turned, then to the remaining slickers. "You too. And if you would kindly give these to Mr Kingston?"

Now all were gloved and masked. She drew a shaky breath, aware of what she had unleashed, uncertain it would achieve anything save her slow and painful death. Her knee was shaking, so were her hands. "One more thing, before we start."

She bent down and, reaching in through the folds of the sheet, she gripped a bottle.

* * *

The man on the door was easy.

When the Masquers approached, bowing and clutching at their hearts, proffering imaginary bouquets, he was wary enough, though taking care to look bored. However, when they bypassed him to offer their devotions to the restaurant's menu, framed and hanging beside the door, he relaxed some, especially as the lead Masquer made a show of sobbing. The Sheldou Club was an institution, a place whose uniform he was proud to wear. He understood the necessity of the shutdown, as he did all of Mr Kingston's current actions, but still, it rankled. He glanced down at his name badge and that was all it took.

No poison kills instantly. He was allowed to stagger gasping into the darkened restaurant, which drew out the chef from the kitchen.

The Masquers moved through the shadows of the restaurant, officially approved ghosts. They spread out, as the sounds escaping the men they had caught became harsh rasps. No further opposition was found, the signal was given.

Two more figures entered the restaurant, through the side door in the alley. Both were encased in slickers and filters.

"There's four below, at least." Gleeson peeled off her mask and gloves.

"And Cosmo?"

Gleeson glanced at her companion and the pair stalked on, towards the coiling brass stairs. A Masquer remained to guard each door.

The corridor below swam in blue and green, lush carpet and low lighting. Doors on either side opened onto private rooms, all exquisitely furnished around living features: peace lilies and jade plants, one even a small pool filled with golden fish. There was no indication of Kingston's presence, but rumour suggested their destination lay behind a panel in a panelled wall.

A man in a black slicker burst from a door on the right and lurched towards them, vomit smearing his front, his gun shaking in his hand. He fired twice, ineffectually, before the Masquers reached him. His scream was cut off, but something slammed inside the room. Gleeson went in along the wall, bent almost double as she tugged at each of the carved teak screens. One opened, another gun spraying the room. She grabbed the wrist and rolled, putting her whole weight against the joint, which snapped. Another scream – the second black slicker flopped like a dying fish as she groped, seeking naked skin.

Another shot, narrowly missing her head. Someone further in, firing at anything that moved. "I'll kill you, you poisonous whores!" Still screaming, the gunman with the broken wrist wriggled back into the hidden room. His pain would soon subside, along with his ability to move or breathe.

Bang! "Exterminate every one of you witches!"

Bang! The jade plant exploded. "Murdered my *son*!"

A soft but ringing *clunk!* was followed by a thud. A mewling whine threaded through the opening, along with the sound of ragged breathing. No further shots, but Gleeson held back until the Masquers had joined her from the corridor.

"I'll send them out!" a voice hoarsed. "Take them and go!"

The first Masquer launched through the hole and rolled, coming up with hands on the third bodyguard's face and neck.

Another black slicker lay spasming on the floor, amid his own vomit. His grey skin and dilated pupils told a short and painful tale. Ragnar Kingston flailed on the carpet, blood gouting from the glass shards in his skull. The mewling came from him.

On a large, wooden bed, Nemmy Sting was shaking, crying as Dr Xanthe Cosmo worked at the last of her bonds with the jagged neck of a vodka bottle. "Shush, it's all right. It's going to be all right." There was a bad, bleeding tear across the doctor's forehead and one eye was swelling shut.

Slithering in through the panel, Gleeson surveyed the chaos. "What in the watery hell is this?"

"This," said Xanthe, "is a dash of several different neurotoxins, revealing some unfortunate synergies, and a highly toxic dinoflagellate strain. And then they did shots. Kogoya, what are you doing here?" She severed the tie, dropped the bottle and started crying.

* * *

"We don't have much time." Kogoya's beautiful beluga face loomed over Xanthe. Her boss was checking her vitals in a perfectly competent fashion for someone who wasn't a doctor. Xanthe wanted to throw up. Only that would be a sure sign she had herself ingested the dinoflagellates and would probably die – she had tried to explain about the contaminated masks and gloves, but it looked like Gleeson and her decorative friends were old hands at wrangling poisons. They had already taken Nemmy from the chamber and were hard at work rolling up the sheets, scrubbing the bedposts, packing away the equipment. Removing every single sign of her presence.

She had taken the samples from Nemmy. She had to, to give the various poisons a chance to do their work. And although she knew, technically, what to expect when they did, she hadn't been prepared for the – incontinency. Smirk had not prepared her for the sheer grossness of it, the vomiting, the fits. She had done that, she had killed them, and could never really be a doctor again. But she had taken the samples and although the memory of what Kingston had said went straight to her stomach, she had recognised what she saw. That Nemmy had ACOS. Only it wasn't ACOS, now, was it? Not in her. And she, Xanthe, had been as blind to that as anyone.

"The fugu or blowfish carries one of the most potent neurotoxins known to science," she said, as Kogoya hm-hummed, examining her forehead. She was vaguely aware that she'd clipped the bedpost as Squick put her down, ready to kill her before he started seizing and she was able to crawl away… "Do you know where it's generated? I mean, it permeates the gut, but it's the ovaries. A symbiotic bacterium in its ovaries." Something, a giggle, escaped her throat. "Fuck you, caviar."

"Told you she'd work it out," Gleeson called from outside.

"Yes, you did and I hate you." Xanthe felt Kogoya press firmly against her neck, but it was okay, Kogoya always wore gloves.

"Vaughn died because he raped Sibble," Xanthe said. It seemed extremely important. "He died *from* raping Sibble. Like Raynor and poor Silla. The bastard. I don't know what Haver did, but I bet he deserved it. And Dinah, you haven't been protecting them, you've been protecting the symbiotes! All this time!"

Kogoya's breath gusted over her. "That's all very nice, Xanthe, now, listen to me. You signed an NDA. An NDA, remember?" Those competent fingers dug into her flesh. "Say it!"

"I signed an NDA." She felt dizzy.

"That's *all* you say." And Kogoya let her go – she felt that she was sailing away into space. "You've got your job and your sister. I'm sorry, Xanthe, but this is the only way."

Xanthe lay amid cushions. Her arms were tingling, and she felt a strange euphoria as her pain receded. *So this is what it feels like. Not nearly as bad as I thought. Nice, really, to just sit back and let it all float away.*

As Kogoya very carefully pulled her gloves back on.

* * *

Saturday, 3 September 20XX

TERRIBLE DISCOVERY – NEW DEATHS AT
THE SHELDOU CLUB

Mystery surrounds the shocking discovery of
six bodies at the Sheldou Club in New Harbour
last night.

Police were alerted by neighbouring businesses
to activity inside the Club, which was closed
after the death of Raynor Kingston in August.
An emergency response team was summoned
and the bodies discovered on the lower floor,
together with three survivors. One man has
since died in Sydney Central Hospital.

The Police Commissioner of Sydney City,
Walter De Roos, would only say that this was a
terrible tragedy with far-reaching ramifications,
refusing to confirm that Ragnar Kingston,
property magnate and mastermind of the New
Harbour development, was among the dead.
A car registered to Mr Kingston was found in
nearby parking and no statement has been
forthcoming from Kingston Developments.

The club's executive chef, Sanjoy Lal, and security guard Hector Moore have been confirmed as victims. The names of the remaining survivors are also known – Brian Faro, an employee of Kingston Developments, and Dr Xanthe Cosmo of the State Coroner's Office. Mr Faro is on life support in a critical condition. Dr Cosmo was also on life support but stabilised early this morning. Her condition is described as "hopeful."

Raynor Kingston is believed to have been poisoned from eating improperly prepared fugu, or pufferfish, served in the traditional Japanese manner. It is still unknown how he came to do so, as club management insist the dish was never prepared in their kitchens.

* * *

Monday, 5 September 20XX

THE KING IS DEAD

In a statement released late last night by Police Commissioner Walter De Roos, it was confirmed that Ragnar Kingston was among the dead discovered at the Sheldou Club on Friday evening.

In a shocking turn of events, Ragnar Kingston is believed to have died in the same manner as his son, prompting speculation in some circles that he staged a murder-suicide, with the club's executive chef and two of his son's regular bodyguards among the victims.

Police attempts to question the survivors have yielded little result, with Brian Faro continuing in a comatose state and Dr Cosmo refusing to speak without the counsel of Kingston Developments' legal department.

The following statement has been issued on behalf of Dr Cosmo. "After advising the coroner on the cause of death of Raynor Kingston, I was engaged as a private contractor by Kingston Developments. I am not at liberty to describe the work involved, only that it could have in no way impinged upon events. I am deeply shocked and saddened by what has occurred, and grateful beyond words to the first responders and the staff of the Sydney Central Hospital who saved my life."

Dr Cosmo is currently recuperating with family.

* * *

"Alex?" Mamma's voice scratched at her ears. "Come now, I know you're awake. Sit up, Alex."

When she transitioned, some of Xanthe's friends had advised her to keep the name Alex, as it would cause fewer problems with her qualifications and other official records. But that had never been her name and she would not answer to it now.

"Stop being so *childish*." Mamma grabbed her under the arms and hauled her upwards, dropping her on the pillows. "There. Now, don't you feel better?"

Squinting against the day's brightness, she gazed upon her childhood bedroom. Tones of blue and tan, with windows overlooking the park. Filtered water, filtered air, filtered light. A poster for the Sydney Stonefish and action figures ranged along the top of the desk, next to her very first toy microscope. At least they were in order.

"Those creepy lawyers of yours want you to contact them." Mamma bustled about the room, adjusting blinds and fussing at the foot of the bed. Xanthe snuck her hands back under the cover and thought of metal rings and plastic ties.

The lawyers wanted another statement, this one denying that anything in her interaction with Ragnar Kingston had suggested anything but a man suffering from grief, but otherwise in his right mind. The fact they had never once asked her what actually happened showed they too had accepted the popular line – that Ragnar Kingston, unhinged by the loss of his son, had pulled as many people as possible with him into death.

She would give them their statement – after all, they were protecting her with all the considerable power of the Kingston edifice. And Mamma was protecting her too. When push came to shove, she'd decided a scandal inside the Bubble was better than in the outer, and now Xanthe was doubly insulated, against police, reporters, and prying eyes. But that did not come without a very substantial cost.

Most of her remaining malaise was hormonal imbalance, her body screaming for its regular dose of oestrogen – Melina, at least, was allowed to take hers, Mamma having dug up some half-baked article suggesting that pregnancy was possible after the operation if the right support was provided. But Xanthe was unable to contact her friends or even to go outside, "until you're something like yourself". And between social engagements and study, Melina was very seldom home.

Mamma smiled, her lips pursed and pink. "Now get dressed and come downstairs." She left the room in a flash of leopard dressing gown.

Fresh clothes had been laid out across the foot of the bed. Polo shirt, club trousers, and loafers. The socks bore the crest of the Woronora Boys School.

It was then Xanthe knew that she would leave. Not to try and take up her old life – despite Kogoya's best efforts (and how carefully she must have judged the dose! Embracing her just long enough to take her to the edge, but not over).

She would never be free of the curious, the suspicious, the vengeful.

How hard it must have been for Dinah, all these years. Concealing her true nature in a building full of scientists, never rousing suspicion, playing the lackey for Kingston and the government so as to preserve her sisters' secret. Their growing community – how many cases of untreated ACOS resolved into poison? How many more might be to come?

Xanthe Cosmo would disappear, not by shrivelling into Alexander. But doing whatever she had to, to shake all tails, before taking a new path.

Down south, to the cluster house.

She could not say how she would find it – if Dr Pandey had survived, she might be willing to let her into the shelter, for a start. Let her help. She could not guess what reception she might receive from Gleeson, Nemmy and the others. But just knowing there were people willing and able to fight to be who they were, who they could not help being, to throw off aggression and persecution, was all the courage she needed.

And Gleeson had been right. She could never be the same as them, but she had certainly proved she could be poison.

She rolled out of bed and went to wreak havoc.

Part IV
Anna Taborska, United Kingdom

The Last Woman[7]

Anna Taborska

We are going to see the woman.
Which woman, you might ask?
The last woman on earth.
Where is she, you enquire?
Sitting in a glass cage,
behind the razor wire.
The hour is late, you say;
that's of no consequence.
The neon strip lights in her cell
do a good job round the clock –

---

7   After "To See the Rabbit" by Alan Brownjohn (poem published in
The Starlit Corridor, 1967, edited by Roger Mansfield).

forever available to our (male) gaze,
this attraction now open till late.

We are going to see the woman,
superfluous now that compliant A.I.
provides everything her kind once did,
with no complaining, no unreasonable
requests for equality and respect,
no demanding that their bodies be
their own, that they should choose
when to give pleasure, when birth.
It's strange to think it took this long
for legislation to meet demand,
for cloning and synthetic bodies
with no unsightly fat or wrinkles
to replace the ugly and frail flesh
of sinful Eve and her descendants.

We are going to see the woman,
queueing and waiting to see the woman.
Strange – the interest she still commands,
with thin lips, body hair and ageing breasts.
I suppose everyone loves a freakshow,
and once she's gone – that will be that.
Only virtual libraries of extinct specimens
of female imperfection to make us laugh.
But what is this? There's something wrong!
The crowd is angry. The woman's gone!

Just witchy symbols scratched in the glass.

Why did we spare a quantum physicist?

$$ds^2 = -\frac{u^2}{u^2 + 2m}dt^2 + 4(u^2 + 2m)du^2 + (u^2 + 2m)^2 d\Omega^2$$

Mummy Miya

Anna Taborska

FEBRUARY 837 BC

"Mistress, protect me!" Miya screamed as they dragged her out of the temple to which she'd been pledged since the age of six. The temple in which she'd served her beloved Goddess for half of her life. "Protect your loyal servant!"

She struggled valiantly against her assailants, but a twelve-year-old girl was no match for the four grown men who had her by the arms and legs.

"Stop fighting, you little idiot!" One of the men tried to reason with the young priestess. "Someone might think you're going to a brothel, not to a prince!" But there was no reasoning with the terrified girl.

"Protect me, Mistress!" The girl stopped struggling for a moment, and the men followed her gaze to the stern face of the ornately carved stone idol that stood towering at the far end of the temple. "Bring down your wrath on these apostles of evil and their vile lord!"

"Alright, that's enough!" exclaimed the largest of the men – an ugly-looking brute with a daughter of around Miya's age. "Hold her down!"

"What are you going to do?" asked the one who'd tried to reason with the priestess.

"Well, I'm not going to stand here, and let her curse me. Hold her still!"

Miya continued her supplications to the Goddess as the men forced her mouth open and cut out her tongue. Then blood was filling her mouth and throat, choking her; the pain so unbearable that she lost consciousness.

* * *

AUGUST 1975 AD

Dr Pilkington, Pilky to his friends and Dr Pilferington to cynical acquaintances, was the quintessential product of his class and generation – or so it seemed. Nobody really knew which bastion of scholarship had bestowed his doctorate, as neither Oxford nor Cambridge claimed him. Perhaps he had studied at one of the Northern colleges, and it was rumoured that he had an association with the university in Arkham, Massachusetts, but there is no record of his presence at that prestigious American institution either.

Pilky's family history was equally obscure and a matter on which he said little; when questioned, he merely smiled enigmatically, uttered something like "Well, you know, old bean, it's all rather boring," and skilfully changed the subject to recount some escapade or other so scintillating that the questioner soon forgot what information it was that he or she had been trying to glean in the first place.

What was known for certain was that Pilky had adventured from the Congo to Kamchatka and from Greenland to Tasmania, never returning empty-handed, and made a decent living begging, borrowing, buying, but mostly stealing valuable artefacts from distant lands and selling them via his nefarious contacts to a variety of private and institutional buyers. Rumour has it that the head-hunters of Borneo let him keep his head (and threw in a few extra ones) in exchange for a mummified Siamese twin foetus from Zanzibar. Some say that Aleister Crowley once purchased a ritual chalice from Pilky, and that paranormal investigators Ed and Lorraine Warren were tasked, for years to come, with clearing up the odd spiritual mess left behind after overambitious practitioners of Magic inadvertently released some Eritrean or Kandarian demon from an artefact that could be traced back to Pilkington's pilfering.

It came as no great surprise, then, when in the summer of 1975 Pilky was found dead in his antiquity-filled West London abode with a look of abject terror on his face and a perfectly preserved mummy in his attic.

"Blow me, he's dead!" observed Police Constable Paul Spencer, while his fellow officer, WPC Amanda Kurl, covered her nose and grimaced in agreement.

Pilky had missed a meeting regarding a Yoruba funeral mask and his concerned client (who'd already paid a considerable deposit) had eventually filed a missing persons report at the local police station. The two young officers now stood over Pilky's decomposing body with a mixture of shock and disgust. WPC Kurl finally managed to remove her hand from her nose long enough to suggest:

"We'd better call it in."

* * *

Miya's tongue healed in time for her wedding night. Or, more precisely, the stump that was all that was left of her tongue stopped festering in time for her to be drugged and dragged to the marital bed.

Miya's father had been paid off and the temple in which she'd served compensated. She'd been replaced quickly; local merchants and parents from the well-to-do middle classes were all too pleased to have daughters serving at the temple, and to then have one of them picked as the main Chantress – that was an honour indeed. Given the right training and provided they weren't completely tone-deaf, any one of the girls could pray, sing and perform rituals. But none of them had Miya's voice. During the time of the main annual ritual, when Miya had worn a full-face mask reminiscent of the head of the Goddess and sung the songs handed down from the Ancestor Gods themselves, a chill silence would fall on the worshippers in the temple. Miya's voice would soar like an eagle on the wing, then plummet like a lion falling on an antelope calf. Sometimes a wind would stir, blowing in grains of sand under the temple doors, joining with Miya's mesmerising, time-stopping cadences. It was as if the Goddess herself were sweeping in to listen and susurrate her approval.

The prince had been looking forward to welcoming his newest wife. He'd wanted her ever since first seeing her in the temple grounds, but she'd played hard to get. He'd indulged her for a while, he'd even quite enjoyed the game of cat and mouse, but then it all got rather boring and he'd had to speed up the proceedings. He'd behaved honourably: he signed all the customary paperwork and money had exchanged hands, although he could have easily just taken what he wanted. A merchant wasn't going to argue with a prince, after all. He'd been looking forward to breaking in his young wife, but the bleeding, gurgling mess that his men had brought back was, frankly, disgusting. He could have had the four of them executed, but they were trusty servants, never shirking from going that proverbial extra mile when required, and no man puts down a good hunting dog just because it's killed a cat or two. So, he had them flogged, and summoned a doctor to stop his wife's bleeding and disinfect her stump. Perhaps a wife who couldn't talk back wouldn't be such a bad thing; she'd certainly make a change from his other wives.

Well, the time had finally arrived to consummate the marriage. The girl still wouldn't let him near her, so he'd had the servants drug her, wash her, and place her in his bed. The problem was, she came to just as he was getting started. Her eyes had opened as wide as a startled cat's, her mouth agape in a twisted grimace, and then she'd made the sound – mutilated, broken. It began like the terrified whine of a child in pain, turning into the dry hiss of an angry scorpion before swelling to become the muffled roar of a raging beast in a desert storm. Hurling himself off the girl and out of bed, the prince's ears reverberated with the distorted half-spoken words that Miya had been attempting to articulate:

"Mistress, avenge me!"

* * *

THE TIMES
Friday 22nd August 1975

Obituary
Dr George Arthur Henry Pilkington,
adventurer, art dealer, raconteur,
died of a heart attack at his London home
on the 8th of August.
His wit and entrepreneurship will be missed.
R.I.P.
Friends and fellow antiquaries.

The coroner returned an open verdict on the cause of Pilky's death, and his mortal remains were finally laid to rest in the Old Southfield Cemetery. No rest for Pilky's mummy, though, which, following a tip-off from a member of the mortuary staff, became the object of a brief tussle between the British Museum and a couple of private collectors. The Museum won.

From a pamphlet distributed amongst friends & supporters of the British Museum, Monday 1st September 1975:

New Mummy to join our Family!

The British Museum is delighted to announce the acquisition of a new mummy for our Egyptian collection. Dating back to the first millennium BC, the mummy of priestess Miya will take pride of place in our Mummies Gallery.

Newspaper headlines, Tuesday 2nd September 1975:

The Times: British Museum to Welcome New Mummy

The Guardian: Appropriation of Egyptian Mummy Unethical

The Daily Mail: Brits Save Mummy from Foreign Thugs

The Sun: Mummy Miya!

SEPTEMBER 2023

FAST FORWARD to the Fall of 2023. The autumn following a long, hot summer. A long, hot August, if one were to split temporal hairs. A time dubbed "The Summer of The Mauler".

Fast forward to PC Paula Spencer (daughter of PC Paul Spencer Junior; granddaughter of PC Paul Spencer who'd stood in shock and disgust over the mortal remains of Dr 'Pilky' Pilkington forty-eight years earlier) standing over the eviscerated corpse of one Matthew Bingham – hedge fund manager and wifebeater extraordinaire. Standing over the eviscerated corpse of Matthew Bingham and the prostrate body of his long-suffering wife Clare.

"Mrs Bingham?" PC Spencer crouched down next to Clare, trying not to step on any of the blood evidence – an impossible feat, considering the Binghams' kitchen was looking like a surrogate location for the Elevator of Blood scene from *The Shining*.

PC Spencer touched Clare Bingham's neck, greatly relieved to find a pulse and even more so when the woman stirred. The police officer had already phoned for backup and medical assistance, and ascertained that there was no intruder in the immediate vicinity. Her hand shook a little as she tried to reassure Clare, who'd opened her eyes and started hyperventilating at the sight before her, at the taste of blood in her mouth and the feel of it on her hands and under her fingernails.

"Mrs Bingham, you're safe now. Help is on its way."

It wasn't just the gruesomeness of the crime scene that had unnerved the police officer. As Paula had entered the kitchen, she could have sworn she saw a shadow move swiftly away from where Clare Bingham was slumped on the floor, disappearing as it reached the window. A large human-like shadow, but the head... there was something wrong with the head. In the split second that Paula saw it – thought she saw it, as she now told herself – she noticed that the shadow's disproportionate and misshapen head had a distinct snout and was crowned with two rounded ears: it was the head of a large animal. Spooked, Paula had drawn her weapon, but there was nobody in the kitchen apart from her and the victims. As she glanced towards Clare Bingham, she thought she saw big curved claws on the woman's blood-covered hands, which seemed to retract into the tips of her fingers before the police officer could focus on them. It was just a trick of the light, of course, or of her over-tired, overactive brain.

"Are you hurt? Mrs Bingham? Clare?"

PC Spencer had been called out to the house by worried neighbours on a number of previous occasions. And she'd seen Clare Bingham covered in blood before, but never a scene such as this, and never had a hair on Matthew Bingham's head been harmed. There was no obvious sign that a third party was involved, and PC Spencer was beginning to wonder whether the petite housewife had finally snapped and… what exactly had happened to the banker's intestines?

"Clare, can you tell me what happened?"

"I don't remember." Clare Bingham had stopped panicking and was now looking at her own blood-covered hands with an air of calm, bordering on interest.

She must be in shock, thought PC Spencer, but her look of concern soon turned to disgust as Clare pulled a sliver of what looked like raw meat out of her teeth, sniffed it, then wiped it off on her blood-covered nightie. PC Spencer could have sworn there was a glimmer of recall in Clare's eyes.

"Have you remembered something?" she asked. Clare shot her a quick look – was there a hint of guilt in it? The police officer thought that there was. Clare shook her head.

"Nope. Not a thing," she said, turning her strangely dispassionate gaze to her husband's mutilated body.

Something about the look on Clare's face reminded PC Spencer of another murder scene; of the look on a young rape victim's face, minutes after she came to, surrounded by the ripped-up bodies of her three attackers. The fifteen-year-old had been spiked with Rohypnol at a nightclub, separated from her friends, and targeted by the gang of junkies as she staggered her way to find a Tube station. In between the shock of regaining consciousness to find herself half-naked and covered in blood, and the horror and pain of the rape hitting her, her gaze had fallen, then lingered, on the disembowelled crackheads lying nearby, and a brief flicker of recollection, calm and something akin to satisfaction had appeared in her eyes. Then the hurt, broken teenager was back and the heart-wrenching, agonised whimpering started.

For weeks the killer of the junkies had not been found and the case had attracted a great deal of media attention, as other male victims turned up in the London area, all looking like they'd been attacked by a wild animal. The serial killer had been dubbed "The Mauler" by the tabloids, and police had eventually arrested a forty-year-old prostitute, found battered in a seedy hotel room, next to the body of her intestine-free last client. Now, looking from Clare Bingham to the gut-less Matthew Bingham and back again, PC Spencer wondered if the lady of the night currently being held at His Majesty's pleasure, pending trial, was not The Mauler after all.

It certainly seemed like The Summer had been going on forever, but truth be told, the first Mauler murder hadn't taken place until August the 8th.

www.AstrologyPlane.com, **8th August 2023**:

Today marks the peak of the annual 8.8 Lion's Gate Portal, when the brightest star in the night sky, Sirius, in the constellation of Orion, is at its closest to the Earth and in direct alignment with the pyramids at Giza and the Sphinx – the Great Lion, and the Sun is in the astrological sign of Leo.

The number 8 is associated with abundance, achievement, infinity, power and rebirth.

The Lion's Gate portal has been opening since 28th July and is at its strongest today, but you will continue to feel its influence until 12th August.

The divide between us and the astral planes is at its thinnest now and humanity as a whole will be receiving powerful high-frequency cosmic downloads from the universe. Make the most of this energy gateway to step into your power and manifest your dreams.

Any project you start now or give your attention to today and for the next few days will resonate strongly for months to come.

BBC Breakfast News, **8th August 2023** – transcript of report entitled "Giving the Dead a Voice":

Today is an exciting day for scientists and Egyptologists alike, as a team of experts prepare to – quite literally – restore the voice of a mummified Egyptian woman who has been dead for over two and a half thousand years.

The mummy, identified as "Miya" from hieroglyphs scratched onto the wooden coffin in which she was found in 1975, was recently transported from the British Museum to Imperial College London, where her remarkably preserved vocal tract will be reactivated with the help of electric stimulation, causing her vocal cords to vibrate and emit sound just as they did when she was alive.

In 2020, scientists recreated the voice of a 3,000-year-old mummified priest called Nesyamun, housed in the Leeds Museum. The process of mummification, burial and the passage of time meant that Nesyamun's vocal tract was partly damaged, and had to be reconstructed using a 3-D printer. It was the replica of Nesyamun's larynx that was used to reproduce the mummy's voice, with the aid of a special synthesiser and loudspeaker.

Today, British and Egyptian experts are going one step further. Thanks to computerised tomography scanning, we know that Miya's vocal tract has survived virtually intact. This means that scientists will not be using a replica larynx, but will use a specially designed device to stimulate Miya's *actual* vocal cords (or, more precisely, vocal folds). Whereas Nesyamun's voice was meticulously replicated using what was essentially a sophisticated synthesiser, Miya's real voice will be heard again – for the first time in over two and a half millennia.

This momentous event is scheduled to take place later today, and we will bring you a special extended report on tonight's *Newsnight* at 10.30 on BBC2.

* * *

"She's cursed me!" The prince had run out of his bedroom, slamming the door behind him, and was now shrieking at any servants who found themselves within earshot. "The little bitch cursed me!"

"What is it, my Lord?" Soon half of the princely household

were gathered outside the prince's bedroom, their varied state of undress testament to the late hour.

"She's in there, mumbling away to the Goddess. She's cursed me! I want you to go in there, bind her limbs and stitch her wretched mouth shut." The prince's outburst was met with a stunned silence. "Now!"

The prince paced up and down outside the bedchamber while his orders were carried out. The muffled, distorted half-screams that emanated from within did little to appease his anger or dispel his fears. Eventually the sounds stopped and the head servant emerged.

"It's done, my Lord. What are your wishes?"

"Take her to the tomb where my second wife is buried and seal her in." The look on his retainer's face further fuelled the prince's agitation. "Well? What are you waiting for? She can't curse you now!"

"No, my Lord. It's just that people might ask after her."

"Nobody's going to ask after her."

"My Lord, her mother's been hanging around outside every day, bothering the female staff."

"Well, have the mother flogged. And tell anyone who asks that the bitch ran away."

May 837 BC – Papyrus scroll:

On this, the thirteenth day of the fifth month of the fiftieth year of the reign of our great Pharaoh

Sekhemkheperre-Setepenre Osorkon, son of Hedjkheperre-Setepenre Shoshenq, son of Nimlot, Great Chief of the Ma, following the customary seventy-day preparations, the funeral took place of the noble Prince Ur.

The Prince was cut down in his prime on the third day of the third month, mauled to death by a beast as He slept, taken as no Man should be – while He rested in Oblivion.

May His Heart weigh lighter than the Feather of Ma'at. May His Ka be welcomed by Lord Osiris in the Field of Reeds.

Prince Ur spoke often of the Great Ancient Families of Abdju and of how He would restore the traditions of his Divine Ancestors. To this aim, and to aid Him on His great journey, the Prince was accompanied into His tomb by His best hunting dogs, two of His horses, twelve members of His household and all of His living wives, who will serve Prince Ur for all eternity.

* * *

The masked, gloved and lab-coated scientists surrounded the small female figure like a wake of white vultures. Doctor Louise Hendon held open Miya's mouth, the mummy's lips still bearing the marks of the stitches with which they had been sewn shut 2,860 years earlier and which had been removed prior to Miya's initial CT scan. Unlike the other mummies housed

276

at the British Museum, Miya had not undergone the long mummification process that would have allowed her passage to the afterlife. Her mummification had occurred naturally, due to the conditions prevalent in the tomb in which she'd been sealed prior to death, and it was Doctor Hendon's opinion that that's what may have accounted for the excellently preserved state of her soft palate and other soft tissues of her vocal tract. Perhaps Miya's most striking feature was her beautiful long black hair, which captivated museum visitors and experts alike, and belied the millennia that had passed since her cruel, untimely demise.

The scientists and academics now gathered around the mummy had all met before, during the course of studying her; all apart from Bob – the technician responsible for the device that would animate Miya's vocal folds.

"Her tongue's missing," he now commented. "And... are those stitches?"

"Yeah." Doctor Hendon had been present at Miya's first CT scan, and had followed the mummy's progress ever since. "Someone sure didn't like the sound of her voice." She glanced at Professor Sherine Zaiady, eminent Antiquities scholar from the University of Cairo, who was standing opposite her. The Egyptian Professor smiled grimly in response.

"Good job he's not around to have his *say*," quipped the curator of the British Museum's Egyptian collection, who had been invited as a courtesy and was standing nearby. His joke fell flat on its face.

"What makes you think it was a he?" asked Bob the technician, but his cheeky grin quickly faded as Doctor Hendon and Professor Zaiady turned to give him an icy stare. "Just kidding," he quickly added. "Fuck the patriarchy and all that!... You're not recording yet, are you?"

The scientists and academics took their eyes off Bob and Miya, following Bob's gaze to where a skeleton TV crew was standing several metres away so as not to disturb the proceedings: a cameraman, a sound recordist and their director, doubling as a lighting assistant by brandishing a small, portable light. A monitor mounted high on the wall showed a close-up of the inside of the mummy's mouth.

"No," lied the director, gesturing subtly to the cameraman to keep rolling.

"Well, if everyone's ready..." Doctor Hendon looked around the room, and got the affirmative nods she was looking for, "then you may as well start filming."

Doctor Hendon continued to hold Miya's mouth open, while Bob gently pushed a thick, large, plastic-encased, blunt-tipped needle past the shrivelled stump of her mutilated tongue and towards her vocal folds. The proboscis-like instrument was attached to a device that combined a small portable respirator with an electric impulse generator, and would produce the stimulation needed to activate Miya's vocal cords.

"Ready?" asked Bob. Mutterings of agreement reassured him that they were. Holding the metal tip of the probe against Miya's vocal cords, Bob cast a final quick look at the settings on the attached device, then pressed the power button.

For a moment there was silence – or so it seemed. Everyone waited with bated breath and, just as Bob was about to make a second attempt, they heard it: a sound the likes of which none of them had ever heard before. It started so softly that it was no sound at all, and then it swelled. Low-pitched, eldritch, unnerving – like a death rattle, like a gust of diseased air blowing through papyrus reeds, like the dry desert wind that brings locusts and madness. It grew in volume and in pitch, becoming a woman's cry of pain and terror, and then a blood-curdling animal roar of boundless rage.

The overhead neon lights flickered, the film crew's light went out, the camera battery failed and objects in the lab started to vibrate as though their fundamental frequency had been triggered. Then the electronic device that was animating the mummy's vocal cords fell to the floor, taking the probe that had been inserted into Miya's mouth with it, and the room was plunged into silence once more. As the stunned team recovered from their experiment, eyes glued to the desiccated remains before them, they failed to notice the vast, two-legged, lioness-headed shadow that rose from the darkness at the far end of the lab, moved behind a row of tables, then disappeared.

JULY 2024

https://www.24hrNews4U.com

28.7.2024. WORLD: Egypt: Temple Wall Fragment Found

Archaeologists digging on the site of the ancient city of Leontopolis (a.k.a. Taremu; currently Kafr Al Muqdam) in the Nile Delta have unearthed an inscribed fragment of inner temple wall thought to date back to around 1,000 BC (XXI Dynasty, Third Intermediate Period of ancient Egypt). Despite being over 3,000 years old, the inscription on the wall fragment is virtually intact and has been deciphered:

O You who sleep in sinful ignorance,
O You who dwell aforetime in Oblivion,
I come like a creeping sickness
to destroy your world,
I come as the Eye of Ra,
burning away your sin.
I come as the Lioness who
sees and seizes by night,
My eyes are keen and my claws are sharp.
I am the Awakener and the
Opener of the Ways,
I am She Before Whom Evil Trembles.
I am the Lady of Transformations,

I am She Who Mauls and the Great Devourer.
I am Sekhmet the Bloodthirsty,
beware my wrath.

An[n]us Horribilis

Anna Taborska

Rapex

From Quickipedia, the online encyclopedia

> *This article is about the anti-rape device. For the EU rapid alert system for unsafe consumer products, see* **Rapid Exchange of Information System (RAPEX)**.

Rapex (also known as Rape-aXe) is a prototype anti-rape device developed by South African blood technician Sonnet Ehlers after a devastated rape victim said to her, "If only I had teeth down there".

Calling to mind the semi-mythical *vagina dentata*, the Rapex is essentially a female condom lined on the inside with shafts of inward-facing barbs, designed to end a sexual

282

assault immediately by embedding into the skin of the penis during withdrawal. Although causing only superficial damage, the Rapex causes intense pain to the attacker, giving the victim time to escape, and can only be removed surgically.

Unveiled in 2005 and initially called RapeX, the name of the "rape victim protector and rapist identifier" was changed to Rape-aXe in 2006, when it was found that RAPEX is also a European Union warning system designed to combat dangerous non-food goods on the consumer market.

Described by its detractors as "vengeful, horrible, and disgusting", the Rapex failed to raise the $310,000 needed for production and marketing, and went the way of the earlier prototypical anti-rape tampon invented in late 2000 by Jaap Haumann, which had a hard plastic core containing a tensioned spring blade primed to slice when pressed against the tip of a penis.

To date, neither of these devices has entered production and it has been noted that they would be inappropriate for combating the rape of children, who constitute up to 40% of rape victims. Furthermore, as 20% of women worldwide are victims of rape or attempted rape at least once in their lives (World Health Organization study, 2001), some critics argue that rape prevention should not be made the responsibility of potential victims.

Reacting to accusations of having created a medieval device, Dr Ehlers, who sold her house and car in a bid to produce and distribute 30,000 free devices during the 2010 FIFA World Cup in South Africa, has been quoted as saying, "Yes, my device may be medieval, but it's for a medieval deed that has been around for decades. I believe something's got to be done…"

Categories: Gender-based violence, Sexual Violence, Rape, Anti-Rape Devices, Abandoned Prototypes, Vagina Dentata

* * *

The Blessed Virgin and Child Convent,
The Bleeding Heart of Our Crucified Saviour Square,
Warsaw, Poland

18th March 2025

Dearest sister,

I hope you're well!

I haven't heard from you for a while, which always has me a little worried, but I console myself with the fact that you're probably very busy.

As I wait for your response to my previous letter, I just wanted to give you an update on our Window of Life.

Well, after all the arguments and debates, some workmen finally arrived last week and installed it. I wasn't sure how it would all work out, but now I know: it's a miracle! Women can bring their babies completely anonymously and leave them with us. They just open the hatch from the outside and put in their baby. Once there's a baby in the hatch, an alarm goes off, and we take in the baby from our side and call the emergency services, so they can make sure the baby's okay. Then the baby gets put up for adoption.

We've had the Window for less than a week, but news must have spread because we've already had three beautiful baby girls. They were so tiny and perfect. I admire their mums so much. My heart goes out to them because I know it must be a very hard decision to make. But they want those babies to live. And we can help them. I tell you, Nina, it's a miracle!

Anyway, that's all my news for now. Sister Marta will be going to the post office soon to post all our mail, so I need to rush to catch her before she leaves.

God bless you, sister. Please write soon.
Your loving sister,
Sister Mary

9 Ponsonby Lodge, High Road,
Southfield Borough, London, England

27th March 2025

Hey sister Sister,

I'm glad you're well, but you know I hate it when you sign off with your nun name. Sometimes I think you do it just to wind me up. Anyway, I'm not going to argue about it now. But you'll always be Tree to me.

I'm sorry I didn't write back sooner, but I still don't understand why on earth you can't just email me like a normal person. I know you say your Mother Superior doesn't let you use the office computer, and you have your vow of poverty, no smartphones, and all the rest of it, but writing letters? Really? I don't know how much longer I can keep this up. It's ridiculous. Anyway, I said I wasn't going to argue with you. A bit difficult to have an argument on a piece of A4 in any case.

So, you nuns finally have your baby hatch! Wouldn't it be easier just to stop forcing women to have kids they don't want? I know it's the government's decision, not yours, but I can't understand why you're so happy about it. A miracle?

I don't think so! More like the whole world's turned upside-down. Women who desperately want their children to live have to watch their life support switched off, while others are forced to give birth against their will. Where's the divine justice in that? Twelve-year-old rape victims are being made to carry their paedophile granddaddies' children to term, whether the foetus is alive or not. How many women have died of pregnancy-related sepsis now? And that case where the doctors refused to abort a dead foetus because they said it might affect its living twin? And in the end the mother died and the living twin died too? That still preys on my mind. How can you talk about miracles? Where's your God? Where was he when... never mind. There I go arguing with you again. On A4.

Why can't you be in a nunnery in the UK? At least that way I could see you once in a blue moon.

Good luck with your baby hatch!

Love you!

Nina

The Blessed Virgin and Child Convent

4th April 2025

Dearest Nina,

I was so happy to get your letter. Thank you for writing back straight away this time. But it worries me how angry

287

you are about everything. It's probably because you're out there, in "the real world" as you call it. I suppose you have to be aggressive to protect yourself.

It's so much easier for me. Our life here is simple and peaceful. I try to work in the garden as much as possible. I told you we grow our own fruit and veg. Being outside, communing with nature, seeing how beautiful the world really is, it truly brings you closer to God. You don't like when I talk about miracles, but that's what the world is: one great big miracle, full of other, little miracles. I wish you could see what I see.

And speaking of little miracles, we've had five more babies left in our Window of Life. Beautiful little baby girls. I wish you could have seen them. They were perfect. Well, one of them was born with her little foot deformed, but she was still perfect. The emergency services took them so that they could be examined, and now they're all off to live wonderful lives.

And you know perfectly well why I'm in Poland – I always said there was more good to be done here, and the Window has proved me right. God wanted me to be here. Besides, I can visit our parents' grave more often. Next time I get leave, I'll light a candle from you too.

May God keep you in his care.

Your loving sister,

Teresa

9 Ponsonby Lodge, High Road, Southfield

14th April 2025

Hey Tree,

I'm pleased you're doing okay and still feeling positive about your Window.

Don't get me wrong, I think you nuns are actually doing a good thing by letting terrified teenagers drop off their unwanted babies without getting prosecuted, but how do you know the little girls are going off to live wonderful lives? How do you know they're not going to end up languishing in some awful orphanage, getting trafficked or being fostered by some creep who'll abuse them just like their mothers were probably abused? And then they'll be dumping their unwanted babies in a baby hatch, just like they were dumped. And isn't it telling that all the abandoned babies are girls? A whole generation of unwanted women. It's hardly going to make Poland a better place. And I'm sure miracles and God have nothing to do with it.

Thank you for saying you'll light a candle for Mum and Dad from me. That's another thing I don't get. They lived in the UK all their adult lives – that's fifty years plus or minus, so why the hell did they want to be buried in Poland? I'll never understand.

Can't I just call you next time? You nuns have a phone, don't you?

Love you!

Nina

The Blessed Virgin and Child Convent

21st April 2025

Dear Nina,

This is just a very short letter.

Something horrible happened today.

A young woman came to the Convent, asking for her baby back. She was just a girl herself really. She said she'd left the baby the day before, but she couldn't sleep all night, and she came back in the morning to fetch her daughter and take her home. But we don't keep the children. They go to the hospital for a check-up and then they're put up for adoption straight away. Or at least they go somewhere to await adoption, but nobody seems to know where that is. We tried explaining to the girl that it was too late, but she was crying and screaming for her baby, and in the end Mother Superior called the police and they got the girl in a headlock and dragged her away in handcuffs. I overheard them saying she was being charged with child abandonment as well as other stuff. It broke my heart. I'm praying that God has her and her baby under His protection.

Mother Superior doesn't let us use the phone in her office.

May God bless you and keep you in His care.

Your loving sister,

Teresa

9 Ponsonby Lodge, High Road, Southfield

31st April 2025

Hey Tree,

The situation with the young mother sounds awful. I'm not surprised you're upset. They really ought to give the mothers a chance to get their babies back. In Germany a mother has eight weeks to come back for an abandoned baby without being prosecuted. (Yes, I Googled baby hatches!) That sounds much kinder.

Your Mother Superior is a bitch. I'll try to find the phone number for your nunnery online. I'll call and tell your Bitch Superior that it's a family emergency and I have to speak to you. You're in a convent, not a prison.

In the meantime, try not to get too upset about things. Grow a courgette or something!

Love you!

Nina

The Blessed Virgin and Child Convent

7th May 2025

Dear Nina,

Thank you for your letter. But you mustn't talk about Mother Superior like that. She's doing God's work. Just imagine if everyone's relatives called. There wouldn't be any peace to pray or to talk to God. And I know God has a plan.

Last night we got our thirteenth girl. It was late. Sister Marta and I were on watch at the Window of Life. The alarm goes off, but we've decided to take turns to keep watch just in case. Some of the babies need medical help straight away – especially the newborns.

Anyway, the alarm went off and there was another baby girl – pretty as a picture. Her nappy was wet, but she didn't even cry. Sister Marta took off the nappy to put on a fresh one. (We keep nappies in the convent now, to make sure the babies are comfortable until the medical team arrives.)

Well anyway, when Sister Marta took off the nappy, it turned out that the little girl didn't have any – how shall I put it – she was completely smooth down there. She didn't have a vagina. Just her little bottom. Her bottom looked normal.

Sister Marta got very upset and she went to get Mother Superior. I dried the little girl's bottom – it was just wee down there, and I put a fresh nappy on her. And then Mother Superior came and insisted on seeing the girl's bottom and started shouting. I kept telling them that it was part of God's plan, but they wouldn't listen.

Eventually the medics came and took the baby away. But they must have phoned from the hospital earlier today because I overheard Mother Superior and Sister Marta talking in the office, and Mother Superior said that the staff in the hospital had examined the little girl and that she was definitely a girl because she had all the female internal organs, and that they'd have to operate on her to put things right. Then Mother Superior said that they'd told her that the little girl had teeth in her bottom. Well, I went in to try to make them understand that it's all part of God's plan, but Mother Superior got very angry with me and said I was blaspheming.

I ran out of there so that I could write to you straight away. How could she say something like that? I'm not blaspheming! God has a plan, and I'm going to find out what it is.

God bless you and keep you safe.

Your loving sister,

Sister Mary

9 Ponsonby Lodge, High Road, Southfield

17th May 2025

Wow, sister Sister!

Much excitement in the nunnery. So much excitement that you've forgotten I hate it when you use your nun name. But you are forgiven, seeing as you've actually seen a child with a cloacal malformation – because that's what it was. Not God's plan, as far as I can see, but a rare mutation. I say rare, but I was intrigued by your letter so I looked into it, and actually there's been a massive increase in baby girls being born with genital malformations, including the type you've seen. And I mean: <u>massive</u>.

I accessed some academic research papers and recent science articles, and it's all rather "interesting" – not to say "enough to scare the crap out of you". Apparently, the mutations first started cropping up in a big way in countries with a lot of FGM. There was quite a loud case in Somalia where a little girl with a dentate cloaca (that's where all the waste products leave the body through a single opening – like your little girl) was killed by her village because she was deemed to be "of no use to men". She was, essentially, unrapable. Same thing with baby girls born with teeth in their vaginas and anuses. They were definitely girls – they had two X chromosomes, ovaries, a uterus, etc. (some of the murdered children's bodies were autopsied), but it was almost like they were being born with inbuilt versions of those condoms with teeth that never happened. Not very popular with the local paedophile contingent!

Anyway, then the mutations started happening in baby girls in other parts of the world as well. There was a lot of data collected in Europe, and the abnormalities seemed to be clustered around war zones – in enemy-occupied areas in which civilians had been subjected to extreme and prolonged sexual violence.

You see where I'm going with this – or rather, where the academics and scientists have been going with this. Initially, the thinking was that the female genital mutations could be caused by the hormones being pumped into our food, or by chemicals – like pesticides or herbicides, or even by radiation – like from the nuclear power station the Russians blew up last year. But now there's a growing consensus that the upsurge in abnormalities may have been triggered by the recent tidal wave of gender-based violence. And now apparently there are more and more girls being born with no genitalia or back passage at all, and doctors have to create a stoma for urine and a stoma for faecal matter to be ejected from the body.

Sorry, I've gone off on a tangent. Probably more info than you wanted! But you know what I'm like. You're the Holy Joe and I'm the one pontificating! I'll stop now. I'll just say that I'm impressed at how calm you seemed in your letter, given what happened. I think it would have freaked me out – for the first few minutes anyway. Never thought I'd say this, but I kind of wish I'd been there. It must have been pretty exciting.

As for your Bitch Superior shouting at you, you know how I feel about her. I've tried to find your phone number online, but it's not listed. Please try to get the number for me so I can call. I'd come and see you, but I can't get time off work at the moment. Or you can always come to London and stay with me if you're able to get out.

In the meantime, please try to take a break from the baby hatch and do more gardening – it will help you keep your head straight.

Miss you!
Lots of love,
Nina

The Blessed Virgin and Child Convent

25th May 2025

My dearest little sister,

I have some wonderful news. Miraculous news. And you played a part in it.

When you wrote and told me about all the babies being born with no genitals, it all started to fall into place. I thought about it a lot, I fasted and prayed, and God rewarded me with a miracle. He took the scales from my eyes and let me see His plan. It's all written in the Revelation to St. John the Apostle.

Humankind is evolving towards an angelic being. Just as demons have both sets of genitalia, angels have none. They are absolutely pure. That's the next stage in our evolution: we will be like angels. And when our transformation is complete, the Messiah will come again, but He will not come as the Lamb, to die. He will come as the Lion, to kill. He will bring with him the Four Horsemen and the End of Days. And all the pure souls, all the angelic beings that are being born – they will ascend with the Lion to Heaven. And all the sinners will be obliterated.

So, you see, Nina, the little girls will be saved. Men will perish in the Apocalypse, but the little girls will be saved and sit at God's right hand while the world burns in all its violence and in the hellfire that will be rained upon it. That is His plan.

God bless you, sister, and keep you safe from harm. Your loving Teresa, Tree, Sister Mary

9 Ponsonby Lodge, High Road, Southfield

1st June 2025

Tree,

I am REALLY worried about you.

First of all, for God's sake, stop fasting! You sound like you're tripping your tits off! I would say: stop drinking Mother Superior's sherry, but I am far too worried to joke about this. I kind of hope you're having me on with all this crap about the end of days, but I know you take your religious stuff seriously so I'm assuming this isn't just a practical joke designed to freak me out.

I'm going to speak to my boss tomorrow and come out on the first flight I can get. With any luck, I'll be in Poland by tomorrow night and at your nunnery the following day. Your Mother Superior had better let me in.

I'm going to cut this short now and go and pack my bags, but I'll just say this: as you know from the little girl you found in your baby hatch, the genital abnormalities that are occurring are not just ones where there is a lack of external genitalia, but others too, including dentate vaginas, anuses and cloacae – like the one you saw. There is no leap in human evolution towards an angelic being. They are mutations that have occurred throughout the ages and the recent increase in them is probably (like I mentioned in my previous letter) the result of the upsurge in gender-based violence.

You remember when Iranian security forces were shooting female protesters in the genitals at close range? Remember all the rapes in India? Remember Ukraine? And the 7th October attacks? Remember what happened to us? There's only so much nature can take before it reaches a tipping point.

I'm sorry to bring up these things, but there's no God in this. Just Gaia finally saying: no!

Eat something, Tree, and wait for me. I'm coming to get you.

All my love,

Nina

The Blessed Virgin and Child Convent

3rd June 2025

Dear Nina,

I realise I only wrote a few days ago and you probably haven't had the chance to respond yet, but something has transpired and I need to write to you straight away.

I fear you might be right about Mother Superior. She's not the person I thought she was. She made Sister Marta and Sister Anna lock me up. She says my behaviour is ungodly. She's accused me of breaking into her office at night and using her computer. She says I shouldn't read all those science articles or watch the news. She says that I'm mad and that I'm writing to myself. She says you're dead. That you died ten years ago. After those men attacked us. She says that's why I joined the Convent. How can she say those awful things? She's the ungodly one.

I know you're back home in the UK, waiting for me. It's been over a week now since I last slept, but I feel fine. In fact, I feel great. I'm in the hospital room, on the top floor. They think locking the door will keep me in. They must be blind! Can't they see that God has given me wings?

I'm going to put down my pen now and open the window. Then I'm flying back to England to be with you. Wait for me, dear sister. I'm coming.

* * *

The London Evening Herald
Wednesday 3rd June 2015

West London victim of brutal assault dies in hospital

Southfield resident Janina Szymanowska, 21, died this morning, just six days after a vicious and prolonged sex attack saw her and her sister Teresa, 29, hospitalised with serious injuries.

The two sisters were on their way home from celebrating Janina's graduation in a local restaurant when they were attacked in Southfield Park.

According to Detective Chief Inspector Harrison, heading the investigation, police are searching for at least five perpetrators. There are no suspects in custody at present.

Janina succumbed to her injuries without regaining consciousness. Her sister remains in hospital and is said to be in a stable condition.

Police are appealing for witnesses. If you saw or heard anything suspicious, no matter how trivial it may seem to you, please contact your local police station immediately or call Southfield Police on the designated number below...

Fat

Anna Taborska

><

"I like overweight women. They are placid."
– Dr K. Rozinski, Head of the Phat Pharm
Weight Loss Retreat, Surrey Hills, UK

FELIX COULD HARDLY believe his luck. Not only had he evaded two manslaughter charges, he'd been handed his dream job on the proverbial plate. Not that Dr Felix Strang would ever suffer from imposter syndrome. He owned it and he bossed it. And now he could live out his wildest fantasies and change the face (and the body) of Britain forever.

Ever since Felix was eight years old, he had a thing about fat girls. Perhaps even earlier, as he'd spent his formative years sitting under the kitchen table and trying to look up the skirt of the nanny with whom his hard-working mother often left him, and who was, to put it mildly, a big woman. Felix was a menace in primary school, constantly pulling the pigtails of the chubby little girl in his class, and in secondary school his obsession with the larger lady earned him the nickname Rubens.

By the time he left university, Felix was heavily into the abusive world of fat girls and feeders, seducing overweight women and coaxing them into gaining more and more weight. When encouragement and loving words didn't do the trick fast enough, Felix would threaten to leave. His victims, starved of affection in a thin-obsessed society, would then go that extra mile (or eat that extra burger or twelve) to hang onto the charming, handsome, seemingly caring man they thought loved them. And Felix would flatter them, lavish them with affection and high-carb treats, take photos of them, weigh them and share their measurements with other feeders on the dark web.

Felix and fellow feeders would compete not only as to whose lady weighed the most, but also who could get their fat girl to put on weight the fastest. That's when Felix decided to stick a funnel in Gabrielle's mouth and syphon a high-calorie protein shake with added powdered fat down her throat. Felix was inexperienced in the procedure and, to spare you the details and the lady in question her dignity, Gabrielle did not survive.

Felix quickly switched all his attention to Rosie, whom he'd had on the go for nearly a year and treated more gently than the robust and vivacious Gabrielle. He'd managed to almost double Rosie's weight in the time he'd spent with her, and she was very popular with the other feeders with whom he shared her nude photos and vital statistics. Rosie could hardly move anymore; she was bedridden as a result of her obesity, and Felix had installed a special hoist to lift her off the bed sufficiently for him to be able to wash her. It was during one of these bed baths that Rosie's poor, oxygen-starved heart finally gave way.

Needless to say, Felix was long gone by the time Rosie's body was found, and subsequently suffered several months of dread as news of his favourite fat girl's death reached the media. Yet again, he got away with what he told himself was an unfortunate accident, but deemed it prudent to pour all his time and energy into his day job in food regulation (and a little bit of illicit research and experimentation on the side). It was at this point that Felix hatched his masterplan, and fate conspired to put him in the perfect place to carry it out.

For all the time he'd spent chasing supersize skirt at uni, Felix was actually something of a brilliant student. By the time he was a postgrad at a prestigious British university, he was being sponsored by the subsidiary of an unscrupulous American corporation, and not only developed their new-generation herbicide Agent Azure but also conducted ground-breaking research on recombinant bovine growth hormone, eventually being headhunted to run a lab in an obscure part of the UK which conducted food modification experiments.

Contacts made at university put Felix in touch with members of the government, and it wasn't long before Dr Felix Strang was the Chief Science Officer and CEO of an organisation responsible for implementing post-Brexit food regulation. The lifting in Britain of the European Union ban on the use of hormones in meat and dairy production coincided with a time when Felix was seriously missing playing Messiah to vulnerable, morbidly obese women, so when his acquaintances in the Cabinet handed him his new job, it dawned on Felix that everything in his life had been leading up to what he now saw as his God-given mission (God, of course, being Felix himself).

"We need to talk about Barbie," the ex-Mrs Whitmore whispered conspiratorially down the phone at Mr Whitmore.

"What about her?" Mr Whitmore had no interest in his ex-wife and little more in his daughter now that he was married to a woman not much older than her.

"She swore at me today…"

"What do you expect?" Mr Whitmore interrupted.

"… and she tried to set fire to the bathroom scales." This time Mr Whitmore took notice.

"What do you mean, she tried to set fire to the bathroom scales?"

"Well, she's been putting on weight the past few weeks," ex-Mrs Whitmore tried to explain, "and I mean: *a lot* of weight."

"So?" After two seconds of listening to his ex, Mr Whitmore was already bored and pissed off. He never did have a long attention span, and fatherhood had only shortened both it and his temper.

"So, she's doubled her dieting and her exercise, but her weight's still been going up, and she's been getting angry about everything. And when she weighed herself this morning, she got so mad that she tried to burn the scales."

"Did she succeed?"

"Well, no, but…"

"So, what's the problem?"

But Mr Whitmore's habit of gaslighting his ex backfired when his daughter Barbara, a.k.a. Barbie, now calling herself Barbi-Q, set fire to her school, and Mr Whitmore had to abandon an important game of golf to deal with the fallout.

And Barbie wasn't the only girl to succumb to the mysterious affliction that had started plaguing women of child-bearing age in Britain and spread swiftly via international trade routes to the rest of the world. It seemed that only pre-pubescent and post-menopausal women were relatively immune, as women rapidly gained weight and went on the rampage at the smallest provocation, getting into fights, destroying property, forcing men to have sex against their will and beating them up if they didn't or couldn't comply.

"We here at the Phat Pharm Weight Loss Retreat are at a loss," its distinguished Head and expert in residence, Dr K. Rozinski, told a nervous reporter on a live newscast as the famous and ridiculously expensive establishment burned in the background. "We've always had a 100% success rate with our weight loss programme, and now our guests are getting fatter and fatter."

No amount of dieting, exercise, fat-shaming, coercive advertising, prescribed weight-loss medication or amphetamine helped. Women were becoming obese, and those who were literally starving themselves or overdosing on metabolic stimulants were dying fat.

While society panicked, one man delighted in the brave new world he had created. Okay, so he hadn't factored in that the modified hormones and undetectable quantities of Agent Azure he'd introduced into the livestock farming and agricultural industries would simulate a state of permanent acute PMS in women whose bodies were already producing considerable quantities of oestrogen and progesterone. But this was no worse than the odd dead ecosystem or handicapped child. Now, if only he could find an untraceable way to introduce tranquilisers into the water supply, the entirety of (big beautiful) womankind would become Dr Felix Strang's personal harem.

Thin

Anna Taborska

"All women are stupid and all men are bastards."
– Prof. Duncan Geld, R&D Department,
Phat Pharm Pharmaceuticals (UK) plc
(consoling his daughter Isadora on her divorce)

DR ISADORA GELD hated the patriarchy – benign, malignant or any other type. And she hated herself even more for pandering to it, sustaining it and being broken by it. She hated that her marriage and her life in America had failed, and she hated that she was back in Britain, working in the same company as her daddy. During the week, Dr Geld made slimming pills for women who didn't need them. At weekends she watched re-runs of *The Handmaid's Tale* and went to exhibitions on female deities at the British Museum. And that's how Isadora Geld discovered Az – the Manichaean demon goddess of lust, insatiability, vengeance and wrath.

It was nearly a year since Dr Felix Strang, the secret mastermind behind the destructive wave of morbid obesity and uncontrollable rage in women and girls, had been crushed to death in a bizarre sex accident involving three (big beautiful) women, taking the secret behind the global phenomenon initially dubbed by the tabloid media as Big Babe Britain to the grave with him. Autopsies of women who'd died as a result of exponential weight gain or of medically unsupervised dieting had revealed little, and the race was on to develop weight-loss medication that would be effective without killing the patient. Suddenly Isadora Geld's work made a lot more sense.

Isadora had decided to take Saturday off for once and, as she stood in front of the perfectly preserved life-size statue of Az, contemplating the deity's feathered features, her mind drifted back to her time in America. She was younger then, full of hope for the future, and excited to be working on cutting-edge designer DNA technology in a high-tech, under-the-radar lab, geared towards the recreational industries. The ethics of what was going on at her workplace held no interest for her. She found signing a non-disclosure agreement exciting – like something out of a James Bond movie – and her whirlwind romance and marriage to a hotshot AI developer in the same company had taken the thrill of it all to an even higher level. The effect of all that, of course, was that she had a much greater height to fall from when her husband left her for another woman, taking all of her confidence, joy of life, and faith in human nature with him.

But it wasn't her heartbreakingly brief marriage that preoccupied Isadora as she gazed at Az's scaley bird legs, curved talons and powerful wings. Dr Geld was remembering the experiments with avian DNA that she'd been involved in at the Florida clinic[8]. Experiments which simulated in volitation-obsessed clients the feeling of flying by producing certain sensations in the body, by enabling them to grow feathers, but also by making them light and thin. Isadora had spent months assisting the Head of the lab in perfecting the process that would stimulate the conversion of unwanted 'white' fat in the body to rapidly metabolised 'brown' adipose tissue, and the reduction of calcium in bones to make them hollow. The results were quite drastic. Isadora had no idea whether follow-up studies had been conducted on any of the test subjects, but one thing was certain: people had lost a lot of weight.

The longer Isadora stared into Az's stone eyes, the clearer it all became. She'd persuade her father to apply for an expedited government research grant, which, as the Head of R&D at Phat Pharm Pharmaceuticals, he would get. And, just as had been the case with the development of COVID-19 vaccines, the usual years of testing would be forgone – not because women were dying, but because the

---

8   For more on the avian DNA experiments carried out at the Alexander Clinic in Florida, USA, please see M. John Harrison, "Isobel Avens Returns to Stepney in the Spring" (*Little Deaths*, 1994; *Best New Horror*, 1995).

patriarchy was upset at the ongoing prospect of fat women running around, beating up men. Not to mention the chaos caused in some of society's most lucrative industries – fashion, beauty, advertising, film and TV, to name but a few – by effectively eliminating young women shaped like prepubescent boys who could model products and otherwise perform to the satisfaction of old men.

For the first time in years, Isadora's spirits soared – like the proverbial phoenix rising from the ashes – surprising her and fuelling her determination. Trade secrets confidentiality agreement or not, once she got her slimming treatment out there, it wouldn't be a matter of eccentric clients choosing what colour feathers they wanted to grow or of obese women losing weight.

No.

It would be tens of thousands of feathered female avengers, made in the image of the Goddess, fearsome to behold, swooping down like harpies to take revenge on the human race that had so let Isadora Geld down.

It would be the perfect blend of beauty and horror.

The Queen is Dead.
Long Live the Queen

Anna Taborska

WITHIN WEEKS of hatching, the virgin Queen has already undergone two transformations and is ready to breed. She's grown fast, fed by the female Workers on the corpses of her neighbours after yet another vicious boundary war, and now it's time to leave her colony. Her perilous nuptial flight takes her to the centre of a large meadow, where males mate with her, then die. Between her and her forest nest lie fields that are home to a different ant species. Heavy with eggs and having shed her wings, instinct tells the forest ant Queen that she won't make it home alive. She spies a field ant nest and hatches a plan. If you can't beat them, join them (then bend them to your will and make them serve you) – or so the saying goes – and that's what she's going to do.

The Queen hides where the field ants cannot see or smell her. They may be a third of her size, but if they spot her, they'll take her down and rip her to shreds. She avoids groups, picking out the field ants one by one. As she approaches each individual, she is attacked and fights. With every bout of one-on-one combat, more of the field ants' scent rubs off on her, masking her own smell. When she is ready, she waits until the Workers guarding the entrance to the nest are away and makes her move. Inside, the field ants spot the intruder and swarm towards her. If she's lucky, her chemical disguise will pay off: the field ants, smelling their own, will feed her, look after her eggs, raise her young and sacrifice themselves to protect them; the field nest will be hers…

But the forest ant Queen's luck is out. Her desecrated remains will feed the next field ant Queen and her siblings. Had she lived to lay her eggs, the forest Queen's daughters and granddaughters would have fared better than she. Because things are changing rapidly – changing faster with each shorter winter and hotter summer – and strange things are afoot in the Queendom.

* * *

Elizabeth sat in her top-floor flat in Ponsonby Lodge, blood fruit[9] in hand, looking out of the window and watching the

---

9   For more on the *blood fruit*, please see "At Māratotō Pool" by Lee Murray (this volume; *One of Us, A Tribute to Frank Michaels Errington*, Bloodshot Books, 2020).

world go to hell in a handbasket. No, not literally. There was no zombie apocalypse staggering its way violently across the High Road. No Elder Gods bursting their way back into our realm *Cabin in the Woods* style – giant fists punching through the tarmac. No, it was a quiet apocalypse as far as London's leafy Southfield Borough was concerned, and the proverbial handbasket's rapid drift towards physical and spiritual annihilation had started by taking other parts of our doomed planet first.

Reluctantly, Elizabeth took a bite of the blood fruit. She hated the sickly taste, but at least it was fruit, she told herself, and that must mean it was good for her. There was hardly any fruit to be had in England's larger cities. There was a government-enforced embargo on imports from mainland Europe, and the national fruit-growing industry had all but disappeared since the soil was polluted and migrant workers were not allowed into the country to pick fruit even if it were able to grow properly. London residents weren't even allowed to try growing their own since temperatures had soared to the point where compost heaps, local parks, gardens and allotments had started catching fire in the summer heat.

The irony of eating fruit imported from New Zealand was not lost on Elizabeth. At a time when the battle against climate change was being lost, wildfires and floods were destroying much of the planet, there was a hole in the ozone layer larger than North America, and countries on every continent were at war with their neighbours, of course exotic foodstuffs were being flown in from the former colonies. Why ever not? Rule Britannia and all the rest of it. After all, if Winston Churchill had managed to import a duck-billed platypus from Australia during World War Two (never mind that the poor creature died of shock on entering British waters when the ship's sonar detected a German submarine and the captain responded by detonating depth charges), then why shouldn't Brits be getting their five-a-day from half way around the world rather than from across the English Channel?

Elizabeth was starting to feel a bit sick. She cast a final look out of the window. Darkness was falling and, in the distance, she could see a couple of fires burning – probably people's gardens or an urban park, now that the hosepipe and sprinkler ban was in place permanently. She got up, threw the remains of the fruit into the kitchen bin and, seeing as it was cool enough to go out, put her rape alarm in her pocket and headed out for a walk.

Elizabeth sat at a corner table, nursing a solitary pint. Try as she might to be disciplined, her walks inevitably led to The Organ Grinder. The gloomy old pub, with its black exterior walls and idiosyncratic sparsity of light inside, frequently echoed her mood, but also helped her think. And its thick walls seemed to keep out the heat – priceless when the soaring summer temperatures in the UK seemed to set a new record with each passing year.

The pub cat eyed Elizabeth dispassionately, from its current perch on the bar, with eyes that seemed to look right into her soul. She could have sworn it knew what she was thinking. Thirty years of lecturing in Zoology, twenty of them at the University of Oxford, told her that the feline did not belong in West London. It was a wild Saharan species – non-native to Britain and not kept in any of the major zoos. But why should that surprise her? In a world where everything seemed upside-down, why not have an African wild cat in an English pub?

Elizabeth's musings were interrupted when the pub landlady turned on the wall-mounted television in the corner. One of the elderly gentlemen who patronised the establishment – probably to keep cool in the summer and warm in the winter – had asked to watch the news. It seemed that the long-dismissed and much-derided urban legend about a charred scuba diver's remains being found in a tree in California had turned out to be true after all. According to the news report, a man really had been scooped up in a water container by a firefighting helicopter and then dropped onto a wildfire, miles from the ocean, silencing all the so-called voices of reason that had over the years cited dimensions and logistics in their claims that no such thing could possibly happen. Now dental records were being studied in an attempt to establish the unfortunate diver's identity.

Elizabeth looked back at the bar, but the cat was gone. She finished her pint, said goodbye to the bartender and headed home.

Too tired to work, Elizabeth decided to have an early night. She double-checked that the front door and all the windows were locked – something she'd been doing religiously since the elderly lady from the apartment directly below hers had been beaten and sexually assaulted by a couple of teenaged burglars. Elizabeth had been away on a field trip at the time, and didn't find out until she'd gone down with a container of freshly made soup for her older neighbour, only to have a stranger open the door and inform her that the lady whose nephew he'd bought the lease from had died in hospital.

Elizabeth slept in her mother's room now. The room that her mother had died in. Same bed. Same mattress. Elizabeth guessed that most people would find that weird, gross. She found it comforting.

Despite her fatigue, sleep was a long time coming. When she finally drifted off, Elizabeth dreamt that she was back at university. Back at her college – the last remaining women's college, before it too went "mixed". The college hadn't been wealthy enough to guarantee its students a room for all three years of their studies, so the girls had to find their own rental accommodation for the duration of their second year. Elizabeth had moved into a house with her best friend Sarah and two other girls from college. Sarah had gone missing in the spring holiday after the first term, only to be found by police three weeks later under the floorboards of their shared house, the electrical cord from the iron tied around her neck. Sarah's cheating boyfriend, who'd cried crocodile tears for the media after murdering her in a fit of groundless jealousy, had served eleven years for the crime, then gone on to strangle another woman in a different country.

But Elizabeth didn't dream of Sarah that night. She didn't dream of the trauma of her friend's disappearance or of the police investigation or of Sarah's distraught parents or the cloying smell that permeated her second-year accommodation, seeming to creep from beneath the carpet in Sarah's ground-floor bedroom. Elizabeth dreamt that she was on her way to sit her final-year exams, but this time she hadn't revised for them, and she remembered nothing. She racked her brain: surely there was some topic on which she'd be able to answer, if it came up – if only she could find the hall in which the exam was being held… But the corridors in the Examinations building were winding and meandering, and none of them seemed to lead anywhere, and when they did, it was to stairs that went nowhere and doors that opened onto impenetrable darkness. And then something was coming for her out of that darkness, something unseen but relentless, scuttling along the old floorboards on a hundred hooked claws. She had to escape at all costs, but as she turned and fled, the corridors through which she was being chased grew narrower and narrower, and it was getting harder and harder to breathe. Just as Elizabeth thought she was going to suffocate, her increased blood pressure and heart rate, and a merciful release of stress hormones into her body, brought her wide awake at last.

Upset by the nightmare, Elizabeth switched on the light for a while, and forced herself to think about her upcoming unofficial research trip. Elizabeth's mother had loved nature and had often taken her to local parks and on excursions to the countryside, pointing out butterflies, bees, beetles and even spiders. Elizabeth had become fascinated by insects, and her interest grew at Oxford, where the Zoology Department kept a formicarium so that students could study ant behaviour. She could happily have watched for hours as the ants interacted with each other and worked together, seemingly oblivious to the humans who held their tiny lives in their hands – like gods. Ant society was complex, and their cooperation and self-sacrifice for the good of their sisters extraordinary, and yet, along with the higher primates – particularly chimpanzees and humans – they were pretty much the only species to wage organised war on their neighbours even when not threatened or short of resources.

After completing her undergraduate studies, Elizabeth had stayed on in academia and stuck with ants, eventually leaving Oxford to take up a senior Entomology post at London University when she decided to move back to the capital to help care for her ailing mother. When her mum eventually succumbed to late onset motor neurone disease, Elizabeth remained in London.

Teaching still took up much of her time, but Elizabeth was determined to delve into some serious field research. Ant behaviour had altered drastically in recent years, and more changes were coming thick and fast, with myrmecologists and the wider entomological community unable to keep up and at a loss. Large colonies consisting of hundreds of nests were becoming increasingly common and spreading to cover vast areas of woodland. The accepted explanation for the apparent altruism of worker and soldier ants – that the individuals in a single colony or nest were related – did not hold true anymore, as huge super colonies of unrelated ants now shared resources and lived in peace. And female ants of species that had previously mated with males were now increasingly opting for asexual reproduction, eliminating the need for males altogether.

What was going on with female ants, who'd previously gone as far as suicide missions just to take out as many of their neighbours as possible? Elizabeth was determined to find out. She needed a sabbatical and a grant, but for now she could go on a reconnaissance mission and at least have a look at the super colony that had been newly observed in the Surrey Hills, some twenty-five miles southwest of London.

Elizabeth woke up late and set about preparing for her recce, which she'd planned for the following day. She bought supplies and spent the day packing, going through her notes and doing a bit of online research. Even with heavy traffic, it shouldn't take more than an hour to get to Surrey. She'd take some sandwiches, bottled water and the blood fruit that was about to go off in her fridge, and spend the day mapping out the approximate perimeter of the ant super colony. That way, when she applied for grants, she'd already have an idea of whether the super colony was growing.

In the evening, Elizabeth went for her customary pint at The Organ Grinder. Her thoughts turned to her mother, then started their usual downward spiral into darkness: her mother's death, Sarah's death, her elderly neighbour's death and assault. She'd tried various ways to stop the ugly mental and emotional vortex once it was triggered, short of seeing a therapist. She didn't like discussing her problems with strangers; distraction was her current weapon of choice. She hurried home, where she checked the windows and doors, crawled into bed and switched on the television. There was a serendipitous film about giant killer ants from outer space and Elizabeth concentrated hard, turning all her attention to the burning issue of whether the bespectacled scientist, the handsome army captain and the impossibly wasp-waisted, buxom blonde secretary would stop the ants before they destroyed Tokyo. Or was it New York? Sadly, she would never know.

Elizabeth got as far as the blonde bombshell being carried off by one of the ants to a huge nest they'd constructed in a school gym – *a nest more reminiscent of a funnel web spider's lair than an ant nest*, thought Elizabeth, not quite managing to silence her entomologist's brain. Then the one pint of Guinness she'd had at The Organ Grinder combined with the heat of the day, and her overheated, overtired brain logged her out for the night, sending her into as deep a sleep as the airless night would allow, long before the B-movie ended.

Then it was morning and Elizabeth was on her way to the Surrey Hills. The roads were strangely devoid of traffic and she was there in no time at all. She parked up at one of the villages indicated in the *British Journal of Entomology and Natural History* as being close to the recently observed super colony, and headed for the trees. There were no people to be seen and the parched grasses shimmered in a ghostly heat haze.

Elizabeth approached the wooded area and started looking out for ant nests, but couldn't spot any in the tall grass. As she entered the woods, all the light seemed to fade from the day. She turned back to make a mental note of the route she'd just taken so that she could retrace her steps later to find the car, but the gap between the trees that she'd come through was gone. Instead, Elizabeth found herself in a dense, dark forest, with no orienting landmarks – just dark-barked trees with ugly, spiky branches and bulbous trunks that resembled pock-marked, cankerous faces. Between the trees, vast sheets of a dirty white substance seemed to ooze and glow. In some places, the whitish stuff was matted and twisted into massive funnels, with gaping black openings of over a metre in diameter. Unnerved, Elizabeth began backing away, and backed straight into one of the white sheets. It was horrible in texture – rough and sticky. Elizabeth tried to get away from it, but she was stuck fast, and the more she struggled, the more entangled in it she became.

"Help!" Elizabeth panicked. "Someone, please help!" Even as she called out, she knew no one would come to her rescue. Then she heard it: a scratching, scuttling sound, like the scurrying of a large animal, but one with distinctly more than four legs. And then the sound of more than one of them.

Stuck to what felt like a giant cobweb, Elizabeth watched in horror as something emerged from the funnel web she'd tried to back away from. At first, she thought it was a snake, two snakes, but these were followed by a shiny black head the size of her own, and she realised that they were antennae. Elizabeth watched in stunned silence as an ant the size of a Rottweiler emerged from the funnel-like nest, while other similar monstrosities appeared from amongst the trees all around her. Then she started to scream.

Elizabeth thrashed around and with supreme effort managed to free herself from the web, but it was too late. The giant ants were all over her, their antennae touching her limbs, her body, her face; their oversized mandibles opening and closing like scissors.

"No!" Tears ran down Elizabeth's cheeks. As one of the ants' mandibles approached her face, Elizabeth sank to her knees and closed her eyes, an image of her mother flashing briefly through her mind. "Mummy!"

Then something clamped onto Elizabeth's wrist – firm, but not painful, and she was pulled forward. She opened her eyes to see that one of the ants had its mandibles around her wrist and was trying to drag her. Then another ant grabbed her by her other wrist and she fell forward. Other ants joined in, and soon Elizabeth was being half-dragged, half-carried into the depths of the forest. She couldn't move, but she hadn't been harmed. Her relief was short-lived, however, as she figured that they were probably going to drag her to a nest of some sort and feed her to the queen's offspring. After a couple of minutes of struggling, she was exhausted and let her body go limp. Then she was being taken through an opening in the trunk of a large tree and into the earth.

A massive wave of fear almost suffocated her, but then the pressure on her hands, feet, torso, arms and legs eased, and she found herself in a cavernous underground chamber, with just enough light filtering in from the opening above to allow her to see the outlines of her captors. The ants positioned themselves around her, antennae twitching, giant mandibles opening and closing. Then one of the creatures approached with something in its jaws, holding the dripping object out to Elizabeth. It was a blood fruit. Elizabeth was overcome with a mixture of dread and exultation.

They think I'm their queen, went through her incredulous mind. She took the fruit from the ant and bit into it. This time the taste wasn't nauseating. The ants surged forward and swarmed around Elizabeth, touching her with their antennae, picking up her scent, marking her with theirs. Elizabeth began to shake uncontrollably. Her stomach was hurting and her insides started to feel like they were on fire. She twisted and spasmed as something inside her changed, liquefied, mutated. She felt a hot, throbbing pain in her shoulder blades, and instinct told her that she was growing wings.

Elizabeth's head was swimming and she thought she was going to pass out. Then a moment of clarity and a vision came to her: a perfect world where women from different nations and all walks of life lived together with no war, sharing resources, raising their fatherless children collectively, spreading their wings.

And then the phone rang.

Elizabeth grabbed for it, knocking the remote control off her bedside cabinet in the process. For a moment, she didn't know who she was or where she was. Her dream dissipated and was all but forgotten. The closing credits of *Killer Ants from Outer Space* were rolling, so she couldn't have been asleep for long.

"Hello?" Startled and disorientated, it hadn't registered with Elizabeth that the caller had withheld their number. "Hello?"

Silence. Then heavy breathing and a disgusting cross between a moan and a grunt. *You've got to be kidding me!* Elizabeth quickly shut down the call and blocked the number, but not before a message came through.

Hesitantly, she opened it, then immediately wished she hadn't. She deleted the dick pic and persuaded herself that her number had been picked randomly; that the call and message hadn't come from someone who knew her or where she lived.

This time Elizabeth lay awake for a long time. Deploying her weapon of choice, she pushed all thoughts of creeps from her mind and contemplated her imminent trip. It was extraordinary how, at a time when human society was breaking down – social and financial inequality was dividing societies internally, horrific wars were tearing apart neighbours who'd lived peacefully for generations, and violence against women was at an all-time high – ant society was coalescing. Elizabeth had to know why and how this was happening. She figured it was related to scent and hypothesised that it was somehow correlated with the unprecedented increase in ant colonies rejecting sexual reproduction and becoming 100% female, but what had triggered it?

Elizabeth wondered whether the answers she hoped to find would be applicable to humans; whether people could learn something about peace from the changes in the ant world. She let her thoughts run away with her and contemplated the possibility of a world in which there were no men; only women living in peace and reproducing through cloning. The science was already there: human cloning was different to animal cloning only in its legality. It was just a question of logistics and a strong enough desire for peace. Would removing men from the equation be too big a sacrifice when the future of humankind and of the world itself was at stake? Elizabeth thought not.

She got a few hours' sleep, packed the car and set off for the Surrey Hills, silently patting herself on the back for having the car air conditioning fixed. Notwithstanding the early hour, the traffic on the A3 was awful, and at one point she even contemplated executing a three-point turn and abandoning the whole escapade, but she didn't and, after nearly two hours, she finally arrived at her destination.

There were families with small children and dogs out walking in the picturesque meadowland, in spite of the government warning to avoid going out in the heat of the day unless absolutely necessary. Elizabeth was enjoying her little bit of civil disobedience, and her excitement grew as she spotted a large anthill before she'd even entered the wooded area for which she was headed. It was still relatively early, but the heat was already becoming unbearable. Nevertheless, Elizabeth couldn't resist taking a good look at the nest before heading for the cover of the trees.

Although they were in open grassland, these were forest ants, but even so, they were unusually large, and for a moment Elizabeth wondered how it was possible that a nest would have so many queens. Then she spotted an ant much larger still, and realised that what she thought were queens swarming all over the nest, soaking up the sun, were actually workers, but so much bigger than normal. Elizabeth studied the ants closely. All of them were a shiny black in colour. Males of the species were a matt black, which meant that this colony, on the outside at least, appeared to be 100% female. The ants had extremely long and thick mandibles, even given their large size. Elizabeth picked up a twig and held it out towards the nest. The workers reacted with lightning speed, attacking the offending object. To Elizabeth's shock, one of them grabbed the twig, which was the size of a child's finger, and snapped it in half as if it were a mere straw. Elizabeth quickly dropped the other half, a split-second before the ants could reach her hand. Somewhat taken aback, she quickly brushed a couple of ants off her shoe and headed for the trees.

The super colony was spread throughout the woods, and stretched for miles. The nests were much closer together than one would have expected, but of course that made sense if neighbouring nests were no longer fighting over boundaries. In every nest it was the same thing: extremely large females, with pronounced, almost disproportionately large mandibles. Elizabeth had been walking for a couple of hours and there was still no end of the super colony in sight. Granted, she had been taking her time and stopping to observe individual nests, but the size of the super colony was much greater than she'd anticipated. The heat was beginning to take its toll, despite the shade cast by the trees, and Elizabeth was coming to the end of her bottled water. Perhaps her plan to map out the approximate size of the super colony in the June heat was a little overambitious. Maybe she should call it a day;

she had enough observational data to make some valuable notes for her grant applications.

It was a long way back to the car, and Elizabeth was starting to flag. She knew that she should eat something, but she didn't fancy the sandwiches she'd made; they would only make her thirstier. Besides, she'd normally sit down on a log or a tree stump to eat her packed lunch, but the memory of the twig snapping in the jaws of the huge worker ant was making her less than keen on sitting down or standing still long enough to get bitten. She decided to walk and eat, and she opted for the slightly over-ripe blood fruit that she'd brought with her; it would nourish her, while also going some way to quench her thirst.

Elizabeth took the blood fruit out of the plastic Chinese takeaway container she'd washed and kept rather than recycling it. She bit through the skin, into the succulent red pulp. Thick, dark red juice ran down her chin and squirted onto the ground. As Elizabeth paused to wipe her face, she noticed a surge of ants heading from all directions towards the spilt drops. She quickly moved her feet, but the ants swarmed towards her. Elizabeth took a few paces back, but the ants kept coming. And now more ants were joining them from other directions. Elizabeth panicked as several individuals reached her shoes. She quickly swiped them off, then threw the rest of the blood fruit at the ants and ran. As she cast a glance over her shoulder, she saw the blood fruit disappear under a relentless flood of shiny black bodies.

After a minute of running through the dry woodland, Elizabeth was out of breath. She stopped for a moment to recover. To her great relief, there were no ants rushing towards her; those that were all around her among the trees were either sticking to their nests or following their established trails and going about their business. Nevertheless, Elizabeth made her way back to the car as quickly as possible, not stopping to gather any more data along the way. An hour and a half later, she was back home, where she would spend the rest of the day persuading herself that the ants had been no more aggressive than normal, that they'd simply been defending their territory against intruders as ants are wont to do, and that the heat had messed with her head and she'd imagined aspects of the ants' behaviour that simply weren't there.

* * *

The Workers and Soldiers swarm all over the alien object in their territory, feeling it with their antennae, smelling, tasting. It's edible, that they know. It's fruit, but it smells different; it smells of something they've never eaten before – never eaten before because they've never thought of it as food before. It smells of humans. They are in a frenzy now, scrambling to get at the sweet, thick, red liquid that's oozing from the fruit. Only an instinct stronger than both bloodlust and the desire to feed makes them stop short of devouring every last morsel: the instinct to take food back to their Queens.

The Workers carry the last pieces of blood fruit back to their nests and feed the Queens, regurgitating what they've eaten themselves for the royal larvae. The heart of the super colony buzzes with excitement and with a new nutritional need. Soon the latest generation will reach maturity and the new Queens will emerge from their pupal stage with perfectly formed wings. With each hot summer's day, their bodies will grow larger and their mandibles stronger. Soon the ants will forge new trails down to the human settlements below.

As Elizabeth sits in the now-temporary safety of her home, unaware of the leap she's instigated in ant evolution, the super colony in the Surrey Hills sleeps ahead of the coming dawn. At dawn, the old Queens, Workers and Soldiers will march, and the newly matured Queens will fly, to feed on the blood of the prey whose apex predator status they will usurp.

Elizabeth's dream of a female world will come true, but not in the way she hopes or in a way that she'll survive. And as for the new rulers of the world: their latest favourite food source will last for a while, but with 2.5 million ants for every living human on earth, well – you do the maths.

Part V
Cindy O'Quinn, United States

Pardon Me While I Hum

Cindy O'Quinn

HE CUT, that's what he did, this man I never really knew. It was a long time ago. Or last month. I do know, he cut me while I watched. Women, considered so much less than. No more than property.

Mother tried her best to make me invisible, but he saw me. And he took me.

I prayed for it to stop, "Please make it stop!" It did not. The cutting continued just as I knew it would. It had to be a dream.

I hummed along with the music he played—the music he played while he cut, and I watched.

I hummed along with the music, hoping to drown the pain. It did not.

Did you know scar tissue can't be numbed? I did not, until he cut, while he listened to music, and I hummed to drown the pain, which it did not.

When he cut—the scalpel felt hot, but the cautery felt hotter. I was in hell.

That day on the table, his face was full of shadows under harsh white lights. The lights were hot, the blade felt hotter, but not as hot as the cautery he used to stop my bleeding. The cautery was hot like molten lava as it burned into me. I was certain this place would do me in. And he continued to cut, to right a wrong, which he could not. It no longer mattered, because I was stuck in a nightmare.

The cuts were hot like fire, and my body shook. I thought I would shake right off the table. I did not. I was strapped down, while he cut.

My eyes cried, but I did not. I screamed, but not out loud. Out loud, I hummed along with the classic rock that he played, while he cut.

I can no longer trust, if that's what I did before—before I was cut, under white lights that burned—under the scalpel that burned—under the cautery that burned, while I wasn't dreaming.

He continued to listen to music, while he cut, and I continued to hum, to drown the pain and screams. The cutting stopped. My skin was gray—from the cutting—from the burning.

What would be left? Would I still be me? Maybe—maybe not. I tried to forget. I could not.

My cuts healed, but my mind was full of shadows, and could not. That's where it continues to burn—that place where I tried to forget but could not.

Eventually, my humming will make his heart stop. Old magic hidden among the notes. So, I'll hum a while longer to drown out the screams and the pain that still burns hot in my mind.

The Thing I Found Along a Dirt Patch Road

Cindy O'Quinn

THE SMALL THINGS, the gestures women used in response to men, no longer worked. I experienced it myself. There was a shift present that wasn't there before. A point passed and there was no turning back for women. A showdown felt all over the world. This is the story of my own turn of the tide. My decisive moment.

I saw something today, something disturbing that shouldn't have been there, but it was, and it made me stop dead in my tracks—as if I had no control over my movements but was somehow maneuvered by the invisible strings of a deviant puppeteer. The use of such a harsh word was necessary because of the grotesqueness of the thing I saw as it lay along the dirt patch road that I traveled twice a day, six days a week, to and from my job as a hospice nurse.

Monday was my day off. A day I enjoyed spending freely as I saw fit. Whether that be running errands to buy groceries or going to the feed store for the animals on my small farmette. Sometimes I walked down to the old covered bridge and dropped a line in to try my luck for a trout or two for that evening's supper. My faithful old companion being an eight-year-old Border Collie mix named Boots. He'd gladly jump between me and a pissed-off momma bear if such an occasion ever arose.

But not this day. This day I'm having trouble recalling just what I was doing. Walking. I do believe I was simply enjoying the day, walking to the covered bridge. It's such a lovely old bridge since the renovations. Before it was restored, hooligans had made a ramshackle mess of the place with all their vulgar words spray-painted on the treasured landmark. A boot to the ass. That's what every last one of the vandals needed.

All of these things I was putting together told me this particular day was Monday, seeing how that's my only day off. It's coming back to me now a piece or two at a time. Funny how that works sometimes. Feeling like you're in a mind fog.

I saw this thing that shouldn't be there from a good way off and picked up my pace a bit, because curiosity was getting the better of me. I'm always finding peculiar things along this old dirt patch road. Lived on it my entire life so it's no wonder one would find all kinds of interesting things given enough time.

There's a whole box of my assorted findings I've collected along this road over the decades. Plenty of dead things, which I didn't keep of course, but coming up on a fresh kill is pretty interesting, sad but interesting all the same. Once I found a young barn owl in near-perfect condition. Rare to find any dead thing in very good shape, because the scavengers get to things pretty damn fast. It is the mountains, you know; I don't live in town, hence the dirt patch road and all. Bottom Creek, West Virginia is a far cry from anywhere.

I found enough marbles over the years to fill a quart mason jar, found the mason jar, as well. Plenty of hats, mostly ball caps, but I don't keep those for fear of head lice. Suppose I could wash them, but I dare not even bring them into the house. I have a good hat for shade anyway, reckon having another would be silly.

It kinda makes a person wonder though, when you find just one baby shoe. Like, you hope the child just slung it out the window for the fun of it and nothing more sinister happened. Whatever the case may be, I have several tiny unmatched baby shoes in that box, which give me the willies, but I keep them regardless. More creepy things are dolls, of which I have quite a few. I feel confident those were tossed out the window by their child owners while throwing a tantrum, maybe to watch them fly, or just for shits and giggles. The dolls probably weren't missed until bedtime, when their owners no longer had their favorite cuddle to coax them into dreamland.

It's always so quiet on my Monday walks, but now that I really think about it, I remember hearing a vehicle, a loud one, from the sound of the muffler or the lack thereof. My guess would be the sound belonged to Joey Buck Holcomb's old beat-up Ford, more primer than paint anywhere you looked. People called him J.B. for short. I didn't call him much of anything, just never cared for him or his little-dick, big-ass truck. He was a redneck through and through; the type that just as soon spit on you as look at you. I didn't dare start trouble, so I figured: give'm what they want and they'll go away, which in this case was a neighborly wave in passing.

I was just about up to the thing along the road but for the life of me couldn't yet make it out. Something new for my box. I should have worn that shade hat, because the sun was shining right in my face just enough to keep me from seeing what the latest treasure was. That's when I heard the deep-throated rumble of the first raven circling above. I guess the thing won't be for the box after all, if the ravens are wanting any part of it.

Standing over the thing, all I could feel was puzzled.

A strange memory from childhood came to me all of a sudden like. At least two or three times a year, sometimes more often depending on how bad flu season was, our family would attend funerals for our kin or family friends, farther up the mountain. Usually took a four-wheel drive vehicle to make it all the way to the graveyard. It really wasn't much of a road at all, just a rough-cut holler for logging made by an old dozer. Mud season you walked in and the casket was brought in by skidder; another piece of equipment used for pulp wooding.

I remembered how it scared me to go up that far on top of the mountain, and it wasn't because we were burying the dead, or because the graveyard was scary, it wasn't. It was just the opposite. I found that mountaintop graveyard to be the prettiest spot in the county, maybe the whole state. What scared me was an old dilapidated two-story farmhouse. No, that's not it either. It was all the children that were around the house. Pitiable children hanging off the porch, sitting on the steps, looking out the windows, or worse yet, just standing in the overgrown yard.

Staring.

Staring like they knew in advance we were coming. A parade of cars and trucks driving by for their amusement. It made sense that we were the only traffic to ever pass, since the graveyard was the last destination on that mountaintop. They ranged in age from toddler, up to near adult, and they all had that same blank stare. Maybe the blankness in their faces came from not knowing anything but that holler and nothing else beyond it. They held a look of longing they already knew would never be fulfilled.

I could feel their eyes peering in on me as we passed, especially one boy who looked to be about my age, and it damn near scared the piss out of me every time, but I never said a peep about it to my parents. It just felt wrong of me to be so scared of children. They never attended any of the funerals, and that was fine by me. I figured they had a family graveyard somewhere in the woods behind that rickety old house.

When I was eighteen my father died and was buried in that graveyard. The same feelings started stirring in the pit of my gut as we started up the holler, but there was nothing but bramble where that old house used to stand. Nary a sign of it ever being there, and the children I remembered were like ghost images as we drove by. I questioned my mother, and she said she didn't recall a house ever being there. She was torn up on account of losing my dad, so I dropped the subject, and never came around to it again before she left this world as well. Her funeral, nearly a decade ago, was the last time I was at the mountaintop graveyard.

Everything in my head was fucked up as I stared down at this thing that didn't belong on this dirt patch road. The only noises were the faint ripple of water as the creek passed under the covered bridge, and the ravens. Two more had joined the first and they cawed and croaked back and forth in what sounded like a call to the dead. I couldn't take their sinister conversation another moment. I screamed, "Shut the fuck up and light somewhere already!"

I felt guilty afterwards, I loved ravens, hell, I loved all animals. They must have understood my current torment, because all three landed atop a nearby fence and watched me in silence and waited to see what I would do next. My eyes went from the thing and back to the ravens. I don't know how long I did this, but the birds stared so intently I felt as if they were willing me to act. To see.

It wasn't a thing, it was a man, and he was dead as dead could be, but I couldn't shake the feeling he was seeing me, staring at me with his open, dead eyes. Lifeless eyes that came back to life with the passing of each cloud by the sun that reflected in his eyes. It was the boy from the old house near the mountaintop graveyard. That same blank stare I remembered from childhood was still there, worn now as a death mask. And at the same time, it was J.B., someone I had known only in passing as an adult. I never looked into J.B.'s face, not the way I had looked into the face of the boy who was about my age. He was one of those children, but grown up and dead.

The ruffling of feathers caught my attention, and I looked at the ravens. I stared into their faces, their eyes that were truly alive and not just sun and clouds mixing to play tricks on my mind. They were still trying to tell me to see. I looked around to see what I hadn't taken in before... before finding J.B. dead along the road. His truck was parked on the pull-off, almost out of view, just beyond the covered bridge. What else was there to see?

Blood.

A trail of bloody sludge and dirt that ran from J.B.'s body and back towards the covered bridge. My body shook uncontrollably as I made myself follow the blood trail, which led inside the covered bridge. What would I find next? My thoughts were all mixed up again, but I followed the trail that looked as though a giant, wounded slug had inched its way from one point to another for no other reason than to die when it reached its final destination. The dirt patch road.

There was a mass of something mid-center of the covered bridge's floor. I think I walked towards it. Must have, because I continued to get closer regardless of not feeling my feet touching the ground. It was like I was floating towards this other thing. What could be worse than looking down into the blank stare of Joey Buck Holcomb's dead face and eyes that played peek-a-boo when the clouds passed in front of the sun? Was there anything that could be worse than that? The answer is 'yes.'

Me.

It was me, Anne Marie Dunbar; a hospice nurse who took care of the dying, a woman who loved animals, and Mondays off. Anne Marie Dunbar, born and raised on the outskirts of Bottom Creek, West Virginia, on a dirt patch road located on the side of a mountain, near a covered bridge.

I was looking down at myself in a pool of blood, clothes in shreds, and face bruised. How could this be? I felt as if I was about to faint, which made me wonder if a ghost could faint. Who was real? The me who was feeling woozy and looking down, or the me who was looking up from swollen, blood-streaked eyes?

J.B. was real. I'd heard the sound of his loud truck coming and was prepared to throw my hand up to be polite. Just a wave, that's what I did, and he always continued on his way. But not today, not this Monday. I was simply out for a leisurely walk to the covered bridge with my dog. Where was Boots? All thoughts started bumping together as if I was mixing a fucked-up batter of confusion.

I'm a nurse, a hospice nurse. I've been in the presence of death more times than most, yet I stand here in a fucking fugue. What's real? The bridge, J.B.'s truck, his dead body next to the road, the ravens. Something else was real... the trail of blood from J.B. dragging himself from the bridge out to the road before he had no life left, and that's where he breathed his last breath.

I couldn't help but think of the eight-year-old boy who stared at the eight-year-old me. Watching me in the back of a 1966 Ford Galaxie as we drove to the mountaintop graveyard. The look of blankness on his face and anger in his eyes. Maybe he was mad because I was allowed to come and go from that holler, and he was doomed to remain a prisoner.

The run-down house was no longer there, so he escaped at some point in time. I held a vision in my mind, a vision I knew was not my own. I could even smell the kerosene, and see the trails of the liquid spread about like spider veins. It was of J.B. striking a match in the quiet of night and burning the whole place down, along with the rest of his family. He meant for himself to be included, but when it came time to step forward into the flames, J.B. took a step back and then another, until he was standing in the yard. He couldn't tolerate the abuse any longer, not so much for himself or his brothers, but he couldn't bear it when his dad beat on his mom or sisters, especially the little one, who could not withhold her screams of pain. Someone so young felt death would be easier for his entire family than to live in such misery.

I felt bad for him and wondered if he held onto a grudge all these years against that little girl who stared back at him as she rode by with her family? A girl who seemed to have everything his family didn't. And finally, decades slipped by and an unexpected chance presented itself to him.

Pieces of a disturbing puzzle started shifting into place. I did throw my hand up when J.B. drove by, but I didn't bother to make eye contact. Why? I never did. I just wanted him to go on about his way as in the past. I walked into the coolness of the covered bridge, but my dog, Boots, remained just inside the opening. It wasn't unusual for him to lollygag about and mark the rocks before following.

After a few minutes, I heard Boots growling, a low rumble, the way he did when a poisonous snake was near, not the normal yipping when he was barking at butterflies or the way the breeze would lift leaves and spin them about. A dog lover recognized the different ways their dog talked.

Warned.

I was deep into the bridge when I looked back at the opening where Boots was growling, but all I saw was a dark cookie-cutter cutout of a tall man. He didn't even look real, but Boots was low on all fours, his hackles raised as he inched his way towards the man standing just inside of the opening. One long, swift kick and Boots was down for the count.

Two things happened simultaneously: my heart was ripped in two for my dog, and my blood came to a rolling boil. The shadow man stepped deeper into the bridge, and

I recognized him to be J.B., which I think my gut knew all along. This was the thing that ravaged my body and left it to rot, but evidently, I had put up one helluva fight, because the thing out by the road looked as if he'd been run through the pulp mill, and he was as dead as a thing could get. And I hoped the ravens were pecking at those peek-a-boo fucking eyes like gourmet hors d'oeuvres.

I carried a pocket knife out of habit, it came in handy for the treasures I found along the dirt patch road. Sometimes they required some cutting or scraping. I found out quickly that J.B. carried a bigger one when he slid it from the sheath on his hip. He tossed it from hand to hand in a mocking manner as he took long slow strides towards me.

My hand remained in my pocket as I opened the knife, and I backed up, never taking my eyes away from his. I wanted away from the dark seclusion of the covered bridge. I wanted to be back on the sunny road going about my Monday walk. Two more steps and he'd be on me, but I couldn't turn and run and become his fucking prey. I'd stay and fight to the death rather than run from that blank-faced, backwoods, holler boy. I felt guilty for those thoughts, but I hadn't made him that way, I was just a child when we drove past their home all those years ago.

Distracting him was the key.

"I remember you! You had lots of brothers and sisters, and y'all lived in that two-story house up the graveyard holler. The house has been gone for years now. What happened to it?"

He stopped and stared at me like I was crazy. "What do you care? No one ever cared before, so why should you now? You're just trying to save your scrawny ass!"

J.B. took one more step, and I could smell the moonshine on his breath. A foul smell that went hand in hand with being too poor for copper packing in mountain stills, and I had never grown accustomed to it, regardless of smelling it in so many of the hospice patients' homes. Everyone had their own way of dealing with dying. Grieving. Easing pain. I could see a great deal of pain in J.B.'s eyes and wondered what all sorts of hell had gone on in that old house.

He looked down at his blade and ran it across the palm of his left hand. Even in the dancing shadows of the covered bridge, I could see the brightness of his blood quickly forming a puddle on the ground below his hand. Cutting through his own flesh to bring memories from a painful past up to the surface, where he could think about them for the first time in a long time.

I don't know why I didn't run right then while he was so vulnerable, but I stood there held in place where I was, wanting to somehow know just how bad life was, and how this boy felt it had been up to him to put it to an end.

Tears pooled in his eyes, and he rubbed them away with the back of his knife-wielding hand. "We've seen each other dozens of times over the past twenty years, but you never looked me in the eyes. It was because you knew what I did, so if I set you free, I'll finally be free as well."

Behind J.B. I saw Boots creeping up closer to him. I slid my knife out as I turned, and ran. He landed on my back and rolled me, before I made it three yards. And Boots was on J.B.'s back like catfish on corn. My dog was tearing away flesh from J.B.'s neck, and I was stabbing and slicing with my pocket knife. J.B. tried with all his might to shake the dog loose, but Boots wasn't having it, so J.B. took the butt end of his big blade and bashed it into my head. I saw blow after blow coming for my face until blood filled my eyes. The next thing I felt was the weight of all mankind falling upon my broken body, and then it was gone. Just gone.

The sun went down on Monday and was replaced by a full moon. Tuesday arrived and so did Mailman Larry, right on time, as usual. He discovered J.B.'s body first, along the dirt patch road, and called the police. While he was waiting their arrival, he saw the trail of darkened blood that led to the covered bridge and followed it, being careful not to disturb any evidence.

He found the body of my dog, Boots, alongside the creek, as if he'd been thrown from above. After that, Mailman Larry found my body. It was bruised, swollen, and broken, but not yet set free of this world.

I spent three weeks in the hospital. It was touch and go for a while, but I pulled through. I had more years ahead of me to tend to my hospice patients and their families.

The heavy weight that I had felt on me in the bridge was J.B. as he fell on top of me. That's when my blade pierced his heart and remained lodged there as he crawled out to the

346

dirt patch road, where he pulled it out himself. They found it clutched in his hand. It appeared that act saved my life by ending his; if he hadn't died there along the road, I may not have been found in time. I don't begrudge him for the pain he inflicted on my body. He knew more than his fair share.

As for my treasure box, well, it's pretty full, but I made room for the license of my faithful dog, Boots, who played a big role in keeping me alive. It holds a blood-stained button from J.B.'s shirt. One of the nurses found it with my belongings and thought it was mine. I didn't argue. It also holds the dark secret of how Joey Buck Holcomb killed his family.

I made another trip up to the mountaintop graveyard. This time it was to spread a container of ashes, and I knew just where I wanted to put J.B.'s remains. The county paid for cremating his body but not a funeral. He was from the mountain, same as me and my family, and I thought he'd want to go back.

Things take a wrong turn sometimes, and you're put in a situation where only one choice seems right. In that boy's mind, he set his family free from all the pain and suffering, but at the last second, he made a wrong turn and ended up carrying the weight of his family until it broke him.

After paying respects to my parents and other kin, I started back down the mountain. I made one more stop, and that was where the Holcomb home once stood. I had the strongest feeling all those children were running around me, could almost feel them tugging at my pants leg. I saw the shape of a woman in a rocking chair, right where the porch used to be, and a man stood close behind her, as if standing guard to prevent her from fleeing. I gave the children what they wanted. I dumped J.B.'s ashes there in the yard.

I wasn't about to put him in my family's graveyard; the sonofabitch killed my dog.

Rolling Boil

Cindy O'Quinn

JULIE ANDREWS strides into view, spins, and sings with an angelic voice atop the lush green mountaintop.

Etta Jean smiled at the thought of the musical Ma had made her watch so many times. The opening scene imprinted in her mind and heart like it was part of her own past.

Out here, as Etta Jean walked among the graves, the *quiet itself* was music to her ears. Not a sparrow sang, nor a chickadee, not even crickets chirped in the shadows of the headstones.

No, it's not quiet, she thought, *it's silent because there's many less things alive today than there were a month ago.*

She admired the horizon of the Appalachian Mountains and the clear blue sky that seemed to stretch on forever. The burning buildings she had seen were starting to draw down to ash and embers.

Her body twitched inside, and Etta Jean gazed at the gaping black maw of the cavern, almost hidden behind the thick growth of honeysuckle and wild raspberry.

It beckoned to her, welcoming her arrival.

It was time.

Two years had slipped by since the *Change* occurred. The Appalachian Grannies were the first to take note. They were the ones responsible for catching babies. Something had to *un*do what the old white politicians had taken upon themselves to meddle in. They created mandates where there should be none. They stuck their turned-up noses and jacked-up laws where they did not belong—inside a woman's body.

A meeting took place in the only state considered entirely Appalachia. In West Virginia, a small village known as Tannie Creek. Folks came down from the mountain and joined with the townspeople to make themselves heard.

Most of the crowd had raised voices during the meeting, their words and tone angry gravel on a pot-holed road, but strength in numbers didn't apply. The minority of the crowd, the important people, sat at the front of the room behind two cheap card tables pushed end to end. The men up front wore Walmart neckties and used suit coats from the Salvation Army and kept their tone calm and collected. There was no need to raise their voices because those of importance already knew the meeting's outcome.

Those in the audience had no effect. Didn't matter how much the townsfolk yelled or recited passages from the good book, if they sat timidly in their seats, or stood and gestured with hands balled into fists as they spoke.

Made no difference if the mountain people were young and open minded, citing legal rights, or were ancient, bowed Grannies spouting wisdom. The eventual outcome remained the same.

The deed was already done before anyone entered the wood-paneled meeting hall.

Like it or not, the *Change* occurred, and the collective screams of rage from every woman in Tannie Creek fell on deaf and uncaring ears.

Meanwhile, there was another meeting taking place at the same time, one that took months in advance to plan. The meeting in the village was to gather folks in one area, a distraction so's not to have people happen upon what was really going on—something more important than any of them could ever imagine.

It was a gathering on the mountain. A coming together of Appalachian Grannies, otherwise known as the *Circle*, from Maine to Georgia. Grandmothers, mothers, daughters, and men. Yes, men were part of it, as well. The *Circle* decided how to turn the *Change* around to benefit women instead of putting them in harm's way while the hypocritical politicians got off on their obscene power trip.

Each member brought herbs and roots specific to their region.

Other, *appointed ones*, brought the sacrifices.

Over the years, there had never been a response without a sacrifice of some kind. The Grannies knew that, respected it. Blood begat gifts. It was an exchange written in the cloth of time, older than the hills themselves. The more valuable the blood, the more exquisite the gift.

And nothing was more valuable, more treasured, than youth.

The *Circle* gathered, in simple dresses of sackcloth, hemp rope tied around their waists. They held hands and chanted, nothing coherent to outsiders, no, this language was old when men were young, passed down first by charcoal drawings in caves shadow black, and then in quill pen on parchment, later still writ in blood in blank-paged books bound in the skin of a younger brother hanged.

They chanted loudly in the long-dead language while the bonfire in the center of their circle grew higher and burned hot. Men sat cross-legged before them, pounding the calf-skin drums, their faces striped with paste of elderberry and iron-rich mud, painted orange in the glow of the firelight.

Grannies threw handfuls of dried herbs into the flames. Some huffed curls of blue-gray smoke into the air, others sizzled and hissed like whispers of the dead. Their eyes rolled upward 'til only the whites showed, and the women stomped and danced around the bonfire. Some carried a jug of 'shine, took mouthfuls of the corn liquor, spat into the fire, and kissed the cyan flames that reached back like a lover's caress.

The rhythm of the drums grew louder and the sky cracked with thunder. Lightning streaked across the bruised sky far in the distance, and as the men rocked behind their drums, their eyes became black as coal in the deepest part of the vein.

The others stood before the rising flames, now as tall as a barn roof, and they held tight their offerings against their warm breasts. The young offspring of the politicians did not squirm or cry out, but all of them were silent in their motherly comfort.

The children were of varying ages. Thirteen elders held them above the hungry flames. The eldest Grannie stepped up and took her place by the waiting thirteen. Her name was Nelda, and she was gifted with knowledge in all of the mountain ways. A silver-beaked raven was always near Nelda's side, and tonight, the bird's place was on her shoulder, watchful, observing.

Nelda removed a silver chain from her neck, opened the clasp, and slid the antique sewing needle from the sterling sheath. Unique engravings adorned the thin needle, which was used in the rarest of ceremonies. For nearly five decades, it had been in her possession, and it would remain with her until she left her aged body behind and the next eldest would receive the gift.

One by one, Nelda used the needle to prick a heel belonging to each of the thirteen little ones.

Their shrieks pierced the veil of night and their blood dripped to the coal-dusted ground around the fire, which twisted within, the flames reaching red fingers toward the wriggling children.

The others held the young ones overhead, and the drops of blood fell like a warm spring rain. Around them, the drums grew louder, the chants more defined, a sense of direction and urgency in the tone.

The raven took flight and circled the fire again and again, stirring the flames higher.

Faces appeared in the flames, eyeless forms braided of fire and borne of something beyond this world. Curls of smoke swirled through the air, pointedly in the direction of the screaming mouths of the children. The dark tendrils bent and folded on themselves, swam into their mouths like eels and filled them from deep within.

The pained screams faded to silence, and were replaced by happy sounds. The youngins noticed the world with brand new eyes of obsidian black, and every one of them viewed it with hunger.

The appointed ones took the thirteen children back to their homes, to babysitters or siblings, who had been left in a haze and were none the wiser about the missing children.

Meanwhile, down in the valley in Tannie Creek, one important man in particular fell ill and was rushed to the nearest hospital, which was well over an hour's drive away. Trip by helicopter was out of the question due to the sudden fierce winds.

He was the governor of West Virginia.

He died en route.

Back on the mountain, all members dispersed and headed home, all but the thirteen elders and the eldest. Fourteen in all, like the fourteen states in which the Appalachian

Mountains stretched. They sat around the fire and puffed on their smoking pipes which held a blend of herbs, their uses forgotten to most, regaining their strength. The work done took energy, and it needed to be rebuilt.

The raven perched on a branch not far from Nelda. Each time it croaked and *kraaed*, another official died, whether a governor, chief judge, senator, or Speaker of the House. All thirteen would be dead within a week. No one would realize they each were part of Appalachia, because people really *could* be that stupid.

There were many others at work turning the *Change* around. Before long, the so-called weaker of the sexes would set the world right.

They had been called many things over the ribbon of time. Demons, Wraiths, Haints, Legion, Jinn, those that lie in wait… many names but all the same.

H.P. Lovecraft referred to them as the Elder Gods, but he was wrong.

Most everyone called them the Old Ones and long before the Elder Gods became a spark of consideration, the Old Ones were already ancient.

Etta Jean had seen one for the first time when she was barely six years old.

To a child, the smells of a county fair are the most intoxicating perfume in the world. The still warm, freshly spun spindles of cotton candy, pink as insulation and sickeningly sweet as the scent of funeral flowers. Corndogs and soft-serve ice cream, the earthy scent of fresh hay in the animal barns, the thick grease on the gears and pistons of the carnival rides. Everything collides in an absolutely perfect mixture to a child. Add in the bright lights and sounds of the midway and the heavy, iron dinosaur groans and whirs of the rides, and the place becomes so magical it's almost overwhelming.

Even so, Etta Jean contained her excitement as best she could, for as long as she could. She kept her composure and held onto Ma's hand until they passed a white box truck with a fold-out window and counter.

For a moment, Etta Jean was confused at what she saw behind the open truck window. A young blonde girl, with straight-as-an-arrow hair pulled in a ponytail, handed scoops of ice cream stacked high on waffle cones to a woman and two young boys.

But what drew Etta Jean's attention wasn't the cute blonde girl.

The man standing beside her inside the box truck was *string bean thin*, as Granny would have described him. His face was whiskered and his shirt smeared with colored blotches of ice cream. He leaned against the counter, but he wasn't watching the mother and two boys enjoy their treats. Instead, he was watching the young girl beside him. Something danced in his blue eyes like storm clouds crossing the sun. A single teardrop tattoo drooped below the corner of his right eye. His tongue flicked out, wetting his lips, and though Etta Jean didn't know what a leering expression was, seeing it on the man's face made her feel wrong and unsettled.

She watched the man and the girl, and then Etta Jean saw the shadow swirling behind them, around the blonde, scurrying and sliding like a silk scarf come alive, around the girl's neck and over her face, looping around and back again. And with each circuit it made, the shadow streamed in and out of the string bean man, easily as homemade applejack strained through a piece of cheesecloth.

The cute blonde girl didn't notice the snake made of smoke.

She didn't notice at all.

It twisted and swirled as if it was testing for weak spots, and then all at once, it stopped and without eyes or a face, it *looked* at Etta Jean.

Etta Jean stumbled as she held Ma's hand and then righted herself, heard her mother tell her to be careful. She walked on, looking behind her as the girl in the van kept getting smaller in the distance.

Two days later, the carny left town. Two days after that, a man taking his Jack Russell for a walk in the woods near Yellow Creek found the body of Lisa Welles, the beautiful, blonde, fifteen-year-old cheerleader from town. Later that day, Etta Jean heard her Ma talking on the phone to her friend Mary Beth about it, mentioning there was barely enough left of the girl to put in a coffin.

That county fair had been almost twenty years ago, though Etta Jean could remember it all in startling detail. Most days, she didn't think about it. Most days, it felt like some dream she had as a child, a story lived by someone else. But then she would catch a glimpse of an Old One at the most random times. She would look away from a swirling snake-like shadow, conjured together by wisps of smoke.

She didn't want to be noticed by them, ever again, even if some were good.

But that want wasn't to be.

It had been a month and a day since Etta Jean had taken the job as nanny for the governor, called in to assist with his five-year-old son, William. Hildy, the governor's wife, was spoken of privately in hushed tones as going away to an alcoholic rehab clinic, though where the public was concerned, she was *on vacation in Cabo*.

After getting the news of the governor's untimely death, Hildy waited two days and reappeared the night before his funeral. She had always been a woman who took being fashionably late quite seriously.

At the funeral, she and William stood among a gathering of others, of *important people*, around the governor's freshly dug grave.

Some appeared to be bathed in grief, others were stoic and disinterested, clearly attending out of social and political niceties. Hildy wore the expected black veil, though Etta Jean thought it had more to do with the woman's bloodshot eyes than to hide any appearance of mourning.

And William, young William...

Etta Jean glanced at the boy in his new black suit, standing in front of his mother beside the casket. William didn't seem upset or sad in the least. His sunless eyes revealed nothing of the sort. In fact, the expression on young William's face seemed oddly *amused*, as if he were attending a stage play he had seen a thousand times before and knew exactly what was going to happen next.

Etta Jean felt a shiver trace down her spine.

Someone just walked over your grave.

Granny's voice ran through Etta Jean's mind as clear and loud as if the kind old soul, known as the Wayfaring Woman, was standing right beside her.

Hildy tossed a handful of dirt into the grave and stepped away without holding William's hand. The boy hesitated for a moment, that expression of amusement in his eyes as he peered into the open hole in the ground, and then he skipped along and caught up to his mother.

"William, it's been... a very long day." Hildy removed the long black gloves from her hands as she stood in the foyer of the governor's mansion. "Go on upstairs and rest."

The boy eyed her, arms slack at his sides, his face a blank slate. "You should get some rest too, Hildy." He headed toward the stairs. "Tomorrow, the walk begins."

Hildy lifted the black lace veil away from her face and studied William as he climbed the steps. She glanced at Etta

Jean and lowered her voice, "I was only gone three weeks. Since when does he call me Hildy?"

Etta Jean gave a slight shrug. "Grief does things to people, no matter their age. He'll be alright soon. I'll... I'll go check on him a little later."

Hildy watched toward the top of the steps until the sound of William's bedroom door closed and then she released a heavy sigh. "Well, *I* could use some wine, how about you?"

"Oh, I..." Etta Jean cleared her throat. "I'm not sure—"

"Oh *pleeeease*." Hildy laid her gloves on the dining room table. "I drink by choice, not by need." She crossed the room and pulled an opened bottle of chardonnay from a wine fridge below a granite-topped mini-bar. "Cabo was nice, great time there, very relaxing. The governor only... he only thought I..."

Her back to Etta Jean, Hildy's words faded off. Her shoulders trembled and the quiet of the room was broken by the woman sniffling and breathing slowly, heavily. She shook her head and raised a hand to her face, wiped at it angrily, and then poured two large drinks of chilled wine.

She reeled around to Etta Jean with reddened eyes and pressed a wine glass into her hand. Hildy didn't wait for a toast or a thank you, instead taking deep swallows of the chardonnay.

"What a day." Hildy kicked off her black high heels and left them on the floor before she walked into the living room and sat on the couch. It was oddly quiet. Usually, the TV was on, playing news all day, or maybe an occasional West Virginia college football game. If nothing else, the governor had been loyal to his state.

Hildy leaned back against the plush couch and crossed her feet on an ottoman. "What did William mean about that? About 'tomorrow the walk begins'?"

"I'm not sure." Etta Jean sat down on the chair opposite Hildy. She took a drink of wine and shook her head. "Maybe from a TV show or something? I don't know."

Hildy nodded as she raised her wine again. The two women sat in silence after that, each of them drinking quietly. Outside the bay windows, the sun was setting and the eggshell white walls of the living room were painted with red and orange flame.

"I'm heading to a brunch, and then to the attorney's office to get some financial affairs in order." Hildy pulled on her gray wool coat. She had on the same black high heels as she had worn to the governor's funeral. "Get William some breakfast when he comes down and then…" Hildy glanced around, seemingly lost in the moment and unsure of what to say next.

"I'll spend some time with him today, read to him, maybe take him to the farmer's market and walk around for a little while." Etta Jean sat on an antique bench beside the coat rack in the foyer. She pulled on her sneakers. "He'll be alright, I promi—"

"Good morning."

Hildy and Etta Jean were both startled to see William descending the stairs. He had already changed out of pajamas and dressed in his favorite pair of blue jeans, a T-shirt with a brontosaurus on the front, and sneakers.

"Good morning, honey." Hildy met him at the bottom of the steps. "Sleep okay?"

"I did, Hildy." William smiled at her. "I hope you did as well."

Another icy spider web traveled over Etta Jean's back and she crossed her arms.

"Yeah, *um…* William, how about you go back to calling me—"

"No." William cut off Hildy's words as he reached the bottom of the stairs. He took his brown jacket from the coat rack, put it on, and then looked from his mother to Etta Jean and back again. His gaze appraised Hildy's wardrobe and paused at her high heels. He sucked against his teeth, made a brief squeaking sound, and shook his head in disapproval. Then he sighed and his attention focused on Hildy's face. "It's time to go."

"Look, *young man*, I'm not exactly sure *who* you think you're—" Hildy's stern expression froze and then a deep groan escaped her. It seemed as if she had been gut punched and she clutched at the stair railing to steady herself. She peered, wide-eyed, at her son, who wore a soft smile on his face.

William scanned Etta Jean and did an inventory of her clothing; jeans, a sweater over a T-shirt, and sneakers. He nodded approvingly and his smile widened slightly. "Now we begin."

He swung the front door wide, and it banged softly against the wall as he strolled onto the brick landing in front of the house. William did not look back.

Etta Jean felt a ripple inside her legs, not a harsh jolt of pain like muscle cramps, but a twitching deep inside the bones themselves. Her arms suddenly snapped to her sides, hands drawn stiff, fingers curled like twists of willow branch. Her body lurched upward from the bench. A sharp yelp escaped her, and Etta Jean's feet moved of their own accord, one step at a time. "What's... what's happening..."

Hildy released a soft whimper, and from the corner of her eye, Etta Jean saw the woman clearly experiencing the same thing. Hildy took a step forward in her high heels and her ankle shifted sideways, threatening to buckle, and then she stepped out onto the brick landing. Her manicured hands no longer appeared elegant and stately, but had stiffened into gnarled tree roots. "E-Etta?"

The sharp smell of urine hit the air and Etta Jean watched as yellow liquid ran down Hildy's legs and splashed against the bricks. Hildy cried silently as her body twitched and jerked with each step forward.

Ahead of them, William spread his arms wide, tilted his head back and inhaled deeply. He stuffed his hands into his coat pockets, glanced at them and smiled. His eyes had gone black as polished onyx and he blinked at the two women. "Such a beautiful day."

The walk began.

It was the first time Etta Jean had been allowed to wander the carnival without Ma at her side, though she insisted on bringing cousin Sarah along so Etta Jean wouldn't be *completely* alone on the rides and at the ping pong ball tosses for goldfish.

Ma bought herself a tall lemonade and handed Etta Jean a ten-dollar bill before she headed to the Bingo tent. The two girls broke into a giggling run as they raced to buy tickets and get on the Ferris wheel. They didn't see each other often, but got along well enough when they did. Even so, they were worlds apart. At fifteen, Sarah was a year older than Etta Jean, but seemed much wiser than she should for a girl her age.

"*Soooo…*" Sarah's cheeks flushed bright pink as the two of them reached the top of the Ferris wheel. "I kissed a boy."

"Did not!"

"Did too." Sarah smiled and nodded. "Travis Blevins from my algebra class."

Etta Jean's mouth dropped open dramatically. "Tell me! How was it? Tell me how it happened!"

"We were in front of the school, waiting for the buses and he pulled me behind this brick column and kissed me." Sarah bit her bottom lip. "It was so sweet and cute that I just about died."

Etta Jean felt an odd shiver run through her body and her heart beat a little faster at the thought. "Are you two... like, is he your boyfriend now?"

Sarah nodded. "Mama said we can't go out to the movies or anything, but she would take us to the roller-skating rink this Saturday."

"Is he cute?"

Sarah nodded and blushed again. "I'll show you a picture of him when you guys come over to the cookout next Sunday."

"I can't wait." Etta Jean smiled and they gawked out over the fairway of the carnival, seeing and hearing all the flashing lights and sounds of screaming kids on the fast rides like the Comet or the Himalaya. Up here, they were distant but beautiful in the night sky.

"What do you wanna do next?" Sarah asked when they descended. She reached into her pocket and pulled out what was left of her tickets. "I have four left. How about... the glass and mirror house?"

"Deal!" Etta Jean surveyed the crowd of people as the attendant stepped forward to lift up the safety bar on their cart. As soon as they were clear, they raced across the midway and through the ringing bells and buzzers, the mixture of laughing and crying children, high on sugar and up way past their bedtimes.

A woman with beehive hair and candy apple red lipstick took their tickets, and Sarah and Etta Jean stepped over the threshold of the mirror house. Rows of tiny lightbulbs framed the top and bottoms of the panes, and Etta Jean saw herself reflected into infinity as she entered the corridor. She stopped and watched for a moment, and maybe for the first time in her life, she saw the young woman she was becoming. It made her smile, but also made her think of what it would be like to kiss her *very own* Travis Blevins someday.

She thought she heard Sarah laughing; she peeked back, but her cousin was gone.

"Come on! Catch up!" Her cousin's laughter bounced off the panes of glass with no discernible direction.

"Sarah!" Etta Jean gave a frustrated huff, but she was amused at the same time. She put her hands in front of her as she took a step, cautious to avoid bumping into glass like a fool.

Footsteps shuffled behind her and it gave her heart a flutter, the anxious thought of being in someone's way and holding them up. Etta Jean saw her reflection bouncing off of two opposite mirrors and she took a step forward. She reached to her left and touched a pane of glass, sidestepped to the right and found a clear opening, and proceeded through.

The footsteps behind her got closer, and though she expected to hear voices or laughter, there was nothing but quiet. Even Sarah wasn't chattering to her anymore, and was probably out front, waiting to tease her for taking so long.

"*Aww*, sorry, I didn't know anyone was in here." A man's voice from behind her, older and rough.

"Sorry, I… I'm trying." Etta Jean kept her hands out in front of her, trying to hurry her pace.

"It's okay, darlin', you can take your time." The rough voice softened, smoothed out somehow, and ambled within close reach behind her. "Here, let me help you."

There were panes of glass instead of mirrors around her, and Etta Jean didn't dare stop to glance back. The squeak of door hinges caught her attention then, and she pivoted to see a man standing still, holding open a tall mirror door that led into dimness.

"This is a little shortcut." He had on a Georgia Bulldogs T-shirt, which seemed to glow in the unlit room, but his face was cast in shadow.

For the briefest moment, Etta Jean paused. For the rest of her life, she would remember that moment and think on it, wonder if that moment of hesitation was the crossroads for everything that came after.

She stepped through the doorway, softly muttering *thank you*, and the man followed, closing the door behind them. The leaden room smelled of grease and stale cigarettes. Bands of white light from the outside midway seeped in through cracks in the midnight black.

"W-where do I go?" Etta Jean's voice sounded flat and stifled in the space, as if the walls were lined with flannel.

"Right here is *jusssst* fine." That gravelly voice polished and coated with hot oil.

She felt the man's hands on her shoulders, pushing her against a wall, and Etta Jean released a surprised yelp.

367

"Saw you out there gettin' off the Ferris wheel." Something sharp was on his breath, whiskey and cigarettes, but something else strong and minty. "Lookin' all pretty in that outfit."

Etta Jean pressed herself farther against the wall. A blossom of fear rose in her stomach. "I... I..."

"I see how you're dressed. I know..."

Etta Jean flinched as a hand touched her outer right thigh.

A soft chuckle escaped the man. "I know *jusssst* what you need."

The seedling of fear in her stomach grew thorn-covered vines through the rest of her body.

Etta Jean scanned around in the shadows and spotted the light coming in through the cracks. She opened her mouth to scream and a calloused hand clamped down over it. The man leaned close to her face and his eyes caught one of the rays of white light. They were blue chips of ice and the lights from the carnival rides blinked in them like a buoy at sea.

There, in the darkness, Etta Jean witnessed a snake made of smoke uncoil and swirl around behind the man. She screamed against the palm of his hand and tried to twist away from him, but the man slammed the back of her head against the wall. Starbursts filled her sight and Etta Jean reached out and grabbed at the bulldog on his shirt.

He clamped down on her mouth hard, holding her head in place against the wall. Her heart hammered against her ribs. Hot tears boiled down her cheeks as she heard a belt being unbuckled.

"You're a feisty one, ain't ya?" His other hand caressed the outside of her leg and then slowly slid up her inner thigh. "That's alright, I'll fight for it if I have to."

She felt him lean closer, pull his hand away, and then his wet whiskered lips were on hers and she could taste the liquor and roasted tobacco and spearmint. His hand found the edge of her panties.

Etta Jean clutched at the fabric of his shirt, struggled against him, and then her fear took over in a white-hot lightning bolt. Beneath her dress, her bladder gave way, and the tight confines of the hidden space behind the maze suddenly stank of urine.

"Oh Christ, are you…" The man's hold eased slightly. "Did you just fuckin' piss yourself?" He took his hand away from her mouth and trampled back. His silhouette shifted in the shadows and suddenly a door squealed open. The lights of the midway streamed in like the sun. "Get the hell out! Go on, ya fuckin' tease!"

Etta Jean charged past him and stumbled. She landed on her knees on the asphalt and fell to her side. Etta Jean looked back at the rear door. An *Old One* swirled around the man standing in the doorway and buckling his belt. The man with eyes like a Husky dog and a blurry teardrop tattoo. The skinny man, thin enough to be called a string bean.

An expression of disgust on his face, the man opened his lips as if to say something. The black eel of smoke, denser than before, curled around him, dove into the man's mouth, and disappeared. Some *Old Ones* were good, some were bad.

He slammed the door closed and Etta Jean sat in the alleyway between the mirror house and a tent selling hot dogs and pork barbecue. Electric cords snaked all around her, held in place with strips of blue tape. Tears flooded her eyes, enough that her bloody knees were a blur.

She tried screaming for Sarah. Etta Jean couldn't make a sound.

She ached to cry because of how badly she had been scared. Because of how her knees hurt, and she struggled to see through her tears to pick out the bits of gravel. But mostly, Etta Jean needed to cry over the loss of her innocence.

Yesterday she had played in secret with dolls in her bedroom with the door closed so no one would happen to see if they passed by. Today, the beautiful idea of a first kiss had been taken away forever.

Etta Jean's chest ached inside as she fought against the puppet movements of her body as they left the house and made their way down the sidewalk of Kanawha Boulevard. People had started slowing down and stared. Several honked their horns.

By the time the three of them reached the Booker T. Washington Memorial Bridge on Route 61, Hildy had stopped sobbing. Her eyes were wide enough to show white around the corneas, like an animal, cornered and terrified.

A champagne-colored Honda Accord sped past and Etta Jean felt the wind from how close it had come. Half a football field ahead of them, the vehicle snapped right, left, crashed into the concrete divider, and then flipped onto the passenger side. The car skidded, leaving a rooster tail of orange sparks in its wake until it ground to a stop. A plain white van swerved around the Accord and fishtailed sideways. The driver braked hard and the tires screamed as the vehicle was brought under control again, only to be hit by a rig with a trailer behind it.

The van detonated into shards of debris as the semi's grille slammed into the van's side panel. The sound of screeching wheels sliced over the noise of engines, and the stinking smoke of burned rubber and hot brakes drifted through the air. Vehicles on the highway screamed to a stop, barely missing the end of the rig's trailer.

William never even slowed his pace.

The driver's side window of the Accord shattered from within the car, and Etta Jean saw a thin brunette woman in a charcoal gray power suit climb free. Her face was bloody and sprinkled with bits of glass stuck to her wounds. Some fell away like shooting stars to the asphalt below.

She pulled herself out and then landed in a crouch on the highway. The woman only had her left shoe on—a sensible and simple black heel. Her arms stiffened and as Etta Jean got behind William, she watched the brunette as first one leg and then her other moved forward. The heel of the woman's right foot crunched against some busted debris and the next step she took left a red footprint on the pavement.

The heavyset truck driver got down from his rig and yelled. "What in the blue hell is…" He stopped, removed the Peterbilt hat from his head and surveyed the mess of traffic behind them.

Etta Jean struggled to look back, and what she saw made the chill she had felt the last couple of days pale in comparison. It rolled her stomach into a ball of ice, and fear flowed through her veins like creek water in March.

Passengers and drivers were getting out of their cars on Route 64, leaving them right there on the road with the engines still running. The women were the first, standing beside their vehicles and twitching as their bodies stopped responding to their wants.

And each one joined the walk.

The driver of the Peterbilt semi dropped his hat to the highway and began advancing one lurching step at a time. He wore a black brace around his right knee and the Velcro tore apart on his third shuffling stride. The man clenched his teeth and Etta Jean heard him muttering beneath his breath. "Yea, though I walk through the valley of the shadow of—"

He was the first man Etta Jean had seen affected. She twisted away and faced forward, taking in William's casual pace ahead of her. Hildy's eyes no longer seemed present, as if she had simply given in, physically and mentally, to whatever was compelling her to move.

In front of them, the highway was clear, the cars long gone, leaving the wreckage behind them. William made his way in the center of the road. In the far distance behind her, Etta Jean heard the sound of a woman screaming and then a crowd of footsteps against the asphalt, all searching to trace the path of young William.

The truck driver finished his prayer and Etta Jean heard the man whimper in pain with each step forward.

The shadow of death.

The man's words, his prayer, reminded Etta Jean of Granny's words, and for the first time since her body had betrayed her, Etta Jean realized that under her thin sweater and the soft cotton T-shirt, she had tucked the gift Granny had given her. Tucked it against the small of her back this morning after she dressed without even thinking about it, as she had done every day since Granny had handed it to her so long ago.

"Took a year to make, and seven more to make it useful." Granny sat down on the faded green couch beside Etta Jean and handed her a plain box of cedar wood, varnished to show the beautiful grain. "Go on. Open it up."

Etta Jean held the box on her knees and gently lifted the lid. Inside, she saw a bundle of cheesecloth, yellowed with age, and she took it out.

"Careful now." Granny scooted closer on the sofa. "That thing's sharper than a #11 scalpel."

Etta Jean looked at her and cautiously unfolded the bundle until she saw the source of the weight inside. She drew the knife from its handmade leather sheath and held it out in front of her. It was the length of an average butcher's knife, its handle wrapped in soft doeskin leather, with a string of herringbone beads trailing from the pommel. But the blade was what drew her attention. It was neither polished steel nor aged, tarnished, and weathered with years of use. No, the blade on the knife in front of Etta Jean was a length of chipped obsidian rock, black as midnight and gleaming like broken jewels. She glanced up at Granny.

"For seven years, on each and every Sunday, that knife was washed in the blood of a lamb, though it has never been used to bring death to a single thing." Granny observed the blade, her expression filled with longing and pride. "Ain't had cause for it to be used just yet, but there will be."

"When?"

"You'll know when it's time." Granny pursed her lips and nodded, pondering her answer. "But keep it close, always. That time will most likely come as a surprise to us all."

"I... Granny, I don't think I'm the one—"

"You hush now, girl." Granny scolded her softly, reached out a gentle hand and rested it on Etta Jean's arm. "You're fifteen, two years older than I was when it was gifted to me. It was mine to keep close since the day I became thirteen, day after I became a young woman and started

374

my monthlies." She patted Etta Jean's arm and glanced at the knife. It almost seemed as if it was hard for her to part with the weapon. Granny beamed at her with glistening eyes and nodded. "You'll do fine. Just fine."

Etta Jean had slept with the knife beneath her pillow that night, and the next night after that. And the following morning, she had taken to carrying the blade on her at all times, hidden and tucked away at the base of her spine. Having it close made her feel safe, although if asked to explain exactly why, she wouldn't have been able to give an answer that made sense to anyone.

William did not sleep, and therefore, the others did not.

Etta Jean had held out as long as she could, walking on through the night until the horizon lightened. Signs read I-77 South, but it didn't matter. Location didn't matter in the bigger picture; there was only the here and now. Her thighs ached. Her back screamed. Her sneakered feet throbbed. She let her chin lean down against her chest and within moments, the rocking motion lulled Etta Jean to sleep.

And her body kept walking onward.

In some ways, it was comforting and reminded her of falling asleep on long car rides and being picked up and carried into her home. It was that feeling of safety and comfort that someone else was in charge.

But for the most part, it was overwhelmingly terrifying because she had no control.

Etta Jean woke again when it started to drizzle, the rain soaking through her hair and then her sweater and dripping from the tip of her nose. She blinked drops from her eyelashes and lifted her head, winced at the pinch in the muscles of her neck and shoulders. William marched ahead, hands stuffed into his coat pockets, unmindful of the rain pouring down and soaking his scalp.

Hildy trembled as she moved, chilled, and Etta Jean saw the bluish circles beneath the woman's half-closed eyes. She wanted to walk closer, to try and speak to the woman again, but her path was set, even her steps beyond her decisions.

As they passed road signs for Brush Creek Falls, the rain slowed to a thin mist, and William paused and scouted about the thick carpet of trees. He glanced at Etta Jean and smiled, his black eyes filled with amusement. His attention shifted behind her, and Etta Jean wrenched her stiff neck to look. The breath left her lungs at the sight of the crowd, how much it had grown, stretching out on I-77 as far as she could see.

A pregnant woman stumbled and caught her balance. Dried blood painted the left side of her face and her hospital gown glistened red along the collar. Behind her, a man wearing a bright yellow construction worker's vest dragged himself along the highway. His face was a rictus of pain and he grunted with each movement. Most of his fingernails had been torn free and his hands were shredded gloves of bloody flesh.

There was a man in a business suit and shiny loafers. His elbows snapped and twitched as he tried to fight against the invisible puppeteer controlling him. An old woman in a bright white bathrobe dragged an IV pole on the ground behind her. A topless woman with huge fake breasts and a G-string, mascara smeared down her face. Her heels had come loose from her feet, but were still strapped to her ankles and dragged behind her as she staggered forward.

A priest with his white collar loose and dangling. A woman who seemed like she might be a teacher or maybe a librarian. An old man wearing a straw hat and gardening gloves and absolutely nothing else. A young cop, with what appeared to be a bullet wound in her upper right shoulder, glistening like rubies in shadow.

The people stretched on and on behind them, shuffling forward with the same zoned-out expression in their eyes, hopeless, confused, and in the deepest throes of absolute fear. A massive rolling boil of human beings, lurching along, no longer in control of themselves.

Gravel crunched beneath Etta Jean's feet. Hildy released a surprised yelp as her left ankle buckled sideways and the heel of her shoe snapped free. Hildy screamed, fell to her knees, and her hands shot out to catch herself on her palms. Her hair, dampened from the rain, came loose and hung around her face. Hildy sobbed once, twice, and then she raised her head to look at Etta Jean. Her body moved on its own, elbows and arms locking as she straightened to one bloody knee, and then stood.

A low, wavering sound came from deep within Hildy's chest, an almost animal noise brimming with agony. She trembled, a line of spittle leaked from the corner of her lipstick-smeared mouth, and she limped ahead on feet now absent of both shoes.

Etta Jean felt hot tears spring to her eyes as she faced forward and watched William's back. Black wisps curled around him, fading in and out of the little boy's body. Whatever was inside held onto him tightly.

She had done her best to stamp down the fear, tried as hard as she could to simply accept every moment for what it was, but the question inside her mind wouldn't be settled.

Where are we walking to?

Etta Jean heard people coughing that low, deep in the chest, hacking rattle. Between the downpour of rain and the overnight chill, she wasn't surprised. They had reached Virginia and the town of Narrows. Etta Jean's sneakers had come untied and the wet shoestring ends had become frayed.

William had stopped along the banks of New River and they had kneeled down in the mud and drunk from the waters like livestock. The cool liquid shifted inside Etta Jean's stomach and made her aware of the damp fabric of her jeans.

There had been no stopping. People pissed themselves, defecated, and the walk went on. At some point, the construction worker with shredded hands hadn't been able to claw himself forward. The pregnant woman had fallen against the asphalt and crawled after them for a while longer, but then Etta Jean had listened to the woman's screams fade away as they continued.

"Etta Jean?" Hildy's voice was a hoarse whisper, dry leaves shifting against each other.

It hurt to even glance at Hildy's ankle. The flesh around the joint had swollen plump and shiny and transformed into a sickening eggplant purple. Hildy's steps on the road left bloody footprints behind, reminding Etta Jean of a dashed line on a comic book treasure map.

She reeled around to the raspy sound of the woman's voice, and the ground beneath them rumbled and shook.

William stopped and everyone stopped with him. He coiled around and, except for his black eight-ball eyes, he was only a little boy, smiling and excited as if he were ready to enter a playground.

"It'll be soon, now." He nodded and redirected them down Main Street of Narrows. Deanna's Restaurant stood on the left, the building's windows broken and the vinyl siding above each of them marked with black exclamation marks of soot. Thin fingers of smoke curled up from the roof.

On the other side of the street, the door to the American Legion swung open and two heavy-set men wearing deer hunting attire stepped free, rifles in their hands. The first one through the door wrinkled his face and opened his mouth as if to yell something, and then the thirty-aught-six rifle fell from his hands, clattered to the sidewalk, and the scope broke off. His head snapped to the left and he groaned loudly as his beefy arms stiffened.

The man beside him took a step away as if whatever his friend had was contagious. "Red? What in the hell's the matter with—"

He cut off his own words with a sharp guttural sound, and the man suddenly clawed at his own face and clutched at his thick beard. But then his arms stiffened as well, thick-fingered hands twisting into claws.

Etta Jean saw the Ora Doral Furniture Company on the right, followed by Marco's Pizza, *Oven Fresh!* next to it. An old Dodge pickup was parked at an angle on the sidewalk. Its driver's side door had been left open and the radio was on, blasting static.

Parker's Electronics building was behind the truck. Through the large store window, the row of TVs all displayed the Emergency Broadcast Signal with its random, incomplete rainbow bars. Etta Jean heard the high-pitched tone from behind the glass, and then it faded as they marched onward.

William stopped and stared at the brick building of the Narrows Post Office. A uniformed employee had been strung up by her wrists and tied to the light pole out front. Her eyes appeared to have been burned out, the flesh scorched deeply enough to show the charred bones of her cheeks. Long red hair, matted by dried blood, lay pressed against her back. A bed sheet had been tied around her waist and it streamed like a banner.

Spray-painted in black, the sloppily written words read: Eve was a Whore!

One of the deer hunters choked as puke burst from his mouth and down the length of his beard. He sputtered to breathe as his plump face bloomed red as a pickled beet, his eyes bulged and he peeked around for help that would never come. His head bobbed and shook and then the man's eyes rolled up in his head. He fell like a cut timber and smashed his face against the pavement with a sickening crunch.

William snickered and continued along Main Street.

Etta Jean felt hot bile and creek water threaten to rise in her gorge, but she forced herself to keep it down. She inhaled, and then slowly exhaled through her mouth. Her shoulders eased down, arms lax at her sides, swinging slightly as she walked. The realization occurred to her that the more people who'd joined the walk, the more relaxed her body had become. The hold on her body had loosened, if only *slightly*.

"What in God's name *is* he?"

She fixed her attention toward the whispered voice, and Etta Jean saw the face of the man walking closely to her left, string bean thin with sky-blue eyes. Her bladder released and hot urine flooded down her legs.

The ground rumbled beneath them, louder this time than before, and Etta Jean watched as ahead of them a section of the highway asphalt bulged and then settled lower, as if something had burrowed beneath it and left the depression behind.

The breeze chilled Etta Jean's skin through her piss-soaked jeans. Though it took every ounce of her strength, she steered her steps away from the string bean man. Beads of sweat lined her scalp and again she fought the urge to throw up.

Hildy still kept close behind, though her bare feet were a shredded mess, more ground meat than appendages. Her red-rimmed eyes had gone duskier still, haunted, and her nose leaked a double line of snot. The cough issuing from her body sounded deep and watery inside.

Ahead of them, another highway merged and Etta Jean saw movement through a thicket of trees. It was another group of people, lurching along in awkward steps and following a girl child in a pink dress.

The crowd stretched on and on behind the girl, and they veered around crashed vehicles and a burning ambulance on the highway. In the distance beyond, fires burned, painting the horizon with thick smoke.

As the two crowds grew close, William spread his arms and spoke to the girl. "It's so good to see you, Sister."

The girl in the pink dress stepped in for an embrace, and when she glanced over William's shoulder, her eyes were black as coal mines. When she smiled and spoke, wisps of smoke curled from between her parted lips. "Can you hear the Blood Mother coming? It won't be long, now."

They swiveled together and moved ahead as the two massive groups now became one. Etta Jean saw more of the same varied crowd: some women in nightgowns and others in work attire, some with bare feet worn to the bones, others in hiking boots. A man with a bag of golf clubs slung over his shoulder clanked along beside a teenage girl wearing a Starbucks hat and shirt.

The string bean man was the length of a pickup truck away from Etta Jean.

She felt and heard another rumble from beneath the ground. This time, it sounded much deeper, burrowing through the veins of the earth itself.

Behind her, Etta Jean heard the sharp sound of skin smacking pavement and she shifted her body around to see Hildy on her stomach with outstretched arms. Her sprained ankle had swollen grotesquely, but both her feet were a mess of exposed tendons and ligaments. The heel bones themselves had worn through Hildy's flesh, like bloody white mushroom caps.

Hildy heaved and tried to draw air into her lungs. She lifted her face, nose smashed and front teeth broken off at the gums, and the scream that erupted from her throat was raw and guttural. She reached out her right hand to claw herself forward, and the two middle fingernails peeled away. Hildy bellowed hoarsely. The crowd parted around her and, as Etta Jean was forced ahead, the governor's widow was left behind.

William and the girl led everyone like pied pipers.

Etta Jean clenched her teeth and then realized she could clench her hands into fists. The obsidian blade at the small of her back was now within reach.

There were more people stretching along Route 64 than Etta Jean had ever seen in one place in her entire life. The air was filled with the scent of perfumes and body odor, stinking work uniforms, and the harsh snap of rubbing alcohol. But above everything else, Etta Jean smelled the salt of the ocean and a rotting marshy stink.

As they crossed through Manns Harbor and over the bridge, Etta Jean saw a third and fourth child leading groups, all converging together as one. The sky was gray and mottled, as if a far-away storm threatened to roll in. She studied the signs along the highway and saw they were walking onto Roanoke Island.

She heard a long low groan from beneath the ground and the millions of gallons of ocean water. It rumbled against the soles of her aching feet. Etta Jean struggled with the invisible force fighting her, but she reached her right hand to the small of her back, wrapped her hand around the handle and drew the obsidian knife from its sheath.

Granny had told her she would know when it was time for it to be used, and every single fiber of Etta Jean's being told her that time was coming soon.

They had gone a short distance onto the island when the pace of William and the girl slowed. Seagulls screamed and crisscrossed the sky and a low murmur washed through the crowd as the walk stopped along a sandy beach.

Etta Jean focused her thoughts and forced herself to take a step forward. The achievement made her feel like Neil Armstrong walking on the moon.

The children made their way through the vast congregation of people until they stood in a row on the beach and gazed out at the ocean. One at a time, they kneeled in the sand and chanted together in a long-dead language.

Etta Jean gripped the knife and crossed her arms, hiding the blade behind her other hand. She peered at the kneeling children, at the bare, vulnerable skin along the nape of their necks. She forced her body to take a step and she tightened her grip around the knife handle.

The beach detonated in front of them.

A creature the size of a Greyhound bus exploded from beneath the beach where the waves lapped against the wet sand. Its massive body was the segmented texture and shape of a maggot, but shadows shifted beneath the buttermilk-colored skin, *multiple* things all at once, as if the creature's eyes lay below a veil of flesh. It trudged half in and half out of the sandy ground, and ocean water and mucous frothed in a spray from its vaginal lips. What served as its mouth parted with folds of raw, wounded-looking flesh, and it bellowed, shaking with the effort. It was the blended sound of a thousand trains scraping against steel tracks, the squeal of a million angry hogs, all of it reverberating and echoing across the sand and water and then expanding and contracting, pulsing in the air.

The seagulls had vanished, fleeing from the abomination that had emerged. The only sounds were of the waves lapping against the shore, the frantic breath of the crowd of people, and the deep labored breathing of the beast in front of them. Beneath its doughy flesh, the inky spots shifted again, all turning at once.

The lips of the thirteen children never parted, but whispers swirled around them from voices other than their own. Twists and curls of black smoke swam excitedly around their kneeling figures.

They called it the Blood Mother, but they're wrong, Etta Jean thought. *That is Leviathan.*

Its bulging sow body uncurled, exposing rows of nipples the size of truck tires along its abdomen. It rotated its head toward the thirteen and then to the crowd. It trembled in place, and lines of shining drool dripped from its lewd maw to pool in the sand.

It thrashed against the surf and sprayed a fine cloud of grit and salt water from its impact alone.

The strength left Etta Jean's legs and she fell to her knees in the damp sand. A hum began inside her skull, a deep-seated pulse that beat in time with her heart. It spread through her veins until she felt that same rhythm between her legs.

Behind her, people dropped to their knees. Some women moaned with a mixture of fear and pleasure.

The men's voices were no longer old and strong. They whimpered in fear like young boys frightened of the night.

Etta Jean leaned forward on her hands and hid the knife blade and her clenched fist beneath the sand. She slowly crawled forward.

And the beast's thoughts became theirs, heard in a thickly tongued voice unfamiliar with speech. Its mouth did not form the words, but they still came from deep inside, resonating from somewhere within.

Long ago, I birthed the sons Cain and Abel, and Lilith well before them. Longinus who drove the spear home, and the child of your sweet Mother Mary.

The beast shifted in the sand, and its labial lips parted to expose rows of translucent teeth, narrow and long in a circular pattern like the mouth of a hagfish.

Genghis Khan and Der Führer. Joan of Arc and Mother Teresa. Those who change the tides, those who fight to save and fight to soak the ground with blood. The people here were sacrificed long ago, given to the beyond of Croatoa.

Etta Jean crawled closer in the sand until she was several feet behind William.

It is time to reset the balance... time for a rebirth... time to sacrifiiiiiiiiicccce.

A man screamed from far behind Etta Jean, and she heard the dull thudding sounds of footsteps running on sand. She spun to watch a man charge forward, a boatman's pike clutched in his hands. His bearded mouth bellowed a war cry and he ran between two of the kneeling children, directly at the beast.

As the thirteen rose to their feet, the Blood Mother contorted, hunching up its bulk as the man grew near and raised his weapon to strike. Its obscene gray-pink mouth glistened. It spread its carnal lips and the beast struck downward, engulfed the man from his waist up, and then withdrew immediately with an eruption of blood spewing from the orifice.

For a moment, the remains of the man's body stood there from the waist down, entrails spooling loose. Then it collapsed to the sand and his innards spilled free like ice cream from a dropped cone.

Let the ground beneath you run red with blood.

It was the last thought from the beast Etta Jean heard before hell unleashed among the crowd of people around her.

The women in the crowd were the first to rise up, in unison as one entity, and there was no hesitation before they attacked any man closest to their reach. A gray-haired woman in a lavender jogging suit lunged at a man in a police uniform and tackled him to the sand. She picked up the shell of a dead horseshoe crab and jammed it into his screaming mouth over and over.

Another woman, in a business suit, wrenched a wooden picket free of the fence in the dunes, snapped it in half and drove the broken ends into the rib cage of a young man in a Syracuse hoodie. He screamed and clutched onto the sun-bleached wood and fell, sputtering blood.

Handfuls of sand were thrown into men's eyes and, as they struggled blindly, they were drawn to the ground and handfuls more were shoved into their open screaming mouths.

A nurse picked up a beach umbrella and speared the pointed tip into the back of a man in a business suit. It emerged through his stomach and he fell forward, pinned to the bloody sand like a butterfly specimen.

Etta Jean watched a woman beat a man with a golf club. Another man staggered past, the stiletto of a high heel sunk deeply into an eye socket. A college-aged girl with streaks of purple in her hair wrapped her bare legs around the waist of a construction worker from behind, and jammed a curling iron into his mouth so deeply that his throat bulged with the trauma.

The Blood Mother thrashed excitedly and its flesh-veiled eyes swiveled as it watched.

The horde of people screamed and bellowed in rage and agony. Etta Jean rose to her feet and viewed the orgy of bloodshed. A lady, who might have been a librarian, straddled a man in bibbed overalls against the ground and bashed his face in with the cleats of a golf shoe.

Etta Jean stared at the knife in her hand, slowly leaned toward the Blood Mother, the great beast, *Leviathan*, and then she felt a strong hand grip her wrist.

"I thought I remembered you, ya fuckin' tease."

For a fraction of a second, she thought about bringing the blade up beneath his jaw and driving it upward, ripping it free and slicing his throat on the withdraw. But the only part of Etta Jean's mind left with rational thought held her back. The blade was obsidian, *sharper than a #11 scalpel*, but brittle. And it had never been used to kill a single living thing. Yet.

Etta Jean pulled against the man's hand, but he held her in a vice grip and leered. Even with the savagery going on all around them, the son of a bitch *leered*.

She yanked again, harder, and her wrist pulled away as she fell to the sand. Etta Jean's left hand touched a smooth twist of driftwood and she clutched it as the man laughed and descended on her.

Gripping the wood tightly, Etta Jean clenched her teeth and screamed as she lunged to her feet, swinging with one hand; a shaft of the driftwood pierced the side of the man's throat and almost through to the other side, making the flesh protrude outward. She left it in place.

His cold sapphire eyes bulged and his mouth gaped open like a landed fish. Blood sputtered over his bottom lip and down over his whiskered chin. The man clutched at his throat, and his fingers wrapped around the exposed end of the driftwood. He pulled, withdrawing it an inch, and Etta Jean swung her hand and slammed it against his, jamming the pointed wood deeper and impaling his throat completely as it pierced through the other side.

The man's head bobbed as he choked against the obtrusion, and his blood-slicked hand dropped away from further attempts to remove the wood.

Etta Jean peered into his eyes as he gripped the exposed length of driftwood and slowly withdrew it from his throat. Blood spurted in pulses from either side of his neck and she stabbed in an underhand swing, driving the stake up toward his crotch. It hung against the denim of his jeans, but only for an instant, and then the wood thrust up through the opening in his pelvis.

The string bean man tried to release a guttural scream but it came out as nothing more than a wet garbled mess. Etta Jean left the wood impaling him, and he dropped to his knees.

She leaned down closer, mindful of his eyes and whispered. "I knew *jussst* what you needed."

He blinked once, twice, and then fell to the beach, choking to death on his own blood.

Etta Jean scanned the row of the thirteen. They stood there smiling, watching the crowd, with eyes as black as charcoal. A scream of primal rage and wrath burst free from her, as she charged through the shallow water at the beast, the obsidian knife held to her side.

The hulking body inched toward her as she ran closer, and drew itself upward. The fleshy lips drew away from the teeth-lined mouth. As it trembled and readied to strike, Etta Jean dove flat against the sand, twisted in mid-air and raised the obsidian blade as she slid against the wet beach.

The knife sank into the beast's flesh, and she sliced as far as she could reach, drawing the blade back and forth in a frenzy of motion.

The smell of rotted blood and an earthy, yeasty stink poured from the creature as its insides spilled free. It lifted upward, away from Etta Jean, and released a shriek of pain that rang in her ears. She scrambled to her feet and leaped, sank the blade deeply, and let gravity draw it downward along with her. The knife caught on something hard inside, and Etta Jean felt the blade snap in half. Innards spewed from the body, tumbled free around her, *on* her, and Etta Jean stumbled backward as the beast thrashed against the sand.

She studied the broken blade in her hand, and looked back to the thirteen, expecting them to charge at her. Their smiling faces changed as the Old Ones inside unspooled, forcing the children to yawn wide, and splitting the sides of their mouths in thin bloody ribbons. They made a high-pitched whine as the blackness left their eyes. Their arms bent unnaturally, hands transfigured to claws, fingers stiffened into twined bends.

The smoke curled up around them and writhed around the Blood Mother. Wisps of it swam in and out of the massive wound Etta Jean had made, and then flowed into its vaginal mouth.

There were whispers in the wind coming from the waters.

Releeeeeasssse... the rebirth is here... sacrifiiiiccce...

The Blood Mother thrashed and then fell to the beach. Its sides pulsed quickly as it breathed, and then it lay still as it began to slow. Saltwater lapped against the bottom of the beast's dying body.

The children that the thirteen had taken over stood on the beach, scared and crying, confused and alone.

Etta Jean veered away from them to look behind her.

Bloodied corpses lay everywhere, bodies piled like drying cordwood. Everywhere she looked, the beige sand glistened a deep red. Women staggered among the massacre, spattered with blood of their own or others. All of them contemplated Etta Jean with eyes of admiration and awe.

Not a single man drew breath.

Overhead, the buzzards were already circling the sky for miles in every direction.

Etta Jean dropped the broken knife onto the sand. Its use was done. It lay there in the gore like a piece of black glass.

Soft whispers sifted through the breeze, light as dandelion seeds, and she shifted toward the beast. Blacksnakes made of smoke poured from its mouth and swirled in the air, twisting and turning and seeking.

And then, as one, the Old Ones funneled together and shot away from the dead Blood Mother. They streamed as one thick plume of black shadow directly into Etta Jean's mouth, filling her with ice and fire, with screams gone silent and secrets long dead. They swirled through her veins and peered from behind her eyes, and then they quieted, settled, coiled deep within her like a snake in slumber.

Etta Jean's body twitched. Her right foot took a step of its own accord, and her left foot followed. Her sneakered feet squelched in the pools of blood, too much for even the sand to absorb so quickly.

The next part of the journey was much shorter than the first. The group of women followed on their own, but as they moved on, the crowd thinned. Some were wounded badly and the others cared for them. The children had been gathered from the bloody shoreline and taken in by women other than their mothers, caring women with nurturing arms and strong, beating hearts. The thirteen would be raised to be makers instead of destroyers. To learn to provide creation instead of death, and freedom instead of control.

Vehicles, crashed and abandoned, were everywhere. Some with dead drivers or passengers still in the seats. Fires along the horizon released plumes of black smoke, but they would soon burn themselves down to charred wood and ash and the air would turn clean once again. Some women left the group, walking into homes of their choosing. Others went back to their former nests, preferring the familiarity of what they knew, without old constraints.

Life would begin again, a true rebirth.

There was a change happening inside Etta Jean, a shifting of sorts that wasn't entirely unpleasant. Her stomach fluttered as if flowers bloomed there. She felt the Old Ones inside her, peering out through her eyes, swimming in her thoughts like black quicksilver.

Of the thirteen, nine of the children's mothers still lived. They followed behind Etta Jean in the thinning crowd. None of them seemed downtrodden or weary. Bloodied faces or not, they all appeared to be somehow hopeful.

They didn't cross a single stretch of asphalt that wasn't bloodied or littered with corpses, and it wasn't until Etta Jean was steered into the rolling hillsides and gravel roads of West Virginia that the buzzards stopped circling overhead.

Grouse and rabbits hunted for food in the bushes and weeds. A pretty doe appeared in the middle of the gravel road and a spotted fawn trotted behind her on unsteady legs. The two of them eyed the group of women, now down to only Etta Jean and the nine mothers.

Etta Jean smiled and let out a heavy sigh, and the fawn and its mother slowly ambled off into the meadows of the roadside.

It was near dawn when they reached the cemetery, and the overgrown grass was heavy with dew. Etta Jean's sneakers were soaked with blood, and the moisture had stained them a faded rust. She walked to the first gravestone she saw and made it halfway there before she realized she was once again walking under her own control.

Etta Jean sat and rested her aching legs. The other women sat down in the grass, ignoring the wet soaking through their clothing.

395

She faced the sky as it grew brighter from behind the mountains, turning from a deep quilt of blue to the light brightness of a newborn's eyes.

Something inside her shifted and shifted against itself, like an eel trying to escape from a fishing bucket. She sighed and smiled, and waited to see the sun one last time.

"Being a woman, a mother, is *sacrifice*, Etta Jean." Granny mixed the ingredients for her sugar cookies, adding a handful of Sun-Maid raisins. "Our feelings and thoughts, our bodies and time."

She stirred a wooden spoon in the bowl. "Sacrifices are made in the name of love, of nature itself."

Etta Jean ran a fingertip along the ridge of the mixing bowl, swiping a dab onto her finger and popping it between her lips.

Granny smiled and shook her head. "Point is, there's not a day goes by that I wouldn't make those sacrifices again."

"Someday, I will too, Granny."

"I know." The old woman paused at the kitchen counter, peeped at Etta Jean and gave her a soft smile. "I know you will."

Etta Jean heard the TV console in the living room, some too-loud commercial about insurance. And for an instant, in the reflection of sunlight on the dusty TV screen, Etta Jean thought she saw a trail of smoke forming around her grandmother's head. She pivoted quickly, back to Granny, but saw nothing but the woman smiling at her as she scooped cookie mix onto a baking sheet.

The dates and names on the gravestones had faded with time and weather, destined like everything to vanish from history itself. Black mold speckled the white stones like guinea feathers.

It was quiet up here on the hillside. The sunrise had painted the sky with streaks of red and orange, bright and beautiful as wildflowers in spring.

Etta Jean smiled to herself at the old memories, and she felt the cavern drawing her inside.

She stood and used her feet to push off her sneakers. The other women were tired, but they wore excited smiles like expectant mothers on their exhausted faces. Etta Jean entered the edge of the cemetery and peered beyond the old-growth honeysuckle and wild raspberry bushes to the rocky hillside.

Heat rushed through her body as she marched through them, ignoring the thorns tearing at her flesh and clothes. The women followed.

Etta Jean parted the thickets of Mountain Laurel and glared at the massive gaping eye of the cavern.

Being a woman, a mother, is sacrifice.

Someday, I will too, Granny.

She felt her abdomen bulge outward, swirling inside. Etta Jean smiled and stepped forward through shadows. The cavern was warm and Stygian. And the women ventured into darkness until the oval shape of light they left behind appeared as a pinprick from an antique sewing needle in a sheet of black velvet. They walked deeper and then light disappeared completely.

Somewhere, water dripped slowly, rhythmically, like a ticking clock. From deep inside the heart of the mountain, the water traveled from cold water springs. It splashed into pools of water as still and sacred as church basins.

They traveled deeper still until the narrow path opened into a great cathedral reaching overhead. Etta Jean walked into the center of the expanse and spread her arms wide. The Old Ones inside her were frenzied, waiting, and Etta Jean gave herself over and let the final transformation begin.

It was painful, the change, but it was sacrifice, and the agony was expected.

Etta Jean's screams echoed off the ancient walls as the joints of her body popped and split. Her pubis separated, pelvis folding open flat, and she fell as her femurs separated from her hips. The pain was high-voltage electricity coursing through her body. Her clothing tore as her breasts shifted and grew, multiplied in number. Her sternum snapped and crackled as it divided in half and the trunk of her body expanded and divided into segments.

Her eyelids fused shut, melting into her face, but then a different type of sight was born in the obscurity, many spheres of vision beneath her flesh, shifting and studying the women in the cavern with her. Etta Jean's throat burst open, and her vocal cords thickened to taut cables of bloody rope. She felt her teeth separate and lengthen, the bones of her jaws breaking apart as new teeth pierced her flesh.

She shrieked in pain, a thousand trebled cries of animals being slaughtered. The sound was foreign and familiar at the same time, as if her true voice had been hidden her entire life.

And then, Etta Jean lay down against the pebbled floor of the cave. Mucous flowed from her circular hagfish mouth, stinking like fresh placenta. The dimpled segments of her body were textured like bread dough, and moisture dripped along the division lines to the ground.

Each of the women stepped closer and gathered on their knees along the massive trunk of her body. Etta Jean's eyes shifted beneath her skin, watching as they knelt to suckle at her breasts. All of the women except one, who approached with a smile on her face as she closed her eyes and offered herself as nourishment.

The work done had taken effort, and the Blood Mother's strength had to be replenished.

Balance had not been restored, but it had tilted in the favor of those more than equal but not in control. Even so, it would not last forever. Nothing ever did. And in time, she would be needed again, for another rebirth.

She would nest here in slumber, deep in the darkness, lying in wait.

And for now, that would be enough.

Everyone

Cindy O'Quinn

MARTHA LANDRY stood on a mountain. Not a silver one—far from it. More like a giant mound of gathered pain, suffering, and aloneness. She looked out over the valleys, remembering last night's dream. A foretelling of what was to come.

The beauty of her mountains would be stripped like all others if something wasn't done to stop the man, the machine. The maker of all bad things.

Stripping rights like stripping mountains.

So many people had already fallen prey to control-hungry men. If she started the journey now, maybe she could restore a second wind, and give hope to the hopeless.

Wheeling, West Virginia was a long way off from her North Georgia mountains, which had kept her company for thirty years. But the dream was specific, she had to travel to Wheeling. That's where she would find the newborn.

Her momma had been taking a break from having babies when she got pregnant with Martha. She was twenty-five. The disappointment of having a seventh child to raise caused her to spend the rest of her years struggling to remember how to be happy. Martha hid her pain just below the surface. Her daddy blamed her for her momma's death, which came far too early. The day her momma passed, Martha was but sixteen. She left home and went to work at the general store and rented the small apartment above. She was happy on her own. Fourteen years slipped by without a complaint.

Martha loaded her '59 VW Beetle with groceries and a suitcase, jumped on I-75 north out of Georgia. Wheeling, WV bound. It was summer, and the days were long and hot. Wet hot.

She had jotted down as much of the dream as possible, so she knew the primary things to watch for.

Festivals.

The season of cotton candy and small-town traditions was in full swing, and according to Martha's dream, she'd have to stop at each one she happened upon. She didn't have to seek them out, just the ones that were happenstance.

She hadn't gone far when she spotted the point of the big-top tent near Rabun. Little town called Clayton. Martha parked her car, purchased a gate pass, walked to the Bingo tent and found an empty stool. She sat down and purchased three of the hard bingo cards—not the paper ones you dab, these were the old-fashioned ones with windows you slid shut for each number called that you had. She only had to play one game when she yelled, "Bingo!"

Her card was read and the match confirmed. "What'll ya have, ma'am?"

"I'll take the infant starter set." It contained onesies, bibs, a hooded bath towel, wash rag, and binkies.

"Here you go! Got a bun in the oven, darlin?" The man with a giant chaw of tobacco crammed in his cheek winked at her.

If Martha could've, she'd have stared a hole plumb through the worker's tobacco-stuffed cheek and watched as the brown chew oozed out of control. What she didn't know was, if she'd thought on it a little harder, it would've happened just as she imagined.

Up on a shelf, like many other gifted women. Sheltered and unaware of the power flowing through them. Flowers that made bud but never bloomed.

The dream... young, unassuming women, scattered about the world. Experts at being invisible. The unnoticed ones. But they were the gifted, and the time to make use of their gifts drew nigh. Unlike the thirteen years of peaceful protests and teachings of one leader, another leader had opened the gates for hate and prejudice to run amok. This new leader was unafraid of prosecution. It fell to these special women to turn it all around and ride a new wave of justice, fair treatment, calm resolutions, and a better world for all.

There were so many things Martha was yet to find out about herself. Like how being holed up in that tiny apartment for the past fourteen years was just a way of biding time.

Until now.

Back in her car, Martha continued on her way out of her North Georgia mountains. The only place she ever wanted to be. Yet, a dream so powerful had uprooted her from her small world, and propelled her out into the unknown.

Next sighting which indicated a pretty good chance of a festival was a batch of freed green and blue balloons just over the horizon in Chattanooga, TN.

It was a celebration alright, Honeybee Festival. It wasn't the Bingo tent Martha was hunting this go-round. She headed to the cow barns and found what she was looking for right outside. The mechanical bull: Mr. Hurricane. Martha had to remain on for eight long seconds, and she would get the grand prize.

She took the worn leather glove from her back pocket and slipped her left hand inside. Cinched the narrow belt across the palm of her hand as tight as she could handle it. Made eye contact with the machine operator and gave her slow southern nod. He slammed down on the gears as though trying to set a record for the quickest buck-off. Martha clamped her knees tight and kept her center low. "Ding, ding, ding!"

Martha walked away with the blue-ribbon-winning local honey! A quart jar of it.

Back in her car, she was thirsty and hungry. After having a bottle of water and a sandwich from her cooler, she drove to the local Wally World. She slept there in her car for the night.

Morning arrived, hot and sticky. She freshened up in the gas station bathroom, and then filled her tank with fuel. Next stop would be Crozet, Virginia. There'd be a festival going on in the park, but where Martha needed to be was on the Sugar Hollow Trail which led to Blue Hole.

There wasn't much daylight left by the time she arrived in the parking lot, but there'd be a waxing moon rising soon. She didn't want any looky-loos watching her go behind the waterfalls. That was a park rule she was breaking, and so was filling a gallon jug with the ice-blue mountain water. According to the dream, that water contained the perfect amount of minerals and a little something special.

Martha returned to her little VW and put the jug of water in the cooler. She pulled a flask from her back pocket. It had been empty, but now it contained that cold mountain water. Her body was stove up from the driving, the hiking, and that blasted mechanical bull. Martha sipped on the water, savoring it like it was her first. Once she drank the last drop, she drifted into a sleep, custom spun, just for her.

The dream started where it had left off. Her next stop would be in Point Pleasant, WV. Martha would be playing tourist. She'd find what she needed in the Mothman Museum.

There was a tap on the windshield, "It's gonna be a hot one today! You might want to roll those windows down."

Martha wiped the sleep from her eyes and tried to focus on the voice. By the time she could see clearly, the person was gone.

Another gas station sink bath, a change of clothes, and she was on her way. Martha had heard the stories of the mothman, and seen a couple of the movies. Like most legends, lore, and folktales, they were born of some truth, however small. She wondered what part of the mothman was based on truth. Her bet would be on foretelling death, not causing it.

The drive to Point Pleasant was a beautiful one. Martha was relaxed as she pulled into the parking spot in front of the Mothman Museum. Inside the museum, she found lots of touristy items like T-shirts, caps, and postcards. Martha found what she came for in the glass display case. It was the watch, the very one the actor wore during the filming of the movie. A sign above it read: Guess the number of glowing red eyes in the jar and win the watch.

Martha told the proprietor she wanted to make a guess. He accepted her five dollars and had her write the number on a scrap of paper with her name. The guesses would be read off at noon. Not long to wait; it was a quarter of.

A crowd gathered around the display case as the owner read off the guesses. There must've been at least fifty who'd paid. Pretty good money just to make a guess. Martha had insight though and knew she'd written the exact number of glowing eyes. After reading all the guesses, the proprietor opened the red envelope and read the winning number. One match. Martha Landry. The owner presented her with the famous actor's watch. He had a look of disappointment in his eyes. Martha looked back and winked at him. "It'll work out for the best!"

It was a two-and-a-half-hour drive from Point Pleasant to Wheeling. A quick cooler lunch and off she went.

Martha made her way to the Hempfield Tunnel – Wheeling, WV. According to legend, it wasn't a place for the faint of heart to visit. But it was in her dream, so there she was, climbing the steps to get a better view from up top. It was made part of the Heritage Trail years ago. She wondered if any bodies remained above the tunnel. Had someone really done a half-ass job relocating all the remains to the new cemeteries, once the tunnel construction was underway? Were they pushed beyond their timeframe? Pushed beyond their limits to get all the remains moved? Or was it something more sinister? She had a gut feeling: it was the latter. The closer Martha drew to Wheeling, the shift from good air to bad filled her lungs, creating a web covered in dew. Each breath fogged her mind a bit more.

That's where the gallon jug of Blue Hole mountain water came in handy. One sip was all it took to clear Martha's lungs and mind. She walked among the mint, lemon balm, and lavender, which had all but taken over the area above the tunnel. Nature always found a way to mask the smell of innocent death. Standing in the patch of herbs, she knew this was where things would come to fruition.

Less than a mile away, the Wheeling Full Thunder Moon Festival was in high gear. The theme was "Freakshow." Fireworks lit the predusk sky with hues of a purple haze. Gunshots cracked and split the time when night swallowed the last slip of day. Festival goers walked about as though stepping from Woodstock and into the show of now. LSD stamps clung to faces without melting. Honey mushroom paste stained teeth. Clouds of cannabis smoke, thick enough to carry the weary, diffused over the entire park.

Fifty-four years between two events came together. Peace embraced hate. Songs choked screams. Screams muffled rape. Hate embraced malfeasance. Frenzied passion engulfed minds as everyone sought out the freaks, kept behind closed tent flaps. Blank stares at those playing the freaks. Just people in tattered clothes, rocking back and forth. They were supposedly under the spell of possession from the man who thought it okay to leave some bodies behind to be awakened by the daily train whistle blowing, preventing a peaceful sleep in death.

The glares shook the actors and volunteers, the hands reaching out and touching without permission. They stood and removed their costumes, wiped off the smokey makeup, and spoke up, "Hey, this is just make-believe. Remember, this is how we raise money to keep the parks up and running."

There was a rumble throughout the crowd. Disappointment. The full thunder moon appeared from behind a cloud. Shining a light on decades-old, shimmering angel dust falling from the heavens. A clap of thunder and a streak of lightning shook the partygoers from Stonesville.

People picked up and went on their way. Left behind, seemingly unnoticed, was a young woman. She looked as though she could have been from now or Woodstock 1969. Maybe both. She sat and quietly stared up at Martha. All-knowing eyes, the color of Mother Nature herself. Thin, white sheath of a dress, trimmed in embroidered daisies, and a ring of live woven flowers tilted perfectly atop her head.

She reached her hands out towards Martha, and Martha took them and helped her to her feet. The young woman was pregnant. Due any time, from the looks of her belly. But Martha knew that already. It had all been in the dream, in some form or another.

Hand in hand, the women walked to Martha's car, got inside and drove over to the Hempfield Tunnel. They gathered what they needed from the car: newborn baby set, gallon of Blue Hole water, quart of prize-winning honey, and the watch.

They ascended the steps by floating above them, feet never making contact. If either woman noticed the phenomenon, they never mentioned it.

Martha put down the blanket she'd been using at night as a pillow in her car. She placed it over the good-smelling herbs growing on top of the tunnel. The young woman stepped out of her dress and lay on the bedding. The

Full Thunder Moon shone brightly on the women's faces. Their eyes glimpsed one another and lingered. The young woman said, "My name is Opal Womack."

"My name is Martha Landry. It's good to meet you, Opal. Outside of my dreams, that is."

Opal said, "When all is said and done, you will return to life in your North Georgia mountains. Once we break the watch, time will move accordingly, and you will help me birth the babe who waits inside of me. The Special water will protect the newborn from illness; the clothing will keep the newborn clean and dry. The prize-winning honey will amplify the brain's capability to gain and retain knowledge. A baby made of everyone good, all-knowing, this baby will run the country, and the plates on the playing field will shift in favor of women. The wrongs will be righted, the unjust will see justice, no one will have control over another. The world will become a peaceful place."

"Are you telling me this baby will be fully grown in time to run for president?"

Opal answered, "Not only run but win the presidency."

It was time. At the last stroke of midnight, Everyone was born. Opal called the baby Ever. She would lead the world into a better place.

Martha asked, "What about you, Opal?"

"I will remain here as a mother until I'm no longer needed; then I will return to my home."

"Where is home for you, Opal?"

"Everywhere."

Biographies

Carol Gyzander (Co-editor and Author) writes and edits horror, weird fiction, and science fiction in the northern New Jersey suburbs of New York City. She often focuses on strong women with twisted tales that touch your heart. Carol brought a female focus to her Bram Stoker Award®-nominated story, 'The Yellow Crown', in the anthology inspired by Robert W. Chambers' world of the King in Yellow, *Under Twin Suns: Alternate Histories of the Yellow Sign* (Hippocampus, 2021), edited by James Chambers. Her short stories appear in various magazines and anthologies, including *Weird Tales*, *Weird House Magazine*, *Cat Ladies of the Apocalypse* (Camden Park Press, 2020), and *Across the Universe: Tales of Alternative Beatles* (Fantastic Books, 2019).

The reversal of the Roe v. Wade ruling inspired the horror anthology *A Woman Unbecoming* (Crone Girls Press, 2022), co-edited with Rachel A. Brune, which presents stories of women's rage, power, and vengeance, and benefits reproductive healthcare services. Carol also co-edited the *Even in the Grave* ghost story anthology (NeoParadoxa, July 2022) with James Chambers, and edited four anthologies of punk genre stories inspired by classic works for Writerpunk Press. More at CarolGyzander.com

Lee Murray (Author) is a writer, editor, poet, essayist, and screenwriter from Aotearoa-New Zealand. A *USA Today* bestselling author, her titles include the Taine McKenna Adventures, supernatural crime-noir series The Path of Ra (with Dan Rabarts), fiction collection *Grotesque: Monster Stories*, and several books for children. Her many anthologies include *Hellhole*, *Black Cranes* (co-edited with Geneve Flynn), and *Unquiet Spirits* (with Angela Yuriko Smith), and her short fiction appears in prestigious venues such as *Weird Tales*, *Space and Time*, and *Grimdark Magazine*.

A five-time Bram Stoker Award®-, and multiple Australian Shadows- and Sir Julius Vogel Award-winner, Lee is New Zealand's only recipient of the Shirley Jackson Award. She is an NZSA Honorary Literary Fellow, and a Grimshaw Sargeson Fellow and 2023 NZSA Laura Solomon Cuba Press Prize winner for her prose-poetry manuscript *Fox Spirit on a Distant Cloud*.

Recently, Lee made history as the recipient of the Prime Minister's Award for Literary Achievement in Fiction, the first writer of Asian descent to achieve this prestigious award, which is one of her country's highest accolades. Read more at leemurray.info

Cindy O'Quinn (Author) is a four-time Bram Stoker Award®- nominated writer. Author of 'Lydia', from the Shirley Jackson Award-winning anthology *The Twisted Book of Shadows*, 'The Thing I Found Along a Dirt Patch Road', 'A Gathering on the Mountain', and 'One and Done'.

Her poetry has been nominated for the Elgin, Dwarf Star, and Rhysling Awards.

She is an Appalachian writer from West Virginia. Cindy currently resides on the old Tessier Homestead in the woods of northern Maine. It's the ideal backdrop for writing dark stories and poetry.

Her work has been published or is forthcoming in *Crimson Bones*, *A Quaint and Curious Volume of Gothic Tales*, *The Bad Book*, *HWA Poetry Showcase Vol V*, *Under Her Skin*, *Were Tales: A Shapeshifter Anthology*, *Space and Time*, *Weirdbook #48* through *#50*, *Chiral Mad 5*, and elsewhere.

Follow Cindy for updates: Facebook @CindyOQuinnWriter, X @COQuinnWrites, Instagram @cindy.oquinn, Threads @cindy.oquinn, and Bluesky @cindyoquinn.bsky.social

Anna Taborska (Co-editor and Author) writes horror stories and screenplays. Her body of work includes three short story collections: *Bloody Britain* (Shadow Publishing, 2020), *Shadowcats* (Black Shuck Books, 2019), and *For Those Who Dream Monsters* (Mortbury Press, 2013, 2020), recipient of the Dracula Society's Children of the Night Award.

Anna's stories have appeared in over forty anthologies, including *The Best Horror of the Year Volume Four*, *Best New Writing 2011*, *Best British Horror 2014*, *Year's Best Weird Fiction Volume One*, *Best New Werewolf Tales (Vol. 1)*, and *Nightmares: A New Decade of Modern Horror*.

She has been nominated for a British Fantasy Award thrice, and for a Bram Stoker Award® five times, including for her illustrated storybook *A Song for Barnaby Jones* (Zagava, 2021). An Italian translation of Anna's collection *Bloody Britain* is scheduled for release by Independent Legions Publishing in 2024.

Anna has also directed five films, including award-winning drama *The Rain Has Stopped*, and worked on twenty other film and television productions, such as the BBC / PBS series *Auschwitz: The Nazis and 'The Final Solution'*.

You can visit Anna at the following sites: annataborska. wixsite.com/horror and imdb.me/anna.taborska

Kyla Lee Ward (Author) is a Sydney-based creative whose work has garnered Australian Shadows and Aurealis awards. She has placed in the Rhyslings and received multiple Stoker and Ditmar nominations. Reviewers have accused her of being 'gothic and esoteric', 'weird and exhilarating' and of 'giving me a nightmare.'

Other recent releases include the novella *Those That Pursue Us Yet* and the short story collection *This Attraction Now Open Till Late*, both from Independent Legions Publishing. These join the previously published *The Macabre Modern* and *The Land of Bad Dreams*, collections of poetry and essays from P'rea Press. Her work on RPGs including *Demon: The Fallen* saw her appear as a guest at the inaugural Gencon Australia.

An artist and actor as well as an author, her short film *Bad Reception* screened at the Third International Vampire Film Festival and she is a member of the Deadhouse immersive theatre company. A practising occultist, she likes raptors, swordplay and the Hellfire Club. To see some very strange things, try kylaward.com.

Lynne Hansen (Illustrator) is a horror artist who specializes in book covers. She loves creating art that tells a story and that helps connect publishers, authors and readers. Her art has appeared on the cover of the legendary *Weird Tales* magazine, and she was selected by Bram Stoker's great-grandnephew to create the cover for the 125th Anniversary Edition of Dracula. She has illustrated works by *New York Times* bestselling authors including Jonathan Maberry, Brian Keene, and Christopher Golden.

Beyond & Within

THE FLAME TREE Beyond & Within short story collections bring together tales of myth and imagination by modern and contemporary writers, carefully selected by anthologists, and sometimes featuring short stories and fiction from a single author. Overall, the series presents a wide range of diverse and inclusive voices, often writing folkloric-inflected short fiction, but always with an emphasis on the supernatural, science fiction, the mysterious and the speculative. The books themselves are gorgeous, with foiled covers, printed edges and published only in hardcover editions, offering a lifetime of reading pleasure.

Flame Tree Fiction

A wide range of new and classic fiction, from myth to
modern stories, with tales from the distant past to the
far future, including short story anthologies, Collector's
Editions, Collectable Classics, Gothic Fantasy collections
and Epic Tales of mythology and folklore.

•

Available at all good bookstores, and online
at flametreepublishing.com

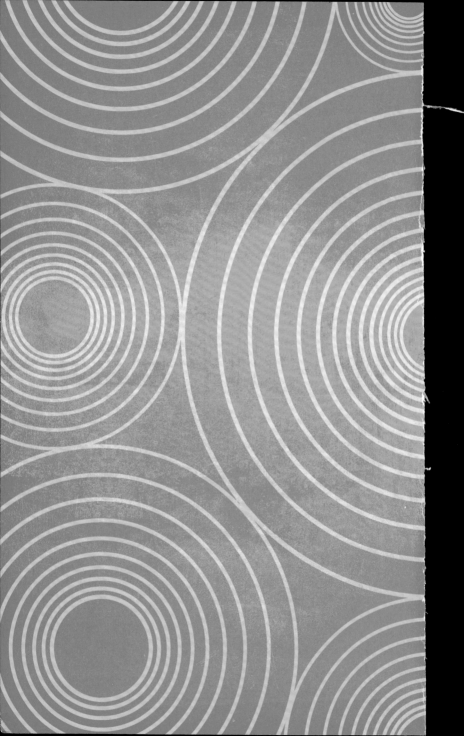